About the Authors

Initially a French/English teacher, **Emma Darcy** cha... d careers to computer programming before the happ... demands of marriage and motherhood. Very much a pe... le person, and always interested in relationships, she ... ls the world of romance fiction a thrilling one and the ... allenge of creating her own cast of characters ver... ddictive.

US... Today bestselling author **Kat Cantrell** read her fir... Mills & Boon novel in third grade and has been scr... bling in notebooks since she learned to spell. She's a f... mer So You Think You Can Write winner and for... er RWA Golden Heart finalist. Kat, her husband an... heir two boys live in north Texas.

Joa... na Neil had her future planned. She enjoyed her wor... as an infant teacher and didn't envisage any ch... ges to her way of life. But then she discovered M... & Boon. She was surprised to find how absorbing an... interesting they were and read them on a regular ba... s. The more she read, the more she had the ov... whelming desire to write one. Encouraged by her fa... ly, she persevered until her first book was accepted, a... after several books were published, she decided to w... e full time.

D0928616

Tropical Temptation

Tropical Temptation: Exotic Propositions

EMMA DARCY

KAT CANTRELL

JOANNA NEIL

MIX

Paper from
responsible sources

FSC

FSC C007454

This book is produced from independently certified FSC™ paper
to ensure responsible forest management.

For more information, visit: www.harpercollins.co.uk/green

Printed and bound in Spain
by CPI, Barcelona

MILLS & BOON

First Published in Great Britain 2020
By Mills & Boon, an imprint of HarperCollins*Publishers*
1 London Bridge Street, London, SE1 9GF

TROPICAL TEMPTATION: EXOTIC PROPOSITIONS © 2020
Harlequin Books S.A.

His Most Exquisite Conquest © 2013 Emma Darcy
From Ex to Eternity © 2015 Kat Cantrell
His Bride in Paradise © 2012 Joanna Neil

ISBN: 978-0-263-28217-7

HIS MOST EXQUISITE CONQUEST

EMMA DARCY

CHAPTER ONE

A DEARLY BELOVED daughter buried in the wrong plot.

A man digging up a grave.

A dog running amok in the memorial garden, knocking off angels' heads.

What a Monday morning, Lucy Flippence thought as she drove to Greenlands Cemetery, having been given the job of dealing with these situations. Just when some slack time would have been very handy, too, it being her sister's birthday. It would be really nice to take Ellie out to lunch, especially since Lucy was dying to see her in the wildly colourful new clothes with the new hairdo.

It would be like a complete makeover and highly due, given it was Ellie's thirtieth birthday. For the past two years her sister had been drowning in blacks and greys and taupes, and so caught up in being Michael Finn's personal assistant, she didn't have any other life—not one man sparking her interest.

Right now Lucy had quite a fresh understanding of this disinterest in men. The nasty incident in the Irish pub at Port Douglas had spoiled her weekend away with friends. The guy had started out a promising prince and turned into a horrid frog. It seemed to her they all did, sooner or later. At twenty-eight she had yet to meet one whose shining armour remained shiny, regardless of circumstances.

Even so, she wasn't about to give up on men. She enjoyed the exciting high of a new attraction, loved the sense of being loved, if only for a little while. It was worth the hurt of being disillusioned. As long as she lived, she was going to be out there, experiencing everything that looked and felt good. It was what her mother had told her to do—her mother who'd married her horrible frog father because she was pregnant with Ellie.

'Don't ever make that mistake, Lucy. Be careful.'

She was.

Always careful.

Especially since she didn't want to have children, didn't want to pass on her dyslexia, blighting another life with it. Putting a child through what she'd been through at school was not an act of love, and the problems didn't stop there, either. The incurable disability blocked a heap of avenues that normal people simply took in their stride.

The thought of an innocent baby being born with a wrongly wired brain like hers triggered a strongly negative recoil inside Lucy. She would not risk that happening. Which meant, of course, she would probably never marry—no real point to it if having a family was out of the question.

There was, however, always the hope of meeting a prince who didn't care about having children, or perhaps one who had a genetic fault of his own and would be happy to simply settle with having each other to love. She hadn't ruled out these possibilities. They bolstered her resolve to keep moving on, making the most of her journey through life.

The cemetery on the outskirts of Cairns came into view. It was aptly named Greenlands—everything being so very green as it usually was up here in far north tropical Queensland, especially after the big wet and before the oppressive heat of summer. August was always a pleasant month and Lucy was glad she wasn't stuck in the office, closed off from the lovely sunshine.

As she drove the van into the parking lot, she spotted a man wielding a shovel beside one of the graves. He looked elderly and Lucy instantly decided he wouldn't be dangerous to approach, not that she was frightened of doing so anyway. Her appearance invariably disarmed people.

She loved putting herself together in a fun outfit. The Sunday Markets at Port Douglas were always great for crafty stuff. The wooden bead necklaces and bangles she'd bought yesterday, along with the tan leather belt, and sandals that strapped in criss-crosses up her lower legs, looked fabulous with the white broderie anglaise miniskirt and peasant blouse she was wearing today. Her long blond hair was piled up on top of her head to show off the cute dangly wooden earrings, as well. She didn't look like officialdom and that was half the battle in getting people to confide in her.

The elderly man caught sight of her walking towards him, and stopped digging, leaning on the long handle of his shovel as he watched her approach, looking her up and down as most men did, regardless of age. She could now see two large plastic bags of potting soil lying on the ground beside him, and behind them was the top of a rose bush.

'Well, you're a pretty sight for sore eyes, girlie,' he greeted her, his mouth slowly curving into a wistful little smile. 'Visiting a loved one?'

'Yes, I always visit my mother when I come out here,' Lucy said with her own wistful smile. The man's face was so lined and dotted with age spots she guessed he was about eighty, but his body had a spry wiriness that undoubtedly came from keeping himself active.

'Your mother, eh? Must have died young,' he remarked.

Lucy nodded. 'She was only thirty-eight.' Ten years older than Lucy was now—a fact that lay constantly in the back of her mind, urging her to pack as much into her life as she could.

'What took her?' the man asked sympathetically.

'Cancer.'

'Ah, that's a hard death.' He shook his head sadly. 'Guess I should be grateful my wife went quickly. Heart gave out. Coming up seventy-five she was. Almost made it to our diamond wedding anniversary.'

'You must have had a happy marriage,' Lucy commented, wondering if it was really true. She had observed that some couples stayed together because they didn't want to face the turmoil of breaking up.

'My Gracie was a wonderful woman.' There was love and longing in his voice. 'Wouldn't have swapped her for anyone. She was the best, the only one for me. I miss her so much….' Tears welled into his eyes.

'I'm sorry,' Lucy said softly, waiting until he'd re-

covered his composure before asking, 'Are you planting that rose for her?'

'Yes,' he answered huskily. 'Gracie loved roses.
Especially this one—Pal Joey—because it has such
a beautiful scent. Not like those hothouse roses they
sell in shops. Here...' he bent down and picked up the
bagged rose bush, pointing out the one yellow rose in
full bloom '...come and smell it.'

She did. The scent was stunningly strong and beautiful. 'Oh, that's lovely!'

'I brought it from our garden. I couldn't let my Gracie lie here without some part of our garden, and this
was her favourite rose.'

'Well, Mr...?' Lucy raised her eyebrows quizzically,
needing his name.

'Robson. Ian Robson.'

'Lucy Flippence,' she responded. 'I have to tell you
I'm from cemetery administration, Mr Robson. Someone reported you digging at a grave and I was sent out
to investigate, but I can see there's no harm being done.'

He frowned over any possible interference to his
plan. 'Only want to plant the rose.'

'I know,' Lucy soothed. 'What you're doing is fine
with me. You'll tidy up afterwards, won't you? Leave
your wife's grave looking much nicer than it was before, take the empty bags away?'

'Don't you worry, Miss Flippence. I'll not only do
that, but you can count on me tending to this rose bush,
feeding it and pruning it so it will bloom beautifully
for my Gracie.'

Lucy gave him a warm smile. 'I'm sure you will, Mr

Robson. It's been a pleasure meeting you. I'll go visit my mother now.'

'God bless,' he said in parting.

'You, too.'

As she walked on Lucy had no doubt that Ian Robson had been a prince to his Gracie. That kind of devotion could only come out of a true love which lasted a lifetime. However rare that was, it was comforting to know it did happen—could happen for her if she was super, super lucky.

She stopped at her mother's grave, sighing heavily at what Ellie had insisted be printed on the headstone:

Veronica Anne Flippence
Beloved Mother of Elizabeth and Lucy

No 'Beloved Wife of George,' because that would have been a huge lie. As soon as their mother had been diagnosed with terminal cancer their father had deserted them. Not that he would have been any help during those long months of suffering. Every time he'd come home on leave from his mining job in Mount Isa he'd ended up getting drunk and abusive. Better that he had left his daughters to look after their mother, but the desertion certainly demonstrated there was not even common decency in his character—a frog of the worst order.

Ellie had found out he'd had another woman in Mount Isa and was leading a double life—a cheat on top of everything else. Lucy was glad he had dropped out of their lives. She still hated him for not giving her mother the love she had deserved. There'd been no roses in their marriage—none that Lucy could remember.

'It's Ellie's birthday today, Mum,' she said out loud. 'I'm sure you know that. I bought her a gorgeous butterfly blouse and a lovely green skirt to go with it. She's fallen into a dowdy rut and I want to break her out of it. You said for us to always look out for each other, and Ellie does more than her fair share of that, helping me over hurdles I can't leap like everyone else because of my dyslexia. I'm trying to help her to meet a prince. Guys notice colourful people. She has to give herself a chance, don't you think?'

Lucy smiled at what Ellie had told her over the phone this morning—that her long brown hair was cut and dyed auburn. That was a step in the right direction. If her sister would just lighten up a bit, have some fun, show she was enjoying herself… Guys liked that. In fact, they gravitated towards women who emitted a joy in life.

'If you can perform a miracle, Mum, it would be fantastic if two princes showed up for Ellie and me today. Okay? That would be a birthday to remember.' Lucy heaved another big sigh at the improbability of this happening. 'In the meantime, I've got to go and collect some angels' heads so they don't get damaged any more than they are already. Bye now.'

When she reached the memorial garden, she stood aghast at the number of headless angels. The dog must have been a huge German shepherd or Great Dane. It sure had run amok here. She picked up one head, realised how heavy it was, lay it back down and went to bring the van closer to the garden. It took her an hour to load them all up for transport to the stonemason.

Checking the time, she decided that job could wait until after lunch. If she didn't get to Ellie's office before twelve o'clock, her sister might go off somewhere by herself. Lucy could call her, but surprising her was better. What was a birthday without a nice surprise?

Finding a parking space close to the Finn Franchises building was impossible. Lucy ended up two blocks away from the Esplanade, where it was located. She half ran the distance and managed to arrive at Ellie's office just a few minutes after noon. Having paused long enough to catch her breath, she knocked on the door and opened it enough to poke her head around it to check if the room was occupied. Ellie—a brand-new Ellie—sat at a desk.

It put a wide grin on Lucy's face as she asked, 'Okay to come in?'

'Yes.'

Given the affirmative, she literally bounced in, twirling to shut the door behind her, then dancing over to the desk in an ecstasy of delight over the dramatic change in her sister's appearance. 'Ooh…I *love* the hair, Ellie,' she happily enthused, hitching herself onto the edge of the desk for a close look at the new style. 'It's very sexy. Gives you that just-out-of-bed tumbled look and the colour really, really suits you. It complements the clothes I picked out for you brilliantly. I have to say you look absolutely marvellous. Now tell me you *feel* marvellous, too.'

The slightly uncertain expression on her sister's face cracked into a smile. 'I'm glad I made the change.'

Then, typically Ellie, she turned attention away from herself. 'How was your weekend?'

'Oh, so-so.' Lucy waved her hand airily, then pulled a woeful grimace. 'But I've had the most terrible morning.'

She didn't want to relate the frog in the Irish pub episode. No negatives about men today, with Ellie looking so beautiful. Lucy rattled on about the rose planting at the grave and the dog damage in the memorial garden, describing the scene and what she had to do about it, how heavy the angels' heads were....

It was a really good story, yet Ellie was clearly distracted from it, her gaze sliding away, fixing on some point at the other end of the room.

'Angels' heads...' a male voice said in a rich tone of incredulous wonder.

It sent a weird quiver down Lucy's spine. She didn't know if sound vibrations could squeeze her heart, but something did. She whipped her head around, feeling an instant urge to check out the owner of *that voice*.

And there he was—tall, dark and handsome, the perfect image of a storybook prince!

CHAPTER TWO

EVERYTHING IN MICHAEL Finn's mind was blown away by the vision of stunning femininity perched on the edge of Elizabeth's desk. The legs hit him first—long, beautiful legs, glowing with a golden tan, their shapely calves accentuated by straps running up from her sandals. A white frilly skirt ended at midthigh. A white peasant blouse hung off one perfectly rounded shoulder. A mass of shiny blond hair was piled loosely on top of her head, some curly strands of it escaping whatever pins she'd used.

Her face was turned towards Elizabeth, but there was certainly nothing jarring about its profile, and a fascinating dimple kept flashing in her cheek as she talked, her voice lilting with animation. Arty earrings swayed against her lovely long neck, bangles jingled on her arms as her hands waved around in graceful gestures, and the story she was telling was as mesmerising as the rest of her.

'Angels' heads…?'

The words spilled from his mouth, escaping from the bubble of incredulity bouncing around his brain. He could hardly believe the heart-grabbing impact she was having on him, and her mention of angels added to the sense of an out-of-this-world encounter.

He was used to sizing women up before deciding if he was willing to put the time into having an ongoing relationship with them. He never rushed into a decision because it was so tedious breaking off the connection when he found it didn't suit him. But the *rush* he was feeling with this woman in his sights triggered a wildly rampant compulsion to forge a connection with her right now before she could disappear on him.

Her head turned towards him. Surprise lit her lovely face, her eyes widening as she stared at him—big brown eyes with amber sparkles in them. Shiny coral lipstick highlighted her lush, sexy mouth as it dropped open to emit a breathy, 'Wow!'

It echoed the *wow* zinging around Michael's mind, and he felt himself stirring as her gaze flicked over him, uninhibitedly checking out his physique. Her open interest in him was like an electric charge. He had an erection in no time flat—which had never happened to him at a first meeting with any woman, not even when he was a randy teenager. At thirty-five, this was a totally new experience and a slightly discomforting one. He prided himself on always being in control.

'Are you Ellie's boss?' she asked, her head tilting as though her mind was racing through possibilities between them.

Ellie...? It took him several moments to wrench his thoughts away from the rage of desire burning through his bloodstream, and connect the name to Elizabeth. 'Yes. Yes, I am,' he finally managed to answer. 'And you are?'

'Lucy Flippence. Ellie's sister. I work in cemetery administration, so I often have to deal with angels,' she said, as though needing to explain to him that she wasn't off the planet, but an ordinary human being with a proper job to do.

'I see,' he said, thinking she wasn't the least bit ordinary.

She hopped off her perch on the desk and crossed the floor to him with her hand extended. Curvy hips swayed. Perky breasts poked out at him. She was tall, slim and so exquisitely female that all his male hormones were buzzing.

'Pleased to meet you.' Her smile was entrancing. 'Okay if I call you Michael?'

'Delighted.' He took her hand and held on to it, the soft warmth of it making his skin tingle with excitement at this first physical contact.

He suddenly registered movement at his side, reminding him he'd just come out of a serious business meeting with his brother. Harry was stepping up, expecting an introduction. Was he feeling the same impact, wanting Lucy's attention turned to him, centred on him? Michael fiercely hoped not. He didn't want to fight his brother over a woman, but he would with this one. A highly primitive sense of possession was swirling through his gut.

His eyes telegraphed hard warning-off signals at Harry as he turned to make the introduction. This was no-go territory. Don't make a contest of it. They had always respected each other's interest in their targeted women, but Lucy had to be a magnet for any man. Even as he said, 'This is my brother, Harry,' Michael willed him to accept he had first claim.

His heart swelled with satisfaction when Lucy left her hand in his grasp and simply raised her other hand in a blithe greeting, tossing a 'Hi, Harry!' at his brother in a kind of bubbly dismissal.

'Charmed,' Harry purred at her.

The flirtatious tone didn't raise so much as a flicker of response. Her gaze instantly connected to Michael's again, the warm brown eyes appealing for understanding and, to his mind, much more than that to come from him. He felt her reaching out, wondering, wanting....

'I don't know if you know, but it's Ellie's birthday today,' she said, 'and I thought I'd treat her to a really nice lunch somewhere. You won't mind if I take her off and she's a bit late back, will you, Michael?'

Lunch...*yes,* he thought exultantly. He couldn't wait to have more of this enchanting woman.

'Actually, I'd decided to do the same myself,' he quickly informed her. 'Lunch at the Mariners Bar.'

'Oh, wow! The Mariners Bar!' Her eyes sparkled with golden lights. 'What a lovely boss you are to take Ellie there!'

'Why don't you join us? It will be a better celebration of her birthday if you do.'

'I'll come, as well. Make a party of it,' Harry put in, instantly supporting the idea.

Four was better than three, Michael decided. Harry had to know now that Lucy wasn't interested in him, and he could entertain Elizabeth, which took the onus of doing that off him.

'I only booked a table for two,' his PA inserted, pulling them back to arrangements already made.

'No problem. I'm sure the maître d' will make room for us,' he stated, oozing confidence as he smiled at Lucy. 'We'd be delighted to have the pleasure of your company.'

Her smile of delight was turned to her sister. 'Well, a foursome should be more fun, don't you think, Ellie?'

There was a touch of irony in Elizabeth's reply. 'Certainly no awkward silences with you, Lucy.'

She laughed, seeming to sprinkle sunshine at everyone as she happily declared, 'That's settled then. Thank you for asking me, Michael. And it's good of you to join in the party, too, Harry.'

Michael wasn't interested in having a party.

What Harry called his tunnel vision—usually applied only to his work on the franchises—had kicked in with a vengeance on Lucy Flippence. He saw no one but her. His entire focus, physical and mental, was on her. He wanted her completely to himself.

It didn't occur to him that it might not be a good idea to bed his PA's sister.

All he could think of was how to get her there as fast as he could.

CHAPTER THREE

LUCY COULDN'T BELIEVE her luck. The prince liked her, wanted to be with her. And what a prince he was, not only drop-dead gorgeous, but a billionaire to boot! Ellie had said enough about the Finn Franchises for her to know this guy was seriously wealthy, but had never mentioned he was also seriously sexy.

Which gave Lucy pause for thought as they made their way out of the building and across the Esplanade to the boardwalk that ran along the water's edge of the park leading to the marina. Was there something *wrong* with Michael Finn, something that had put Ellie off being attracted to him? Was he a terribly demanding boss? Lucy wasn't keen on *demanding* men. If he had struck himself off Ellie's possibility list, Lucy needed to know why before jumping in the deep end with Michael Finn.

Though it was a beautiful day and her heart was singing. There was no reason not to enjoy this exciting attraction while it was still lovely and shiny. As soon as they paired off on the boardwalk, the two of them in front, Ellie and Harry behind, Michael gave Lucy a smile that tingled right down to her toes.

'Tell me about yourself, Lucy,' he invited. 'How did you come to be in cemetery administration? You look as though you should be a model.'

He had silver-grey eyes—very distinctive, like the rest of him—and she was thrilled that he was interested in her, if only for a little while. Words bubbled out in an effervescent stream. She told him about her experience of modelling—its advantages and disadvantages—then tour guide jobs she'd had, and he laughed at the amusing stories about people who'd made guiding both difficult and hilarious at times. Moving on to her stint in the dance studio, she was prompted to ask, 'Do you dance, Michael? I mean, do you like dancing?'

It was a strike against him if he didn't.

He grinned at her, half singing, 'I've got rhythm... you've got rhythm....'

She laughed in delight.

'Our mother insisted that Harry and I have dancing lessons when we were kids,' he went on. 'Said it was a mandatory social skill and we would enjoy it in the end. We grumbled and groaned at having to miss sport for girlie dancing, but she was right. You could get the same adrenaline rush out of dancing as you can out of sport.'

'A case of mother knows best,' Lucy remarked.

He winced ruefully. 'She always did.'

Seeing the change of expression, Lucy softly asked, 'Does that mean your mother is not still with you?'

It drew a quizzical look. 'Don't you recall the plane crash that took both my parents?'

'No. I'm sorry, but...'

'It was all over the newspapers, the media....'

She wasn't about to admit that her dyslexia made

reading newspapers too difficult. 'How long ago was this?'

'Close to ten years.' His frown lifted. 'Maybe you were too young to take much notice. How old are you, Lucy?'

'Twenty-eight. And just over ten years ago my mother died of cancer. I didn't take much notice of anything for a while, Michael.'

'Ah…understandable.'

His face relaxed into a smile again and Lucy was highly relieved that a sympathetic bond had been established. She pushed it further, saying, 'I don't have a father, either. He deserted us before Mum died. It's just me and Ellie now.'

'Do you live together?'

'Yes. We share an apartment. Ellie is a wonderful sister.'

The voice of her wonderful sister shattered the lovely build-up of understanding. It was raised in extreme vexation, crying out, 'That's because you're so annoying!'

Startled, Lucy instantly swung around, anxious that nothing go wrong today. Michael turned, too. Seeing that she'd drawn their attention, Ellie rolled her eyes at her companion and huffed in obvious exasperation before saying, 'It's okay. Harry was just being Harry.'

Guilt swirled around Lucy's mind. Had she inadvertently lumped Ellie on her birthday with a man she didn't like, spoiling the nice lunch her sister had been anticipating with Michael? Being completely star-struck by the storybook prince, Lucy might have been blindly selfish in so quickly agreeing to a foursome, not really consulting Ellie about whether it was okay with her.

'Be nice to Elizabeth, Harry,' Michael chided, 'It's her birthday.'

'I *am* being nice,' he protested.

Ellie didn't lose her temper over nothing, Lucy thought, taking proper stock of Michael's brother. He was a very manly man, his white T-shirt and shorts displaying a lot of firm muscle and smoothly tanned skin. The slightly bent nose stopped him from being classically handsome, but the riot of black curls and the bedroom blue eyes gave him a strong, rather raffish attraction. He exuded a confidence that probably meant he was used to being popular with the opposite sex, but he'd be dead in the water with Ellie if she perceived him as a playboy.

'Try harder,' Michael advised, dismissing the distraction by lightly grasping Lucy's elbow and turning her away with him to continue their stroll together.

She couldn't dismiss it so easily. 'Does Ellie dislike your brother, Michael?' she asked, hating the feeling that this foursome had been a very bad idea.

If it was, she had to break it up, regardless of the miracle meeting with this man. A real prince who was truly, deeply attracted to her would pursue a relationship, anyway. It wasn't fair to Ellie, messing up her birthday with a man she found hard to tolerate. Better for them to dump the men and go off together, though that was tricky with Michael being Ellie's boss.

'I don't think it's a case of *dislike,*' he answered with a slightly wry grimace. 'I've never known anyone to dislike Harry. He's a natural charmer, but he does tend to ruffle Elizabeth's feathers with his flirting.'

There was flirting and *flirting,* Lucy thought, and some of it could get a bit icky.

'Don't worry,' Michael went on. 'He'll behave himself now. I've warned him.'

That made no difference if, deep down, Ellie couldn't abide the man. Lucy needed to have a private word with her, suss out the situation to her satisfaction. Impossible right here. They had walked past the park with the children's playgrounds, and were level with the swimming lagoon. Another ten minutes' stroll would bring them to the Mariners Bar, Hopefully, she would get the chance to be alone with Ellie in the cocktail lounge before they went into the dining-room.

In the meantime there was no point in not making the most of Michael's company.

'We'd got up to dancing,' he reminded her with a grin, the grey eyes lit with amused curiosity. 'Modelling, tour guiding, dancing—how did this lead to cemetery administration?'

'Oh, there's a lot of stuff in between,' she said airily. 'I was doing a beautician course while the dancing was paying off. That led to jobs in a department store and two of the holiday resorts up here.' She slanted him a twinkling look. 'I do a great foot massage and pedicure if you ever need one.'

He laughed. 'A woman of many talents.'

She loved the sound of his laugh. It echoed in her ears and seemed to ripple down to her heart, where it tripped her pulse into racing overtime.

What was she going to do if his brother was a frog? *Please don't let him be,* she silently begged. It would ruin this highly promising lunch.

Michael kept asking her questions, seemingly intrigued by her, which was a lovely feeling. Most guys wanted to talk about themselves. He gave her the sense that he'd never met anyone like her before and he couldn't get enough of her, not right now, anyway. Whether that would last... Well, nothing usually did, not on this kind of high, but Lucy couldn't help revelling in it.

Of course, he wouldn't be intrigued by her at all if he knew the truth—that she didn't just flit from one job to another because she was attracted to something new and different. More times than not she ran into an unavoidable snag because of her dyslexia, and she was either let go or moved on before she had to suffer the humiliation of being found wanting again. Her disability was a curse she had to live with, but she was determined to enjoy the good times in between being stumped by it and having to pick herself up and try something else.

Right now the promise of having a very good time with Michael Finn was thrilling her to bits, though she still had to check with Ellie that what was happening was okay with her. She wanted her sister to have a happy birthday. Men came and went in Lucy's life. Ellie was the only person she could count on to always be there for her.

They'd passed the yacht club and were on the path to the cocktail bar adjoining the restaurant when Harry called out to them. 'Hey, Mickey! I'll buy the girls cocktails while you see the maître d' about our table.'

Mickey? Mickey Finn. Lucy rolled her eyes. That was such *boy stuff!* Maybe Harry was simply an overgrown boy, irritating Ellie with his silly immaturity.

'Okay.' Michael tossed back the response, apparently accustomed to being called Mickey by his brother, and not minding it.

Whatever… The arrangement between them would give her some time alone with Ellie in the cocktail bar—time enough to check if the current scenario sucked for her sister.

Michael left them at the bar, striding swiftly into the restaurant to speak to the maître d'. Harry led them to a set of two-seater lounges with a low table in between, and saw them settled facing each other.

'Now let me select cocktails for you both,' he said, the vivid blue eyes twinkling confidence in his choices. 'A margarita for you, Elizabeth.'

It surprised her. 'Why that one?'

He grinned. 'Because you're the salt of the earth and I revere you for it.'

She rolled her eyes at his linking her character to the salt-encrusted rim of the glass that was always used for a margarita cocktail.

Though it was clever, Lucy thought, openly conceding, 'You're right on both counts. Ellie loves margaritas and she *is* the salt of the earth. I don't know what I'd do without her. She's always been my anchor.'

'An anchor,' Harry repeated musingly. 'I think that's what's been missing from my life.'

'An anchor would only weigh you down, Harry,' Ellie put in drily. 'It would feel like an albatross around your neck.'

'Some chains I wouldn't mind wearing.'

'Try gold.'

He laughed.

This quick banter between them gave Lucy pause for speculation. 'Do you two always spar like this?' she asked.

'Sparks invariably fly,' Harry claimed.

Ellie gave him an arch look. 'I would have to admit that being with Harry is somewhat invigorating.'

Lucy laughed and clapped her hands. They were playing a game, scoring points off each other. It wasn't bad at all. 'Oh, I love it! What a great lunch we'll all have together!' She cocked her head at the man who was certainly ruffling Ellie's feathers, but quite possibly in a way her sister found exciting under her surface pretence of indifference. 'What cocktail will you choose for me?'

'For the sunshine girl…a pina colada.'

She clapped her hands again. 'Well done, Harry. That's *my* favourite.'

'At your service.' He twirled his hand in a salute to them both and headed off to the bar.

A charmer, Michael had said, and Lucy could now see how it was. Ellie was attracted to Harry but she didn't trust his charm, maybe thinking he was a bit too slick with it. She should just ride with it, enjoy it, let her hair down and not care where it led.

Lucy leaned forward to press this advice on her sister. 'He's just what you need, Ellie. Loads of fun. You've been carrying responsibility for so long, it's well past time you let loose and had a wild flutter for once. Be a butterfly instead of a worker bee.'

An ironic little smile tilted Ellie's mouth as she drawled, 'I might just do that.'

'Go for it,' Lucy urged, excited by the possibility that

both the brothers could be princes. 'I'm going for Michael. He's an absolute dreamboat. I'm so glad I wasn't held up any longer at the cemetery. I might have missed out on meeting him. Why didn't you tell me your boss was gorgeous?'

'I've always thought him a bit cold.'

Lucy threw up her hands at her sister's lack of discernment. 'Believe me. The guy is hot! He makes me sizzle.'

Ellie shrugged. 'I guess it's a matter of chemistry. Harry is the hot one for me.'

Chemistry...yes! That explained everything. There was nothing *wrong* with Michael. Quite simply, there was no chemistry between him and Ellie, and no one could make that happen. It either did or it didn't. Lucy had met some really nice guys in her time, but there'd been no point in dating them. They just didn't do it for her.

She sat back contentedly, the narky questions that had been niggling at her making a complete exit, leaving her free to fall in love again.

She grinned at Ellie. 'Brothers and sisters...wouldn't it be great if we ended up together, all happy families?'

It was a lovely fantasy! Totally off the wall, because Lucy knew she wasn't good enough to hold on to a man of Michael Finn's calibre. Today was hers. Probably tonight. Maybe she would have him for a week or two if she could manage not to be found wanting by him.

'I think that's a huge leap into the future,' her sister commented, rolling her eyes at Lucy. 'Let's just take one day at a time.'

Sensible, as always.

And completely right, as always.

But Lucy was flying high and didn't want to be brought down to earth.

That could happen tomorrow or the next day or the next....

Today she was over the moon and wanted to stay there.

CHAPTER FOUR

WHILE LUCY DIDN'T believe in big dreams for herself, she saw no reason for Ellie not to have them. Her sister was brilliant at everything. No one could find fault with her. However, her personal life certainly needed brightening, and Harry Finn looked like the right man to do it if she'd simply fling the door open and let him in.

'You're always so sensible, Ellie,' Lucy chided, wanting her to lighten up and take a few risks for once.

'Which is something I value very highly in your sister,' Michael said warmly, picking up on her words as he appeared beside them and seated himself next to her on the lounge.

'Oh, I do, too,' she quickly agreed, liking him all the more for appreciating this quality in his PA. She bestowed a brilliant smile of approval on him as she added, 'But I also want Ellie to have fun.'

'Which is where I come in,' Harry said, also catching her words as he came back. His eyes danced with wicked mischief as he gazed at Ellie. 'Starting with cocktails. The bartender will bring them over. Here are the peanuts and pretzels.'

He placed a bowl of them on the table and settled

himself beside her, throwing her a challenging look that mocked any resistance to having fun with him. She flicked him a sizzling glance in return.

Definitely something hot going on between them, Lucy thought, and gave Harry an approving smile as she asked, 'What cocktail did you order for Michael?'

'A Manhattan. Mickey is highly civilised. He actually forgets about sunshine until it sparkles over him.'

Lucy laughed at the teasing reference to herself as the sunshine girl. 'And for yourself?'

'Ah, the open sea is my business. I'm a salty man, so I share Elizabeth's taste for margaritas.'

'The open sea?' Lucy queried.

'Harry looks after the tourist side of Finn's Fisheries,' Michael answered. 'I take care of buying in the stock for all our franchises.'

'Ah!' She nodded, understanding why Harry was dressed the way he was.

She knew Finn's Fisheries was a huge franchise with outlets all around Australia. They not only stocked every possible piece of fishing gear, a lot of it imported, but the kind of clothing that went with it: wetsuits, swimming costumes, shorts, T-shirts, hats. The range of merchandise was fantastic and Ellie had told her Michael dealt with all that.

She knew about the tourist side, too, having been a tour guide herself. There were Finn dive boats offering adventures around the Great Barrier Reef, Finn deep sea fishing yachts for hire, and for the really rich, the exclusive getaway resort of Finn Island, where she'd never been but would love to go.

Harry couldn't be too much of a playboy if he was

responsible for keeping these enterprises running successfully. She noticed that his white T-shirt with the tropical fish had the emblem of Finn Island printed below his left shoulder, and wondered if he'd come from there this morning. Maybe if she and Michael hit it off really well, he would take her to the glamorous getaway.

Lucy decided she could not have wished for a more exciting situation—Ellie and Harry, she and Michael. The conversation over cocktails zipped with good humour. Ellie drank a second margarita, definitely loosening up, hopefully throwing caution to the winds. A thirtieth birthday was not a time to be overly sensible.

Lucy wanted her sister to have the best possible day.

Which led to making *the mistake!*

They were handed menus as soon as they were seated in the dining-room, and instead of waiting for the others to start talking about the dishes listed, as she usually did, the fact that they were at a top-line restaurant gave her the confidence to say, 'I bet I know what you're going to order, Ellie.'

Her sister raised her eyebrows. 'What?'

Lucy grinned at her. 'The chilli mud crab.' It was her absolute favourite dish.

'Actually, I can't see that on the menu,' Michael said, glancing quizzically at her.

'Oh, I didn't really look. I just assumed,' she replied quickly, silently cursing herself for being an impulsive idiot.

Revealing her disability to a man she wanted to impress—a man as smart as Michael Finn—would make him lose interest in no time flat, and she would shrivel up inside if he got that look on his face—the look that saw her as defective. Hiding her dyslexia was always the best course. Now she had to cover up the stupid mistake.

Pretending to study the menu properly, she asked, 'What have you decided on, Michael?'

'The steak.'

'How about sharing a seafood platter for two with me, Elizabeth?' Harry said, leaning closer to point out the platter's contents on the menu. 'You get crab on it, as well as all the other goodies, and we can nibble away on everything as we please.'

Lucy instantly warmed to him even more—a sweet man, not only caring about her sister's pleasure, but also taking the meal selection heat off herself.

'Harry will eat the lion's share,' Michael warned.

Harry instantly raised a hand for solemn vowing. 'I swear I'll give you first choice of each titbit.'

'Okay, that's a done deal,' she said, closing the menu and slanting him a smile.

'Sealed with a kiss,' he said, bright blue eyes twinkling wickedly as he leaned closer still and pecked her on the cheek.

'You can keep that mouth of yours for eating, Harry,' she snapped, probably on the principle of give him an inch and he'd take a mile.

He grinned. 'Elizabeth, I live for the day when I'll eat you all up.'

'That'll be doomsday.'

'With the gates of heaven opening for me,' Harry retorted, his grin widening.

Lucy couldn't help laughing.

Ellie heaved a long-suffering sigh and shook her head at him. 'You are incorrigible.'

'A man has to do what a man has to do,' he archly declared, sending Lucy off into more peals of laughter.

He *was* fun. And totally irrepressible. She suspected that Ellie was holding out against him because she got a kick out of the sparring, as well as not wanting him to think she was an easy catch.

However, their selection of a seafood platter for two didn't help Lucy with choices. She would have to order the same as Michael, which was okay. The steak should be very good here.

Michael was amused by Harry's determined assault on Elizabeth's defences, amused by her determined resistance to his charm, too. Most women would be lapping it up. His brother was going to have to work hard to win this one over, but the battle served to keep them occupied with each other, leaving him free to pursue the connection with Lucy.

He'd been quite stunned when Elizabeth had turned up at work this morning wearing the gorgeous butterfly blouse—totally atypical of her usual style in clothes. A birthday gift from her sister, she'd said—a sister who was as different from her as chalk and cheese. She was so right about that. He could see Elizabeth as a schoolma'm. Lucy promised to be a delicious array of exotic cheeses, and tasting all of it had already become a must-do in his life.

And despite her choice of *white* clothes today—very sexy white clothes—she was definitely the butterfly, flitting from job to job as though they all had some sweet nectar for her, tasting and moving on, clearly enjoying everything that life could offer her, wanting a whole range of experiences.

Including him.

Saw him, liked him, wanted him.

His head was still spinning with the excitement of her uninhibited response to their meeting. No games, no pretence, no guard up—just lovely open Lucy letting him know she found him as sexy as he found her. It was a struggle not to be in a constant state of arousal.

He thought of Fiona Redman, his most recent ex, who'd definitely been into female power games. The convenience of having her as a sexual partner did not stack up against the annoyance of being expected to toe her lines. No woman was ever going to decide for him when he should work and when he shouldn't. The success of Finn Franchises had been top priority in his life ever since his father's untimely death, and that was not about to change any time soon.

However, he would certainly make time to satisfy this sizzling lust for Lucy. It probably wouldn't last long. The sheer novelty of her would wear off and the usual boredom or irritation would set in. He had never come across the magic glue that could make a relationship stick. He always found fault somewhere and that was the end of it. Quite possibly the fault was in him. Whatever… he was going to enjoy this woman as long as she stayed enjoyable.

The waiter returned and took their orders. Lucy chose the steak, too. Wanting to share everything with him? It was absolutely exhilarating being with her, especially when she turned those big brown eyes on him, the golden specks in them glowing with warmth.

'You said dancing lessons interfered with sport, Michael. What did you like playing?' Dimples flashed in her cheeks as she spoke.

He smiled reminiscently. 'Everything in those days—cricket, baseball, tennis, soccer, rugby.'

'Not now?'

'They were mostly schoolboy passions. I still play tennis, but only socially. I have a couple of games of squash during the week to loosen up from too much desk work, and usually a round of golf at the weekend.' She looked sublimely fit, probably from dancing, but out of interest he asked, 'What about you? Any sporting passions?'

'I can play tennis, but like you, only socially. At school I mostly concentrated on athletics.'

He grinned. 'High-jump champion?'

His instant assumption surprised her. 'How did you guess?'

'Long legs. Great shape, too.'

And he couldn't wait to have them wound around him in an intimate lock.

'You're obviously in great shape yourself,' she retorted, her eyes simmering with the same kind of thoughts, driving his excitement metre higher. Then, as though taking a mental back step, she added, 'I also play netball with a group of friends once a week. I always keep up with my girlfriends. Men can come and go, but real friends stay in your life.'

'You don't count any men as real friends?'

'A few gay guys. They're lovely people. Lots of empathy and caring.'

'No straight ones?'

Her dimples deepened as her luscious lips twitched into a provocative little smile. 'Well, sooner or later most straight men turn into frogs.'

'Frogs?' he repeated, needing enlightenment. He'd heard 'empathy and caring' loud and clear but 'frogs'?

Her eyes danced teasingly at him. 'You suddenly turn up in my life and everything about you shouts that you're a prince amongst men.'

A prince. That was a surprisingly sweet stroke to his ego.

Her hands lifted in a helpless gesture. 'But how do I know you won't turn into a frog tomorrow?'

'Ah!' he said, understanding. 'You've been with guys who haven't lived up to their promise.'

She shrugged prettily, the off-the-shoulder sleeve of her peasant blouse sliding lower on her upper arm. 'It happens,' she said in airy dismissal. 'I'm hoping not to be disappointed with you, Michael.'

The seductive challenge sizzled straight to his groin. He was up for it, all right. He wished he could whizz her straight off to bed. How long would this birthday luncheon go on—main course, sweets, coffee? At least another hour and a half. He'd give Elizabeth the rest of the afternoon off, take Lucy to his penthouse apartment. Although...

'Do you have to get back to work this afternoon?' he asked.

'Yes, I do,' she answered ruefully. 'I have to deliver the angels' heads to the stonemason, take the van back to the office, then visit the people who own the burial plot that's been mistakenly used, and hopefully persuade them that one burial plot is as good as another.'

'Tricky job,' he said with a sympathetic wince.

'Not really. It's a matter of getting them to empathise with the bereaved parents who have just laid their daughter to rest—how terrible it would be for them to have her dug up again,' Lucy explained. The caring in her voice moved something in his heart, reminding him of laying his parents to rest, the final closure.

Caring, empathy…he sensed something quite special in this woman. She wasn't just fantastically sexy. There was much more to her. So far it was all good.

'Are you free tonight?' he asked, not wanting to wait any longer to have her to himself.

'Yes.'

Her smile promised an eagerness that matched his for a more intimate encounter. Which made his hard-on even harder.

Fortunately, the waiter showed good timing in arriving with their main course. Their conversation moved to food as they ate their steaks, which were perfectly cooked, asparagus on the side with a touch of Béarnaise sauce, and crunchy roasted potatoes.

Lucy was into cooking, loved experimenting with different combinations of ingredients. Better and better, Michael thought, looking forward to enjoying many meals with her. She had an infectious enthusiasm for life that made her company an absolute delight. He was wondering if she'd ever cooked frogs legs after bidding a frog goodbye when Harry claimed his attention, leaning an elbow on the table and pointing a finger at him.

'Mickey, I have the solution to my problem with the resort.'

The problem that had brought him to the office

this morning—the discovery that the resort manager was feathering his own nest at their expense. Michael frowned over the interruption. He didn't want to talk family business with his brother when he had plans to make with Lucy.

'You have to clear that guy out, Harry,' he said tersely—the same advice he'd given earlier. 'Once you confront him you can't leave him there. The potential for damage…'

'I know, I know. But it's best to confront him with his replacement. We walk in and turf him out. No argument. A done deal.'

Why was he persisting with this discussion here? 'Agreed,' he said impatiently. 'But you don't have a ready replacement yet and the longer he stays—'

'Elizabeth. She's the perfect person for the management job, completely trustworthy, meticulous at checking everything, capable of handling everything you've thrown at her, Mickey.'

That rocked him. Was Harry off his brain, wanting to mix pleasure with business? The way he'd been madly flirting…was he seriously attracted? This didn't feel right.

'Elizabeth is my PA,' Michael stated firmly, giving his brother a steely look.

Harry dug in regardless. 'I'm more in need of her than you are right now. Lend her to me for a month. That will give me time to interview other people.'

'A month…' Michael frowned over the inconvenience to himself. Harry did have a point. He needed a replacement for Sean Cassidy pronto.

'On the other hand, once Elizabeth gets her teeth

into the job, she might want to stay on,' Harry said provocatively.

Michael glowered at him. 'You're not stealing my PA.'

'Her choice, Mickey.' Harry turned to her. 'What do you say, Elizabeth? Will you help me out for a month… stay on the island and get the resort running as it should be run? My about-to-be ex-manager has been cooking the books, skimming off a lot of stuff to line his own pockets. You'll need to do a complete inventory and change the suppliers who've been doing private deals with him. It would be a whole new challenge for you, one that—'

'Now hold on a moment,' Michael growled. 'It's up to me to ask Elizabeth if she'll do it, not you, Harry.' This on-the-spot decision didn't sit well with him, particularly with his brother virtually railroading him into it, yet it was a credible solution to the problem.

'Okay. Ask her.'

Michael heaved an exasperated sigh, disliking the sense of having been pushed into a corner. 'It's true,' he reluctantly conceded. 'You would be helping us out if you'd agree to step in and do what needs to be done at the resort. I have every confidence in your ability to handle the situation. Every confidence in your integrity, too. I hate losing you for a month….'

He grimaced at the prospect. She was his right hand in the office, always understanding and delivering whatever was needed. Gritting his teeth, he muttered, 'I guess someone from the clerical staff can fill in for a while….'

'Andrew. Andrew Cook,' she suggested, which meant she had already decided to go with Harry.

'Too stodgy. No initiative,' Michael said, hating the idea of having to do without her.

'Absolutely reliable in doing whatever task he's set,' she argued.

'I take it that's a yes to coming to the island with me,' Harry noted, grinning from ear to ear.

She shot him a quelling look. 'I'm up for the challenge of fixing the management problems, nothing else, Harry.'

Good! Michael thought. Elizabeth wasn't about to mix business with pleasure. If that was on Harry's mind, as well as solving his predicament, she'd spike his guns and serve him right, given that he'd have to put up with Andrew Cook while she was away.

'That's it then,' he said, resigned to a month of having to spell out everything to his *pro tem* PA.

'A whole month! I'll miss you, Ellie,' Lucy said wistfully.

Ah, yes! A month of Lucy without her sister possibly butting into their relationship, Michael thought, realising and appreciating the one upside of this situation. It could have been tricky having his PA an ever-present watchdog while he bedded her sister. Absolute freedom from that felt good. A month might very well be the limit of this currently hot connection, anyway—everything done and dusted before Elizabeth returned to take up her position with him again.

'The time will pass quickly enough,' she assured Lucy.

The waiter arrived with the sweets they'd ordered when he'd cleared away their main course.

'We need to get moving on this,' Harry muttered as he dug into his chocolate mud cake.

'As soon as possible,' Michael agreed, looking forward to having intimate time with Lucy.

'Today,' Harry decided, checking his watch. 'It's only three o'clock now. We could be over on the island by four-thirty. Have him helicoptered out by six. We leave here when we've finished our sweets, hop on the boat....'

'It is Elizabeth's birthday, Harry,' Michael reminded him. 'She might have other plans for today.'

'No, I'm good to go,' she said.

Great! he thought. No delay to what he wanted.

'What about clothes and toiletries and stuff?' Lucy put in. 'You're going for a month, Ellie.'

'You can pack for her, Lucy,' Harry said decisively. 'Mickey can take you home, wait while you do it, take Elizabeth's bags and arrange their shipping to the island.'

'No problem,' Michael said, smiling at Lucy. 'I'll give you my phone number. Give me a call when you've finished work and I can come by your apartment this evening.'

She'd be there all by herself. Perfect!

Her eyes danced with pleasure as she agreed to the plan, and her smile was full of sensual promise.

Michael decided he didn't care what Harry did with Elizabeth.

Let them sail off into the sunset!

He was going to make hay with the sunshine girl!

CHAPTER FIVE

LUCY WAS NERVOUS. Excited, too. Much more excited than she usually was about having a first date with a new man, which was probably what was making her so nervous. Plus the fact that Michael Finn was a high-flyer and she had never connected with anyone from his level of society. She was definitely out of his league in any social sense, and more than likely he only wanted a sexual fling with her, which she might as well accept right now and not get herself in a twist about it.

Regardless of his intentions, she wanted to be with him, wanted to experience him, so no way was she going to back off at this point. Besides, a Cinderella could win a prince. Miracles could happen. Failing that, if the worst came to the worst, she could write off her time with him as a case of real lust being satisfied. Because while she had certainly fancied other guys in the past—not like this, not nearly as strongly as this—Michael Finn had her in an absolute tizzy of lust.

Just thinking of him, she was squeezing her thighs together, and when she'd been in the shower earlier, running her hands over herself, dying to know how it would feel with his hands caressing her naked body.

Even now as she prepared the Thai salad to go with the prawns she'd bought on the way home, her stomach muscles kept contracting.

He'd be here soon—another ten minutes or so. The apartment was tidy. The table was set. She'd changed into a yellow wraparound dress with a tie belt that could be easily undone, and underneath it she wore her sexiest white lace bra and panties, wickedly intent on knocking his socks off, though he probably wouldn't wear socks. Or shoes. Easily slipped off scuffs, she decided, like hers. She'd deliberately left off jewellery, not wanting it to get in the way. Her only adornment was a frangipani flower she'd picked off the tree in the front yard and stuck in her hair.

She imagined him wearing shorts and an open-necked sports shirt that could be pulled off in a second. Would he have a hairy chest? Not too hairy, she hoped, but having such thick black hair, and obviously loaded with testosterone, he was bound to have some. She couldn't wait to see, to touch. Her fingers were tingling with anticipation.

The doorbell rang.

Her heart started pounding.

Please let him be a prince tonight, she wildly prayed. *Please let him not do or say anything to put me off him. I want this night to be perfect.*

The rush of desire steaming through her made her legs feel weak as she walked to the door and opened it. Her breath caught in her throat at seeing him again— so stunningly handsome, and the silver-grey eyes shining with pleasure at seeing her. She barely managed a husky 'Hi!'

His smile was dazzling. 'I've been looking forward to this moment ever since we parted this afternoon,' he said, the lovely deep tone of his voice sending a thrill through her.

'Me, too,' she said, smiling back. 'Come on in, Michael.'

He was wearing shorts and a sports shirt—navy and red and white, a strong combination that emphasised his alpha maleness. He handed her a bottle of wine as he stepped into the living-room. 'To go with whatever you've planned to feed me.'

She laughed. 'It's only a light meal. It was a very substantial lunch.'

'Perfect!' He matched the word to the glance encompassing her appearance before adding, 'It's a light wine, too.'

A very good one, she thought as she glanced at the label—Oyster Bay Sauvignon Blanc. Almost giddy with excitement, she certainly didn't need alcohol to feel intoxicated, but she asked, 'Do you want to open it now?'

'When we eat,' he said dismissively, taking in her living space. 'This is a wonderfully welcoming room, Lucy. Did you do the decorating?'

It was a fairly standard two-bedroom apartment, one bathroom and an open kitchen combined with the living area, but she was proud of how they had turned it into their home, and Michael's approval of it was especially pleasing. She set the bottle of wine on the kitchen counter so she could use her hands to gesture at various items as she answered him.

'Ellie bought the basic furniture. I added the cushions and the wall posters and the rug in front of the lounge. We wanted it to be a cheerful place to come home to, and with the walls and floor tiles being white, the whole place virtually begged for bright splashes of colour.'

'You've done a brilliant job.' He gave her another dazzling smile, setting off a fountain of joy inside her. 'My mother was great at using colour to please the eye, too.'

Being compared to his mother felt like a huge compliment. Lucy beamed at him. 'I'm glad you like it.'

He shook his head slightly as he moved towards where she stood in front of the kitchen counter, 'There's nothing not to like about you, Lucy.'

The lovely low throb in his voice set her stomach aflutter and her heart leapt into a wild gallop when his hands started sliding around her waist. Her own hands automatically lifted to his shoulders as he drew her closer, gently pressing her lower body to his. The silvery-grey eyes darkened with a storm of feeling, searching hers for a reflection of the same storm.

'I don't want to wait any longer,' he said, the plea edged with urgent demand.

'I don't, either,' she admitted without hesitation, every atom of her body yearning to know all of him.

Her lips were already eagerly parted as he bent his head to kiss her. When his mouth made contact with hers—an incredibly sensual first taste—her head whirled with the sudden roaring of her blood. She moaned softly, deep in her throat, as his tongue slid over hers, sweeping her mouth with acute sensation. The kiss fast became more fiercely demanding, driving her into a wild response. The lust that had been simmering since the first moment of meeting flared into passionate need.

Her hands buried themselves in his hair, fingers raking through the thickness of it, grasping his head possessively. His hands clutched the cheeks of her bottom, scooping her hard against him, pressing her so close his erection furrowed her stomach, exciting her further with his strong arousal. Her whole body started aching for him. Her thighs quivered with the fierce desire to feel him inside her, and the rush of hot wetness between them begged for instant satisfaction.

The gloriously devouring mouth suddenly abandoned hers, breaking away to snatch air in ragged gasps. 'Lucy...' It was a groan of wanting.

'Yes... Yes...let's do it.' The response spilled straight off her tongue.

In a spurt of frenetic energy she pushed herself out of his embrace to lead him into her bedroom. 'Come on,' she urged, untying the belt of her dress, taking off the light garment and tossing it onto the lounge as she passed, turning as she reached the bedroom door, looking back to see how he was responding to her wanton invitation.

He'd spun around and was facing her, but seemed stunned into immobility, an incredulous look in the eyes that were raking her from head to toe. His glittery silver gaze lingered on the white lace panties and bra long enough to make the wetness hotter and turn her nipples into bullets.

'You do want me?' she asked provocatively, wondering if he was more used to leading the action than having a woman doing it.

'Oh, yes! Madly!'

The vehement reply shot a bolt of elation into a gurgle of laughter.

He tore off his shirt and hurled it on top of her discarded dress. He did have hair on his chest—a nest of black curls across the centre of it, arrowing down to where his hands were unfastening his shorts. Fascinated, she watched as he pulled them down and stepped out of his remaining clothes. More black curls framed his manhood, which was magnificently primed for action.

Her insides quaked with anticipation. Nevertheless, she never forgot caution, and didn't this time, either. The urge to step back and touch him was irresistible. She took him in her hand, fingers gently stroking the silky skin of his strong shaft as she lifted her gaze to his, appealing for understanding. 'I need you to wear a condom, Michael.'

'Right!' he said, sucking in air and shaking his head as though trying to clear it, while reaching for his shorts again and extracting a packet, holding it up for her to see. 'I did come prepared.' He raised a quizzical eyebrow. 'You're not on the Pill?'

She slid her other hand up his chest, spreading her fingers into the black curls. 'Yes, I am, but that's not protection from everything.' Her eyes flashed him a look of troubled uncertainty. 'I don't know who you've been with before me, Michael.'

He frowned. 'I assure you I'm clean.'

'I want you to be, but I won't risk my health,' she pleaded.

His mouth twisted into a rueful grimace. 'Fair

enough!' He lifted a hand to her cheek, a sympathetic look in his eyes as he stroked where she usually dimpled. 'You've been with a frog who lied to you?'

She grinned at his pick-up on frogs. 'No. I just believe in being careful.'

He grinned back. 'Okay. I'll see a doctor tomorrow. Get a clearance. Can we do without condoms then?'

She flung her arms around his neck, her eyes dancing with relief and pleasure as she rubbed her body invitingly against his. 'You're looking ahead to more of me?'

'Much more,' he assured her in his deep-throated voice.

She lifted herself up on tiptoes and kissed him, deliriously happy that he had so readily accepted her conditions, and he didn't see her as a one-night stand.

He instantly took the initiative from her, claiming her mouth with wildly erotic passion, clamping her body to his, driving up the urgency of the desire churning through both of them. He broke the raging intimacy of their kissing long enough to command action. 'Put your feet on top of mine, Lucy.'

She did and he walked her backwards, keeping her locked to him, the movement making her acutely aware of the hard muscular tension in his thighs, in his entire body. Her breasts were brushing the broad hot wall of his chest, tingling with excitement. Her skin felt electric, buzzing with sensory overload. She couldn't wait to be completely naked, too, feeling all of his maleness everywhere.

As soon as he'd turned into her bedroom, one of his hands slid to her bra clip and unfastened it. Impatient for all barriers to be gone, she unwound her arms from his neck and stepped off his feet, quickly pushing the straps from her shoulders, flinging the bra away, grabbing the top of her lace panties and pulling them down enough to lift her legs out of them.

Michael was wasting no time, either, tearing open the packet of condoms, sheathing himself. She straightened up and for one sizzling moment they looked at each other, revelling in the sight of their sexuality completely open to view. He was perfect, Lucy thought, absolutely perfect, and the glittering desire in his eyes told her she was just as excitingly perfect to him.

He startled her by suddenly swooping and lifting her off her feet, crushing her to his chest. It was a smallish room. The bed was close by, a couple steps away.

'You bring out the caveman in me,' he said gruffly.

She laughed, bubbling over with elation at the possessiveness of his action. When he carried her onto the bed, the same streak of possessiveness swept through her as she wound her legs around his hips in aggressive ownership.

Take me, take me. The words were pounding through her mind, the fierce need to take *him* thrumming through her whole body. She was open to him, dying for him, and he didn't keep her waiting, plunging inside her so fast she gasped at the glorious sensation of the aching emptiness being totally filled, powerfully filled.

She clutched him to her, wanting to hold him there, wanting to hold on to this awesome moment, live her awareness of it to the full. 'Michael...' She breathed his name—the man who lived this moment with her.

'Open your eyes, Lucy,' he commanded.

She hadn't realised she'd closed them, keeping the

high mountain of feeling to herself. But yes, she wanted to share it with him, have him share what he was feeling with her. She opened her eyes wide and caught the fierce intensity in his—the need to know, the desire to take all that she was.

'Keep them open.'

She did, watching him watch her as he began a rhythm of retreat and thrust that slowly escalated to a faster and faster beat, on and on until she was arching, bucking, writhing with the pleasure of it, the excitement, the exquisite tension, building, building to a crescendo of almost agony, teetering on the unbearable. She cried out, her eyes wildly demanding release, her hands clawing his back, her feet goading him on in desperate need, her heart seemingly on the point of bursting.

'Yes…' The word hissed from between his teeth and his eyes blazed with sheer animal triumph as he drove himself into her as deeply as he could, and the agony shattered, melting away on wave after wave of ecstasy emanating from the spasms that convulsed around him.

'Yes…' she echoed, with a moan of sweet pleasure, feeling him pulsating, too, his body shuddering in his own explosive release, his chest heaving for breath, and when he collapsed on top of her, it seemed his heart was drumming in sync with hers, a testament to their utter togetherness.

Long may it last, Lucy fiercely willed.

She'd never had a man like Michael Finn in her life.

She wanted what they had right now to go on and on forever.

Of course it wouldn't…couldn't.

Loopy Lucy—which was what the kids at school had called her—was not good enough to hold on to this top-of-the-scale man for long. *Just cherish the moment,* she told herself. *Hug it tight.* Make it a memory she could hold on to. Unless she suffered amnesia or Alzheimer's disease, nothing could take great memories away from her.

They were hers forever.

CHAPTER SIX

Wow!

For a while it was the only word in Michael's mind. He had been conscious enough of his heaviness on top of Lucy to roll onto his side, but he took her with him, ensuring their togetherness continued. She hooked her leg around him, as intent as he was on maintaining their intimate connection. Her incredibly sexy breasts were softly heaving against his chest. Her warm breath was wafting over his throat. Her arms embraced him as though she wanted to stay clamped to him forever.

She was…amazing!

So uninhibited about showing her desire for him, voicing it, moving on it… no woman in his memory had ever been so actively inviting, making him feel he was amazing to her. His heart started thumping again as he recalled her peeling off her yellow dress, revealing the lovely curve of her back, the long glorious legs and her cheeky bottom fringed in white lace. Then stepping back to stroke him…

His mind had been so blown by her he might well have forgotten the condoms if she hadn't brought up the safe sex issue. He was glad that she had. It was best to be careful. They had no history between them. Only today. But there were going to be a lot of tomorrows. He'd get a health clearance as soon as he could, do away with the condoms so there'd be nothing between him and the whole sensual experience of Lucy Flippence.

His PA's sister...

Amazing!

She was certainly the best possible consolation prize for losing Elizabeth to Harry for a month.

When Michael grew too soft for her to hold him in, she sighed and moved her head to look at him, her big brown eyes shiny with pleasure, a smile of contentment curving her mouth. 'That was fantastic, Michael,' she said happily.

'Fantastic!' he agreed, grinning in turn.

'Shall we go and have a shower together?'

'Nothing I'd like better.'

She laughed, disentangling herself from him and rolling off the bed. 'I'll go and turn the taps on. We don't have a mixer in the shower and you have to be almost a rocket scientist to get the temperature right using both taps. I don't want you to get scalded and—' her eyes danced teasingly '—I don't want you to have a cold shower, either.'

She made him laugh. She made him feel happy. He suddenly realised he hadn't felt this happy for a long time. The sunshine girl... He smiled over the aptness of the name as he followed her to the bathroom.

Showering together was another sensual delight, caressing each other with soap, doing what should have been foreplay, except they'd been in too much of a hurry. He loved her breasts, large enough to fill his hands and firm enough to hold their beautiful shape. The areolae were brown, a very distinctive frame for her enticing nipples, which he'd definitely pay more attention to later this evening...though possibly not much later. He was hardening again under Lucy's erotic ministrations.

'Mmm...' she murmured, looking down at him and cocking her head with a considering air. 'Maybe we should do what we have to do first, or we might never get it done.'

'What do we have to do?' he asked, dropping a kiss on her forehead.

'Pack a bag for Ellie. And we could open your bottle of wine and eat what I've prepared.' Lucy met his gaze, eyes twinkling with mischief. 'Not that you look as if you need to build up your strength, Michael, but it might be even better if we wait a bit.'

'Okay.' He didn't mind waiting, knowing what was coming. 'Elizabeth won't need much,' he informed her. 'She'll be wearing the island uniform while she's on duty, the same as Harry had on today—white shorts and T-shirt with the Finn Island emblem. She'll be supplied with those clothes.'

'So, it's toiletries, make-up, underclothes....' Lucy turned off the taps, stepped out of the shower, grabbed a towel for herself and handed him one as she listed the items to be packed. 'Pyjamas, dressing-gown, the gorgeous caftan I bought her for swanning around in.' She grinned at him. 'It will certainly catch Harry's eye.'

'I'm not sure that would be doing your sister a favour.'

The remark earned him a sharp look. 'You think he wouldn't be good for her?'

Michael shook his head. 'I didn't mean that.'

'What then? Ellie is very dear to me. I don't want her hurt.'

He shrugged. 'I simply have the impression she doesn't approve of my brother. The way he flirts...'

'Mmm...probably doesn't trust him yet. I think she was badly let down by a guy about two years ago. Put her right off men. Harry will have his work cut out winning her over, but she is attracted to him. No question.' Lucy wrapped her towel around her, tucking it in above her breasts.

'What about you?' he asked, wrapping his own towel around his waist.

'What about me?'

'How long have you been unattached?'

'Oh, a couple of weeks,' she answered, waving an airy hand as she headed out of the bathroom.

'You weren't devastated by the break up?'

'Not at all. I'd been going off him for some time and I finally called it a day.'

She entered a second bedroom. He followed, watching as she opened a built-in wardrobe and lifted down a medium-size travel bag from the top shelf. 'This should do,' she said, smiling at him as she turned to lay it on the bed, waving at a chair in front of a computer desk. 'Take a seat while I pack.'

He sat, noting that Elizabeth's room was very different from Lucy's—no vivid colours, less random clutter, more orderly, somehow not as endearing in personality. 'Why did you go off him?' he asked, curious about Lucy's dislikes in a man.

She rolled her eyes. 'He was getting to be a control

freak, wanting everything his way. In my book, relationships should be a two-way street. I am not going to be told what to do, what to wear or what to say, and he actually started answering for me when people asked me questions....' She threw up her hands.

'No respect for the person you are,' Michael deduced, liking her stance for individuality.

'How come you're unattached?' She tossed the question at him, returning to the wardrobe to fetch clothes.

'I wasn't available enough for the last woman I was involved with. She thought I should take off from work any time at all, specifically when she wanted me to.'

'Ah!' Lucy grinned at him as she brought an armload of garments to the bag. 'No respect for your position.'

He nodded. 'Altogether too self-centred.'

She shook her head, wryly remarking, 'It starts off good. You think it's going to be great. Then it all goes downhill.' Her eyes sparkled brightly at him. 'Let's make a deal, Michael. I won't try to change you and you won't try to change me. If we don't gel as we are, then we accept that and part with no hard feelings.'

'Sounds good to me.'

He didn't want to change one thing about Lucy Flippence. Her directness and spontaneity were a delight. He imagined her last guy had been the type to want to catch a butterfly, put it in a bottle, poison it and pin it to a board so it could never fly away and attract anyone else's eye. She was well rid of him.

'I'll just grab Ellie's toiletries and make-up from the bathroom and pack them before I add the good stuff. Don't move. I'll be right back,' she instructed.

It was strange being in his PA's bedroom. It actually felt like an intrusion of her private life, which he'd known nothing about until Lucy had enlightened him. He hoped Harry would be careful with Elizabeth, not treat her feelings lightly if he pursued the attraction that Lucy was so sure of.

Maybe a trip over to the island might be a wise move, to check out what was happening between them. In a month's time Michael wanted a fully functional Elizabeth back in the office with him, and that might not be how it would end up if his brother messed with her emotions.

Lucy waltzed back in with her plunder from the bathroom.

'Are you free this coming weekend?' he asked her.

'Free as a bird,' she answered blithely, placing Elizabeth's essentials in the bag.

Or a butterfly, Michael thought, smiling over his image of her. 'We could go over to Finn Island, see how your sister's doing, stay Saturday night and enjoy the facilities ourselves.'

Her face lit with delight and she clapped her hands in excitement at the prospect. 'I'd love that, Michael.'

'I'll call Harry tomorrow, set it up.'

'Wonderful! I know about Finn Island, of course— exclusive getaway, open bar, gourmet food—but I've never been there. Do you go often yourself?' she asked as she returned to the wardrobe to select more clothes.

'No. Harry oversees everything to do with the island.'

'I didn't mean for business.'

'For pleasure?'

'Yes. I imagine it's very romantic.'

Michael laughed. 'With the right companion, yes. It's not such a paradise with the wrong one.'

'Well, I hope it will be paradise for us,' she said, grinning at him while proceeding to load up the bag. 'This should see Ellie through. She can tell me on the weekend if she needs more.' Having zipped it shut, Lucy grinned at him again. 'Now food and wine and fun in the kitchen.'

Michael was happy with that program.

She led him back to the living room, where she whipped away her towel, picked up the yellow dress, put it on—without underclothes—and turned to him as she did up the tie belt, her eyes dancing teasingly. 'This is safer for me while cooking, but you can keep your towel, Michael.'

He did, enjoying the idea that he was as accessible to her touch as she was to his in the wraparound dress. She quickly provided glasses and he opened the bottle of wine, while she removed a prepared salad and a plate of prawns from the refrigerator.

It was fun in the kitchen. Lucy was playful, provocative and positively entrancing. She had a wonderfully expressive face and he loved watching it as she talked and laughed, loved how her dress swished with the sway of her hips and the bodice gaped with each movement of her breasts. She was so delectably female, absolutely adorable and incredibly sexy.

The meal they sat down to was perfect: prawns cooked in a Thai dressing with a touch of ginger and chilli, accompanied by a very tasty salad. Lucy ate with uninhibited relish. Just watching her enjoy the food was erotic. She emitted a joy in life that Michael realised he'd been missing ever since his parents had died.

There'd been pleasures—many of them, from many sources—but this unadulterated sense of joy bubbling over... His mother had been like that, as though every day the sun shone just for her, and life was always beautiful. The gift of happiness, he thought. Lucy had it, too. Maybe he had found the woman he could spend the rest of his life with.

The fanciful thought surprised him. What had it been—about nine hours since he'd met Lucy? She made an incredible impact, but it was far too early to be entertaining any thoughts about a future with her beyond the month he'd given himself. As she'd said herself, it starts off good then it all goes downhill. Right now it was great, but 'downhill' was probably on its way, sooner or later.

After they had cleaned up after their meal they returned to the bedroom, both of them intent on a slower build-up to ultimate intimacy. Michael loved Lucy's total lack of inhibitions, her innate sensuality, the exquisite delicacy of her tantalising caresses. She inspired him to stroke, kiss and taste her all over, revelling in her responses. It was an act of extreme control to hold off taking her until she begged him to do so, intense need making her voice shrill. His own excitement was at fever pitch and their coming together was even more incredibly satisfying than before.

He was conscious of a wildly primitive elation, almost a sense of triumph in bringing her to such a powerful peak of wanting him. She climaxed almost immediately and he exulted in the hot creaminess of her as he drove towards his own climax—a fiercely ecstatic release that left him floating in a sea of joy.

When he finally kissed Lucy goodbye that night, he carried the joy with him. How this relationship would turn out—whether they'd be compatible as a couple or not—he didn't know and didn't care. He was going to take whatever he could of Lucy Flippence until the joy of her ran out.

CHAPTER SEVEN

Lucy was on cloud nine. Michael had wanted to be with her every night this week. Even on Wednesday evening, when she played netball with her friends, he'd come to the gym to watch her in action, and quite happily suffered being introduced to a group of hot, sweaty women. So far he'd been an absolutely perfect lover, showing no froglike tendencies at all. He was charming, considerate, always ready to laugh with her, have fun, and tomorrow he was taking her to Finn Island, which would surely be paradise.

Her heart was pounding with excitement as she walked along the Esplanade, anticipating their date this evening. Michael had to work late and he'd asked her to meet him at Danini's, a very chic Italian restaurant, at eight o'clock for dinner. He'd booked a table, which was just as well, because there was a crowd of people out and about—lots of tourists enjoying the warm weather, visiting the night markets and filling up most of the tables in the pavement section of the many restaurants catering to them.

'Do you want to sit inside or out?' Michael had asked her before making the booking.

'Out,' she'd answered, preferring the evening breeze off the ocean to air-conditioning, and the hustle and bustle of the street to the relative seclusion of an inside dining-room. She enjoyed watching people, and if she had to wait for Michael to arrive, it would pass the time pleasantly.

As it turned out, she didn't have to wait. Although it was five minutes short of eight o'clock when she arrived at Danini's, Michael was already seated at a table.

'You're early,' Lucy declared, greeting him with a happy smile.

'So are you,' he said, returning her smile as he stood to hold out her chair.

She laughed, instantly feeling giddy in his presence. 'I didn't want to miss out on any time together.'

'Nor did I.'

His eyes sparkled with silvery glints, and Lucy's heart was skipping with happiness as she sat down. A pina colada was on the table in front of her. 'Oh, you've bought me my favourite cocktail, too. Thank you, Michael.'

'Your pleasure is my pleasure,' he said in his deep, warm voice, resuming his seat opposite her.

He was a beautiful, beautiful man. A true prince, Lucy thought, thanking her lucky stars that she had met him. This was an experience she could treasure for the rest of her life.

He handed her a menu, which was always a tricky business for her. 'Have you decided already on what you want to order?' she asked.

He nodded. 'The veal scallopini.'

'I'll have the same.'

'What about sweets?'

She grinned at him as she closed the menu. 'I'll watch what's being served at other tables and see what appeals most.'

He laughed and set his menu aside, content to wait for her decision. A waiter arrived very promptly and took their order, leaving them both to settle back comfortably and enjoy each other's company.

'There's a charity ball at the casino next Saturday night,' Michael told her. 'I bought tickets months ago, more to contribute to the charity than with any intent of attending, but we can join a group of my friends if you'd like to come and dance with me.'

'I'd love to dance with you,' she said truthfully, though meeting his high society friends was a bit of a worry. Regardless of that problem, however, the invitation to the ball was proof he was anticipating a second week with her, which was marvellous.

'Then I'll look forward to it,' he said, looking pleased.

Lucy firmly told herself the invitation also proved Michael wasn't worried about how she'd mix with his peers. On the other hand, he was a man, and on the whole, men didn't look for shortcomings in her. It was the women who could get narky if they thought she didn't fit in with them.

Her friends had all raved over Michael. What woman wouldn't? He had everything!

His friends would undoubtedly be running a more critical eye over her.

The ball at the casino would be a test of whether their relationship could stand up in his world.

Lucy hoped she would pass it with flying colours.

Though Michael had to, as well. For him it would be a test of how well he tried to integrate her with his group of friends, whether he would stand by her side as a true prince would if she ran into difficulties, protect her if she needed protecting. It would be lovely to feel secure with him.

There had been no security in her mother's marriage—not emotional or financial or even physical security—and Lucy knew she would never commit herself to any man long-term unless she was confident she would be safe with him in every sense. Not that she was expecting long-term with Michael, just hoping for longer than her relationships with guys usually ran.

Determined to being prepared when meeting his friends, she gave him an inviting smile and said, 'Tell me about the people we'll be with at the ball.'

Happy to oblige, he described one married couple who ran a wedding bureau specialising in the Japanese market, since it was much cheaper to have a wedding in Cairns than in Japan, with the plus factor of a tropical location. Another couple owned a coffee plantation up near Mareeba on the tablelands. A third couple was making big business out of macadamia nuts, mangoes and other exotic fruits. The rest were singles, but all of them successfully established in various fields—smart, wealthy achievers.

Lucy couldn't help thinking none of them would understand her haphazard way of moving from one job to another. She wasn't *driven* to achieve anything because she had always known her dyslexia would get in the way. Enjoying herself with whatever appealed and was available was the best she could do.

'I won't fit in with them, you know,' she warned Michael. 'I'm from a different kind of zoo.'

He looked totally unconcerned, grinning at her as he lifted his cocktail glass in a toast. *'Vive la différence!'*

The tension that had been building up in Lucy eased. Michael was the only one who really counted, and he liked her the way she was.

Their meal arrived, along with a bottle of red wine to go with the veal. The meat was melt-in-your-mouth tender, the mushroom sauce was delicious and the wine, a full-bodied cabernet sauvignon, complemented both perfectly. Lucy's palate was immensely pleasured by it all and she sat back with a contented sigh when she'd finished eating.

As Michael put down his knife and fork, looking equally replete, she felt a strong sense of being watched. Her skin prickling at being the target of some intense focus, she threw a sharp glance around. Passers-by were streaming past the restaurant, none of them paying any attention to her, but the feeling persisted and her gaze was eventually drawn to a table at the adjoining restaurant.

Recognition of the guy from the Irish pub in Port Douglas came as a nasty jolt. He was staring straight at her, and when he caught her eye he lifted a schooner of beer in a half-drunk, mocking manner, a look of leering triumph on his face. He was with a group of men, probably the same ones who had been at the pub.

They'd been fun at first, flirting with her and her girlfriends, inviting them to dance—fun until they'd drunk too much. They were a bunch of good-looking men who were obviously used to getting their own way with women regardless of their behaviour. They'd yelled abuse after Lucy and her friends when they'd walked out on them.

She'd actually felt attracted to the guy staring at her now—Jason...Jason Lester. He had a gym-toned body, wicked blue eyes and a sexy bristle along his jaw, but by the end of the evening the attraction was stone-dead. And he hadn't liked being rejected by her—not one bit.

Her stomach cramped when he pushed his chair back and stood up, his gaze still trained on her. Alarm crawled down her spine. If he was intent on confrontation... She quickly reached out and grabbed Michael's hand, needing his full attention as her eyes transmitted an urgent warning.

'There's trouble coming our way,' she said quickly.

'What?' He frowned, looking past her to spot what she found disturbing. 'You mean Jason Lester?'

'You know him?'

'Played football against him in my teens.'

She hadn't imagined any connection between them and didn't have time to ask Michael whether he'd liked Jason or not, which drove up her tension considerably when the guy arrived at their table.

'Well, well, here's the honey bee again,' he drawled sneeringly, his gaze shifting to Michael, who was rising to his feet, half a head taller than Jason and more broad-shouldered, but apparently not intimidating enough to stop a jeer at him. 'Pulling in bigger bucks with you, Mickey Finn.'

'You're being rude, Jason,' Michael said tersely, his face set in stony challenge as he added, 'inexcusably.'

'Just thought I'd give you a friendly warning, Mickey.

What looks like all sweetness has quite a sting in her tail.'

'I'd prefer to discover that for myself,' he replied coldly. 'Now if you don't mind...'

'But I do mind. I want the honey bee to spell out why she turned her back on me when she's slept with half the men in Cairns.' The blue eyes lasered hers with vicious spite. 'Well, sweetheart?'

Her face flamed at the slur on her character. That he had made such a nasty crack about her in front of Michael goaded her into a wild reply. 'Even a town slut can have standards, Jason Lester, and you don't meet them.'

'After richer pickings, aren't you?' he retorted, and threw a last mocking look at Michael. 'Just so you know what you're playing with, old friend.'

He left.

Lucy sat frozen, watching him saunter off. It totally appalled her that she'd used the term 'town slut' on top of Jason Lester's numbering her ex-lovers as half the men in Cairns, making it sound as if she was actually acknowledging herself as a slut, which she wasn't. Far from it. But Michael could be starting to see her that way—as a gold-digging slut who had drawn him straight into her bedroom on their first night together.

If Jason Lester and Michael had been friends... If Michael believed him, one man to another... She couldn't think past that, couldn't bring herself to look at the prince who might at this very moment be turning into a frog.

Michael slowly unclenched his hands as he watched Jason Lester make a quick retreat back to the safety of a gang of mates seated at a table in the next restaurant. Typical of him to dive in, hit where it hurt, then run for cover. He'd always been a dirty player on the football field, grabbing guys' crotches and squeezing whenever he could. Harry had got him back in one game, delivering a bit of justice.

Certainly there was no friendship fostered between Lester and the Finn family. He hadn't come to this table to do any favours. His only purpose had been to poison the happy flow of a relationship he wanted to destroy out of some malicious sense of envy. Michael *knew* this, but he couldn't stop himself from wondering how much truth there was in the poison.

The honey bee...

It was an apt name for Lucy, flitting along in her free-spirited way and so sweet to be with in every sense.

The burning question was how many men had dipped into her honey? He might have dismissed Lester's snide crack about half the men in Cairns but for Lucy's retort that even a town slut had some standards. It had been an angry retort, hitting back, yet his own experience with Lucy—her easy, uninhibited approach to having sex—suddenly didn't feel so great to him.

This past week he had been obsessed by the pleasure of her, at the cost of his usual complete concentration on work. Even tonight he'd cut short what he should have done in the office, impatient to be with her again. Had she deliberately gone after his balls because of his 'big bucks'? He'd thought that her joy in sex was part and parcel of her nature, but maybe it was all designed to play him, to take him where she wanted him to go, ensnare him into not looking beyond what she gave him. Was he being fooled by this woman?

He glanced sharply at Lucy as he resumed his seat. Her chin was up at a defiant angle. Her face was taut. No smile. Her whole body looked tense. Her gaze was lowered, seemingly fixed on the table next to theirs, where the waiter was serving sweets. Michael didn't think she was considering what to order for herself, but he decided to pretend that she was. A bone-deep pride insisted that Lester not see he had disturbed either of them in the slightest.

Michael reached over and touched her hand to draw her attention back to him. Her head turned slowly, reluctantly, and when she lifted her gaze to his he saw her eyes were anguished.

Because what she was had been revealed…or because it deeply distressed her to have him think anything nasty of her? There was no certain way of telling at this moment, and he wasn't about to sit in judgement with Lester watching.

Michael quickly composed an indulgent smile and nodded to the next table. 'Do you fancy any of the sweets being served over there?'

'What?' she asked in a dazed fashion.

'You said you wanted to see what sweets other people ordered before you decide,' he reminded her.

'Oh!' There was a second of utter disbelief, almost instantly chased away by immense relief. The frozen look on her face cracked into a smile that showered him with a gush of warmth. 'I wasn't really looking at them.'

He squeezed her hand. 'Don't let Lester spoil your appetite. I love the way you appreciate good food.'

The smile wobbled. 'He was so nasty. I thought…' Her eyes searched Michael's anxiously.

Again he squeezed her hand. 'He's gone, Lucy. We were enjoying ourselves. Let's wipe him out of our minds and keep on enjoying ourselves.'

She looked at him wonderingly. 'You can do that?'

'Yes.' It wasn't the absolute truth, but he grinned at her to lighten the moment and said, 'Though I'm glad you didn't sleep with him. I have standards, too, and Lester doesn't meet them.'

'I hate abusive men,' she said fiercely. 'My father was abusive when he got drunk. It was a huge relief when he dropped out of our lives.'

Michael frowned, wondering what exactly 'abusive' entailed, if there was any bad sexual history that might have led to sluttish behaviour on Lucy's part. 'Do you mean violent?' he asked cautiously.

Lucy grimaced. 'He did hit Mum occasionally. Most of the time, though, he'd just get mean and nasty.'

'What about you and your sister?'

She shook her head. 'We learnt early on to stay out of his way when he got drinking.'

Michael sensed nothing hidden behind her answer and felt relieved that there'd been no sexual abuse. He wished Lucy hadn't made that 'slut' remark. It sat uneasily in his mind, along with Lester's 'bigger bucks' remark.

'Not a happy household,' he murmured, thinking how lucky he had been with his parents.

'It was happy when my father was away in Mount Isa,' she said quickly. 'He lives there full-time now. He's a miner.'

'I see. He came home to Cairns in between shifts.'

'Yes. And it was always a relief when he left.' She shook her head again. 'Mum should never have married him. She was pregnant with Ellie at the time and more or less got trapped into it. She was on her own up here, having come from a broken home herself—no one to turn to—and she tried so hard to hold it all together. I couldn't have had a better mother, Michael.'

'Well, I'm glad of that,' he said sincerely. 'And I'm sorry your father wasn't what he should have been.'

She eyed him curiously. 'What was your father like?'

'He was great. Both my parents were. Harry and I were brought up in a very happy home.'

She sighed. 'Then you must have only good memories of them.'

'Yes.'

'I guess you'll want to give your children the same kind of happy home.'

There was a faraway look in her eyes, as though she was imagining how it might be in the future. *Whoa!* The warning shot straight into Michael's mind. He might have gone there with her before Lester had fired his bolt of poison, but he didn't want a wife or the mother of his children to have earned the reputation of being a slut.

On the other hand, his gut rebelled against giving Lucy up at this point. He'd never had sex this good, and until Lester's intrusion she had been a delight to be with. Michael still wanted to enjoy this relationship. He wasn't looking for any long-term future with her. He just wanted a continuation of what they'd been sharing all week.

The waiter arrived to clear away their dinner plates,

and diverted Lucy's attention to ordering sweets. The rest of the evening was fun and they finished it off with fantastic sex. Michael was content with that, deciding he would simply enjoy one day at a time with Lucy, take the experience for what it was—complete and utter pleasure. If it was his wealth that made her sparkle for him, he didn't care, as long as she kept sparkling. He liked the sunshine. It relaxed him. It made him feel happy.

CHAPTER EIGHT

FINN ISLAND...

Lucy drank in all she could see of it as Michael steered his motor launch closer to the wharf where Harry was waiting for them. They had entered a large bay edged with a beach of very white sand, partially shaded by masses of palm trees. It was a beautiful sunny day and the water was a glorious glittering turquoise. At the centre of the crescent of sand wide wooden decks led up to the main buildings of the resort. On either side, villas were stepped up on hills that were covered with rainforest.

Paradise, indeed, she thought, except for the snake in it. Last night Michael had urged her to wipe the encounter with Jason Lester out of her mind, and she had tried to do that, relieved that Michael's interest in her had not wavered. But somehow it didn't feel right that he hadn't cared about what had been said. Although she had dreaded a negative reaction from him, it didn't seem natural for there to be no reaction at all. Unless he just wanted the sex to continue, regardless of how many men she had slept with.

She'd told herself not to get in a twist about it if

Michael just wanted a sexual fling with her. But if he now saw her as no better than a slut to be used…or even worse, a slut with an eye on taking a slice of his wealth… Lucy hated that thought.

It had wormed its way into her mind this morning and she couldn't get it out. She *had* slept with most of the men she'd dated for any length of time, though not on the first night. It had been different with Michael. The excitement of connecting with him had been so intense that the idea of holding him off until they knew each other better hadn't even entered her head. She'd done what she'd wanted to do, elated that the desire was so mutual.

And he'd made her feel…*amazing.*

Still did.

As though she was the best thing that had ever happened to him.

He was certainly the best thing that had ever happened to her.

Maybe she was worrying needlessly.

He'd been happy in bed with her last night, happy with her company on the boat this morning, touching her with pleasure in his eyes, holding her, kissing her. She'd revelled in the warmth of his manner towards her. If she could just get rid of this uneasy feeling that underneath it all he might have no respect for her, she would be totally happy with what they were sharing.

Harry helped Michael fasten the motor launch to the wharf and led them to a golf buggy for a quick ride to the administration centre, where Ellie was waiting for them. A track wound through the rainforest and underneath the awesome canopy of foliage formed by the incredibly tall trees were masses of tropical vegetation: giant tree ferns, palms, bamboo, hibiscus, native flowers. Lucy wondered if her sister loved working in this environment, so different to city living. Had she found it more relaxing, or was working with Harry a tense situation, given the very personal element of being attracted to him?

Ellie was not one to let down her hair in a hurry, but Lucy hoped she was letting Harry into her life. Two years of strict spinsterhood needed to be broken. Ellie was too young to give up on men. There was pleasure to be had in relationships, even though the guys might turn into frogs after a while. Lucy decided to insist they all have lunch together. It would give her the opportunity to observe what was happening between Harry and her sister.

They alighted from the buggy at a wide wooden walkway dividing the two main buildings. Michael took her arm, tucking it around his, smiling in pleasure at having her with him. Lucy's heart lurched. He was such a beautiful prince. She desperately wanted to be his princess, though she already knew this relationship would not have that happy ending.

Michael would want a family in his future. He hadn't actually said so last night, but she'd felt it in his head and in his heart, and she wasn't the one who'd be sharing that with him. Nevertheless, she still wanted to feel he loved and respected her.

Harry led them into the manager's office. Lucy beamed at her very clever sister, who rose from behind an imposing desk, looking very much in charge of everything. 'This island is fabulous, Ellie,' she immediately enthused. 'What a great place to work!'

'Tropical paradise,' Ellie replied, smiling as she moved out from behind the desk to greet them.

Lucy slipped her arm free of Michael's to rush forward and give her a hug. 'Are you loving it?' she asked, curious to know everything, especially the situation with Harry.

'Not too much, I hope,' Michael semi-growled in the background.

'It's been quite a change,' Ellie said drily, flicking him a sharply assessing look, probably checking if he was badly put out by her decision to leave him for a month. He hadn't grumbled about it to Lucy, but he probably wouldn't anyway, since their relationship had nothing to do with his work, and he'd be conscious of the fact she and Ellie were sisters.

'A good one, I hope,' Harry interjected, drawing Ellie's attention to him.

'Yes,' she answered with a warm smile, which Lucy took as a very good sign.

'Now, Harry, poaching my PA is not on,' Michael declared.

'Like I said before, Mickey—*her choice,*' he replied with an affable shrug.

'Okay, while you two guys argue over my brilliant sister, I want her to show me her living quarters,' Lucy put in quickly, wanting to get Ellie on her own. 'You can mind the office, can't you, Harry?'

'Go right ahead,' he said agreeably.

'Come on, Ellie,' she urged, nodding to the door at the back of the office. 'Michael said your apartment was right here. I want to see everything. And while I'm at it, may I say you look great in the island uniform?'

Ellie laughed. 'Not as spectacular as you this morning.'

Lucy was wearing cheeky little navy denim shorts with a red-and-purple halter top, big red hoop earrings, red trainers on her feet, and a purple scrunchie holding up her long blond hair in a ponytail. 'Am I over the top?' she asked.

Ellie shook her head. 'You can carry off anything, Lucy.'

'I wish....' she replied with a wry grimace, as Elizabeth ushered her into the apartment and closed the door on the two men in the office.

She hadn't carried off the encounter with Jason Lester with any classy panache, quite possibly adding to his nasty slur on her character with her own wild retort, and she wasn't very confident of carrying off being an appropriate companion for Michael at the ball next Saturday night. Jason's accusation that she had come on to one of the Finn brothers because of his wealth might be suspected by Michael's friends. It could also have tainted *his* opinion of her.

Ellie eyed her quizzically, sensing something was weighing on her sister's mind. 'Is that a general wish or...?'

'Oh, nothing really,' she replied airily, not wanting to unload these highly personal problems on her sister. She focused on examining the living-room of the apartment. It looked bright and cheerful, with colourful tropical prints on the cushions softening all the cane furniture. An adequate kitchenette ran along one wall.

A television and sound system were arranged against another. She gestured around, saying, 'This is lovely, Ellie. Show me the bedroom and bath.'

The very modern bathroom had everything any woman could want, and there was no stinginess in the bedroom, either. The queen-size bed had much more space than the king-size singles they had at home. She couldn't help grinning mischievously at Ellie. 'Have you shared this with Harry yet?'

'Actually, no.' She retaliated with, 'Do you want to tell me what's going on with Michael?'

Lucy threw up her hands. 'Everything is happening! I swear to you, Ellie, I've never been this mad about a guy. I'm in love like you wouldn't believe, and while it's incredibly wonderful, it's also scary, you know?'

'In what way scary?'

Because it meant too much that everything feel right between them—so much it made her terribly conscious of shadows lurking in the wings. She flopped onto the bed, put her hands behind her head and stared at the ceiling, knowing Ellie expected an answer, and finally picking a problem her sister would readily understand.

'Michael is smart. I mean *really* smart, isn't he?'

'Yes.'

'So what happens when he finds out that my brain wasn't wired right and I'm a dummy when it comes to reading and writing? So far I've been winging it, as I usually do, but this is far more intense than it's been with other guys, and he's bound to start noticing I'm a bit weird about some things.' She rolled her head to look directly at Ellie, needing a straight opinion from her. 'You've worked for him for two years. Will it put him off me if I tell him I'm dyslexic?'

Her sister frowned in thought, then slowly shook her head. 'I honestly don't know, Lucy. Does it feel as though he's in love with you?'

'Well, definitely in lust. I can't be sure that's love, but I really want it to be. More than I've wanted anything. I want him to care so much about having me, it won't matter that I'm flawed.'

Ellie sat on the bed beside her and smoothed the worried furrows from her brow. 'It shouldn't matter, if he loves you. And stop thinking of yourself as a dummy, Lucy. You're very smart, and you have so many talents.... Any man would be lucky to have you in his life.'

She heaved a rueful sigh. 'Well, I don't want him to know yet. I couldn't bear it if...' She shot a pleading look at Ellie. 'You haven't told Harry, have you?'

'No. And I won't.'

'I need more time. To give it a chance, you know?' A chance to keep this man as long as she could—to have all the pleasure of him—because it was really going to hurt when she did lose him.

'Yes, I know.'

'I've been running off at the mouth about me. What about you and Harry?'

Ellie shrugged. 'Same thing. More time needed.'

'But you do like him.'

'Yes.'

There was obviously a chance for something really good here for Ellie. Harry couldn't possibly see any bad in her. She was clever and classy and sensible, perfectly suitable to be a wife who could manage any-

thing in the Finn world. Definitely not riff-raff—a tag
Lucy suspected might be attached to herself, since she
drifted aimlessly from job to job, living in the moment
rather than planning ahead, because there was really
nothing to plan for, not with her dyslexia blocking any
way upward.

In contrast, Ellie's path forward had always been
clear. The teachers at school had loved her for being so
bright and studious, and she had certainly been driven
by their family situation to make the most of her capa-
bilities, building a career ever since she'd been at business college. To be so good at everything automatically
commanded respect.

Lucy propped herself on her elbow, looking earnestly
at her far more worthy sister. 'Promise me you won't
go off him if things don't work out between me and
Michael.'

Ellie looked surprised at the request, but it was important to clear away any complications in the current mix. When the relationship with Michael lost its
magic, it shouldn't take the shine off Ellie's connection
to Harry. Lucy didn't want sister loyalty to muddy the
waters. That wasn't fair. The idea of the four of them—
brothers and sisters—ending up together was a wonderful fantasy, but Lucy felt compelled to do a reality
check here and now.

'Harry could be the right guy for you,' she argued.
'Let's face it…he's gorgeous and sexy and wealthy, and
obviously keen to have you in his corner. You could be
great together and I don't want *me* to be the reason for
you not having a future with him. I'd be happy to see

you happy with him, Ellie, regardless of what happens between me and Michael.'

Concern and confusion chased across her sister's face. 'But being so madly in love with Michael, you'll be hurt if he walks away from you.'

And who always stood by and tried to make things better any way she could?

Ellie did.

Being the older sister, she had an overdeveloped sense of responsibility, looking after Lucy when they were kids, stepping in when she was bullied at school for her scatty mind, taking charge of everything when their mother became too ill to manage, getting them through all the traumatic turmoil of her death and setting them up as their own little family unit. Ellie was the rock, the anchor around which Lucy had drifted, the one who made a mission of *being there,* no matter what.

No way was Lucy going to cost her sister a chance with Harry Finn.

'I'll muddle along like I always do,' she insisted. 'I'm good at putting things behind me. I've had a lot of practice at it.' She reached out, took Ellie's hand and squeezed it reassuringly. 'You mustn't worry about me. Go for what you want. You deserve a good life, Ellie.'

'So do you.'

'Well, maybe we'll both achieve it. Who knows? I just want to clear the deck for you and Harry. Now tell me you're okay with that.'

Ellie heaved a deep sigh, obviously wishing the situation wasn't complicated. But it was and there was no point in not facing it. 'I'm okay if you're okay,' she finally said, her hand squeezing back, her eyes holding the steady determination that had seen them through many troubles. 'Whatever happens with either of us, we'll always have each other, Lucy.'

'Absolutely!' she agreed, relieved to have this serious stuff settled between them.

It was time now to set about banishing shadows from both their lives. They were here on this beautiful island and two princes were waiting for them. She grinned at Ellie. 'Now let's go get our men!' She bounced off the bed and twirled around in a happy dance. 'Let's have a fabulous weekend, following our hearts' desire and not thinking about tomorrow.'

She paused in the doorway to the living room to give her often too sensible sister a wise look. 'You never know when something might strike us dead, so we do what we want to do. Right?'

'Right!' Ellie echoed.

Life could be very short.

Since their mother had died, that proven truth had never left Lucy's mind. She had to stop thinking of any kind of future with Michael and just take each day as it came.

Forget the shadows.

Live in the sun.

CHAPTER NINE

MICHAEL KEENLY OBSERVED the to and fro between Harry and Elizabeth over lunch. She definitely wasn't resisting him anymore. There was no mocking, no sparring, no challenge being thrown out. Harry didn't tease or flirt. Her smiles held genuine liking. His smiles seemed to trumpet happiness.

The writing was on the wall.

Harry was winning.

Though not necessarily to the point of seducing Elizabeth into taking on the manager's job. She and Lucy had a home together in Cairns and the sisters were close, having only each other as family. He was fairly sure she would return to her PA job when the month was up. As for having an affair with Harry, he thought Elizabeth would be very level-headed about not expecting too much from him, since she had always perceived him as a playboy. It was unlikely that she would end up in an emotional mess over him. She would be guarded against that.

He wondered now about his initial impression that Lucy had no guard up against anything. Accustomed to being with more sophisticated women, who knew how to play it cool, he had been bowled over by her apparent openness, her spontaneity, the way she seemed to freely give everything up to him—with no guile at all. It had been so different to all his previous experience of the opposite sex, but was it real or was it the cleverest artifice that could be used on a man?

Michael felt uncomfortably conflicted by this question. He wanted Lucy to be what she seemed to be. Wanted it too much. He wasn't used to feeling this emotionally involved, and he didn't like it, not when she could be playing him. He needed to settle this doubt. Hopefully, Sarah and Jack Pickard might help do that when he took Lucy to their villa for afternoon tea.

The Pickards had been a fixture in his and Harry's lives all through their teens and early manhood, with Sarah being their parents' housekeeper and Jack being the maintenance man on their property. Harry had transferred them to the island to carry out the same roles here when that suddenly empty homestead with too many memories had been sold.

They were good people. Michael was very fond of both of them. Even more importantly, he trusted their instincts. How they reacted—responded—to Lucy would tell him how they viewed her as a person, a view uncoloured by the lust she continually stirred in him.

Lucy loved the restaurant, a huge open room overlooking the swimming pool and spa decks, the beach and the bay, with lush tropical gardens on either side. The tables were well spaced, making everything feel designed for relaxation, with no crush, no hurry, just divine surroundings and divine food and wine.

Best of all, the mood around the table was relaxed, too. Ellie recommended some of the dishes on the menu, making Lucy's choices easy and natural. There was no sign of any tension between the brothers, so Michael couldn't be worrying too much about losing his PA, and there was nothing but positive vibes flowing between Harry and Ellie.

It was a great lunch.

Followed by an even better afternoon.

Michael took her up to what he called a pavilion villa. This was perched on a hillside overlooking another beach, facing west to catch the sunset. It actually had a private infinity pool at the end of its open deck. Inside was just as marvellous—a white cane lounge suite in the sitting area with plump blue-and-white striped cushions, a kitchenette running along one wall leading to a totally luxurious bathroom, also in blue and white and containing a spa bath as well as a shower definitely built for two, plus a range of bath salts and body oils and lotions in exotic containers standing ready for use.

The bedroom was on a mezzanine level—not missing out on the beautiful view— and featured a king-size bed, lots of cupboards along one wall, a luggage stool where their overnight bags had already been placed and bedside tables with lamps held up by seahorses. There were artistic arrangements of shells and pieces of coral from the reef, a wall-hanging of white net holding fish made of mother-of-pearl, and large candles giving out a faint scent of frangipani.

'This is heaven, Michael!' she declared, swinging around with her arms out in an all-encompassing gesture. *And he is what makes it heaven,* she thought. *This man who is so impossibly perfect.*

Maybe it was all too good to be true, but Lucy wasn't about to let that thought spoil this time with him. He laughed at her exuberance, moving up the steps to the mezzanine level, where she already stood in her rush to see everything.

Her eyes gloated over him, the classically handsome face, the glowing olive skin, white, white teeth, the so masculine body shown off by smartly tailored shorts in a blue-and-grey check teamed with a royal blue sports shirt. Just the sight of his strong, muscular calves made her feel weak with desire. And the great big king-size bed was waiting right behind her.

'Can we have a siesta?' she asked huskily.

He grinned, his silvery-grey eyes twinkling wickedly. 'As long as you don't expect to sleep too much.'

Oh, she loved him, loved him, loved him, locking her arms around his neck in ecstatic possession of him as he drew her into his embrace. An idea sprang into her mind—one that would give her wonderfully free access to all of him. 'Maybe I'll make you go to sleep,' she said teasingly. 'Let me give you a massage, Michael. It would be criminal not to use one of those body oils in the bathroom, and afterwards I could wash it all off you in the spa bath.'

'Well, I can't say no to that.'

'You strip off and I'll fetch a bath sheet and the oils.'

She planted a quick kiss on his mouth, then danced away from him, down the steps to the bathroom, eager to get moving on showing him how good a masseuse she was. He was already naked and throwing off the bedcover and decorator cushions when she returned, pausing a moment to ogle his taut, cheeky butt. In the flesh, Michael Finn had to be the sexiest man alive, and excitement zinged through her at the thought of having all his flesh under her hands.

He turned and caught her eyeing him. 'I think I see lecherous intent,' he said laughingly.

'I was simply measuring your muscles,' she retorted with a grin.

'Fair's fair! You strip off while I spread out the bath sheet.'

She handed it to him, put the oil bottles on the bed-side table and whipped off her clothes. 'Okay, I'm naked, but no looking. This is about feeling,' she insisted. 'I want you to lie facedown, close your eyes and let me have my way with you.'

'As you wish,' he answered agreeably, doing as he was told.

Lucy tried the oils on her skin first, choosing the one with the more exotic scent. She straddled Michael, taking wicked pleasure in sitting on his sexy butt, and dribbled the oil around his shoulders and down his spine, grinning as he shuddered at the sudden coolness on his skin. 'The heat comes next,' she promised, taking sensual delight in swishing her breasts over his back as she leaned across him to put the bottle back on the table.

'I'm getting a breast massage?' he queried, amusement rumbling through his voice.

'No. I was just indulging myself.'

'Indulge as much as you like.'

She laughed and went to work on his shoulders with her hands, gently kneading his muscles. 'You're a bit tight up here. I guess that comes from working at a desk all day.'

'Mmm…that feels very good,' he murmured appreciatively. 'Where did you learn to do this?'

'Part of the beautician course. It's more for relaxing, though, not remedial stuff.'

'I'm all for relaxing. I can take a lot of it.'

'I'm going to give you the whole works.'

He sighed contentedly. 'I love your work, Lucy.'

Love me.

She willed that to happen as her hands revelled in stroking his firm male flesh, feeling the strength of his muscles, loving every part of his physique as she moved over him in a kind of sensual thrall, rubbing his arms, legs, hands, feet. The oil glistening on his skin made him look like an Olympian athlete. The scent of it grew more and more erotic to her. When she told him to roll over so she could continue the process on his front, her pulse leapt into a gallop at the sight of his fully taut erection.

She couldn't tear her gaze off it as she knelt between his legs and ran her hands over his calves and up his thighs. The urge to bend her head and run her tongue around the tip of the shaft was irresistible. He gasped. His eyes opened into glittering slits. She took him in her mouth and he groaned her name repeatedly.

Yes! she thought in wild elation as she lashed him with her tongue and pumped him with her mouth, excited beyond belief by this rabid possession of his manhood. *He's mine…. He's mine!* she thought as her own body creamed in climax.

He jackknifed up, grabbed her, lifted her, pulling

her forward to fit her over him. She took him inside her, riding him, fiercely wanting to drive him over the brink, exploding everything else he cared about into meaningless atoms so that only she existed for him. He cried out as release spurted from him in uncontrollable bursts, and she writhed over him in an ecstasy of triumph. *Mine...!*

He was moaning, tossing his head from side to side. She leaned forward, held it still and covered his face with kisses. His arms encircled her, pulling her down on top of him. She could feel his heart thumping. He rolled with her locked in his embrace, taking the more dominant position so he could kiss her as he willed, his mouth devouring hers in a frenzy of passion, as though he had to make her *his* now. His and his alone.

Lucy exulted in the sense of feeling secure with him. She needed this. It might not be absolutely real for always, but it was real enough for now. His desire for her, this marvellous intimacy, the heart-warming magic of being together...sheer bliss.

Michael didn't want to think. He just wanted to wallow in the exquisite pleasure of Lucy Flippence—what she did to him, what she gave him. Yet it was so much—so much more than he'd ever expected or received from any other woman, and it had happened so quickly. Only a week. He couldn't stop his mind from circling around the situation, trying to weigh what it meant.

Jason Lester's jibe that she was after bigger bucks with Michael could be true. She'd said herself that she belonged in a different zoo to his social circle. Had she sized him up as a mark worth pulling out all the stops for? It actually felt like a stab to his heart to even consider it, which was a warning of how deeply she was getting to him.

He hadn't really had any serious relationships—more a series of attractions that wore off for one reason or another. No woman had driven him to the point of obsession as Lucy did. He couldn't get enough of her, despite the doubts that were now jangling through his mind. Even his concentration on work had been affected this past week, and he never allowed anything to interfere with his control of the franchises.

Had something changed in him?

Did Lucy touch some chord of need that had been kept locked up inside him?

Keeping faith with his father's vision had been more important to him than anything else since his parents had died. Harry felt the same way. It was a strong bond between them. They'd poured all their energy into building on the strong business platform their father had established, possibly at the cost of a more natural lifestyle, though surely it had been in their nature to do what they'd done.

Maybe it was all about timing.

They'd succeeded in achieving what they'd set out to achieve.

Now, with Lucy suddenly bursting into his life, making him acutely aware he wanted more on a personal level…it made him feel vulnerable in a way he'd never felt before. Not in control. Knocked askew.

Again he told himself to just ride with what was happening.

It was too good not to.

Eventually the situation would sort itself out. Maybe with Jack and Sarah this afternoon.

Lucy stirred, lifting her head to smile at him, her dimples flashing endearingly. 'I'd better run the spa bath if we're to wash the oil scent off us before our visit to the Pickards.'

Weird that she'd thought of them at the same time as he had. He'd told her about the invitation on the trip out, explaining their connection to the family, and she'd seemed eager to meet them, interested in their life on the island.

'Good thinking,' he approved.

Her eyes sparkled. 'I'll use the watermelon bath crystals. That will clean us up.'

He laughed. She rolled away from him, off the bed, and headed for the bathroom in a provocative prance, swinging her delectable bottom, leaving a broad smile on Michael's face and the thought in his mind that she made him laugh a lot, putting a happy zing in his life in more ways than one.

The sunshine girl...

He enjoyed the challenge of his work, keeping on top of everything, but when he walked out of his office, Lucy's kind of sunshine was precisely what he wanted, what he needed to put his world in balance. Did he really care if it was his wealth that brought him this?

He'd prefer it not to be, but it was an integral part of who he was, which probably made it a factor in all his relationships. Except with his brother. Telling himself not to let it cloud this time with Lucy, he swung himself off the bed, rolled up the bath sheet and went to join her in the bathroom.

The spa bath was another sensual delight. She insisted on soaping him all over, her body sliding around his, then directed him to sit between her legs, his back turned to her while she shampooed his hair and gave him a scalp massage. He ended up horny and they had sex again—fun sex this time, with the bubbles from the bath crystals swirling around them.

Michael could not remember feeling more relaxed when they finally strolled down the hill to visit Jack and Sarah. He wanted them to find no fault in Lucy. He wanted today to stay as perfect as it was with this woman at his side.

Paradise...

CHAPTER TEN

LUCY WAS NERVOUS about meeting the Pickards. Normally she didn't care if people approved of her or not, but from what Michael had told her, Jack and Sarah were almost like a second set of parents to him and Harry. They *counted* in his life, so it really mattered to her that they like her.

It helped that he was holding her hand, giving her a sense of security with him, and surely they would see he was happy with her. That should help, too. And Ellie would have made a good impression on them. Her sister had real class in every way. Not that Lucy was like her. She wasn't. But they were *family*.

The Pickards' villa was positioned on flat land between the gym and the huge maintenance shed that housed the power generator and the desalination plant providing fresh water for the resort. Within easy walking distance of the administration centre, and bigger than the guest villas, it was a permanent home for them.

They were both on the veranda that ran across the front of the villa, probably eager to greet Michael and his companion when they arrived. Eager to look her over, too. Jack appeared to be spraying plants in tubs placed around the edge of the veranda. Sarah was in a rocking chair, flipping through a magazine.

As she caught sight of them, she put the magazine aside and stood up, calling out to Jack that they were coming. He set the spray-can on the veranda railing, took off his gloves and joined her at the top of the steps. They were both short, lean and wiry in physique, with iron-grey curly hair framing fairly weather-beaten faces—obviously active outdoors people. And they were wearing cheerful, welcoming expressions that eased some of Lucy's inner tension.

'It's lovely to see you, Mickey!' Sarah warmly declared.

'Likewise,' he said just as warmly. 'And this is Lucy Flippence, Elizabeth's sister.'

'My, my...you're not at all alike.' The predictable comment came as she grasped the hand Lucy offered.

'No. Ellie is as sharp as a tack and I guess most people would consider me fairy floss.' Lucy tossed off the remark with a self-deprecating smile.

'I always thought there was some magic in fairy floss,' Jack said, grinning at her as he took her hand and shook it.

She laughed, relieved that he accepted her so readily. 'I think this island is magic, and Michael tells me you've both helped to make it so.'

'Oh, we do our bit. We love it here, don't we, Sarah?'

'Yes, we're very lucky,' she agreed.

'I see you've got your roses growing well, Jack,' Michael remarked.

Lucy was surprised. 'Roses? Here?'

Jack's eyes twinkled with pleasure. 'It was a challenge, but...' he stepped back, his arm swinging out to gesture to the tubs '...coming into bloom now.'

Lucy spotted a yellow bud just opening up. 'Is that a Pal Joey?'

'Yes, it's one of my favourites,' Sarah answered. 'It has such a lovely scent.'

'I know. It's beautiful. I was at Greenlands Cemetery last Monday and an elderly man was planting a Pal Joey rose bush on his wife's grave. He said he couldn't have his Gracie lie there without her favourite rose.'

Sarah's face softened. 'Oh, how very loving of him!'

'They'd been married almost sixty years. I thought it was wonderful. Do you grow them for Sarah, Jack?'

'For both of us.' He smiled ruefully at his wife. 'But should I have the misfortune of Sarah passing first, I shall certainly plant one on her grave.'

She smiled back. 'You do that, Jack.'

Lucy sighed. 'It's so nice to meet married people who are devoted to one another. There's not enough of it.'

'You can make your own world, Lucy,' Sarah said philosophically. 'And how is it that the cemetery features in yours?'

'It's her job,' Michael put in. 'Lucy is in cemetery administration.'

That startled Sarah. 'Good heavens! Do you like it?'

'So far I do. I haven't been in it for long,' she admitted. 'It gives me plenty of opportunities to visit my mother's grave. She died when I was seventeen, and I like to chat to her, tell her what I'm thinking and feeling. It sort of settles me down when I feel a bit adrift, you know?'

She was running off at the mouth as she always did

when she felt nervous. But Sarah didn't seem to think she was weird or anything, taking her hand again and patting it in a comforting way.

'It's very sad, losing your mother so young,' she said sympathetically.

'Yes, though Ellie is great. She takes charge of everything.'

Sarah nodded. 'I can see how she'd do that. She's handling everything very well here.'

'Don't you weigh in with Harry, Sarah,' Michael quickly interjected. 'Elizabeth is my PA. This situation is only temporary.'

'Not my business,' she assured him, stepping back to wave them forward. 'Come on through. I've set up afternoon tea on the back veranda. It has a view of the beach and sea.'

'Can I help you with anything?' Lucy asked as they were led into a large living area encompassing kitchen, dining room and lounge, all furnished in a very homely way.

'I just have to boil the kettle, dear, but stay with me and chat. You can help take the cake and cookies out when the tea is ready.'

'Please tell me they're your peanut butter cookies,' Michael said with relish.

Sarah laughed. 'Would I bake you any other? Go along with Jack now. We'll be out in a few minutes.'

The two men made their exit via a back door. Sarah switched the kettle on, then turned to Lucy, her hazel eyes bright with interest. 'Your sister told me you met Mickey at the office.'

'Yes, it was Ellie's birthday last Monday and I

dropped in to see her. Harry was there, too, and we all ended up having lunch together.'

'You must have seen more of Mickey this week for him to bring you here.'

Sarah was fishing, but Lucy didn't mind answering. 'Every night! It's been amazing! I feel like I'm in the middle of a fairy tale with him. He's such a prince!'

'He is, isn't he?' she said fondly. 'So is Harry. They're both very special men. Like their parents. They were special, too.'

'Michael said he lost them about the same time I lost my mother.'

Sarah sighed. 'A terrible tragedy. But they'd be very proud of their sons. Very proud.'

Realising that this woman had to know Michael's character through and through, Lucy decided to take the risk of confiding how she felt—the doubts she had about how Michael viewed this relationship, whether it could become really meaningful to him in his mind and heart.

She made an ironic grimace and gestured helplessly. 'The trouble is I'm not sure I can live up to him, Sarah. I mean...I'm more or less a Cinderella in his world. He's asked me to attend a ball with him next Saturday night, and I'm scared stiff that I won't fit in with his friends.'

'Don't be scared, Lucy,' the older woman advised. 'If Mickey wants you with him, he'll look after you. He's very like his father. Intense about anything he sets himself to do, and extremely protective of anyone he cares for.'

But did he really *care* for her? That was the big question.

'Then I should be okay,' Lucy said with a smile, thinking she'd probably dug as far as she could dig.

Sarah smiled back. 'I'm sure you will be, dear.'

The kettle boiled and she filled a large teapot that was patterned with roses. Lucy imagined the cups and saucers set outside would match.

'You *are* lucky, Sarah. There were no roses in my mother's marriage,' she wryly remarked. 'If I ever marry, it will only be to a man who loves me enough to give me roses.'

'Can't wait!' Michael announced from behind them. 'I'm going to snaffle a cookie.'

'We're coming!' Sarah chided.

'Fine! You bring the tea. I'll take the plate of cookies and Lucy can carry the banana cake.'

'How do you know it's a banana cake? It's covered in icing,' Lucy pointed out.

Michael grinned at Sarah, his eyes twinkling with certain knowledge.

'It's banana cake,' she conceded.

'You're a treasure, Sarah.'

'Oh, you and Harry always butter me up to get what you want.' She waved to the plate of cookies. 'Take them. We'll follow you out.'

They settled around a large wooden table on the back veranda, which faced a different bay than the administration centre. 'This beach catches the afternoon sun,' Jack pointed out. 'And, of course, we get the sunset view from here.'

As would the pavilion villa up on the hill, Lucy thought happily.

'You have a gorgeous lot of bougainvillea out here, Jack,' she remarked, gesturing to the brightly coloured profusion of them surrounding the veranda.

'They don't mind the sandy soil and sea air. Easy to grow here,' he explained.

'Did you do that wonderful tropical garden around the restaurant?'

Her curiosity about the development of the resort made for an easy, relaxed conversation over afternoon tea. Jack was proud of his work and Sarah was proud of her husband's ability to turn his hand to anything. Lucy coaxed smiles and laughter out of both of them, which always promoted a happy time and reduced any chance of self-conscious tension taking hold.

Michael sat back and watched her charm Jack and Sarah. She had quite extraordinary people skills, focusing on whoever was talking, picking up on their interests, making them seem just as interesting to her. Her smiles evoked smiles, and her laughter was infectious.

When she asked about how the sea water was turned into fresh, Michael quickly suggested to Jack that he take Lucy down to the maintenance shed and show her the process. It would give him some time alone with Sarah, who was a shrewd judge of character. Her opinion of other women he'd brought here had always been spot on.

Jack was only too pleased to show Lucy anything. He was clearly very taken by her. Most men would be, Michael thought, no matter how old. *The honey bee...* Lester's name for her slid into his mind again and he frowned as Lucy and Jack left the veranda together. Lester had given it a sexual connotation, but Lucy had not been consciously sexy over afternoon tea. She was simply...very appealingly female.

'What's wrong, Mickey?' Sarah asked quietly.

He shook his head. 'Just a problem I have.'

'To do with Lucy?'

'What do you think of her, Sarah?'

'A joy to be with,' she answered with a smile.

'Yes,' he agreed. 'Anything else?'

Sarah mused for a few moments before remarking, 'She's quite different from the other women you've brought over here. More spontaneous, artless…'

'Not a scheming gold-digger?' he pressed.

Sarah looked shocked. 'Not at all! Has she done anything to make you think it?'

'I am a very wealthy man,' he said drily.

'That can be intimidating to a girl like Lucy, Mickey,' she quickly argued. 'It can make her think she's not good enough for you.'

'She's beautiful. She's sexy. She's fun. That's a fairly good trade-off, Sarah.'

'If you have a lot of self-esteem, and I don't think she has,' Sarah replied thoughtfully. 'There's not much ego running around in that girl. She focuses on other people, doesn't want the spotlight turned on herself.'

'Because she's hiding something?' Michael queried, wondering if that was the case.

'I don't know. Her comment about being fairy floss compared to her sister made me think she knew she could never compete with Elizabeth, possibly from an early age. So she conceded all that ground and chose a different path for herself—one that didn't demand more than she felt capable of doing.'

'She is the younger sister. Elizabeth called her ditzy,' Michael recalled.

Sarah shot him an ironic smile. 'That's probably a good cover for feeling inadequate.'

He frowned over that possibility. 'I doubt Lucy feels inadequate. She's held quite an amazing array of jobs—model, beautician, tour guide, dancing teacher, amongst other things. It's as though she's drawn to try anything and everything. She dropped out of school to nurse her mother, who died of cancer, and never went back to complete any formal education—said she had no head for study after that. But I think she manages to do quite well for herself.'

'Where was Elizabeth when her mother was dying?'

'At home. Already at business college, so I imagine Lucy did the bulk of the nursing.'

'While Elizabeth prepared to take on the future.' Sarah nodded in understanding. 'Would you say the sisters are close?'

'Yes. Very different but very close. Lucy called Elizabeth her anchor.'

'When she feels adrift…that's what she said about visiting her mother's grave.' Sarah gave Michael a very direct look. 'You don't have a scheming gold-digger on your hands, Mickey. I'd say if Lucy is hiding anything, it's something she feels very vulnerable about. Be careful how you treat her.' His friend's serious expression cracked into a smile. 'She sees you as a prince.'

Michael grinned at her. 'Until I turn into a frog. According to Lucy, most princes eventually turn into frogs.'

Sarah laughed. 'She is a delight, that girl! In some ways, she's very like your mother. A joy to be with.'

Yes.

It was exactly what had been missing from his life, ever since his mother had died.

That was the chord Lucy struck in him—a much deeper need than the lust she stirred. A need for that emptiness to be filled.

'It's been good talking to you, Sarah,' he said appreciatively.

Someone he could trust.

Someone who would never lie to him.

He needed that, too.

If Lucy was covering up something she didn't want him to know, trying to keep him blinded with her fairy floss, he couldn't really trust her.

What did she feel she had to keep hidden?

The number of men in her past?

Maybe he should have questioned her about that last night. Maybe he should do it now. But remembering the anguish in her eyes after Lester had left them with his poison, Michael didn't want to bring that back and spoil this weekend with her. *Let it ride for a while,* he told himself again. But he wouldn't forget that Lucy could be keeping something from him—something that was important for him to know before this relationship went much further.

CHAPTER ELEVEN

LUCY COULD NOT have wished for a more marvellous time with Michael. The afternoon tea with the Pickards had been relatively stress-free. She had not felt any negative vibes coming from either of them. They were really nice people. Michael had then suggested a game of tennis, which had been great fun, followed by a dip in the infinity pool, drinking champagne as they watched the sunset. A romantic dinner for two on the deck below the restaurant had been a highlight finish to their day, eating superb food to the lapping of waves on the beach, under a star-studded sky.

On Sunday morning they slept in after a long night of making love. The fruit platter in the refrigerator was breakfast enough, since they were having an early lunch with Harry and Ellie before setting off to the mainland. Lucy wanted to see them happy with each other, as happy as she felt with Michael.

It was another beautiful, sunny day and harmony flowed between the two brothers and sisters as they sat in the restaurant, enjoying the fine cuisine. Ellie had mused out loud over the choices for each course, making decisions easy. It caused Lucy to reflect how lucky she was to have a sister who cared about her problems.

All through her school years, Ellie had tried to help her with reading and writing. She'd researched dyslexia on the internet and downloaded programs that might untangle the confusion in Lucy's mind. When they hadn't produced a miracle, she'd spent hours and hours coaching her to learn things off by heart. Without Ellie she would never have passed her driving test, which had allowed her to get jobs that wouldn't have been possible otherwise. Lucy owed her sister a debt she could never repay. It was good to see her eyes twinkling happily at Harry. Ellie deserved a prince.

Again Lucy couldn't help thinking how wonderful it would be if all four of them could end up together. That was a *big* dream—an impossible dream—but she was sailing along in a bubble of bliss, until Ellie dropped her bombshell.

They were sitting over coffee when Michael asked, 'Any prospects for the position of manager here, Harry?'

He shrugged. 'A few résumés have come in. I haven't called for any interviews yet. Elizabeth may want to stay on now that she's on top of the job.'

'Elizabeth is mine!' Michael shot him a vexed look.

'No!' The denial tripped straight out of Ellie's mouth.

Lucy was shocked into staring at her sister, who suddenly looked very serious and determined.

Michael, too, was taken aback. 'Don't tell me Harry has seduced you into staying here.'

'No, I won't be staying here beyond the month he needs to find someone suitable,' she replied quietly and calmly.

'So you'll come back to me,' Michael insisted.

She shook her head. 'I'm sorry, Michael, but I don't want to do that, either.'

'Why not?' he persisted.

'Being here this week has made me realise I want a change. To try something different. I'd appreciate it if you'd take this as my notice.'

He wasn't happy. He glared at his brother. 'Goddammit, Harry! If it wasn't for you—'

'Hey!' Harry held up his hands defensively. 'I'm not getting her, either.'

'Please…' Elizabeth quickly broke in. 'I don't want to cause trouble. I just want to take a different direction with my life.'

'But you're brilliant as my PA,' Michael argued, still annoyed at being put out.

'I'm sorry. You'll just have to find someone else.'

The relaxed atmosphere around the table was completely shattered. Everyone was tense. Lucy could hardly believe Ellie had come to this decision. It was like a rejection of both brothers, and the reason she gave… What direction *did* she want to take from here? Shutting herself off from two great careers made no sense.

'Why not try out Lucy as your PA?' Harry suggested to Michael with an airy wave of his hand. 'She's probably as brilliant as her sister.'

Panic instantly welled up in Lucy. *No, no, no!* screamed through her mind. She wasn't Ellie. She could never be like Ellie. She begged help from her sister with her eyes.

'It's not her kind of thing,' Ellie said firmly.

Michael was not put off, turning to remark quizzically, 'You do work in administration, Lucy.'

'I'm the front person who deals with people, Michael,' she stated, her stomach in absolute turmoil. 'I don't do desk work. I'm good at helping people, understanding what they want, helping them to decide.... There's quite a bit of that in cemetery administration. And I like it,' she added for good measure, pleading for him to drop the issue.

He grimaced in frustration.

She reached out and touched his hand, desperate to restore his good humour with her. 'I'm sorry, but I can't fill Ellie's place.'

The grimace slowly tilted up into a soothing smile. 'I shouldn't have expected it. You are a people person and I like that, Lucy. I wouldn't want to change it.'

Relief poured through her at having crossed this tricky hurdle without having to spell out why she'd be such a hopeless alternative to her sister.

'I hope you'll give me a good reference, Michael,' Ellie said, drawing attention away from Lucy.

He sighed and turned to her. 'It will be in the mail tomorrow. I hate losing you, but I wish you well, Elizabeth.'

It was a fairly graceful acceptance of the situation, but Lucy was extremely sensitive to the fact that the congenial atmosphere around the table was not about to resume. Tension emanated from Harry. It was obvious he didn't like this decision, either.

'Thank you,' Ellie said, nodding to Michael.

Case closed.

Except it wasn't.

Stony glances were being exchanged between the brothers. Frustration simmered from both of them. No one chose to eat any of the petit fours that accompanied coffee. Nothing was going to feel good until Michael and Harry cleared up their differences, which could be done only by leaving them alone together. Apart from resolving that problem, Lucy was also anxious to query Ellie about her reasons for leaving the PA job with Michael.

Had turning thirty hit her hard, triggering this sudden desire for change?

Or did the decision have something to do with foreseeing a bad outcome for the relationship Lucy had entered into with Michael? Ellie might not want to be around him if he let her sister down, and maybe she believed that was going to happen, complete with some horrible emotional fallout. If she was acting on that belief…Lucy inwardly recoiled from the idea. She would hate it if anything she did mucked up her sister's career.

As soon as Ellie had finished her cappuccino, Lucy pushed back her chair and rose to her feet. 'I'm off to the ladies' room. Will you come with me, Ellie?'

'Of course,' she said, immediately rising to join her.

The moment they were closeted away, Lucy confronted her, determined to learn the truth. 'Why are you leaving your great job with Michael? He's not happy about it.'

Ellie shook her head. 'It's not my mission in life to keep Michael happy,' she said drily.

'But you always said you loved that job.'

'I did, but it's high pressure, Lucy. I didn't realise how much it demanded of me until I came out here.

I don't want to be constantly on my toes anymore. I want to look for something else—more relaxed, less stressful.'

Was this the truth? Ellie had always been ambitious, and walking away from such a top-level position seemed like a complete turnaround from achieving what she'd aimed for. On the other hand, Lucy knew nothing of high pressure jobs, never having had one, so Ellie might actually need to give it up and move on.

'Then it's not because of me and him?' Lucy asked worriedly, wanting to believe this decision was as straightforward as her sister made out.

'No,' she replied, her eye contact remaining absolutely steady as she laid out what she thought. 'I'm sorry Michael is unhappy about it, but I don't think he'll take it out on you, Lucy. If he does, he's not the man for you.'

Lucy hadn't got that far in her own thinking. Her main concern had revolved around Ellie sacrificing her job out of some sense of protective loyalty. If there were personal repercussions from Michael because of his frustration over the situation…well, that simply wasn't acceptable. He would not be the man for her. It would be frog territory. Lucy was not so blindly in love that she couldn't see that. This was a test he would have to pass or there was not even a small future for them.

She heaved a sigh to relieve the tightness in her chest, gave her sister a quick hug, then looked her directly in the eye. 'You're right. Okay. It's completely fair for you to look for something else. He's just got to lump being put out by it.'

'You can play nurse and soothe his frustration,' Ellie said with a smile.

Lucy laughed, more in the grip of hysteria than from any amusement. She desperately didn't want things to start going wrong between her and Michael, but if they did, she had to be as sensible as Ellie. However seductive a fairy tale fantasy was, in the end there was no escaping from reality.

Michael couldn't recall ever being at serious odds with his brother, but he was right now. He'd lent Elizabeth to him to facilitate the quick removal of a crooked manager. He could tolerate not having her on hand for a month, but losing her altogether had not been on the table.

Just one week over here and she was handing in her resignation as his PA. He didn't buy her reason for leaving him. Something had happened and that *something* had to do with Harry. Michael waited until the two sisters had closed themselves in the ladies' room, safely out of earshot, and unleashed his anger.

'This is bloody nonsense!' he hissed at Harry. 'Elizabeth never showed any dissatisfaction with her work situation. Whatever I threw at her, she ate up, and came back for more. And I paid her what she was worth. She's completely on top of her job. Why the hell would she want to take a different direction? The only thing that makes sense is you've thrown a spanner in the works, Harry.'

'If she wants a different direction, why isn't she staying on here?' he retaliated. 'She's on top of this job, too. It's not me pulling the strings, Mickey.'

'Then what is it?' he demanded testily.

Harry eyed him grimly. 'I'd say it's Lucy.'

'That's nonsense, too! Lucy was just as shocked as I was at Elizabeth's resignation.'

'Wake up, Mickey!' Sheer exasperation laced Harry's voice. 'You're having it off with your PA's younger sister—a sister she's more or less been a mother to after their own mother died. From the moment you took up with Lucy, Elizabeth's resignation has probably been on the drawing board. Seeing how it is for her sister this weekend undoubtedly clinched it.'

'What do you mean?'

Harry rolled his eyes. 'Even to me it's obvious that Lucy's head over heels in love with you. Elizabeth would be well aware that your relationships have never lasted long. You might end up hurting her sister very badly.'

'And I might not!' Michael retorted heatedly. 'I might want to keep this relationship.'

Harry shrugged. 'Whatever... But you introduced a personal element that wasn't there before.'

'What about you? Don't tell me you haven't got very personal with Elizabeth this week.'

'Which is probably why she won't stay on working for me, either,' Harry retorted, then threw up his hands in exasperation. 'I don't know what's going on in Elizabeth's head. I wish I did. I do know that once she makes up her mind, she follows through, so we both have to accept her decision whether we like it or not.'

Michael huffed in frustration. 'Okay,' he conceded. 'It's not your fault.'

'Definitely not,' Harry vehemently insisted.

'Dammit! Why did Lucy have to be her sister?'

'You be careful how you treat her, Mickey. I don't

want your affair with her messing up what I might have with Elizabeth.'

Michael shook his head over complexities he hadn't considered. 'We've never been mixed up like this before, Harry.'

'I'll tell you now. I'm not letting Elizabeth go if I can help it.'

He was deadly serious.

'I'm not about to let Lucy go, either.' Not in the foreseeable future. There was absolutely no point to ending it within a month, since Elizabeth wasn't coming back to work for him. He could let it go on for as long as it pleased him.

Harry nodded. 'So…are *we* sorted, Mickey?'

'Yes, sorted.'

Which didn't mean he liked the situation, but at least he agreed Harry wasn't to blame for it. Elizabeth had pulled the trigger on the professional side, quite possibly swayed by the personal elements of two brothers and two sisters becoming emotionally entangled. Lucy had called her *'the sensible one.'*

Michael castigated himself for not seeing this coming, yet he hadn't known the nature of the relationship between the two sisters when he'd been bowled over by Lucy last Monday. He'd begun to see it more clearly in his conversation with Sarah yesterday, but he still hadn't anticipated this breakaway by Elizabeth.

It seemed an extreme action.

And he resented the assumption that he might treat Lucy badly.

He had never treated a woman badly.

Yet both Sarah and now Harry were warning him to

be careful with how he treated Lucy. That didn't make a lot of sense, either. She hadn't come across to him as a fragile personality, more like a free spirit, flitting around, trying anything that appealed to her. If their relationship took a wrong turn, surely she would flit somewhere else, not fall in a heap and need massive support from her sister.

Regardless of what he thought or felt, Elizabeth's decision had been made and there was no point in sweating it. He didn't regret picking up with Lucy even if it had lost him his PA. She could become very important to his life—a joy not to be missed or set aside. And he still had three weeks of having her to himself before her sister returned to Cairns—time for the relationship to consolidate, if it was going to—without any outside influence interfering with it.

Michael didn't believe being 'head over heels in love' meant a relationship was on unbreakable ground. It was probably a fair description of how he felt about Lucy right now—infatuated to the point of obsession. But this could be a fairy floss stage, melting into nothing in the end.

He wanted to share a deep, abiding love with a woman.

As his father had with his mother.

He needed more time with Lucy to know if she was *the one* he'd been waiting for.

If she wasn't, he would let her down as lightly as he could.

She might see him as a frog, but he sure as hell wasn't a gross cane toad!

CHAPTER TWELVE

LUCY COULDN'T HELP fretting over the impact of Ellie's decision. The goodbyes after lunch had a strained edge to them, and Harry had called up Jack to drive her and Michael to the jetty in the golf buggy, not choosing to do it himself. She sensed he couldn't see the back of them fast enough, and Lucy was sure he'd be very quickly demanding more explanation from Ellie. He was no longer wearing the expression of a winner.

Michael was harder to read. He chatted to Jack on the way to the jetty in a normal manner, and he held her hand, which was comforting. Jack helped him cast off, and it wasn't until they had left the island behind that Lucy plucked up courage enough to ask, 'Do you feel Ellie has let you down, Michael?'

He made a rueful grimace. 'I can't say I understand her reason for resigning, but every person has the right to choose what to do with their life. I won't argue with that but...she'll be a hard act to follow. It's going to be difficult finding someone to fill her shoes.'

Lucy tried to explain how Ellie might feel. 'I think it has to do with her turning thirty. And the apartment is paid for now, so she doesn't have to feel responsible about keeping a roof over our heads. If you've got that security you can afford to cut free a bit. I guess that's where she's at, Michael.'

He shot her a quizzical look. 'I wondered if it had anything to do with us being connected.'

Lucy shook her head. 'Ellie says not.'

'You asked her?'

'Yes. It just seemed too coincidental somehow. Although I had cleared it with her yesterday morning— like, whatever happens between you and me shouldn't affect what she and Harry could have together. The same should have applied to her job. I told her I'd just pick myself up and move on if it came to us parting.'

His mouth twitched with some private amusement. 'You would, would you?'

'Not easily,' she said archly, pleased that he wasn't grumpy. 'But I would. It's not good to hang on to things that have to be put behind you.'

He laughed, took one hand off the steering wheel of the motor launch and reached out to draw her into a hug. 'That's my Lucy!' he said warmly, and dropped a kiss on her forehead. 'I love the way you look at things.'

Love... Her heart drummed with happiness.

On the work front he was definitely put out by Ellie's resignation, but there was no overflow of negative feeling onto what they had together. He was still a prince to Lucy. She laid her head contentedly on his shoulder and sighed away all her inner angst.

'Thank you for a wonderful weekend, Michael.'

He planted another kiss on her forehead and gave her a tighter hug. '*You* made it wonderful.'

Pure bliss! Michael had passed this test with flying

colours. The only nasty little niggle remaining in her mind was the possible fallout between Ellie and Harry. Lucy *wanted* him to be her sister's prince.

Later that evening, after Michael had left her apartment, she headed straight into Ellie's room to email her. The great thing about modern technology was the common practice of using shorthand texting that cut out a lot of letters in words. Lucy could manage this simplified communication fairly well, though Ellie could get the gist of any garbled stuff she typed, so it wasn't a problem, anyway.

She kept it short.

M & I R OK. R U & H OK?

As soon as she woke up the next morning she rushed to the computer hoping for an answer. A new message popped into the inbox and yes, it was from Ellie. It opened with a smile sign, which instantly put a smile on Lucy's face, then the confirmation: H & I OK.

Still two princes, Lucy thought happily, and the week passed brilliantly without anything happening to put even a slight crack in that sweet belief. It gave her more confidence about going to the ball with Michael. She was sure he would smooth over any shortcomings she might have in the company of his friends.

On Saturday he took her out to lunch, saying they probably wouldn't be fed until quite late tonight so they might as well enjoy a good meal early in the afternoon and have plenty of energy for dancing. He drove them to the Thala Beach Lodge, which was located between

Cairns and Port Douglas and perched on top of a steep hill with magnificent views of the coast and sea.

The restaurant was open-air, with high wooden ceilings and polished floorboards, and their table for two overlooked the rainforest that covered the hillside down to the beach. Lucy once again covered up her dyslexia, remarking to the waitress that everything on the menu looked marvellous, and asking what were the most popular choices. That made it easy to pounce on the coconut prawns, followed by a chocolate fudge brownie with pistachio nuts, roasted banana and butterscotch sauce. This time it was Michael who chose to have 'the same', which gave Lucy a pleasant sense of complacency about her disability.

Maybe he would never notice it, or by the time he did, hopefully he wouldn't care about it, because there was so much that was good between them.

Like enjoying this delicious lunch together.

Like making love back in her apartment until she had to chase Michael off so she could do all she had to do to look her absolute best for the ball.

Lucy didn't own a ball gown. She had thought of borrowing one of the costumes from the dance studio where she'd worked, but decided the competition creations might look out of place in a crowd that was bound to be sophisticated. In the end, her tangerine bridesmaid dress seemed the best choice. It was a simple, long, figure-hugging shift with a knee-high split at the back for ease of movement. The square neckline was low enough to show the upper swell of her breasts—definitely an evening gown look—and the straps over the shoulders were linked by three gold rings.

With the honey-tan tone of her skin, blond hair and brown eyes, the tangerine colour looked great on her, and the garment was spectacular enough in itself not to need much dressing up—just gold hoop earrings, her slimline gold watch, the gold bangle Ellie had given her on her twenty-first birthday, the gold strappy sandals that were perfect dancing shoes, and a small gold handbag for essential make-up repair items.

She washed and blow-dried her hair, twirling it up into a topknot, and using a curling wand on the loose tendrils that dangled down from it. She kept her make-up fairly subtle, carefully highlighting her eyes and cheekbones, wanting to look right for the company she was to be in tonight, but she did gloss her tangerine lipstick. The dress demanded it and she wanted to look right for herself, too.

Certainly Michael had no problem with her appearance. When he arrived to pick her up he took one look at her and shook his head in awe, murmuring, 'You take my breath away.' Then he gave her a sparkling grin, adding, 'Not for the first time!'

She laughed. 'You do the same to me.'

He was always stunningly handsome, but dressed in a formal dinner suit he was truly breathtaking. Excited simply to be with him, Lucy stopped worrying about other people. She was going to dance all night with this beautiful, fantastic man and have a wonderful time.

However, her exhilaration was inevitably overtaken by nervous tension as they entered the casino ballroom, the need for Michael's friends to find her acceptable rising with every step she took. She tried to reassure herself with the fact that Sarah and Jack Pickard had liked her, but they had been an older couple, probably not as inclined to be as critical as a peer group.

The table Michael led her to was half occupied. They obviously weren't the first of the party to arrive, nor the last. The men stood as Michael started the introductions, and Lucy did her best to fit the names she had memorised to the faces. These were the three married couples he'd told her about, and they eyed her with interest—a new woman on the scene.

'Where did you meet this gorgeous lady, Mickey?' one of the men asked.

'She burst in on me at work and I instantly decided...' his eyes twinkled at Lucy '...I needed her in my life.'

Her heart swelled with happiness at this public declaration.

'Ah! A business connection then,' his friend concluded.

'You could say that. Though my connection to Lucy now extends way beyond business.' He gave her a hug. 'I'm here to dance her off her feet tonight.'

They all laughed. One of the women archly commented, 'He is a very good dancer, Lucy. If you can't keep up with him, hand him over to me.'

'No chance!' Michael told her. 'Lucy has done the dance studio thing. I'm out to prove I can match her.'

'Well, you look like a good match,' another woman remarked, smiling at both of them.

Lucy no longer felt tense and nervous. They were all looking at her in a friendly manner, willing to accept her into their company. Michael had set them on that path with his admiring comments, and they were happy to go along with him. Like a true prince, he'd made the situation easy for her, and she had no trouble carrying on a conversation with these people, using the information he'd given about them to focus on their lives and interests.

Once the band started up, he swept her off to the dance floor. He had great rhythm and was so sexy, Lucy could barely contain the excitement he stirred in her. Dance followed dance. He challenged her with intricate moves and she challenged him right back. Other couples made more room for them on the floor, standing back to watch and applaud their display of expertise. It was wildly exhilarating and they were both breathless when the set ended and they made their way back to the table.

The rest of their party had arrived. More introductions were made. Lucy was on too much of a high to feel nervous about them. Besides, they were all grinning at them, with one commenting, 'You two are hot, hot, hot! That was a sizzling performance on the dance floor.'

Michael laughed. 'I've never had a partner like Lucy.'

'And he's so good I'm only just still on my feet,' she said, sliding her arm around his waist and leaning into him as though close to collapse.

He hugged her shoulders and glanced inquiringly at the men. 'Who's pouring the champagne? My lady needs a refreshing drink.'

Champagne, dancing, fun company, the burgeoning hope that Michael might see her as a partner in every sense… Lucy realised the concern about being a Cinderella at this ball was completely wiped out. She felt like a princess. Not even a clash with Michael's ex in the powder room could dim the stars in her eyes.

The unexpected confrontation with the beautiful brunette was not pleasant. Lucy was refreshing her lipstick at the vanity mirror when the woman beside her turned to face her with a spiteful glare.

'Just who are you?' she demanded.

Startled, Lucy retorted, 'Who are *you*?'

'Fiona Redman.'

The name meant nothing to Lucy. 'So?'

'Michael Finn was mine until a month ago,' she spat out. 'I want to know if you're the reason he dropped me.'

'No. I've only known him for two weeks.'

She gnashed her teeth over that information, her dark eyes glowering meanly at Lucy. 'Well, don't expect to keep him. He's notoriously fickle in his relationships. Business always comes first with him.'

Lucy made no reply. She was recalling Michael's description of this woman as too self-centred.

'He might be as handsome as sin and great in bed, but he'll just use you and toss you away like all the rest,' the woman jeered.

'Thank you for warning me,' Lucy said politely, and made a quick escape, smiling over her mother's old saying, 'the soft word turneth away wrath.' It had always worked for her, putting people off their rants. It was obvious that Fiona Redman was as jealous as sin, having lost 'her catch', and Lucy was not about to let her spoil this brilliant night with Michael.

He hadn't let Jason Lester spoil anything between them.

What they had together was special. It had nothing to do with anyone else. Michael's past relationships simply hadn't proved *right,* just as hers hadn't. As far as Lucy was concerned, a small future with each other remained shining brightly at this point in time.

Michael had taken the opportunity to visit the men's room while Lucy was in the ladies', not wanting to lose any time together. He was washing his hands when another guy claimed his attention, sliding a highly provocative comment at him.

'I see you've snagged the best piece of arse in Cairns.'

Michael frowned at him. 'I beg your pardon.'

'Luscious Lucy.' This was accompanied by a leer. 'Great for sex. Pity she's such an airhead. I enjoyed her for a while. I'm sure you will, too. But trying to put some order into her mess of a mind wore me out.'

The control freak, Michael thought.

The guy flicked water off his hands and made one last rotten comment. 'She should keep her mouth for what it's good at.'

He walked out, leaving Michael untroubled by the 'airhead' tag, but disturbed at having Lucy described as 'the best piece of arse in Cairns.' It made him recall Jason Lester's remark that she'd slept with half the men in the city. Michael didn't believe this was true, certain that Lucy had more discrimination than that, yet it once more raised the question of how many men she had pleasured in the past, and how she had learnt to give so much pleasure.

He told himself it didn't matter.

He revelled in her uninhibited sensuality, her utterly spontaneous response to the sexual chemistry between them. He was glad she was like that, and however it had come about should not concern him. Apart from which, the disparaging comments had come from men Lucy had rejected—men who were missing out on what they wanted from her.

Michael returned to their table, determined to banish the niggles about her past. If she was hiding things she didn't want him to know...so what? He liked what he had with her in the present, and wasn't about to mess with it.

She was already seated, her lovely face alight with interest in the conversation amongst his friends. He took the empty chair across the table from her for the sheer pleasure of watching her smiles, the dimples flashing in her cheeks, the golden twinkles in her sherry-brown eyes, the slight heave of her perfect breasts when she laughed.

Luscious Lucy...

The phrase slid into his mind and stuck there.

They were served a seafood banquet. He watched the sensual way she forked oysters into her mouth, the relish with which she ate chunks of lobster, the licking of her lips to capture any escaping dipping sauce with the prawns, the sheer love of good food that shone through her enjoyment of the sumptuous supper.

Luscious Lucy...

There couldn't be a man alive who wouldn't think of her in those terms. Everything about her was sexy. Michael was strongly aroused simply watching her. It was difficult to contain the desire she stirred in him, the need stealing his appetite, making him impatient for the stack of gourmet food to be eaten and cleared away.

Finally the band started up again. They began with a slow number—a jazz waltz. *Perfect,* Michael thought, gesturing in invitation to Lucy as he rose from his chair. While he skirted the table, she rose from hers, as eager as he was for physical connection. He took her hand. She squeezed his. A few strides and he was swinging her into his embrace, holding her close, legs brushing against each other in the sensual intimacy of the dance.

He was acutely conscious of his erection furrowing her stomach, her breasts pressing into his chest, the warmth of her breath feathering the skin of his neck. He wanted her so badly it was almost a sickness inside him. He wanted her to himself, completely to himself.

The control mechanism in his mind snapped.

The question that should have stayed unasked came out of his mouth in a harsh rasp.

'How many men have you slept with, Lucy?'

She stopped dancing with him.

Her hands slid down to his chest, pushing to create distance between them. She looked up, stared at his face, her eyes blank of all expression, as though she was staring through him at something else.

And Michael knew instantly what it was.

The frog inside him.

He could almost feel himself turning green, and though he wanted to push back that fatal tide of colour, it was impossible to erase the words he had spoken. They hung between them, waiting to be answered—words that might well cost him a woman he wanted to keep in his life.

He wasn't ready to lose Lucy.

He might never be ready to lose her.

She'd become an addiction he didn't want to end.

CHAPTER THIRTEEN

LUCY FELT SICK.

She couldn't understand why Michael had asked that question now, on this night of nights, when everything had seemed so good between them. She had expected it—dreaded it—a week ago when Jason Lester had made that crack about her having slept with half the men in Cairns, which she had made worse with her 'town slut' remark.

Her stomach roiled with nausea.

Had she done something *sluttish* tonight? Lucy frantically searched her mind for some word or action of hers that might have triggered bad thoughts along those lines.

Nothing.

She'd simply been herself.

And if Michael couldn't accept her for the person she was...

'It doesn't matter!' he fiercely muttered. 'Forget I asked, Lucy. It was a stupid question.'

It jerked her into refocusing, meeting his eyes, searching them for truth. 'It does matter to me, Michael,' she quietly stated, hating the fact that he might think her indiscriminately promiscuous.

He grimaced in self-disgust. 'I ran into your latest ex—the control freak—in the men's room. He made some remarks about you. I shouldn't have let what he said bother me, but coming on top of Lester's...' Michael shook his head as though trying to rid his mind of images he didn't want there.

'People who want to cast nasty aspersions on others usually make sex the centre of them. Especially men, I've found. But women, too,' Lucy said, instinctively mounting a counter-attack out of a desperate need to defend herself. 'I was confronted by *your* ex—Fiona Redman—in the ladies' room. Her words were you were great in bed, but you used women up and tossed them away.' Lucy summoned up a wry little smile. 'I didn't believe you were so callous.'

'I'm sorry,' he declared. 'It's just that you're...' He paused, struggling to explain, probably hating that he'd put himself in the position of having to explain.

'What, Michael? Does it bother you that I feel free to enjoy sex as much as you do?'

'No!' He sliced the air with his hand—a sharp, negative gesture. His eyes blazed with intensity of feeling. 'I love how you are with me, Lucy.'

Not enough, she thought. *Not enough.*

Her stomach started cramping.

She clutched it, trying to stop the rolling of pain. Something was wrong. This wasn't just emotional stress. It was too physical. Had she eaten something that was violently disagreeing with her?

Defiantly determined to finish what Michael had started, she lifted her chin and faced him with her truth. 'To answer your question—'

'Don't!' he commanded tersely.

She went on, disregarding his denial of any need for it. 'I've probably slept with as many men as you have women. I've seen no reason not to have the pleasure of sex when it promised to be pleasurable. I've found each experience quite different, because the men were different. And when it came it you, Michael, it was very special.' Tears spurted into her eyes. 'So special…'

Her throat choked up. Her stomach heaved. Bile shot into her mouth. She turned blindly, desperate to get to the ladies' room before she started vomiting.

Strong hands gripped her shoulders, halting any attempt at flight. 'Lucy…' It was a gruff plea.

'I'm sick! I'm going to be sick!' she cried, clapping her hand over her mouth as she doubled over, pain shafting her lower body.

No more talk. Nothing but action, Michael moving her, supporting her, collecting one of his friends along the way to look after her in the ladies' room. Lucy barely had time to sink down on her knees in a toilet cubicle before the contents of her stomach erupted. The convulsions kept coming, even when there was nothing left to vomit. Then she was hit by diarrhoea and that was just as bad. It felt as though her whole lovely night was going down the toilet, along with the relationship she'd hoped to have with Michael Finn.

Michael waited outside the ladies' room, anxious over Lucy's condition and cursing himself for probably contributing to her sudden bout of illness with his stupid question about other men. Everything she'd said back to him was totally reasonable. *Totally.* He should have known it without asking. He should have realised that a free spirit like Lucy would take what she wanted from life and not feel she had to account for it to anyone else. And neither should she.

He'd acted like a jealous man instead of being grateful for having her light up his life, and any sense of jealousy appalled him. It was not the attribute of a rational man, which he'd always prided himself on being. This overwhelming obsession with Lucy had to stop. It was getting out of hand. He needed to pull back from it, be less intense about the feelings she stirred in him.

Though he might very well have wrecked any choice to do anything about it.

Was he now an irredeemable frog in her eyes?

Certainly, he'd killed the light in them—the light that had told him he was special.

She was special.

And he desperately wanted another chance with her.

If she walked away from him tonight, shut the door on him…

His hands clenched. He had to fight, win her back, convince her he would never again make the mistake of holding her to account for anything she might have done before they'd met. Only what they had together was important. That was what he cared about. The future without her in it looked too empty of any joy to even contemplate such an outcome. He would not accept it.

The door to the ladies' room opened. He'd asked Dave Whitfield's wife, Jane, to do what she could for Lucy, and it was a relief to see her coming out. He needed to know what state Lucy was in, whether there was some positive action he could take. Every fibre of his being was intent on changing the situation as it stood.

Jane made a sympathetic grimace. 'Not good, I'm afraid. She's violently ill. I think it must be food poisoning, though the rest of us seem to be fine. Maybe there was a bad oyster in the seafood banquet, and Lucy lucked out, being the one to eat it.'

'What should I do?' Michael asked, feeling helplessly locked out of doing anything.

'I think you'll either have to take her to hospital emergency or...does she have someone to look after her at home?'

'I'll look after her.'

'She might need some medication, Mickey. I'll go back and stay with her until she's okay to get moving.' Jane frowned. 'Though if this keeps up we might have to call an ambulance. I'll let you know if that's the case.'

'Thanks, Jane.'

'It's such a shame!' She shook her head over the mishap as she turned back to the ladies' room.

Shame was right, Michael thought savagely. Shame on him for causing more upset to Lucy when she had started to feel unwell. He had to make up for it, be all she needed him to be. The minutes dragging by felt like hours as he waited for more news. Other women entered and left the ladies' room, glancing curiously at him as they passed. He didn't care what they thought. Only Lucy mattered. He remained on watch.

Finally the door opened and Jane shuffled out, supporting Lucy, who looked completely debilitated—with no colour in her face at all. Even the bright orange lipstick had been wiped off. Her eyes were bleary, as though they'd been washed by a river of tears. Her shoulders were slumped and it was obvious she was too physically drained to stand up straight.

Michael moved quickly to draw her to his side, taking over Jane's supporting role. There was no resistance to his action. Michael suspected she was grateful to have anyone holding on to her.

'She wants to go home, Mickey,' Jane informed him. 'I think the worst is over, but she's fairly shaky. I'll get her bag and fetch Dave. If you give him your keys and tell him where you've parked, he can drive your car to the front of the casino, ready for you to put Lucy in. Okay?'

He nodded. 'Thanks, Jane.'

There was so much he wanted to say to Lucy. but she was in no condition to listen, and he knew it would be selfish of him to push any issues in these circumstances. She needed kindness and comfort.

Jane quickly organised the easiest possible exit from the casino, accompanying them to the car, which Dave had waiting for them. She opened the passenger door and Michael lifted Lucy into the seat and secured her safety belt.

Lucy mumbled 'Thank you' to everyone. Michael quickly expressed his gratitude for his friends' help, anxious to get her home. She was so limp and listless, he worried over whether to take her to the hospital instead as he settled in the driver's seat and started the engine.

'Are you sure you don't need medical attention, Lucy?' he asked.

'Just want to lie down and sleep,' she answered, sounding exhausted.

It was probably the best option, he thought as he set off for her apartment. There wasn't much comfort in waiting for attention in a queue at the emergency room of a hospital, and maybe the worst was over. She wasn't sick during the trip home. Once there, he took her keys out of her bag and carried her into the apartment—a move she weakly protested wasn't needed, but he did it anyway, wanting to hold her in his arms.

He stood her up beside her bed, unzipped her dress, slid it off her arms so it could drop to her feet, before he sat her down and worked on removing her under-clothes and gold sandals. Her skin felt hot and she shivered several times, obviously feverish. He picked out the pins holding up her hair, running his fingers through the falling tresses to ensure they were all gone, before gently lowering her to the pillows, lifting her feet onto the bed and tucking the doona around her.

'Good of you, Michael,' she murmured with a ragged sigh. 'It's okay for you to go now. Thank you.'

She closed her eyes, and the sense of being shut out of her life twisted Michael's gut. If she'd consigned him to the frog species, according to the fairy tale, the only way to change that was for her to kiss him, willingly and caringly. Somehow he had to win his way back into her heart, persuade her to overlook his crass question as to-tally irrelevant to their relationship. Which it truly was.

'I'm not leaving you,' he muttered with fierce deter-mination, sitting on the bed beside her and gently strok-ing her hair away from her hot forehead. 'You're not okay, Lucy. You're running a fever. Do you have any medication here that might lower your temperature?'

She sighed again, whether in exasperation at his

persistence or with her illness, he couldn't tell. Her eyelashes lifted slightly as she answered, 'Bathroom cupboard.'

Her voice was flat. The slitted look she gave him revealed nothing of what she was feeling towards him. 'I'll find it,' he said, and went to the bathroom.

There was a packet of pain tablets that were supposed to lower fever. He took them and went to the kitchen to fill a glass with water before returning to Lucy. He lifted her up from the pillows, fed her the tablets and held the glass to her lips. She gulped down some water. Michael was thinking she was probably dehydrated when she suddenly hurled off the doona, erupted from the bed and staggered towards the bathroom.

Apparently her stomach couldn't tolerate anything in it. Michael had to stand by helplessly as she was convulsively sick again. 'I think I'd better take you to hospital, Lucy,' he said worriedly.

'No…no…' She shook her head vehemently. 'Just help me back to bed. I'll sleep it off.'

Did she want to sleep him off, too?

What could he say?

What could he do?

He tried to make her comfortable again. He dampened a face-cloth and laid it across her forehead, then remembered the cup of ice Harry had been given to suck when he was in hospital with a broken nose. Lucy was definitely dehydrated. He found a tray of ice cubes in the freezer, emptied most of it into a large tumbler and set it on her bedside table. Her eyes were closed again. Not wanting to leave her without any ready access for help, he took her mobile telephone out of her gold handbag and laid it on the bedside table, too.

'Listen to me, Lucy,' he said urgently. 'I'm going to the all-night chemist to ask the pharmacist for advice. Hopefully, he'll have something to settle your stomach. I'll be back soon. Try to suck some of the ice I've left here for you. I've put your phone within easy reach, as well, so you can call me if you need to. Okay?'

'Okay.'

It was barely a whisper of sound. Michael thought she was beyond caring. He hurried out to his car and drove towards the centre of town, where he knew the all-night chemist shop was situated. He was still in two minds about overriding her decision and taking her to hospital. The most important thing right now was to get her well again. Then he could work at making her understand how special she was to him.

He didn't see the car coming at him from the street to his right. The traffic lights at the intersection were green his way. He was focused on where he was going and what he had to do. He felt the impact, then nothing else. All consciousness ceased.

CHAPTER FOURTEEN

THERE WAS A persistent tune penetrating the fog in Lucy's sleep-laden head. On and on it went, until she was conscious enough to realise it was the call-tune of her mobile telephone. Still groggy, she flung an arm out to the bedside table, fumbled around until her hand found the source of irritation. She wanted to shut it off, but some vague memory of Michael leaving the phone beside her to call him made her lift it to her ear.

'Yes...what?' The words emerged in a slurred fashion. Her mouth was dreadfully dry. Her tongue felt furred. It was a huge effort to speak at all.

'Wake up, Lucy!' someone ordered sharply. 'There's been an accident.'

A woman's voice. It sounded like her sister. And saying something about an accident. On the island?

Lucy hauled herself into a sitting position and tried to concentrate. Having pried her eyes open, she could see there was some very early-morning light coming from her window, but it was still an ungodly hour to call anyone.

'What?' she asked again. 'Is that you, Ellie?'

'Yes. Michael was injured in a car accident early this morning. He was badly hurt.'

'Michael…oh, no… No…' Shock cleared her mind in no time flat. The memory of him bringing her home, looking after her, going out to get something for her stomach shot straight into it. 'Oh, God!' she wailed. 'It's my fault!'

'How is it your fault?' Ellie asked worriedly.

'I ate something at dinner last night that upset me. He brought me home. I was vomiting and had dreadful diarrhoea. He left me to find an all-night pharmacy to get me some medicine. I was so drained I must have drifted off to sleep. He should have come back, but he's not here and… Oh, God! He went out for me, Ellie!'

'Stop that, Lucy! You didn't cause the accident, and getting hysterical won't help Michael,' she said vehemently, cutting off the futile guilt trip. 'I take it everything was still good between you last night?'

'Yes…yes… He was so caring when I was sick. Oh, Ellie! I'll die if I lose him.'

She forgot she had probably already lost him. All she could think of was how special he was, how much she loved him.

'Then you'd better do whatever you can to make him want to live,' Ellie sharply advised. 'Are you still sick? Can you get to the hospital? He's in an intensive care unit.'

'I'll get there.' Gritty determination quelled every vestige of hysterical panic.

'Harry was with me on the island,' Ellie went on. 'He's on his way. Be kind to him, Lucy. Remember he and Michael lost their parents in an accident. I have to stay here. Harry's counting on me to take care of business, but I think he'll need someone there, too.'

'I understand. You love him but you can't be with him.'

At least that was good—Ellie and Harry teaming up together. Lucy couldn't let herself dwell on where she and Michael were in their relationship when he was fighting for his life in an intensive care unit.

'I need to know what's happening, Lucy,' Ellie said in a softer tone. 'Please…will you keep me informed?'

'Sure!' Clearly, the situation deeply concerned her sister, too, with Michael being Harry's brother, as well as a man she had worked closely with for two years. 'I'll call you with news as soon as I have it. Moving now. Over and out. Okay?'

'Okay.'

Moving was not easy. Lucy was still weak and shaky. Her head whirled as she forced her legs to take her to the bathroom. Nothing in her stomach, she thought, but was too scared of being sick again to eat or drink anything. Somehow she had to make it to the hospital and not look like the total wreck she saw in the vanity mirror.

Slowly, carefully, she cleaned herself up, brushed her hair and applied some make-up to put colour in her face. Bright clothes, she decided, wanting to make Michael smile…if he was up to smiling at all. She refused to let herself think he might die, though it was impossible to banish the anxiety spearing pain through her heart.

It took a while to put clothes on, since she needed to sit down more than once until her rockiness subsided. She selected the yellow wraparound dress to remind him of the great sex they'd shared, and the pretty shell necklace that might recall their wonderful time together on Finn Island. He would surely want to live to have those pleasures again.

Being in no condition to drive safely, she called for a taxi to pick her up and take her to the hospital. On the trip there she kept wondering where the accident had happened, and how it could have been so serious when traffic in the city had to move at a relatively slow pace. Had Michael been speeding, wanting to get back to her quickly? Had she unwittingly been the cause of it?

Her mind was awash with tormenting questions when she finally arrived at the intensive care unit. Before she could properly inquire about Michael at the nurses' station, Harry suddenly appeared at her side and swept her off to the waiting room, his grim expression filling her with fear. He sat her down and stood over her as he gave her the information she most needed to know.

'It's not too bad, Lucy. His injuries aren't life-threatening. He was hit on the driver's side, right arm and hip fractured, broken ribs, lacerations to the face, a lot of bruising, concussion. The doctors were worried that a broken rib had punctured his liver, but that's been cleared, and bones will mend.' Harry's sigh transmitted a mountain of relief. 'He's going to be incapacitated for quite a while, but there should be no lasting damage.'

'Thank God!' Her own relief was mountainous, as well. 'How did it happen, Harry?' She was still anxious to know that.

'Drunken teenagers in a stolen car ran a red light and slammed into him as he was driving across an intersection. They're all here, too. Needless to say, I don't have much sympathy for them.'

Another huge roll of relief. The accident wasn't Michael's fault. Nor hers. It was simply a case of being in the wrong place at the wrong time, although he wouldn't have been there but for her. Still, the food poisoning was an accident, too, and there was no point in fretting over it. Moving on was the only way to go.

'Can I go and see Michael now?'

Harry grimaced. 'I don't think that's a good idea.'

'Why not?'

'Well, to put it bluntly, he's barely recognisable. It will come as a shock to you. They've stitched the cuts on his face, but it's very bruised and swollen. He's also sedated to keep the pain at bay, and it's best if he stays that way. If you start screaming or carrying on—'

She cut him off very sharply. 'Harry Finn, I nursed my mother while she slowly died from cancer. Nothing is worse than seeing someone you love wasting away. I am no wimp when it comes to facing people who are suffering, and I am not stupid. I care a lot about Michael and no way would I do anything to wake him up to pain. I just want to be with him.'

Surprise at her vehemence gave way to a look of respect for her. He nodded. 'Then I'll take you to him.'

'Good!'

She pushed herself up from the chair and steadied herself for the walk to Michael's bedside. Harry took her arm, which helped her stay reasonably steady. 'Have you called Ellie to let her know Michael will come through this?' she asked, as he led her back to the intensive care unit.

'Not yet. I've just finished talking to the doctors. Since there's no critical danger, they won't operate on

Mickey until tomorrow morning. I've insisted on the top surgeon.'

'I'm glad about that, but do call my sister, Harry. She's anxiously waiting for news.'

'As soon as you're settled with Mickey,' he promised.

It was better if Ellie heard everything from Harry, Lucy thought. She would call her sister tonight, hopefully after Michael had woken up and she had more personal news.

Harry certainly hadn't exaggerated Michael's facial injuries. Seeing him did come as a shock, but she swiftly told herself all this was a temporary phase. He would heal. Harry pulled up a chair for her to sit beside the bed, and she sank gratefully onto it, reaching out to take Michael's left hand in hers, mindful that his right arm had been broken. His flesh was warm. No matter how ghastly he looked, he was alive, and she fiercely willed him to want her in his future.

Though she wasn't sure how much of a future he would want with her. His questioning last night about how many men she had slept with had not left her with a good feeling. It seemed judgemental in a nasty way. He'd told her to forget it, that it didn't matter, but he had brought it up so it obviously meant something to him. Had her answer satisfied him?

She'd become too ill to assess his reaction to it. Whatever he'd thought, he'd been good to her, sticking around, bringing her home, doing his best to look after her. Still a prince, in that sense. She could only hope there wasn't a frog lurking inside him.

Her head ached. Harry had left the room, probably

to make the call to Ellie. Lucy felt too tired to think anymore. Besides, it seemed pointless. There would be no answers until Michael woke up. She rested her head on the bed beside the hand she was holding. The effort to get here had drained her of what little energy she had after being so sick. She slid into sleep without realising it was happening.

A hand gripping hers hard jerked her awake. Michael's swollen black eyes were opened into thin slits. Having drawn her attention, he croaked out, 'Where am I?'

'In hospital, Mickey,' Harry answered, rising from a chair on the other side of the bed to put himself in his brother's line of sight. 'Don't move,' he commanded. 'You have broken bones.'

'How? Why? I can't open my eyes much.'

'You were in a car accident and your face copped a beating. So did your body,' Harry told him bluntly.

'How bad?'

'You'll mend, but it will take some time.'

'It hurts to breathe.'

'Broken ribs.'

'Car accident… I can't remember.'

'Concussion. The doctors warned me you might not regain any memory of last night.'

Lucy shot an inquiring glance at Harry. He hadn't told her that. How much memory might be blotted out? And would it stay blotted out?

He nodded to her. 'Lucy's here. I'll go and fetch the doctor on duty. I was told to do that as soon as you were conscious. He'll answer any questions you have, Mickey.'

Michael squeezed her hand as he shifted his limited vision to her. 'Lucy,' he said, as though he loved her name.

She squeezed back, smiling at him. 'You're going to be okay,' she assured him.

'I remember we had lunch at the Thala Beach Lodge. What happened last night?'

'We went to a ball at the casino. We danced for hours until they served a seafood banquet. Something I ate gave me food poisoning. You took me home, then went out to an all-night chemist to get me some medication. Harry told me a stolen car slammed into you at an intersection—a drunken driver running a red light.'

He shook his head slightly and winced. 'I don't remember any of that.'

'Don't worry about it.'

'Food poisoning…last night… You must feel wretched, Lucy.'

Her heart turned over. Here he was, caring about her when he was all broken up and obviously hurting.

'I'll live,' she said dismissively. 'I had to see you, be with you, Michael. Ellie called me with the news and I was frightened you might not make it through.' She smiled to lighten up the situation. 'I was going to hang on to you like grim death until you did.'

'That's my girl,' he said with a ghost of a smile.

It was so blissful to hear him say that, as though nothing had changed between them.

Harry returned with the doctor and Lucy moved out of the way of any medical checking that had to be done, standing at the end of the bed and holding the foot railing for support. She did feel wretched. A glance at her watch told her she'd actually slept with her head on Michael's bed for over three hours, which should have helped, yet her legs were still weak and shaky.

The doctor went through a schedule of procedures, explaining what would be done and when. He answered questions, then administered an injection of morphine before he left.

Michael turned his attention to her. 'You must go home and rest, Lucy. You need recovery time from food poisoning, and I'll probably be out of it for most of today and tomorrow.' He shifted his gaze to his brother. 'Make her go, Harry.'

'I will,' he promised.

She didn't want to, but saw the sense in it. 'I'll go,' she said, moving around to his side to take his hand again, pressing it with fervent caring. 'I'll come back tomorrow evening. I hope the operation goes well, Michael.'

'Don't worry about it. Hip operations are run-of-the-mill stuff these days.'

She leaned over and kissed his lips very softly. 'I'll be thinking of you every minute,' she murmured.

Harry accompanied her out of the hospital and put her in a taxi. 'Take care of yourself, Lucy,' he said kindly. 'I think my brother will need you in the difficult days to come.'

It was nice that he thought she was an important part of Michael's life. Maybe she still could be if Michael never remembered questioning her about past sexual partners. Initially he had dismissed the Jason Lester encounter. It was the run-in with her most recent ex last night that had reignited the issue in his mind. If that was now wiped out… Lucy couldn't help hoping everything would be right between them.

She desperately wanted to hold on to her prince.

She couldn't bear it if he turned into a frog.

CHAPTER FIFTEEN

FOR MICHAEL IT was a hell of a week. The broken arm was a nuisance because he couldn't use it. The broken ribs gave him pain with every movement, and he had to move. The nurses got him out of bed every day after the hip operation, walking up and down a corridor to ensure his muscles kept working around the piece of titanium that had been inserted.

On top of that was his frustration at having to leave his business to Harry, who was making a good fist of handling the franchises under his instructions, but didn't have the sense of creativity needed to take any new initiatives. Which wasn't really a problem. That could wait for Michael's return. He simply wasn't used to not controlling everything himself. It would have been easier for Harry if Elizabeth had been on hand—the perfect PA—but she was stepping in for him on the island while he was tied up here.

The accident couldn't have come at a worse time, incapacitating Michael when he had no one in the office he trusted to take over in any capacity whatsoever. Andrew Cook was next to useless, needing someone to tell him everything, and there hadn't been time to find a competent replacement for Elizabeth.

The only bright spot in his current life was Lucy.

He was intensely grateful she had decided to overlook his frog blunder at the ball, calling into question her sexual experience. He still didn't remember the car accident, but memories of everything preceding it had come swimming back to him after the hip operation.

He'd actually been afraid she wouldn't visit him again, since he wasn't about to die, but she had turned up on Monday evening and every evening since, chatting to him in her wonderfully bubbly fashion, massaging his feet, giving him her beautiful smile, not at all concerned that he looked like Frankenstein's monster.

Michael had been moved to a private room with his own television to make time pass less tediously. He had no complaints about the care given to him from the medical staff. The physiotherapist was particularly good. His friends dropped in to see him, bringing him gifts to keep him in reasonably good cheer. Harry kept him informed of business issues and was always good company. But it was Lucy who brought sunshine into his room. She made him feel lucky to be alive and very lucky to have her in his life.

Today he was glad it was Saturday, not a workday for her, and she'd promised to visit him this morning. While he waited for her he struggled with the newspaper he'd asked to be delivered to him. It was the *Sydney Morning Herald* and its pages were large. Having the use of only one arm, handling them was awkward, and most of them slid off the bed onto the floor as he tried to separate out the financial section, which he liked to read each week.

He finally managed it, and having found an article

that interested him, he was frustrated again by his vision blurring over the little print. Probably an after-effect of the concussion, he reasoned. The swelling had gone down and his eyes were back to normal, but this was obviously yet another thing he would have to wait out.

He was darkly brooding over the frustrating aspects of his situation when Lucy walked in, all bright and beautiful, instantly lifting his spirits. She'd put up her hair in a kind of tousled topknot, and her eyes were sparkling, her dimples flashing, her smile totally enchanting. She was wearing purple jeans teamed with a purple-lime-and-white top in a wildly floral print, long dangly purple-and-lime earrings and a set of matching bangles.

He smiled. 'You look fantastic, Lucy!'

She laughed. 'I like dressing up. It's fun.'

Fun like a carnival full of happy surprises, he thought.

She'd brought him a surprise, too, holding out to him a perfect yellow rose in a long-stemmed glass vase.

'Look! Isn't it beautiful, Michael? I was out at the cemetery yesterday and the old man who planted a Pal Joey rose on his wife's grave was there. He cut this off for me, but it wasn't quite in full bloom so I waited until today to bring it to you.' She placed the vase on his bedside table. 'Just the glorious scent of it will take away the hospital antiseptic smell and make you feel better.'

'I'm sure it will. Thank you, Lucy.'

'My pleasure.'

She leaned over and kissed him. Desire for her had already kicked in and he wished he could crush her to him, but his ribs were still a problem, so he had to suffer her moving away to pull up a chair.

'Wow! You've made a mess of this newspaper,' she said, bending over to shuffle the dropped pages into a manageable bundle.

It reminded him of the article he'd wanted to read, which was still on his bed, and he needed a distraction from the rush of hot blood Lucy stirred with her sexy derriere bobbing around. 'Just leave them in a pile and sit down, Lucy. There's something I want you to read to me. The little print has me defeated at the moment. My vision keeps blurring. It's an article in this financial section.' He picked it up and held it out to her.

She took it somewhat gingerly and sat down, frowning at the opened page. 'The financial section,' she repeated slowly, sounding troubled. She looked up with a quick, appealing smile. 'Wouldn't it be better if Harry read it to you? Then you could discuss whatever's in it together. I'm simply not into that scene, Michael.'

'Harry has gone over to the island with the guy who's to take over the job of manager as soon as Elizabeth can train him into the job. I don't expect him back until tomorrow. Besides, I don't want to discuss it,' he argued. 'I simply want to know what it says. It's been annoying me, not being able to read it. It will only take five minutes, Lucy. Please?'

The smile was gone. She gave him an anguished look. 'I'd really rather not.'

'Why not?'

Surely it was only a small favour to ask. Why put it off? Why was it a problem to her? She'd lowered her lashes to hide the strange anguish he'd seen, and her body was tensing up as though readying itself to spring from the chair. All this was incomprehensible to him.

'Lucy?' he pressed, needing to have her odd reaction cleared up.

She slowly set the section of newspaper he'd given her on the bed, drawing her hands back to pick at each other nervously in her lap. She drew in a deep breath, then met his gaze squarely as though facing a feared inquisitor.

'I can't, Michael,' she said flatly.

Still it made no sense to him. 'What do you mean... you *can't*?'

Her chin lifted slightly. 'I was born with dyslexia. I've always had difficulty with reading and writing.'

Dyslexia...

He didn't know much about it, only that letters in words got jumbled up to people who had that disability.

Lucy gave a wry little shrug. 'I can usually wing my way through most situations.' Her eyes were bleak with vulnerability as she added, 'But I've been sacked from jobs because of it and dumped from relationships because of it. I know I'm no match for you, Michael. I just wanted to have you love me for a little while.' Tears glittered. 'And you have, quite beautifully.'

It sounded perilously close to a goodbye speech to Michael. 'Now hold on a moment!' He cut in fast and hard. 'This isn't the end for us. I won't have it, Lucy. You're my girl, regardless. What I want is for you to tell me about your dyslexia. Share it with me. You don't have to hide it from me.'

She bit her lips. Her head drooped. Her eyelashes worked overtime, trying to blink away the tears. Her distress was heart-wrenching. She was such a beautiful person, and clearly this disability had been a blight on her life that she'd kept dodging and fighting, determined to make the most of who she was and what she could be. That took amazing strength of character, in Michael's opinion, and he admired her for it. To keep picking herself up and moving on from where she wasn't wanted, and find joy in something else…that was something very few people could do.

As he waited for Lucy to compose herself, his mind raced back over the past few weeks, picking up clues he'd missed. The mistake about chilli crab being on the menu that first day; her habit of choosing specials that were verbally listed by a waiter, when they were dining out, or observing what other people were eating and asking for the same; her panic at the idea of taking on Elizabeth's job as his PA, with Ellie staunchly supporting her, protecting her younger sister from being embarrassed by her disability.

He understood so much more about Lucy now: why she had been the one to drop out of school to nurse her mother, why she'd taken up hands-on jobs rather than desk ones, why few of them lasted very long, why advancement in any kind of serious career would be unlikely for her. The bookwork would be too hard to manage. She'd done what she could, probably relying a lot on Elizabeth's support.

Her anchor…

No matter what happened Lucy would always have her sister, who could be counted on to never waver in her love and support. Michael could see Elizabeth in that role.

He recalled Sarah Pickard's reading of Lucy, and realised now how accurate it was. Being ditzy was a good cover for feeling inadequate, she'd said, while he'd scoffed at the idea of Lucy feeling inadequate about anything. But the dyslexia did make her feel that way, which was why she hid it. Sarah had also been spot on about there being not much self-esteem in Lucy. How could there be if people kept putting her down because of her disability?

'Lucy, I think you're marvellous,' he said softly, wanting her to feel good about herself.

Her lashes flicked up and her tear-washed eyes searched his for truth.

'I do,' he asserted more strongly, holding her gaze with steady conviction. 'No matter how many people have cast you adrift because of your dyslexia, you haven't retreated from the world. You keep on setting out on another path and giving it your best. That drive to keep going, to keep finding joy in the world…you *are* marvellous, Lucy.'

'But…' she frowned at him, a wary uncertainty in her eyes '…you must see I'm defective, too.'

'Who isn't in one area or another?' he quickly answered, thinking *defective* was a particularly nasty word to be attached to Lucy. 'Harry says I have tunnel vision, not seeing anything except what's directly in front of me. You're in front of me, Lucy, and I like what I see.' Michael reached out to her. 'Give me your hand.'

Slowly, she lifted one hand and put it in his. He squeezed it reassuringly. 'I don't care if you can't read or write. I like having you with me. Now smile for me again.'

It was a wobbly smile, but at least there was a glimmer of hope in her eyes. 'I can read and write, Michael. It's just very slow and painstaking. I'm much better at memorising things. That's how I got my driver's licence. Ellie drilled me until I knew all the answers off by heart and could recognise the questions. She's always been great like that, giving me help when I needed it. Though I don't like asking too much of her. I try to get along by myself.'

'You do very well by yourself,' Michael said admiringly. 'I would never have guessed you had any disability.'

She made a wry grimace. 'It's not something I want people to know. I'd rather be seen as normal.'

'You're way above normal, Lucy. You're very special.'

The smile came back. 'My mother used to say that. She used to say my smile was worth a thousand words.'

'She was right,' Michael assured her.

'It doesn't always help, though. The guy I was with before you—the control freak—used to make lists of things he wanted me to do. His handwriting was too hard to work out, so I just ignored the lists and did whatever I wanted. He got really angry about it and called me an airhead.'

'So you walked out on him.'

'Yes. I guess I could have explained, told him about the dyslexia, but I don't like abusive people. My father was very abusive to my mother.' She shook her head. 'I don't want that in my life.'

Michael nodded. 'Quite right! It's not acceptable.'

She beamed a brilliant smile at him and there was sunshine back in the room.

Knowing what he now knew, he should have decked that guy in the men's room for calling Lucy an airhead, though violence wasn't acceptable, either. Instead of standing up for her, he'd been distracted by the sexual angle, which had led him into frog territory. Never again, he silently vowed. No man would like losing Lucy, and bruised egos undoubtedly prompted trying to damage her in the eyes of any other man she favoured.

Michael wondered how much abuse she had suffered because of her dyslexia. 'Your school years must have been hard, Lucy,' he said sympathetically, thinking of teachers who might not have spotted her disability for quite a while, and other kids calling her stupid.

'Yes and no. I was good at sports, which helped, winning me some approval for what I could do, and I did make friends who stuck by me. But schoolwork was a nightmare and I copped some bullying, which was fairly nasty. I was an easy target for those who liked to feel superior.'

'Tell me about it,' he urged, wanting her to unload all she had kept inside and be free of it with him.

Lucy could hardly believe that Michael was so accepting of her disability, not seeming to see any wrong in her at all. He kept encouraging her to talk about it, the problems it had caused her, how she had skirted around a lot of them. She made fun of some of the situations, and it was strangely exhilarating to laugh together about them. Other more distressing experiences drew nothing but sympathy from him, even admiration at how well she'd survived them, not letting them destroy her spirit to find pleasures to enjoy.

They talked all day, and when Lucy finally left Michael, she was almost on a giddy high from sheer happiness. The sense of freedom from having to keep her dyslexia hidden from him was so exhilarating she wanted to dance and whirl around and clap her hands.

Michael liked her as she was.

He might even love her as she was.

And he was very definitely a prince.

CHAPTER SIXTEEN

LUCY WAS IN THE habit of going straight from work to visit Michael. She did not stay long on Thursday evening because Harry was there, making arrangements about Michael's release from hospital on Friday, and Ellie had returned from the island, satisfied that the new manager could handle everything. It had been almost three weeks since she'd seen her sister and was eager to hear all her news and share her own.

Ellie was in the kitchen making a salad when she arrived home. 'Hi, Lucy!' she greeted her with a smile. 'Have you eaten?'

'No. Is there enough for two?'

'Sure! There wasn't much food here so I shopped.'

'I've been with Michael most of the time.'

'How is he today?'

'Still in considerable discomfort but he can manage with a walking stick so they're letting him out tomorrow.'

She nodded. 'Harry told me. I'll be helping in the office until Michael's ready to take over again. I'll train my replacement, too, make sure there's someone competent to assist him when I'm gone.'

'That's good of you, Ellie. Do you have some idea of what you want to do after that?'

'Oh yes!' She grinned. 'There's a bottle of Sauvignon Blanc in the fridge. How about you open it and we'll drink to the future?'

Lucy was happy to see her sister in such high spirits. The month on the island had made a big difference to her. Or Harry had. She opened the bottle of wine, filled two glasses and handed one to her sister. 'Is it a bright future with Harry?' she asked hopefully.

'He's asked me to marry him. And I'm going to, Lucy.'

'Oh, that's great news!' Lucy put down her glass to give Ellie a big hug. 'I'm so happy for you!'

'I'm happy, too. I really believe we're right together.'

Her eyes sparkled. Her skin glowed. Love was beaming out of her. Lucy's heart swelled with joy for her sister, who truly deserved a good man who would always care for her.

Ellie eased back from the hug to give her a searching look. 'How's it going with Michael?'

'Hey! You're not to worry about that. I want you and Harry to ride off into the sunset together without a care in the world. You promised not to let me get in the way, remember?'

'Yes, and I won't, but I'm not about to stop caring about you. I take it you're still in love with him.'

'Oh, I love him to bits and I think he cares about me, too. Though this accident has sort of interrupted things.'

'Lucy, it needs to be more than great sex.'

'I know.' But he hadn't yet remembered asking her

about sex with other men, and that might raise its ugly head again.

'When you phoned me last Sunday, you said he had no problem with your dyslexia. That's good, isn't it?'

'It's amazing! I hated having to reveal it but he was unbelievably nice to me about it. And it's such a relief to have it out in the open, not having to hide it.'

'Then it's made no difference to how he treats you.'

'None at all. I love being with him, Ellie.'

'Well, from what Harry tells me, he loves being with you, too.' Her face relaxed into a smile. 'Who knows? We might all end up in one happy family.'

'We might,' Lucy agreed, but she couldn't quite bring herself to believe it.

Having a lovely fantasy was one thing. Having it become reality was quite another. As much as she loved Michael, marriage was something else. Michael Finn was the kind of man who would want children, and although he admired how she had managed her life with dyslexia, she didn't think he'd want his own children to be afflicted by the disability.

There was no guarantee she wouldn't pass it on to any baby she had. She had kept pushing that unpalatable truth aside in the pleasure of having a wonderful relationship with an absolute prince but it was never going to go away. It was okay for Ellie to have a family. She didn't have the faulty gene. And Lucy was delighted that this was now a solid prospect for her sister with Harry.

As for herself, she had decided long ago that having children was not a fair option so a marriage with family was not going to happen. She thought living together was fine as long as both people were content with the situation. So far none of her relationships had proceeded to that level of acceptance of each other. She would love to be with Michael all the time but the wish for an always future with him was probably a dream that wouldn't come true.

However, she was not about to give up feeling happy with him as long as he felt happy with her. Live each day as it comes, she kept telling herself. One never knew how long a life would be. Michael's accident was a sober reminder of that truth.

As the days went by in the third week since the accident, far from feeling happy with them, Lucy began to panic about the non-arrival of her period. She was never late. The contraceptive pill she used kept her right on schedule with her monthly cycle. Except there was one night when she hadn't taken it—the night of the ball when she'd been too sick to think of it. Then with the shock of Michael's accident, she hadn't thought of taking a morning-after pill, either.

After their splendid lunch at Thala Lodge, they'd made love for hours before parting to dress up for the ball. That long and late sexy afternoon now loomed as the big danger. Yet surely, surely, fate couldn't be so unkind to punish her with an unplanned pregnancy because of one night's unlucky illness. She'd always been so obsessively careful, mindful of her disability and also of the misery an unplanned pregnancy had caused her mother, leading her into an unhappy marriage. It wasn't fair that this should happen to her.

By the fourth week, Lucy couldn't keep pushing the issue aside, couldn't keep desperately hoping this was simply some glitch in her system which would soon correct itself. She steeled herself to take a pregnancy test, needing to know if it was positive or negative. Living in this uncertainty was draining her of any joy in life. Michael had even queried if she was under stress at work. It was growing impossible to be her normal self.

She bought the test kit, rose early the next morning, shut herself in the bathroom and did what she had to do, fiercely willing the result to be negative. She held her breath as she watched the chemicals react. Her heart was a painful hammer in her chest. Her mind chanted *please, please, please...*

There was no kind fate.

As she stared at the positive result the blood drained from her face and the bottom fell out of her world. The shock of it was overwhelming. She fumbled the lid of the toilet down and sat on it, bending over to stop herself from fainting, sucking in deep breaths to clear the whirl of black dots.

Her mind kept railing against the terrible truth. It shouldn't have happened to her. It wasn't fair. The life she had managed so far was spinning completely out of control. She was adrift, more deeply than she had ever been. There was no way back, no way forward that wasn't a frightening blur.

When she felt strong enough she picked up all evidence of the pregnancy kit, took it to her bedroom and hid it in her wardrobe. Her first instinct was always to hide problems. This one was too big to be faced yet. She climbed back into bed, pulled the bedclothes over her head and curled up in the foetal position, wishing she'd never been born.

Time passed in a fog of misery.

Ellie called out to her but she couldn't bring herself to answer. She wanted everything to just go away. Her sister did not oblige, knocking on her door, coming in, asking what was wrong.

'Sick. Not going to work,' she mumbled. 'Tell Michael I can't visit him today.'

'What kind of sick?' Ellie asked worriedly. 'Can I get you anything?'

'No. Just go, Ellie. I want to sleep it off.'

'Well, call me if you need me,' Ellie pressed.

'Mmmh...'

She couldn't *need* Ellie with this. It would spoil what should be a happy time for her sister. It had to be kept hidden, at least until after Ellie's wedding to Harry. Even then, she wouldn't want to be a burden on their marriage.

This pregnancy made everything so difficult.

Especially with Michael being Harry's brother.

Her mind shied away from thinking about Michael. If she told him about the pregnancy and he felt obliged to offer marriage she would hate it, hate it, hate it. It was impossible to see anything working well in these circumstances. Besides, he might doubt it was his child, and she would hate that, too.

Tomorrow she might be able to come to some decision about him. Until she could work it out sensibly it was better not to talk to him at all, so she reached out to her bedside table and switched off her mobile phone, needing to prevent him from calling to ask how she was. She needed time to come to grips with everything.

Michael hated being incapacitated. He could move around his apartment—slowly—and do quite a bit for himself—

slowly—but until his right arm and ribs mended, he was useless in the office. He was trying to wean himself off pain-killers, too, which meant he was in fairly constant discomfort. At least he wasn't so concerned about what was happening with his business now that Elizabeth was here helping Harry. She wouldn't miss a thing, never had.

Though it did amaze him that Harry had decided to marry her. He'd had no idea that the attraction had gone so deep. On either side. He remembered Elizabeth being irritated by Harry's flirting and Harry had definitely considered her a challenge he wanted to win, but it was still a surprise that they felt so much for each other. A good surprise. He had no problem with Elizabeth being his sister-in-law. She was a very admirable woman—Lucy's anchor—responsible, trustworthy, caring, and very smart. Harry had made a fine choice for a lifelong partner.

It had actually spurred him into considering Lucy in the same light for himself. She was very different to her older sister, more endearing in lots of ways. He admired the core of strength underneath her vulnerabilities and she was certainly very caring. Smart, too. Dyslexia didn't limit her intelligence. He knew he wanted her in his life, but his life was abnormal at the moment. This was not the time to be considering a future with anyone.

He spent an hour browsing through some brochures on new fishing gear, having spread them out on the dining-table for easy access. At ten o'clock Elizabeth entered the apartment, bringing his coffee and chocolate muffin from the cafe on the ground floor, as she'd done every day when she'd been working for him.

'How are you doing this morning?' she asked brightly.

'Well enough,' he answered, smiling over their old routine. He'd resigned himself to finding a replacement for her but he doubted anyone could be as good.

'Lucy's not so well,' she remarked, setting the coffee and muffin on the table next to his left hand. 'Must have caught some bug or other. I left her in bed, too sick to go to work, so she won't be coming around to visit you today.'

He frowned over this news. 'I thought she wasn't quite herself the last couple of days. No joy bubbling over. I'll give her a call.'

'Leave it for a while, Michael. She said she wanted to sleep it off.'

'Okay. Thanks for the coffee.'

He waited until lunch time to call Lucy but couldn't get through to her. Her phone was dead. It stayed dead well into the afternoon. It concerned him that she felt too sick to want any communication with anyone. He remembered the yellow rose she had brought him in hospital to make him feel better and on impulse, made a call to Jack Pickard.

'It's Michael Finn, Jack. I have a favour to ask.'

'Ask away, Mickey,' he invited cheerily.

'You know the Pal Joey rose Lucy admired when we were over on the island. Do you happen to have one in bloom?'

'Several. Sarah was commenting on them this morning.'

'Would you cut one for Lucy? I'll send a helicopter over to have it collected. If you'd have it ready to go...?'

'I'll meet the helicopter with it myself,' he promised. 'Lovely girl, Lucy.'

'Yes, she is. Thanks, Jack. It should arrive within the hour.'

He immediately set about making the arrangements required to have the rose delivered to his office before five o'clock, then called Elizabeth to let her know to expect it.

'I want you to take it home to Lucy. Tell her it's from me to make her feel better and ask her to call me. Okay?'

'Will do,' she promised. 'Nice gesture, Michael. I'm sure Lucy will appreciate it.'

It left him smiling. Hopefully Lucy would be well enough to chat to him tonight. She made him forget about pain. He badly missed having sex with her and frequently cursed his broken bones for making him inactive on that front. Four weeks down and probably another four to go, he told himself, determined on making the fastest possible recovery. He just had to be patient. Lucy was still there for him, despite his blunder at the ball.

Lucy remained hiding in bed when her sister came home. Earlier in the day she'd cried herself to sleep and although that merciful oblivion was no longer her friend she was trying to hang onto it, dozing on and off, not ready to face what had to be faced. She heard her door open and Ellie coming into the bedroom, moving quietly so as not to disturb her. She kept her eyes closed, not wanting to be questioned.

'Are you awake?' Ellie asked softly. 'I've brought you a cup of tea and a rose from Michael.'

A rose?

Lucy's mind was in such a mess, it clutched wildly at the hope that Michael truly loved her and would love her no matter what! She hitched herself up, eyes opened wide, heart thumping, only to see Ellie setting down a yellow rose in the same glass vase she had used to take her gift to Michael in the hospital.

Yellow, not red.

Not red for love.

Tears welled into her eyes so fast they overflowed and trickled down her cheeks. Her sister saw them before she could hide the emotional eruption. There was no escape from her immediate concern. Even as she flopped back down on the pillow and closed her eyes Ellie was sitting on the bed beside her, stroking her forehead, asking, 'What's wrong, Lucy?'

'Nothing,' she muttered.

'I don't believe you. Tell me what it is.'

'Just sick.'

'Sick with what? Your forehead isn't hot so you're not running a fever. And why have you got your phone switched off? Neither I nor Michael could reach you today.'

'Didn't want to be reached. Leave me alone, Ellie,' she said plaintively. 'I'm not up to talking.'

'You're hiding, Lucy,' came the voice of certainty.

'No. Just sick.'

'You're sick because you're bottling something up. You've done this before, going into retreat and churning over stuff you don't want to tell me about.'

'Please…let me be, Ellie,' she begged, quickly hiding her face in the pillow to stop the quizzing.

Her sister huffed in frustration. 'Well, at least call

Michael and thank him for the rose. He went to a great deal of trouble and expense to get it for you.'

'It's the wrong colour,' she mumbled into the pillow, tears gushing again.

'What do you mean…the wrong colour?' Ellie continued to probe. 'Michael said it was a special rose you particularly liked. He actually called Jack Pickard for one he'd grown over on the island and had it flown to Cairns by helicopter so I could put it here for you to smell. Now that deserves a thank you call from you, Lucy,' she declared with firm authority. 'I don't care how sick you are over whatever you're sick about. I'm switching your mobile on now and…'

'Don't!' Sheer panic jerked Lucy up, her arm flying out to snatch the mobile from her sister's grasp.

'What on earth…?' Ellie cried in shock.

Lucy clutched the mobile to her chest. 'I can't talk to him! I can't!'

'Why not?'

'Just leave me alone,' she pleaded.

'No, I won't!' Ellie wore her determined look. 'This has gone far enough. Tell me what's wrong, Lucy. I'm not going away until you do.'

Lucy bit her lip. It didn't stop the tears from falling.

'Tell me!' Ellie commanded.

Lucy shook her head. 'You can't fix it, Ellie.'

Her sister took a deep breath. 'Have you found out you've got cancer, like Mum?'

It was such a shocking leap she gasped, 'No…no…'

'Well, thank God for that!' Ellie regathered herself and drove forward. 'We've faced a lot together, Lucy.

It doesn't matter if this can be fixed or not. We face it together. So tell me what the problem is right now.'

Her sister…her anchor…

It was who Ellie was—through and through—and she was not about to let that part of their lives change.

Lucy's resistance collapsed.

This problem did have to be faced, and Ellie was right.

It was better faced together.

CHAPTER SEVENTEEN

MICHAEL PROWLED AROUND the penthouse apartment, banging his walking stick on the tiled floor, too unsettled to sit down and have breakfast with Harry.

'Ask Elizabeth to come straight up here when she arrives at the office,' he commanded his brother.

'Just because neither of them wanted to take calls last night…' Harry began in an overly reasonable tone.

'I want to know why,' Michael insisted. 'And I want to know now!'

'Okay!' Harry lifted his hands in surrender. 'As long as you remember to be kind to Elizabeth. It's not her fault if Lucy's sick and doesn't feel up to chatting.'

'It's more than that,' Michael muttered. 'I can feel it in my bones.'

'Probably because they're broken,' Harry muttered back at him.

'You don't know Lucy like I do,' Michael shot at him. 'I think she might be backing off me now that I'm getting better.'

'For what reason?' Harry eyed him in an assessing fashion. 'I know you've become used to her pandering to your every need this past month. I hope you haven't just been using her for that, Mickey. She is Elizabeth's sister.'

'No. That's not what it's about.' He couldn't forget feeling himself turning into a frog at the ball. Lucy wouldn't desert someone in need and he had been needy since the accident. She was big on empathy and caring. But now that he was well on the mend, other issues could be looked at and acted upon. He didn't want to confide something he was ashamed of to Harry. 'Please…just tell Elizabeth I need to talk to her.'

'Will do,' Harry finally agreed.

He had an impatient wait until Elizabeth did enter his apartment and the wary expression on her face instantly set off alarm bells in his head.

'Good morning, Michael,' she said so formally he sensed her keeping mental or emotional distance from him, which raised his inner tension several notches.

'Elizabeth…' he acknowledged with a nod, waving to an armchair in his living room '…have a seat.'

He propped himself on the wide armrest of its companion chair, directly facing her as she gingerly settled onto the deep cushion. 'What's happening with Lucy?' he asked point-blank.

Elizabeth held his gaze with a hard searching look of her own before calmly stating, 'Lucy is pregnant.'

'Pregnant…' he repeated dazedly, the shock of it sending his mind reeling.

'Because she was so sick the night of the ball, followed up by your accident, she forgot to take her contraceptive pill. Just one night she was off track, Michael. And unfortunately, you'd had a long session in bed that afternoon just prior to the ball. So that's how it happened.'

She didn't have to plead for his understanding. The circumstances were crystal clear. Knowing how obsessively careful Lucy was about safe sex, Michael could picture her deeply distressed by the outcome of this one mishap. He realised this was at the core of her withdrawal from him this past week. It was a big reason. A huge reason. But she should have shared it with him, not kept it to herself.

'Why didn't she tell me?' he shot at her sister.

Again the hard, searching look. 'Do you accept that you're the father, Michael?'

'Of course I accept it! Why wouldn't I?'

'Lucy thinks you might not believe you are. She thinks you're hung up on how many lovers she's had in the past. She said you asked about them that night.'

Michael gritted his teeth, knowing he'd painted himself as a frog, savagely wishing he could change the green into unblemished white.

Elizabeth sucked in a quick breath and continued, 'If it's a concern that will always be on your mind...'

'No!' He sliced the air with his hand in emphatically negative dismissal. 'It was prompted by what other men had said about Lucy but virtually at the moment I was asking the question I realised it was irrelevant to me. Irrelevant to us. And I've regretted bringing it up ever since.'

Elizabeth heaved a huge sigh of relief. 'Well, I'm glad we don't have that problem. I couldn't like you if you thought badly of my sister.'

'I don't. I love your sister, Elizabeth.'

The word slid straight out of his mouth before he'd even realised how true it was.

It evoked a doubtful look. 'Lucy doesn't know that, Michael, and to us *love* is a big word. Please don't use it lightly. Not in this situation.'

'I'll tell her. We'll work it out,' he asserted strongly.

Another sigh. Another doubtful look. 'You know about Lucy's dyslexia. She never planned to marry. Never planned to have children.'

Horror speared into his mind. 'She's not thinking of having an abortion?'

'No. Lucy has too much respect for life to choose that route, but she is upset about the possibility that she'll pass the disability on to her child. And she thinks you might not welcome a…a less than perfect child.'

The mountain of Lucy's vulnerabilities was rising up in front of him. She not only feared rejection from him but rejection of their child, as well. He suddenly had a very sharp memory of Sarah Pickard remarking that Lucy might think she wasn't good enough for him. In fact, Lucy had actually said so herself—*I know I'm no match for you.* This was a mountain he had to scale…somehow.

He shook his head over ever having considered her a possible gold-digger. That was so far from the truth—a million miles from the truth. She hadn't *planned* anything, hadn't expected anything of him, except that he would sooner or later turn into a frog and the pleasure of being with him would be over.

His jaw set in fierce determination. This frog was going to leap every mountain she put in front of him.

This frog was going to be the prince Lucy had wanted him to be.

'Thank you for being open with me, Elizabeth,' he said sincerely. 'I'll take it from here.'

She rose from the armchair, hesitating before heading for the door, her eyes meeting his in eloquent appeal. 'All four of us are going to have to live with whatever you decide, Michael. You must make it an honest decision. Trying to be honourable will only bring more hurt in the end.'

Honourable...standing up when he didn't really want to.

'Lucy and I will always have each other,' she went on. 'You don't have to be a part of her life. You understand? You must be honest so we know where we're going and can work out how best to do it.'

He nodded, seeing very clearly the crossroads where they all stood—two brothers and two sisters. Elizabeth and Harry were solid. They would move forward together. He and Lucy were looking down the barrel of very divergent paths if he didn't make the right moves— moves that had to be right for both of them. At the centre of those crossroads was a child who would tug at all of them, making the paths intersect throughout the future, causing conflict or bringing joy.

Elizabeth was at the door, about to open it, when he thought to ask her, 'How did Lucy respond to the Pal Joey rose you took home with you yesterday?'

Her reply was preceded by a wry grimace. 'She burst into tears. When I asked what was wrong she said it was the wrong colour.'

It made no sense to him. 'It's always yellow.'

Elizabeth sighed, her eyes sad as she answered, 'I think Lucy wanted a red rose from you, Michael.'

'Red...' he repeated, not immediately understanding.

'For love,' she spelled out. 'But please don't give her one unless you truly, truly mean it.'

She left, having made the situation with all its complications as clear as she could.

A great PA, Michael thought.

Then he turned his mind to Lucy and the child who would be theirs.

Decisions had to be made.

He wanted his sunshine girl back. She was dwelling in shadows, some of which he'd cast, others caused by the disability that had darkened many parts of her life—a disability she feared would blight their child's life. Somehow he had to pull her out of those shadows.

He thought of what Elizabeth had said about Lucy never having planned to marry, never having planned to have children. It made perfect sense of her having sex whenever it promised to give her pleasure. There was no moral issue involved, simply a need to feel loved for at least a little while.

Which was all she'd wanted from him. She'd told him so in the hospital when he'd more or less trapped her into revealing her dyslexia. She wasn't expecting to be loved for a long while. Her acceptance of that ruled how she thought, how she lived, making the most of every good moment.

He understood her now.

He understood it all.

And he realised how very critical it was that he make the right decisions.

CHAPTER EIGHTEEN

MICHAEL WAS COMING to talk to her tonight. Harry was bringing him to the apartment. Ellie was virtually standing over her, insisting this meeting be faced. No hiding. No bolting from it. No shutting her mind to the fact that this issue would touch all of them in the future. She had to listen and think very carefully about the decisions she made.

Having been instructed of all this, Lucy felt sick again—sick with nervous tension. She'd barely been able to eat any of the pasta meal she'd made for their dinner. Nevertheless, regardless of how she *felt*, pride demanded that she not *look* sick to the two Finn brothers.

She spent the hour before the eight o'clock deadline making herself appear bright and beautiful, determined to have Michael believe that the sunshine girl would pick herself up and move on, bringing up their child in her own way. After all, she was best equipped to do it, having firsthand experience at living with dyslexia. There was no need for him to concern himself about either of them.

Ellie had assured her that he did accept the child was his—no question. If this was true, he would probably offer financial support, which she would take. It was the sensible thing to do. Her own employment prospects would take a dive, being a single mother. In fact, whatever help he offered she would accept for their child's sake.

Having thought this through, Lucy was feeling a little more settled in her mind when the doorbell announced the brothers' arrival. Her heart, however, rocketed around her chest like a wound-up toy. They were early. It was only ten minutes to eight. She wasn't quite keyed up to face them yet. As Ellie moved to open the door, some self-protective instinct made Lucy step into the kitchen, putting the counter bench between her and the men who had changed their lives.

It wasn't Michael who entered. Nor Harry. Ellie opened the door wide to a delivery guy who was carrying a stunning arrangement of red roses—dozens of them clustered tightly together in a dome shape, and rising from the centre of this was a stick which held an amazing pom-pom of roses to top it all off.

'This is for the coffee table,' the guy said, moving in to place the gift as directed.

He was followed by two more delivery people whom he quickly instructed. 'That one is to go on the kitchen bench...'

More red roses, but fewer of them in this arrangement—a very artistic Japanese style.

'...and that one on the dining table.'

This was more a posy of red roses in a small dainty vase, perfect for its placing.

Fortunately Ellie had enough composure to thank the delivery people and see them out. Lucy was blown

out of her mind. The sheer extravagance of the gift was
dazzling. What it might mean…what it was supposed
to mean…could she believe it? She kept staring at the
roses…so many of them…red for *love*.

The doorbell rang again. Her gaze jerked to Ellie
who was still standing by the door.

'Are you okay, Lucy?' she asked, her hand on the
door-knob, pausing before turning it, waiting to be assured that her sister had herself under control.

Lucy nodded, grasping the end corners of the bench-
top to hold herself steady. Her mind was a whirl. Her
heart was drumming in her ears. Her stomach was
cramping in nervous agitation. Everything she'd thought
of saying to Michael had turned into a jumbled mess.
Just listen and watch, she fiercely told herself. What he
said, how he looked when he said it…that would tell her
where she should go from here.

Ellie opened the door.

Michael entered first—still the most handsome
prince in the world, commanding her total attention
and tugging on everything female inside her. As on
her very first night with him he was casually dressed;
grey shorts, a grey and white striped sports shirt with
buttons down the front—undoubtedly easier for taking
off with his hurting ribs—scuffs on his feet. One of his
hands was gripping a walking stick. The other held a
single rose which wasn't red. It was pink and white.

Confused and hopelessly distressed, Lucy was barely
aware of Harry following his brother in, pausing beside
Ellie, speaking to her in a low voice. It was a jolt when
suddenly they were both gone, the door closed behind
them, leaving her alone with Michael and a roomful of

roses that surely represented some kind of emotional pressure she would have to fight. Panic welled up. She needed her sister standing beside her, needed an anchor to stop her from being drawn into a bad place.

'There's nothing to be frightened of with me, Lucy,' Michael said, his deep rich voice pouring out in a soothing tone.

She swallowed hard, trying to clear the constriction in her throat. 'I'm sorry,' she managed to get out, gripping the counter edge even harder. 'I'm sorry for complicating your life like this. It wasn't meant to happen.'

'I know it wasn't meant to happen but I'm glad that it has.' He smiled at her, pushing one of the kitchen stools closer to where she stood and hitching himself onto the other. 'It doesn't complicate my life, Lucy. In fact, I'm seeing everything very clearly now.'

She shook her head. 'I don't understand.'

'Sit down and relax. We'll talk about whatever you don't understand.'

She unglued her hands from the bench-top, reached out for the stool and dragged it around to the other side of the counter to where Michael was seated, feeling safer with putting solid distance between them. She couldn't allow herself to be persuaded into doing something wrong. Having sat down she gestured to the roses on the kitchen bench beside her.

'You've never said you love me, Michael,' she flatly reminded him, her eyes searching his for any sign of insincerity.

'I'm saying it now.' His gaze held hers with intense conviction. 'I love you and I want to marry you, Lucy.

When we were on the island, I heard you say to Sarah that you'd never marry a man who didn't love you enough to give you roses. What you see here now is a promise there will always be roses in our marriage.'

Pain stabbed her heart. It killed her to say it but she had to. 'I won't marry you, Michael.'

'Why not?'

'It's wrong to marry because of a child. It's what my mother did, thinking it was for the best, but it wasn't. I promised her I'd never do that. No matter how good the intentions, it's bound not to turn out well.'

He didn't look at all deterred by this argument. He rolled right on over it. 'I'd agree that good intentions don't guarantee a good marriage. I think there has to be love between the couple involved for a marriage to work well and from what you've told me, I don't believe your father loved your mother. It's different for us, Lucy. I genuinely want you in my life and I believe you want me. Can you truthfully say you don't?'

'It's not as simple as that!' she cried, agonised by the need to keep on the right track here. 'Our child might have dyslexia too, Michael, and that wouldn't have been what you've planned for yourself.'

'I didn't *plan* anything for myself,' he swiftly replied. 'Somewhere on the back-burner in my mind was the hope that one day I might meet a woman with whom I could have the kind of relationship my father had with my mother. You're that person, Lucy—the woman who lights up my life. And I'm sure our child will light up both our lives, dyslexia or not.'

She couldn't let him just gloss over a condition he'd never lived with. 'You don't know what it's like…the confusion, the frustration, the realisation that you're not normal like other kids. The light goes out sometimes, Michael, and it's hard, learning how to turn it back on.'

The silvery grey eyes glittered with determination. 'Lucy, I promise you it won't be the problem it's been for you. We'll be on the lookout for it in however many children we have, get early professional help if it's needed.'

Children? He was looking ahead to having more than one child with her?

'I've been researching dyslexia on the internet,' he went on confidently. 'There's a lot that can now be done—programs that weren't available to you. But over and above that, we will both be *there* for our children. That's what counts most, isn't it, having a mother and father who love you, who think you're very special regardless of any disability?'

He spoke so caringly, Lucy's resistance to the idea of marriage began to crack. She wanted this man so much and she wanted her child to have a loving father. Yet there was another issue that could stalk and break the happy future together he was painting.

She sucked in a deep breath, released it in a shuddering sigh and looked at him with knowing wariness. 'What if you run into other men I've slept with in the past, Michael?'

His gaze did not waver from hers. 'I haven't forgotten I turned into a frog that night of the ball. I've been intensely grateful that you seemed to let me get away with it, staying by my side these past few weeks.'

'I didn't want you to die, didn't want to lose you, but I wasn't thinking there could be long future for us as a couple,' she quickly explained. 'You made me feel bad that night.'

'I know. And it's made me feel bad ever since. Please believe me when I now say I don't care if you've slept with *every* man in Cairns. If you'll marry me, Lucy, I'll always think I'm the lucky one for getting to keep you.'

The regretful tone, the vehemence of his plea to her…listening to him was playing havoc with her emotions. She so desperately wanted to believe him, yet… 'How can I be sure of that, Michael?'

'Give me the chance to prove it. I want to be your prince, Lucy. I want to love you, protect you, fight your battles for you, be your champion always. If you'll just favour me with your smile…'

The appeal in his voice, in his eyes, was irresistible, tugging at the corners of her mouth.

'…I'll conquer the world for you,' he finished with a flamboyant grin.

A gurgle of laughter erupted from her throat. This was all so impossibly romantic…the stuff of dreams… but it was washing straight through the cracks in her protective armour, swamping her heart, tugging at the love she felt for him.

He twirled the pink and white rose around in his fingers. The beautiful scent of it tickled her sense of smell.

'This rose is called Princess of Monaco. I want to give it to you because you're my princess, Lucy. I want to buy us a home with a garden where I can grow this rose so you'll always be reminded that you're my princess and I love you.' He held it out to her. 'Will you accept it from me?'

A river of emotion in full flood drowned the doubts

she had tried to hold onto. She couldn't stop her hand from reaching out and taking the perfect princess bloom, lifting it to her nose so she could breathe in the glorious scent. She couldn't stop the smile beaming her happiness at Michael—her prince. Her *true* prince.

It spilled into words. 'I love you, too.'

Desire blazed in his eyes. 'I wish I could race you off to bed, Lucy. I'd use that rose to caress every part of you so you'd be totally immersed in its scent and feel totally immersed in my love for you.'

'Oh! I do like that idea!' She gave him a saucy smile as she slid off the stool and rounded the bench to where he sat. 'We don't need to race, Michael. We can get there at a reasonable pace together. Will Harry keep Ellie away for a while?'

'Until I call him to come and get me.'

'Then we can take our time, can't we?'

'Lucy, I won't be able to…'

'But you can turn me into a rose garden and I can take you to the moon, my love,' she said, framing his beautiful face with her hands and kissing him with all the sensual promise of pleasure she could give him without any action on his part that might give him pain.

The fire she lit in Michael's groin demanded instant compliance with whatever Lucy wanted to do. He didn't care if there was some collateral pain. He wanted this intimacy, wanted to love her, wanted to feel her love for him.

She took him further than the moon. She made him burst into heaven and float there, feeling like a king, and he knew with absolute certainty that she would always be the queen in his life. She was the right woman for him. She was the perfect woman for him—an exquisite addiction that would never end. And he silently vowed that nothing would ever mar their happiness with each other.

CHAPTER NINETEEN

IT WAS THE last day of her job with cemetery administration and she'd been asked to supervise the return of the repaired angels' heads to the memorial garden. Lucy was happy to be driving out to Greenlands, wanting to visit her mother's grave. Beside her on the van's passenger seat was a florist box containing the rose she planned to place there.

She arrived before the stonemason and was on her way down the rows of neatly tended graves when she spotted the elderly man who had planted the Pal Joey rose for his wife. She raised her free arm and waved, calling out, 'Hi, Mr Robson! It looks like your rosebush is thriving.'

His face lit up with pleasure. 'Miss Flippence! It is doing well, isn't it? And what have you got there?'

He set off down a cross path to meet up with her.

'It's a thank you gift for my mother,' she explained, pausing to wait for him so he could admire it and have a little chat. He was lonely, having lost his beloved wife.

'Ah! A Princess of Monaco,' he said as soon as he was close enough to recognise the bloom. 'Good choice! Wonderful scent!'

'Yes! My husband-to-be is going to plant one for me when we build our home,' she said proudly.

'Well, congratulations!' he said warmly. 'You look so happy. I wish you both all the best.'

'Thank you. I've never been so happy. It's like a miracle, finding someone who really loves you.'

'I guess you're going to visit your mother to tell her all about it.'

'Yes.' Lucy gave him a confidential smile. 'I think she worked the miracle for me. I asked her to, you see?'

His eyes twinkled at her. 'Then I'm sure she did. God bless you, girlie! Go on now and thank your mother.'

Such a nice man, Lucy thought as she walked on. There *were* princes in this world and she and Ellie were incredibly lucky to be loved by two of them.

Having placed the box at the foot of her mother's headstone, she sat on the lawn facing it, hugging her knees and tilting her head back to look up at the clear blue sky.

'If you're looking down at me, Mum, I hope you can see how magically everything has turned out since Ellie's birthday, and thank you so much if you've been a guiding spirit in it all. This is my last day on the job here because Ellie and I have a double wedding to plan and so much else besides. The four of us are looking at properties for our future homes and trying to figure out what will suit us best. And, of course, I'm three months pregnant and Michael doesn't want me doing too much so the job has to go. I'll still come and visit you though I won't be adrift any more. Isn't that wonderful?'

She heaved a happy sigh and lowered her gaze to the gift she wanted to share with her mother. 'This is the rose Michael gave me when he promised to always be there for me, my knight in shining armour. He chose it because it's called Princess of Monaco and I'm his princess, Mum. Remember how some of the schoolkids used to call me Loopy Lucy because of my dyslexia? I never thought I'd be anyone's princess. Sometimes I can hardly believe it but Michael really does love me. He makes me feel it all the time. And I love him with all my heart.'

Aware that the stonemason may well have arrived in the memorial garden by now, Lucy pushed herself upright and blew a kiss to the headstone. 'Ellie and I will be thinking of you on our wedding day. We know you would have loved to be there, seeing us as brides, and we know you would be proud of us. We followed what you told us—*Never commit your life to a man who doesn't love you and be absolutely sure he's a man you can love for the rest of your life.* We got it right, Mum, so you really can rest in peace.'

She lifted her arms high and twirled around in a happy dance, laughing with the sheer joy of being alive and being loved. She was Michael's princess bride. Nothing could be more *right* for her. And it felt so good.

So...good.

A miracle.

God bless everyone, she thought.

To feel this blessed was wonderful beyond words!

* * * * *

FROM EX
TO ETERNITY

KAT CANTRELL

One

Even the sandpipers were getting more action than Cara Chandler-Harris.

But she was working at this Turks and Caicos resort instead of frolicking in the crystal-blue surf with a nearly naked, oiled companion. Cara would be the sole designer showcasing her fairy-tale-inspired wedding dresses to two hundred industry professionals at a three-day bridal expo. The wedding-dress fashion show was one of the premier events and Cara Chandler-Harris Designs, which was still in its fledgling stages, was poised to explode with this once-in-a-lifetime opportunity for exposure.

Adding testicles into the mix would only drive her to drink.

Cara swept a glance over the woman in white silk standing before her in the Ariel wedding dress and repositioned the model to face forward. Wincing as she knelt for the four hundredth time, Cara stuck another pin through the lace-trim edging of the mermaid skirt.

"Don't forget her heels will be five inches. Not four," her assistant, and sister, Meredith, reminded Cara as she handed her another pin. "And yes, I checked with the airline again. The missing bag with the shoes in it will be here by four o'clock."

"Thanks, honey. I took her heel height into account. Is Cinderella ready to go?" Cara glanced at her sister.

Meredith nodded and flipped her long ponytail over her shoulder. "Won't need more than a slight waist alteration. I did good matching the models with the dresses, don't ya think?"

She had and knew it. Meredith wore her designer's assistant role like a second skin. Cara smiled. "Worried I'm going to fire you for ripping Aurora's sleeve?"

"Nah. I'm more worried about stuff I've done you don't know about yet." With a saucy, cryptic grin, Meredith handed Cara the final pin and hummed under her breath as she tapped out something on her phone.

"You know I hate that song," Cara mumbled around the pin in her mouth.

"That's why I sing it. If little sisters aren't annoying, what are we good for?"

"Herding the rest of the girls into place. We only have three days until the expo starts and we haven't even done one run-through." Her lungs already felt tight to be so far behind schedule. Good God Almighty. Missing luggage, torn dresses and a room with a faulty air conditioner. And it was only their first day in Grace Bay. "Why did I let you talk me into this?"

Cara had no idea how her name had come up to the powers that be who'd selected her for this event. Yes, a small handful of Houston brides had marched down the aisle in her dresses in the eighteen months she'd been in business, and yes, all of them had graced the pages of glossy society magazines. Yes, Chandler *and* Harris were both names everyone in Houston knew. But still. Grace Bay was a long way from Houston.

"Because you recognize my brilliance. Stop stressing. Plans can be altered."

"Dresses can be altered. Plans are carved in granite, and hell has a special level for those who mess with mine."

Meredith waved in two more visions in white who had appeared at the entrance to the pavilion, both barefoot, like the others. All of the models' shoes were in the missing bags.

"Where's Jackie?" Cara glanced back at the empty entrance.

"Puking her guts out," one of the girls responded with a ladylike shudder. "I told her not to drink the water."

Cara frowned. "The resort water is purified."

"Then something else is wrong with Jackie," Meredith said and rubbed Cara's shoulder. "A virus. It'll pass."

"It better. She has to be on stage in six days." A virus. Which could easily be transmitted to everyone else. Cara eyed Jackie's roommate. "How are you feeling, Holly?"

The willowy blonde in the French-lace concoction called Belle stared at Cara blankly. "It's not catching. Jackie's pregnant."

Now seemed like a really good time to sit down. Cara dropped onto the heavy tarp covering the sand, while the other girls squealed over Holly's announcement.

Meredith settled in next to Cara. "I didn't know. About Jackie. I would have—"

"It's not the end of the world. Women get pregnant. Women work while they're pregnant. All the time."

Her sister hesitated and then said, "I'll wear the dress for the run-through."

Thank God Meredith hadn't asked if Cara was okay. She'd had her fill of those kinds of questions two years ago, after her own pregnancy fiasco. Designing dresses had pulled her out of that misery and she didn't ever want to talk about it again.

"You can't wear it. The bust is too small and I can't alter it that much. Not here. Not in a few hours."

But the Asian-themed dress called Mulan wasn't too small for Cara.

The curse of average breasts.

Meredith had gotten Mama's gorgeous Chandler mahogany hair, the voluptuous Chandler body and the gracious Chandler mannerisms. Cara favored Harris blood, and Daddy was well-known for brains and business savvy, not his beauty. Neither Cara nor her father was dog-show worthy, but Cara certainly couldn't have claimed the Miss Texas crown like Mama and Meredith.

Cara staggered to her feet. "I'll wear it."

She'd worn it in the past. Not one dress with her name on the label escaped the Cara Test. When she finished the initial piece-together, she stood in front of the full-length mirror and said, "I do." If the words brought misty tears to her eyes, then the dress was right.

Except she always cried, because she created fantasies of lace and silk and happily-ever-after for someone else. Cara was just a glorified seamstress. A *single* seamstress.

She left Meredith and the chattering models in the pavilion and tottered through the sand to the concrete path leading into the heart of the resort. Twin five-story buildings lay on the outer perimeter and an enormous infinity pool dominated the space between. The pounding clamor of hammers rent the air, and scores of workers shouted to each other as they put the finishing touches on the renovations being executed for the resort reopening at the end of the week. The bridal expo was only a part of the festivities.

She skirted the pool, waited five minutes for the elevator, gave up and climbed the three flights of stairs to Jackie's room, near her own. Cara fetched the miserable girl some soda from the mini-fridge, then slipped into the dress flung haphazardly on Jackie's bed. Cara bit her lip and didn't say a word. Morning sickness sucked, and a dress that had taken Cara countless hours to envision and create likely rated pretty low on the list of Jackie's concerns.

The dress fit. Jogging, a low-carb diet and an extreme amount of willpower for everything except cabernet kept Cara's weight rock-steady. Cabernet calories didn't count.

The mirror taunted her but she didn't glance in it. Couldn't. Her reflection would only show what she already knew—she was always the bride, but never married.

Cara returned to the pavilion—barefoot, because her feet were already killing her and the broken elevator clearly hadn't been fixed yet despite the manager's promises. Cara had worn stilettos all day. Heels were as much a necessity as makeup and jewelry. A Chandler-Harris female did not leave the house unless fully dressed. But after the many problems she'd dealt with today, the last thing she wanted to do later was climb stairs in heels again.

She spent the next few minutes demonstrating to the girls how they should walk down the runway. To their credit, no one made a crack about how modeling was their job. If anyone had dared give Cara design instructions, she'd tell the person where to go, how fast and what to do upon arrival.

This was her life, her career, and nothing was going to keep her from replacing her dream of getting married with a flourishing wedding dress design business.

As Cara stood at the end of the runway going through a couple of more points, the girls shifted restlessly.

"Yummy," Holly whispered to Meredith, her eyes trained on something over Cara's shoulder. "That is one very well-put-together man."

Meredith's eyes widened to the size of salad plates. Cara spun, an admonishment on her lips designed to rid the pavilion of Yummy Interrupting Man. Whatever she'd been about to say died in her chest, and its death throes nearly coughed up her breakfast.

"Uh, Cara," Meredith whispered. "About that thing I did. The one you didn't know about… Surprise!"

Keith Mitchell, the devil in a dark suit, stood in the middle of her pavilion. He crossed his arms and cocked his head. His piercing gaze swept Cara from head to bare feet, lingering on the wedding dress. "Now, this looks familiar."

"Well, well, well. As I live and breathe." Cara fanned herself in mock Scarlett O'Hara style and did her best cat-with-a-canary smile. Stretching those particular muscles stung her face. "It's my very own runaway groom. Still got on your Speedy Gonzales shoes?"

Keith glanced at his fifteen-hundred-dollar Italian lace-ups. "They're functional."

"Lucky for you, sugar." She nodded. "There's the door. Use it."

He grinned, white teeth gleaming. "Sorry to disappoint you, honey, but I'm afraid this is my show."

"What show?" She waved at the wedding dresses and swallowed against the grapefruit in her throat. *Keith Mitchell.* What in the world was he doing in Grace Bay? "You're here to volunteer as my replacement model? I might have a dress in the back in your size."

Ha. Not even one of Keith's long legs would fit in a dress, and besides, he'd exited the womb wearing a suit. An unwrinkled suit because wrinkles did not dare to tread in his world.

Keith. Here in Grace Bay and standing five feet from Cara while she wore a *wedding dress.* Her bare toes curled in mortification. She was naked without her heels.

"Not the fashion show. The whole show." Keith winked, as only he could. "Regent Group hired me to turn this resort into the highest-rated wedding destination in the world.

If I do it right, I'll then have the opportunity to replicate it with their other Caribbean properties."

Oh, God. He was here to star in her very own personal nightmare and take up all the oxygen on the entire island while he was at it. "This is what you're doing now? Weddings? You aren't a particular fan of weddings, as I recall."

"This is the very best kind of wedding. No bride." He chuckled and nodded at Cara. "Or at least that was the intent when I took the job. I stand corrected."

Her blood, dormant for two long years, started pumping in her veins, flushing her face with heat she'd never let on was more than a becoming blush. Cara had generations of gracious Southern women in her DNA.

"I was invited to participate and I design wedding dresses. If you weren't aware, perhaps you need to find a job you're more qualified for," she said sweetly.

Meredith made a little noise in her throat at Cara's tone, likely in warning. Rattlesnakes had a tail. Most men never saw Cara coming.

Keith, who wasn't anything close to most men, just laughed. "I knew. But I wasn't expecting you to be wearing one. Brings back fond memories."

"Save it, Mitchell. What do I have to do to get you out of my way for the next six days?"

His lips pursed as he raked her with a smoldering once-over. With close-cut hair the color of a midnight sky, a body strenuously kept in prime condition and deep caramel eyes, he was unfortunately the very definition of six-foot-three-inches worth of yummy. Always had been.

"Oh no." She shook her head as her body hummed without her permission. "Get your mind out of the sheets. You could have slept with me all you wanted if you'd taken a short walk down the aisle. That barn door's closed to you. Forever."

All traces of yumminess went out the window as his face

hardened. Mitchell the Missile wasn't known for turning around failing companies because people liked his looks. Uncompromising, ruthless and detached—that was the man in front of her. Just like the last time she'd seen him—in her dressing room, forty-seven minutes before the flutist was scheduled to start playing *Canon in D*.

"We're going to be working together, Cara. Very closely. I suggest you get over our unfortunate history and be professional."

The models had gone quiet behind her, but every set of eyes burned into her back.

"Honey, I didn't have much to get over." That was a complete lie but she grinned through it. "I was over it five minutes after you left."

Also a lie. He didn't call her on it, though she was pretty sure he saw right through her.

"Then we have no problem. I'll buy you a drink later and we can catch up."

"As tempting as that sounds, I'll pass. Professionals don't drink on the job."

Keith left the beach pavilion with his head intact, a plus when unexpectedly confronted with an entire roomful of women in wedding dresses. God save him from brides.

He strode through the resort, noting a hundred issues requiring his attention. Tablet in hand, his admin, Alice, scurried after him, logging every sentence from his mouth in her efficient shorthand. She'd long grown accustomed to his ground-eating pace, and the ability to keep up was one of her many competencies.

He appreciated competency.

As he evaluated the construction crews' progress, checked in with the restaurant and catering staff and worked through a minor snafu with the recreation equipment, the image of Cara in that long white dress darted along the edges of his mind.

Not just in a dress, but in charge, running a business she'd created herself.

The harder he tried to forget, the more he thought about her. It was *Cara* but Cara unlike he'd ever seen her before. It was as oddly compelling as it was distracting.

That had not been his intent when he'd selected her for the bridal expo. Her connections were significant and her dresses had created consumer buzz in a tight industry, particularly among the moneyed crowd. Personal feelings couldn't interfere with what he knew this expo needed. Keith only had room for the best, and thorough research told him he'd found that in Cara Chandler-Harris Designs.

The decision to go with Cara was easy. Seeing her again was not.

Cara was a cold, scheming woman, no doubt. *All* women were scheming—or at least the ones he'd dated were—but Cara had proved to be the worst by trying to trap him into a marriage he didn't want. Thankfully, her scheme hadn't worked and he'd gotten out before it was too late.

He would never again make the mistake of agonizing over the decision to ask a woman to be his wife, only to find his effort was all for nothing. It had taken considerably longer than five minutes to get over it, but he'd moved on and rarely thought about his former fiancée…until today.

This consulting job had dominated his focus for the better part of six months. Regent Group had hired him to revive an anemic line of Caribbean resorts, and evidence of the life he'd pumped into this property's veins bustled around him. He thrived on insurmountable challenges.

Cara wasn't but a small, necessary cog in a larger machine and couldn't become a further distraction, no matter how much of a surprise it was to discover he was still dangerously attracted to her.

"Alice, please send a bottle of cabernet to Miss Chandler-Harris's room. Cara," he clarified as he and Alice evaluated the pool area. Meredith drank martinis, with two olives. Obviously quite a few things with the sisters had changed, but not that, he'd bet.

"Yes, sir," Alice responded.

The largest infinity pool in the Caribbean spread out between the two main buildings. The pool's dark basin turned the water a restive navy in deliberate contrast to the turquoise ocean. Intimate concrete islands dotted the outer edge of the pool and would be set up for private dining later in the week.

A breeze picked up strength and rattled the multicolored umbrellas in their stands. Half the stands were empty, yet another in the long list of issues. Many of the thousands of resort projects he'd meticulously approved for implementation had already been done, but not enough. The work teams should be much further along.

Now that he'd arrived, his firm hand would guide the teams into executing the strategy or he'd guide the offenders into the unemployment line.

Keith Mitchell did not allow others to fail on his watch.

In three days, the grand reopening would coincide with a three-day bridal expo. Dozens of merchants, media executives and other wedding professionals composed the elite group of people invited for the resort's relaunch as a premier wedding destination.

Cara's fashion show was one of the highlights of the party.

The image of Cara in a wedding dress continued to compete for his attention. Those bare feet peeking out from under the hem had done a quick, sharp number on his lower half. He'd only ever seen her out of heels when she'd been out of everything else, as well. Naked Cara was a sight worthy of recalling.

They'd had chemistry to spare two years ago, and it hadn't fizzled in the least. A slight miscalculation on his part, but manageable.

The resort manager met him in the lobby, dead center over the inlaid Carrera marble Regent emblem. Elena Moore took his hand in her firm grip. "Mr. Mitchell, welcome back. I'm pleased to see you again."

"Likewise." He'd hired Elena personally and their management styles meshed well. "Show me what you've accomplished."

His last visit had been three weeks ago, and Elena's staffing efforts had dramatically improved since then. Nearly all of the openings in the organizational chart now listed names, and most had received training. They discussed Elena's biggest hurdles until Keith was satisfied with their agreed direction.

Elena showed him to the two-bedroom penthouse suite he'd requested and disappeared. Two pieces of matched luggage bearing Keith's initials sat inside the room, though they hadn't passed the porter. Invisibility—the mark of excellent hotel service. Keith had earned his road-warrior status traveling as many as three hundred days a year, and if he knew anything, it was hotels.

Everything in his life was temporary by design because soon enough, he'd be moving on to the next job. He preferred it that way.

The seventeen-hundred-square-foot suite had been equipped with three flat-screen TVs, a kitchenette and wireless internet connectivity, precisely according to Keith's specifications. When the resort reopened, guests in this suite would have the services of a dedicated concierge, as well.

He tested everything twice. Satisfied, Keith unpacked his clothes and hung his suits in the walk-in closet, taking up only one of the four available racks. He traveled light and alone, always, but guests would appreciate the space.

After calling down to room service for someone to iron his shirts, he washed away the airplane stench in the enormous glass-enclosed shower. Work beckoned but he took a much-needed fifteen-minute break with a frosty Belgian white from the mini-fridge—his preferred type of beer. The staff knew his preferences, as they should and would know the same about every guest in this hotel.

He settled into a solitary chair outside and took a long pull from the bottle. The wraparound terrace offered a 180-degree view of the pristine shoreline, tinted light pink in the dying rays of the sunset. It was a slice of perfection, and those who wished to tie the knot with such unparalleled beauty surrounding them would pay handsomely because every hand-selected staff member paid attention to details.

Keith Mitchell always hit his target.

He worked until his eyes crossed, then slept a solid four hours and rose at dawn to go jogging. He'd barely finished stretching when another early riser came onto the beach a hundred yards down the shore. Normally, he'd give other people a wide berth, as he always opted to be alone whenever he could. It was the nature of consulting to be constantly on the move. Lasting attachments made zero sense and he was typically too busy to get sentimental about the lack of relationships in his life.

But his Y chromosome had absolutely no trouble recognizing Cara, and their brief exchange yesterday hadn't satisfied his curiosity about what she'd done with her life over the past two years. And he had a perverse need to understand why she still got under his skin after all the lies she'd told him.

Keith caught up with her. "When did you start jogging?"

She shot him a sidelong glance. "I might ask you the same question."

He shrugged. "A while back. Not getting any younger."

"Who is?" She threaded brown hair through a ponytail holder and raised her arms in a T, swiveling at the waist. Her red tank top stretched across her torso and rode up to reveal a smooth expanse of flesh. New blond streaks in her hair gleamed against the backdrop of ocean. "Which way are you going?"

He jerked his head to the left and tore his eyes off Cara's body. Reluctantly. "Interested in joining me?"

"No." She curled her lip. "I'm interested in heading the opposite direction."

"Careful. You wouldn't want anyone to get the wrong idea. That sounded an awful lot like someone who isn't over me yet."

"Get your hearing checked."

But she took off in the direction he'd planned to go, face trained straight ahead. He matched her stride and they ran in silence about three feet from the rushing surf. Not companionable silence. Too much unsaid seethed between them for friendliness, faked or otherwise.

The September weather was perfect, still cool in the morning, and later, Grace Bay would hit the mideighties. The first time Keith set foot on Regent's Turks and Caicos resort, he'd immediately designated it the centerpiece of the corporate-wide luxury-wedding-destination renovation. No one would be disappointed with the choice.

After half a mile or so, he expected Cara to peel off or fall to the sand, gasping for air. She kept going, stretching it out to a mile. Impressive. She wasn't even winded. The Cara he'd known had balked at anything more strenuous than painting her nails.

But then, he hadn't really known her at all.

By mutual agreement, they turned around to head back to the resort. At the entrance marker to the private beach, they slowed and then stopped.

Cara walked in circles to cool down and Keith watched her on the sly as he peeled his damp shirt from his chest to wipe his forehead. Her skin had taken on a glow and she'd yet to slather her face with half a cosmetic store. Dressed-to-the-nines Cara he liked, especially when he took her to dinner and got to spend a whole meal fantasizing about stripping her out of all that finery.

This natural version of her hit him with a sledgehammer to the backs of his knees.

No distractions, Mitchell.

Yet, Cara had never stuck to the role he'd assigned her in his life. Why had he been daft enough to believe that might have changed?

She noticed him watching her and crossed her arms over a still-heaving chest. "Tell me one thing. Why me? Out of all the wedding dress designers out there."

"Your name was on the short list. Much to my shock."

"Is it that difficult to believe I can sew?" Her chin jutted out, daring him to say yes.

But it *was* inconceivable that she'd traded a burning desire to trap some clueless male into marrying her for a design business.

"You have a degree in marketing. Two years ago, you were a junior coffeemaker at an ad agency and then, *bang*. Now you're Cara Chandler-Harris Designs, so pardon my mild cardiac arrest. Despite that, your name is highly respected in the industry and I need the best. That's why you made the cut."

Plus, he was curious to find out if she was merely the face of the company. Maybe she had someone else slaving away over the dresses while she took all the credit.

"For your information, *bang* took eighteen months of sleepless nights and several design classes to accomplish. I got an interest-bearing loan. No one handed me anything."

Not even her father? Seemed unlikely that John Harris would have done *nothing* to help his daughter's business.

"Doesn't hurt to have Chandler-Harris on the label either."

"It's not a crime to have connections. If memory serves, the president of Regent Group's board is married to a friend of my mom's. Tell me it's a coincidence you're now working for Regent."

Her gaze sliced into him and he didn't dare grin. But he wanted to. She'd never had so much attitude. He liked it. "All successful people have connections."

"Exactly. And I'm going to continue using mine." The dawn light beamed across her face and caught a wicked glint in her espresso-colored eyes.

Keith filed that fact away—for later, when he might lean on their connection. Though he had no doubt she intended to use her connection to him in an entirely different way than he did. "But wedding dresses?"

"Funny story. I got left at the altar and had this useless dress I'd made myself."

A flash of memory surfaced—Cara in a white dress with hundreds of beads sewn to the top and a stricken look on her face when she turned to see him at the door of her dressing room. He'd stayed long enough to discover the truth about his fiancée. And then left.

"You made that dress?"

With a withering glare, she plopped down in the sand and pulled on a flexed foot. "If you'd paid attention during the wedding plans, that wouldn't be new information."

"If you'd been reasonable about the plans, I might have paid more attention." She'd been like bridezilla on steroids.

"It was my *wedding*, Keith." She closed her eyes for a beat and muttered under her breath. All he caught was the word *professional*.

It had been his wedding, too, a fact she seemed to have

forgotten, but in reality, he hadn't cared about the center-pieces or the color of the cake. He'd given her free rein. Gladly, and then tuned it all out. A wedding was an event to be endured. Much like the marriage he didn't ask for but agreed to because it was the right thing to do.

"So, you made the dress yourself. Then what happened?"

She glanced up at him, her expression composed. "Norah asked me if I could alter it to fit her. So I did and she wore it when she got married later that month. Then Lynn asked me if I could make one for her. I have yet to run out of un-married sorority sisters and friends, so a design business was born."

Norah and Lynn. Bridesmaids number three and four. He had a healthy bit of distance from Houston now, and per-spective on his almost-marriage, but he'd been unprepared for it to feel like weakness to recall details with such clarity.

He should go back to his room and shower. Opening day loomed and nothing productive could come of continuing this conversation. "Do you like it?"

Surprise flitted across her face as she climbed to her feet, pointedly ignoring his outstretched hand. "I do. It wasn't what I envisioned for myself, but I needed…" She took a breath and he had the impression she'd changed her mind about what she'd been about to say. "It was something to occupy my time."

Finally, something that made sense. The design busi-ness was a time killer for an aspiring trophy wife obsessed with finding a husband she'd been unable to snag thus far. Every woman Keith had ever dated wanted nothing more than a free ride and the prestige of being Mrs. Mitchell. Cara was no different.

Except for the part where she started her own business. It was as perplexing as it was fascinating. And he had the feeling she'd been telling the truth when she claimed to have done it with no help from her rich daddy. Keith was thoroughly impressed, quite against his will.

"You come highly regarded for something you fell into accidentally."

"I prefer to think of it as providence."

"So you'd design one-use-only dresses no matter what? Why not something more practical?"

"Ever made a cake?"

"I've eaten cake. Does that count?"

Her eyes rolled. "Sometimes when you bake a cake, it doesn't cook quite right. Maybe it's lopsided or part of it sticks to the pan. Frosting covers a multitude of baking sins. A wedding dress is like frosting. My brides feel beautiful, even if they don't feel that way wearing anything else. I'm responsible for that, and it's amazing."

Frosting was one-use-only, too. Had she chosen the analogy purposely? "You *are* using your marketing degree, then. It's all false advertising in the end."

False advertising. Her best skill.

"Lord have mercy on your cynical soul." She jumped up and brushed sand from the backside of her formfitting jogging pants. No one could fault a man's eyes for straying to the nicely rounded area under her fingers. "One wonders why you asked me to marry you in the first place."

He snapped his focus away from her curves. Her frosting hid a multitude of sins, as well. "Because you were pregnant."

Or so she'd led him to believe.

Two

Cara escaped before she actually sank down into the white sand for a good cry. She slammed the door to the room she shared with Meredith. Hard. Hopefully, her devious sister was still sound asleep. "How could you do this to me?"

The blanket on Meredith's bed moved slightly and incoherent speech rumbled from beneath it.

"Was that English?" Cara ripped the blanket off the bed. "It's like ninety degrees in here. How can you sleep under this?"

Meredith peered up at Cara through slitted eyes. "Which question do you want me to answer? Without a cup of coffee in my hand, you only get one."

"Keith. You knew he was behind the invite." Several people had casually dropped information about his new consulting gig into conversations, but she'd been too busy ignoring anyone who mentioned Keith's name to realize Regent owned this resort.

"Sue me. You needed this expo deal to grow your business. Where's the harm?" Flipping hair out of her face, Meredith sat up, looking as if she'd just rolled out of a lingerie fashion shoot instead of bed. If Cara didn't love her sister so much, she'd hate her. "He's just an ex-fiancé. A guy you are completely over. Right?"

"Totally." *Well, mostly.*

Cara sank onto the bed and brooded. She needed a shower and a sturdy wooden stake to drive through the heart of the walking corpse masquerading as a man named Keith Mitchell.

"Don't protest too hard or you'll hurt yourself. If nothing else, it's a chance for closure. Take it." Meredith's gaze grew keen. "You were fine with this yesterday. What happened?"

"Keith jogs now. Or did you already know that, too?"

Meredith stuck her tongue out. "You two are made for each other. Only insane people get up at the crack of dawn to *run.* Clearly he's lost as many marbles as you have."

"Oh, he's still in possession of all his faculties. What he's lost is his humanity."

"Because he's giving you exclusive worldwide exposure for your dresses? You're right, that's way over the line."

Cara buried her face in her hands and dredged up some Magnolia Grit. She had it to spare or she'd never have made it out of her wedding-day dressing room after losing not one, but two of the most important things in her life. Now would be a great time for that grit to surface. "He only asked me to marry him because I told him I was pregnant. How did I not know that?"

"A lot of guys wouldn't have. He did." Meredith's arms wrapped around Cara and the silent unconditional support nearly undid her. "Still, it's a crappy thing to admit. Even if it's true."

With a sniffle, Cara nodded against Meredith's shoulder. "I thought he loved me."

"One is not mutually exclusive of the other. He probably did love you. Maybe he was going to ask you at some point in the future and you gave him an incentive to speed up the timing."

"Yeah and that worked out."

"Better you found out then that he's a rolling stone. I was never fond of the name Cara Chandler-Harris Mitchell anyway. If you guys kiss and make up, consider keeping your maiden name this time."

She scowled. "I'd rather kiss the hind end of a sweaty camel than Keith."

The knowing smile Meredith shot over her shoulder on her way to hog the bathroom did not improve Cara's mood. "I could've lit the candles on a ninety-year-old's birthday cake from all the sparks shooting around the pavilion yesterday."

"That was Keith's robotic heart short-circuiting."

"You might be over him, but that man is definitely not over you. People make mistakes. Maybe he wants another chance."

"Another chance to crush me beneath him as he rolls away again? Ha."

Lord Almighty. Now she was replaying their conversations through her head. This morning on the beach, he'd been genuinely curious about her life. And okay, he always radiated that carnal come-hither, but more of it had wafted in her direction than she'd been willing to acknowledge.

"Honey, you're a smart girl. Do the math." Meredith leaned on the bathroom door frame. "He didn't invite you here solely for your fantastic wedding dresses. Hell, I can slap some lace on a piece of satin and stick it on some starry-eyed bride. He wants the designer. Not the designs."

"He can want until all the gears in his robotic heart rust. I have a brand-new lease on life and no man, especially not Keith Mitchell, is a part of the plan." Cara elbowed past

Meredith into the bathroom. "And for the crack about slapping lace on satin, you forfeit first dibs on the shower."

Grumbling, Meredith conceded and shut the door behind her. Cara fumed as she stood under the jets.

So. The invitation was a veiled attempt to reconcile, was it? Shattered pieces of her life and her heart had taken a supreme amount of will to recover. There was no way on God's green earth she'd consider forgiving Keith for walking out on her when she'd needed him most.

He was not husband material. Period.

She dressed for the day in her best heels and a flattering outfit—the modern-day woman's equivalent to a full suit of armor.

As the Good Lord clearly felt she deserved a break, the elevator button lit up when she pressed it. A working elevator. About time.

Then the doors slid open to reveal the very man she least wanted to see.

Keith smiled and sizzled her toes with a heated glance at her Louboutin sandals. "Going down?"

"You first." She waltzed in to stand right next to him because she was a professional. An elevator full of testosterone didn't scare her. The idea Meredith had planted—about how Mr. Runaway Groom might be angling for a do-over—*that* put a curl of panic in the pit of her stomach.

Why, she didn't know. There wasn't a combination of words in any language he could utter that would make her crazy enough to try again. And to the best of her knowledge, Keith was fluent in five languages and could order beer in twelve more.

She stared at the crack where the two door panels met and pretended the tension hadn't raised the hair on her arms. Keith's heat instantly spread through the small box and started seeping through her pores. And she'd already

been plenty hot and bothered. He was just so solid and powerful and...*arrogant*.

"Do you run every day?" Keith asked politely.

"Usually. You?" Oh, her mama would be so proud.
Twenty-eight years of lessons on how to smile through
the Apocalypse were paying off.

"I try to. It's great for clearing my head."

Cara bit back her first response—*Is that what happened
to your brain when you cooked up the idea of a second
chance?* "Oh?"

"It's an opportunity to hone my focus for the day ahead."

"Sorry I intruded this morning."

Keith glanced at her but she didn't take her eyes off the
crack. "You didn't. I enjoyed it."

All this civility slicked the back of her throat. Why was
it taking so long to reach the ground floor? The building
was only five stories.

The elevator screeched to a halt, throwing Cara to her
knees. Before she hit the carpet, the interior went black.

Of course. It wasn't enough to be on a small island with
Keith. Now they were trapped in an elevator together. In
the dark.

"Are you okay?" Keith's voice split the darkness from
above her. Obviously he had superior balance in his flat
shoes.

She eased back against the wall, wincing as her ankle
started to ache. Twisted, no doubt. "Fine."

A glow emanated from Keith's hand. "Flashlight app."

"Do you have a call-the-elevator-repairman app? That
would be handy."

"I'm texting the hotel manager as we speak." He sank
to the floor and leaned against the back wall, crossing his
mile of legs gracefully. "At least there's no chance we'll
plunge to our deaths. I think we're stuck between the second and first floors."

"Can we climb out the hatch through the top?"

Keith set his phone on the floor and glanced at the ceiling. "Maybe. I'd have to boost you up. Could you pry the doors apart on the second floor?"

"On second thought, let's see how long it'll take the manager to get someone here to fix it. The temperature in here is cooler than my room. So there's that."

"What's wrong with your room?"

"Air conditioner is flaky."

In the low glow of the phone, Keith's frown was slightly menacing. "Why didn't you report it to the manager?"

"Oh, is *that* what you're supposed to do?" She pulled the sandal off her foot and massaged the offending ankle. Still hurt as if she'd stabbed it with a pair of shears. Well, if nothing else, now she had a good excuse to avoid jogging on the beach with a man who moved so fluidly it made her salivate. "I assume the manager called the same guy to repair it as the one who fixed the elevator. You'd think the consultant responsible for the whole show might have a better handle on this sort of thing."

"My shows always go off without a hitch. Did you hurt yourself?"

"I'm fine."

His phone beeped and he picked it up to tap through the message. "It'll be about twenty minutes. Can you live with that or shall we try the escape hatch?"

Twenty minutes in the close confines of an elevator with her ex-fiancé. If he tried anything, she'd stab him with her heel. There was wood in a stiletto, wasn't there? "I'll wait. I didn't have anything to do today besides lounge around at the pool."

"Me either."

She rolled her eyes. "Yeah, I know. You're the big man on campus. How come you're not CEO of something by now? Too permanent?"

His sculpted lips pursed, and dang it if it didn't set off a flutter to recall how masterfully that mouth could pleasure her body. The curse of celibacy. Her neglected body needed to catch a clue about how totally unattractive Keith Mitchell was.

Well, not on the outside, but on the inside, where it counted.

"I have no desire to be the CEO of anything," he said. "I'm my own boss. I can pick my challenges and move on, instead of being mired in entrenched bureaucracy at a company long-term."

Yep. Meredith had called it. At least Cara had found out about his allergy to commitment before she'd married him. But now she had a ton of other questions.

She should shut up. Being stuck in an elevator didn't mean she had to say everything on her mind. "Just for morbid grins, once we'd gotten married, how long would it have taken you to develop the seven-year itch—six months?"

So apparently she *did* have to hash it out right this minute.

His crisp suit rustled as he shifted into a different position. "I let it go earlier, but let's clear this up now. I didn't leave you at the altar. I'm sure it's more fun to tell the story that way. Gets you a lot more sympathy."

She laughed but it rang hollow. "Semantics, Mitchell."

"It's not. I wouldn't have subjected you to the public humiliation of walking down the aisle to an empty spot where I was supposed to be."

"Well, bless your heart. I really appreciate you sparing me the humiliation of having to call off my wedding minutes before it started. Oh, wait. That *is* what happened. Fill me in on the part where you were acting noble."

If this was a reconciliation attempt, he should stick to his non-long-term day job.

"Cara." He heaved a sigh. "Timing aside, we weren't

meant to be. Our marriage would have been a disaster. Surely you've come to accept that during the last two years."

"That was a lame excuse then and time hasn't improved it. I needed you and you left."

"You needed a wedding and a husband. Anyone with the proper equipment would've done. It just took me a while longer to wise up than it should have."

"I was in love with you!" She curled her hand into a fist and imagined planting it right in his arrogant jaw. A girl could dream. Probably it would break her hand before it rearranged his pretty face.

"Right." He smirked. "Just like I was in love with you."

He didn't believe her.

All vestiges of Southern grace evaporated as a snarl escaped her clamped lips. "Unlike you, I wasn't getting married because of the baby. I was deluded enough to believe we were going to be a happy family."

"That mythical happy family would have been a little difficult considering you lied about being pregnant."

"What?" She shook her head but the roaring in her ears just swelled. "I didn't lie about being pregnant."

"You flashed a fake smile and said, 'Guess what? False alarm.' Convenient how you discovered it moments before the ceremony. That's the reason I spared you the walk down the aisle, because you told me before instead of after."

"False al—" She recoiled so hard, the back of her head smacked the wall. "I had a miscarriage, you son of a bitch."

"A miscarriage?" Keith's pulse stumbled and his lungs contracted. "How is that possible?"

"You've heard of the internet? Do a search." Cara crossed her arms and looked away, but not before he caught the tremble of her lower lip in the phone's glow.

That punched him in the gut. "On what planet does

'false alarm' mean a miscarriage instead of 'not really pregnant'?"

The harsh tone had come out automatically. If he couldn't keep better control over himself, he might check out the escape hatch regardless, which would be very difficult to maneuver with his foot in his mouth. But if she'd really been pregnant, everything he'd assumed about her, about their relationship—hell, maybe even about himself—was wrong.

"Planet Bride-Dealing-With-Whacked-Out-Hormones. It's in the I-Get-A-Pass Galaxy. I didn't want to ruin our special day with something so awful." She muttered "Jerk" under her breath, but she didn't cry.

It was a far tamer slur than the one he was calling himself. Miscarriage. He still couldn't wrap his head around it. "You were really pregnant?"

"Guess you get to keep your genius status one more day."

He was so far from a genius, he couldn't even see the "stupid" line he'd crossed. His temples throbbed with tension and unrestrained nerves.

Miscarriage was the false alarm.

From the moment Cara told him about the pregnancy, he'd been so furious, with himself for not being more diligent about birth control, with how difficult it had been to come to terms with what needed to happen next—regardless of his intense desire to avoid matrimony—and with Cara's happiness over a marriage he didn't want.

Meredith had found him nursing his wounds the morning of the wedding and announced, "Cara needs to talk to you," with such gravity.

He'd fallen on the words "false alarm" like a starving dog on a steak, and as a bonus, he assumed Cara had created a manipulation scheme. Then he'd settled into his role of martyr with ease.

He rubbed his eyes but it only made the sting worse and didn't change what his vision had already told him—

she was telling the truth. "At what point were you going to clarify this?"

"After the ceremony, when we were alone. Figured we could cry about it together and drown our sorrows in expensive champagne I could actually drink." She cocked her head and the heat of her anger zinged through the elevator. "You thought I'd lied about being pregnant? How in all that's holy can you believe I would do something so reprehensible?"

Keith ran a hand across the back of his clammy neck. This conversation was veering into a realm he did not care for. "How could you believe I'd walk out on you if I'd really understood what you meant? Why didn't you stop me?"

Smooth. If she'd just give him a minute to collect his scattered wits, he might formulate a response that didn't make him sound like a callous ass.

I'm so, so sorry. I should have asked more questions. I screwed up.

As always, he could no sooner force such emotionally laden words out of his mouth than he could force a watermelon into it.

"Because I knew, Keith! I could see the relief dripping from your expression. You never invested an ounce of effort into the wedding plans and I blew it off as typical guy hatred of flowers and musical selections. But you stood there, all calm and cool, telling me how we wouldn't have worked out anyway. Miscarriage or false positive, it's the same end. You were looking for an out and I handed it to you."

You're right. I was.

The exit had been calling his name before she'd dropped the pregnancy bomb that then tightened the noose with alarming haste. His first love was a job well done, completed by the sweat of his brow. He'd been fortunate his hard work over the years had resulted in a healthy bank account. Women typically wanted a piece of it. Providing a lavish lifestyle for an unambitious wife who wanted nothing more than to spend his money put Keith off the idea of tying himself permanently to any of them. Only an unexpected pregnancy could have turned the tide.

Of course he'd jumped to the wrong conclusion. Of course he didn't hang around to dissect it. Those dominoes had been set up long before that final showdown. Maybe even as far back as childhood, when he'd watched his mother come home with Bergdorf bags three times a week and trade in her Bentley once a year.

It didn't make him feel any better about what he'd done. "I'm… I… You didn't deserve that."

There was more he should say, but it stalled in his throat. For once in his life, he had no idea how to handle a situation. No idea what to do with the clawing, suffocating guilt lodged in his windpipe.

Keith Mitchell was never caught off guard. Never at a loss for words.

"No, I didn't deserve any of it. But I'm glad it went down like it did. Otherwise we'd be divorced by now."

"That's low. I would have stayed with you for the sake of the baby."

Just as he'd intended to marry her for the sake of the baby. He'd hoped he and Cara might eventually become friendly, like his parents, and have an amicable marriage. She had connections and would be good for his public image, a tradeoff for giving her his name. It was an uneven compromise but one he'd been willing to make.

The baby part of the equation, he did not want to think about. He wasn't cut out to be a father. Despite all the pain, it had worked out for the best.

"I wouldn't have stayed with *you*. That's not the marriage I wanted." She sighed. "I'll probably shoot myself later, but I'm about to agree with you. We wouldn't have worked out. You're a crap-head of the first order, but you did me a favor by leaving. Meredith was right. I needed closure and now I've got it."

The knot in his larynx cinched a notch. Where had this woman *come* from? The Cara of two years ago was a completely different person than the one slouched against the elevator sidewall.

Before, she'd been flirty and fun, someone to spend time with until things ran their course or he moved on to the next job in the next city. He'd never seen their relationship as progressing toward anything serious. When she'd announced the pregnancy, the decision to marry her had come about slowly and painfully. But it took two to tango and Keith never reneged on his responsibilities.

This present-day Cara had an enigmatic blend of strength, wit, drive and determination.

And it was stunning on her.

He cleared his throat. "You said you were in love with me. Is that true?"

She'd never said that before, not even in the weeks before the wedding.

"I thought I was. Now I'm not so sure." She shook her head. "All this time you thought I wasn't actually pregnant? Lord, the names I called you for walking away from a woman who'd just had a miscarriage. Mama would have made me wash my mouth out with soap if she'd heard me."

He cleared his throat. It didn't help shake free the phrase he couldn't withhold any longer. "Cara, I… I'm…sorry. What can I do?"

"You made a mistake and you apologized. It's enough."

"Not for me."

"Sorry, Keith. You don't get to decide. I've already forgiven you."

Her casually tossed-out sentiment blazed past the knot and spread warmth through his frozen chest. Forgiveness. Freely offered. It was a gift he'd never been given, never solicited. Never wanted. Now that he had something so significant…what did he do with it?

She rolled her shoulders. "Now maybe this week won't be as gruesome as I've envisioned."

The overhead lights flickered, then shone steadily, and the elevator lurched. The doors slid open on the ground floor and Cara slipped on her shoe, then climbed to her feet, flinching as her left foot hit the marble in the lobby.

Keith snagged her hand before she could bolt. "Are you going to be able to walk on that ankle?"

Lean on me. I won't let you down this time.

"It's still attached, isn't it? Nothing a good bottle of wine won't cure."

"Let me bring you one. Later tonight."

More questions about the past rose up, struggling to be voiced, such as how it had happened, when she'd gone to the doctor. He wasn't ready to let her go, but neither could he stutter through such an emotional maze. Not now. Later, after he'd processed, his coherency would surely return.

Those espresso-colored eyes danced down to their linked hands and back up again, skewering him. Her intense gaze was full of that mystique he'd begun to suspect had far more depth than anyone realized. Least of all him.

"I'm about Keith Mitchell-ed out for the day. When I said this week won't be as gruesome as I thought, I meant I could dismiss you from my mind without a scrap of remorse."

She slid from his grasp and hobbled across the lobby in pursuit of a goal that had nothing to do with Keith. And shouldn't.

But he'd never been very tolerant of being dismissed, especially not when in the company of a completely different Cara than he remembered. Her business, as best he could tell, was legitimate and indeed the product of a strong work ethic, which he thoroughly respected. Was it possible she wasn't just after a husband any longer? What could have prompted such a big turnaround?

This week had just gotten a whole lot more interesting.

Keith didn't see Cara again until after lunch, when Marla Collins, the expo event coordinator, called a meeting with all the participants. He leaned against a lone table along the back wall of the resort conference room and listened to the spiel from a distance. Alice sat in the first row typing up the highlights, which she would email to him afterward, but he preferred to hear the details firsthand.

His gaze strayed through the seated crowd to Cara's streaked brown hair as she leaned to whisper something in Meredith's ear. Telling her sister about Keith's evils, no doubt. Though she'd probably been doing that for two long years. Cara ran a business now. They likely had more pressing matters to discuss besides the callous ass in the back of the room.

Could she really have forgiven him so easily, in a scant few minutes?

He most assuredly had a hundred more pressing matters to occupy him, and yet the conversation in the elevator this morning never fully left his thoughts. How could it? For two years, he'd been convinced Cara had tried to trap him into a marriage he didn't want.

He'd moved on and had never lost sleep over it. Cara's expo invite was strictly intended to secure the best wedding industry professionals, not expose him to a newly altered reality. And in that mirror, he did not like his reflection. He'd hurt her. Keith Mitchell did not make mistakes.

Marla wrapped up the status meeting and the participants gathered their handouts and electronic devices, chattering to each other as they swarmed from the room. Keith waited for Cara to pass him and invented an excuse to speak to her, but no less than four people lined up to ask him questions or report a problem. He watched her leave with Meredith, never once glancing in his direction. Clearly, she meant to do exactly as she said—dismiss him from her mind. He wished he could do the same so easily.

This brand-new Cara intrigued the hell out of him. He couldn't let things lie between them, not with all her revelations. Not with those bare feet still lingering in his mind's eye. If nothing else, the ledger in his head needed reconciling. While she'd gotten her closure, he hadn't.

"Excuse me," he said to Elisabeth DeBolt, the manager of spa services, who had been midsentence in detailing the color of tile she'd selected for the massage rooms. Details he normally encouraged. But not right now.

He left Elisabeth and the others where they stood and followed Cara out the door.

Cara and Meredith hadn't gone far. They were near the pool, embroiled in what looked to be a fascinating conversation with a maintenance worker's pecs, which the two women's eyes never left. The shirtless pool boy blathered on to the sisters as if he didn't notice, likely used to being ogled by the ladies.

Keith made a mental note to have a word with the recreation manager. This resort would cater to couples, not singles. Shirtless pool boys with the ability to bench-press the equivalent of twice their own weight had their place but not at this property.

As Keith could also bench-press the equivalent of twice his own weight and topped the kid by five inches, Shirtless Pool Boy wisely took off when Keith joined their party.

"Thanks a whole heap, Mitchell. I was enjoying the view," Meredith grumbled. "No matter how good you look in a suit, I can't fantasize about you."

He grinned, his mood considerably lightened. He'd smiled more in the past two days than he had in the past two months. "Why not? Sister code?"

"No, because you're a cretin." She tossed her hair. "Unlike some other people I could mention, I don't forgive so easily. Keep that in mind next time you find yourself in a dark alley."

Cara's cheeks went pink. "I'm standing right here."

"Did I seem confused about that? I wasn't." Meredith crossed her arms and glared at Keith. "Watch yourself. I see that look in your eye. I'm the one who held her while she cried over your worthless hide. Don't you dare break her heart again or the sharks out there will be mysteriously well fed."

"Still here." Cara smacked Meredith but she didn't budge.

They were the same height in their sky-high heels, with the same nose and long, sooty eyelashes, but the similarity ended there. Meredith was a traffic-stopper with her obvious, in-your-face assets, where Cara had a refined beauty that had snared Keith's attention the moment he'd locked gazes with her across the bar, back in Houston. He hadn't even noticed Meredith sitting on the next stool when he'd beelined it over to introduce himself and buy Cara a drink.

Keith saluted Meredith. "Yes, ma'am. No dark alleys. No broken hearts."

"I'm serious, Mitchell." She stuck V-ed fingers near her eyeballs and flipped them around to stab at Keith. "I'm watching you."

"Don't worry your pretty little head about Cara. I'm here to do a job and that's my sole focus."

"Uh-huh. And I'm just here for the pool boys."

With that, she flounced off, leaving him alone with Cara. She wore the same thing she'd had on earlier, which he'd had difficulty fully appreciating in a dark elevator. The lightweight summer skirt and tailored blouse accentuated her curves just as well as the jogging outfit from their predawn run and the outfit's deep shade of peach naturally led to a desire to take a bite out of the creamy swell of her cleavage.

The outside temperature heated, though he'd have sworn it was a balmy eighty degrees five seconds ago. Learning she wasn't a liar and manipulator stirred things below the belt in different, unanticipated ways. Coupled with a brand-new entrepreneur's skin, Cara was suddenly a full package he wanted to rip open with enthusiasm.

She rolled her eyes with amusement. "Meredith has Mama's flair for melodrama. Among other things."

"I've always liked your sister. You like her, too."

"I couldn't do this design business without her." She glanced at him with a slow sweep that dialed up his awareness of how very much he liked dressed-to-the-nines Cara. "Did you want something?"

Yes, he did. It just wasn't the same thing he'd wanted when he left the meeting. "How is your ankle?"

"That's what you chased me down to ask?"

The breeze picked up and flung strands of hair into her face, which he did not hesitate to smooth back. She froze under his fingers. What was he doing? "I'm concerned about you. You're an integral part of the expo."

"I'm fine. I doubt I'll be jogging in the morning. But I'm okay."

"Now that's a crying shame." He'd been looking forward to running side by side with natural Cara, oddly enough. Jogging was supposed to be a solitary sport. That's why he liked it.

His phone vibrated and as he was still on the job, he pulled it out. And swore.

"Problem?" she asked.

"Potentially. I've had my eye on a depression in the Atlantic for a week or so. NOAA just upgraded it to Tropical Storm Mark." He flashed his phone toward her, showing her the map sent by the National Oceanic and Atmospheric Administration. "NOAA app."

"Who has an NOAA app?"

"A consultant hired to turn around a resort located on the leading edge of the Caribbean during hurricane season. I'm good at what I do."

Cara's gaze skittered across his mouth, lingering. "I'm pretty aware of the breadth of your skill set."

Her voice had dropped, turning sultry, and his body hardened in an instant. Yeah, he remembered how hot their kisses had always been. If he could find a way to make up for his mistake, maybe she'd be interested in a repeat of the fun, expectation-free part of their past.

"Are you flirting with me, Cara?"

She smiled and Meredith's shark threat seemed less treacherous in comparison. "Not in the slightest. Your best skill is walking away and I took copious notes. Allow me to demonstrate what I learned."

She pivoted on one sexy stiletto and hobbled after Meredith, leaving Keith standing alone by the pool.

With a tropical storm on the horizon and a grand reopening combined with a bridal expo in two days, Cara was a distraction he could ill afford to indulge. Their history was painful and irreconcilable. Probably too difficult to overcome, regardless of whether she'd actually forgiven him.

Nonetheless, her pointed refusal to engage fanned the flames of his competitive streak into a full-fledged blaze. Once, he'd been eager to disentangle himself from a wannabe trophy wife with zero ambition, and now he could think of nothing else but exploring the new, uncharted Cara.

Keith Mitchell did not back down from a challenge.

Three

"**W**hat do you mean the flight was canceled?" Cara dropped to the bed and flung both shoes at the wall. Since she was a lover not a pitcher, her Louboutins clunked to the carpet well short of the intended target. Just as everything else she'd attempted to do since landing on this island impersonating paradise.

Meredith pushed a couple of buttons on the coffee brewer—her second pot of the day. "C-A-N-C—"

"I know how to spell canceled, smart aleck. *Why* is the flight canceled?"

Her sister shrugged. "Mechanical failure. Pilot's strike. Lost in the Bermuda Triangle. Take your pick. Does it matter? You can wear the dress in the show and I'll run things backstage. People will love the designer taking the runway. Stop freaking out."

"I have to freak out. It's what I do." Cara had already sent Jackie home and the replacement model should have landed at Providenciales Airport an hour ago. Except her flight out of JFK was canceled.

"Let Keith bring you that bottle of wine he offered. You need to relax."

"One day, I'll learn to stop repeating my conversations to you verbatim." Cara scowled and rubbed her ankle, which was not fine despite all her insistence to *that man*. Mentally, she scrolled through her shoe inventory and gave up. Except for her jogging shoes, she'd brought nothing less than three-and-a-half-inch heels. She might not even *own* anything less than three. "I have no interest in being anywhere near Keith."

"I'll drink it then. The bottle he sent last night was not bad."

Cara wouldn't know. She'd refused to let one drop grace her lips. "You can fantasize about him, too, if you want. Or sleep with him. I don't care."

Meredith jerked to a halt, halfway across the room. "Oh, honey. I had no idea you still had feelings for him. Don't clue him in just yet, okay? Make him work for it."

"I don't still have feelings for him!" Cara fell face-first into the raw-silk comforter. Such a vehement denial probably didn't help her case any. Rolling, she stared at the ceiling.

Mad, she had plenty of. Summoning it up took no effort at all.

She frowned when it didn't happen. Well, hell. She might not be as pissed as she used to be, not anymore. He'd been so weird in the elevator after she'd laid into him about being such a sleaze. Weird and speechless, and Keith didn't usually do speechless. He always had words at the tip of his tongue.

That's how she knew he'd told the truth about why he left. And she should have told him about the miscarriage right then and there in her dressing room, regardless of how upset and disoriented she'd been. They'd both made mistakes—his obviously being a lot more flagrant and inexcusable—but it was over with and she had a job to do.

Cara sat up. "I have alterations and so do you. Thanks for being a pit bull earlier and I really appreciated the shark warning, but nothing is going to happen with Keith. In fact, the name *Keith Mitchell* is henceforth banned from being said. Keith Mitchell is like Voldemort to you."

"Creepy on the outside but looks like Ralph Fiennes underneath and has a delish accent?" Meredith waggled her brows.

"Shut up. I'm doing my alterations on the beach. The waves are relaxing, aren't they?" Cara gathered her sewing kit and folded the dress into a bag while Meredith snickered through dumping half a sugar refinery into her coffee.

"Then I'm doing my alterations at the pool. Maybe Paolo will be back, now that your boyfriend's not there to scare him off. Don't wait up," Meredith called after Cara as she exited their hotel room.

The beach was deserted. Everyone currently staying at the resort had a behind-the-scenes role in the bridal expo. The real guests were the wedding professionals who would arrive for the grand opening at the end of the week and then attend the expo featuring the latest wedding trends.

Cara had her pick of beach loungers and arranged a plastic tarp over several to lay out the dress, careful to keep it away from the sand, though the entire expo would take place on the beach. Sand was inevitable. The alterations weren't extensive but she'd handmade all her dresses and every stitch had to be redone carefully. No sewing machine quick fixes for Cara Chandler-Harris Designs.

If the bridal expo worked to increase business as she planned, sewing machines would be a necessary part of her future. Standing orders meant she couldn't take a month to make one dress any longer. Cara threaded a needle and reminded herself she welcomed the influx of business and the opportunity, though Meredith had to convince her of it daily.

This was Cara's life now. She stabbed the needle through the silk spread out over her lap. Weddings were for other women, not her, regardless of how much she wished otherwise. Cara couldn't imagine trusting a man enough to fall in love, let alone marry him. Every day, she expected to wake up and realize she'd gotten over her caution.

Hadn't happened yet. Until then, she'd sew. The surf crashed a few feet away and the cry of gulls floated on a light afternoon breeze. Her life did not suck. She'd found a way to be content instead of deliriously happy, and it was enough.

Sometime later, a shadow fell over the tiny new stitches. Cara glanced up and cursed her stupid quivery heart for lurching even a little bit over the sight of Keith. But sweet Jesus did that man fill out a suit, and he had charm and wit to spare. Once upon a time, she'd thoroughly enjoyed his company.

"Busy?" he asked.

"Nah. I'm working on my tan."

"Sorry, that was a stupid question." He sat without invitation on the next lounger, their knees nearly touching, and his eyes trained on her bare feet. "Is your ankle still bothering you?"

"Geez. That was a lame excuse to talk to me the first twelve times. What's really going on in that pretty little head of yours?"

He grinned and her polarized sunglasses did nothing to protect her from the dazzle. "Do I need an excuse to talk to you?"

"No, you need to take a number. Can't you see how popular I am?" She waved at the empty beach. "Sandals and sand don't mix, ironically enough. That's why I'm barefoot. Stop asking me about my ankle."

Weakness in any form bothered her, especially around Keith, who could scent weakness with the precision of a homing device. Meredith's shark scenario was sweet, but ineffective. Sharks never ate their own kind.

She sighed. Keith wasn't quite the heartless bastard she'd been telling herself for two years. She'd have to stop thinking of him as one.

"Then I'll go with a different excuse. Have dinner with me."

She couldn't help it. Laughter bubbled out before she could choke it back. "No, really. What do you want?"

"That is what I want. But in lieu of that, I'll settle for your advice. The resort wedding coordinator quit with no notice. Her first task was to organize a mock wedding for the expo, and it's in shambles. Is there any way you could walk through the plans with one of the management staff?"

She stared at Keith's inscrutable expression. "You want my help?"

"Desperately and I'm not afraid to beg. I'd compensate you for your time."

Her soul thrilled a little at the thought of a big bucket of masculinity like Keith on his knees, begging. She was five-eight, but even in heels, she never got to be taller than him.

"Money's not the object of my hesitation. It's more that you're asking me for a favor." That brought her up short. He'd owe her. Big-time. And she'd already started thinking of ways to collect, starting with a brand-new fantasy involving Keith and his knees. "Why would you ask me, out of all the people here?"

"Because you've planned a wedding."

"That's rich, Mitchell. How convenient."

"It's not a matter of convenience. I've seen what you can do, and no one else could possibly hope to meet my standards. Except you." Those caramel eyes were on hers, all melty and scrumptious and saying far more than his mouth did.

"So now my ability to plan a wedding is a hot commodity. As I recall, you weren't so keen on it before." She waited for the sting of anger, but it had really and truly fled, dang it. When she'd told him she'd forgiven him in the elevator, it had mostly been because she couldn't resist being contrary, but it seemed to have stuck.

And he wanted her help with *wedding planning*. Nothing got her more excited. Well, almost nothing.

"I can't redo the past. But I can make it up to you now. Name it. Your wish is my command." His scalding gaze rested on her feet again and her toes tingled. She dug them down into the sand where he couldn't see them.

"Don't worry about it." She had absolutely zero desire to find out how he intended to make it up to her. Okay, maybe ten percent desire, but strictly out of curiosity. "I'll help you, but I'll be very demanding and difficult to work with."

His knee swung closer to hers, grazing it as he leaned forward. "Which is no less than I expect. Thanks."

Her breath caught. Of all things, Keith's knee was turning her insides flippy, way down low where all the really neglected parts had throbbed to life. "When do you need me?"

"Right now." That caramel gaze boiled over with searing intensity, holding her captive.

Heat blazed, nearly singeing her uncovered skin. The covered places were pretty hot too and straining to be free of their confines. "You can have me for an hour. Is that long enough?"

"I can accomplish plenty with you in an hour."

Her tongue came out to wet parched lips, and every nerve was screaming to feel his mouth against them instead. "We're still talking about the same thing, right?"

He held out a hand and God above, she was afraid to take it. But she did. He drew her forward, oh so slowly, into his space, where it smelled like ocean and Keith. "I sincerely hope so."

"Great," she croaked and jerked back out of the danger zone. "Let me put my dress in the room and grab my shoes. I'll meet your staff member at the front desk."

"I'll tell her to expect you." He let her pull away, never breaking eye contact as their flesh separated. "And Cara? You and I both know that's not what we were talking about."

She fled before her neglected parts overruled her brain.

By the time she reached her room, she was breathless and mad at herself.

So Keith was hot and really, really, really good at making her body hum. Everything down there needed to *shut up*. This wasn't a vacation and they both had a lot of work to do. Plus, he scared the crap out of her. She'd been down that path and it was not lined with primrose.

The man had serious commitment issues. Her heart wasn't up for another beating, and she could never have a casual tropical island fling with Keith Mitchell. Not then, not now. They were total opposites in that regard. He wasn't interested in long-term. She was.

Besides, Keith had superhero sperm, capable of leaping tall birth control methods. She wasn't even on the pill this time. Abstinence was the only method guaranteed to work.

The reasons for steering clear were piled so high, she couldn't see over them even if she put on a pair of ten-inch heels.

Meredith was gone, thank goodness. Cara so did not want to have another conversation about he-who-must-not-be-named, and on top of that, her sister could read her like an instruction manual. Cara was genuinely afraid of what must be written all over her face—her runaway groom admitted he needed her and praised her wedding-planning efforts at the same time.

That flipped her insides much more powerfully than any heated gaze Keith could shoot in her direction.

Keith waited for Cara at the front desk and shot off some emails so he didn't look like a lovesick teenager hanging out in hopes of accidentally running into the object of his affection. Of course, the things he wanted to do to Cara had a decidedly adult theme. All that heat on the beach had definitely not been one-sided, but she apparently planned to pretend otherwise.

He didn't. This expo would get 100 percent of his attention during working hours, but there was nothing wrong with some after-hours relaxation with an old flame, was there?

Clacking heels announced Cara's arrival, but his Y chromosome had scented her the moment she stepped through the lobby doors. That peach outfit hadn't grown any less mouthwatering as the day wore on, and the sea breeze had teased her hair into a tumbled mess his fingers strained to dive into.

The rest of the lobby vanished. All he could see was Cara.

"I'm here," she said.

Yes, she was. There must be something in the salt air because the first time they'd been together, being in her presence did not drive him batty. Chemistry, they had, but he'd always been able to focus when she wasn't around. Now? Not so much.

And when she was around…well, he was allowing her to be so much of a distraction, he should hand in his resignation to Regent before the sun set.

Or he could get his mind out of Cara's cleavage and act

like the professional he'd insisted she be. Thus far, he'd been the one who'd devolved.

The resort's assistant manager, a native islander who'd been working in local resorts for fifteen years, came around from behind the front desk for an introduction. "Mary Kwane, this is Cara," Keith said. "Mary is filling in until we can hire another wedding coordinator."

Mary sized up Cara and offered her hand. "What are your qualifications?"

Cara shook the other woman's hand and smiled. "I planned a wedding in two months."

"How many guests?" Mary didn't mince words but her work ethic was unparalleled. He hired only the best.

"Five hundred, with two venues and two different themes."

Keith did a double take. Really? Conceptualizing two separate themes was ridiculous, but he eyed Cara with new respect, nonetheless, because she'd also done it while pregnant. Without his help.

Then, because of him, she hadn't gotten to enjoy any of it. His stomach rolled. He'd given lip service to making it up to her, but that wasn't actually possible. Yet she'd let it go, as if he'd done nothing more serious than misplace her favorite earrings.

"I'll leave the two of you to it," he said and escaped.

Keith met with Elena so he and the resort manager could formulate a plan to fill the vacant wedding coordinator position and then he spent an hour alone in his office buried in procurement paperwork. In the next room, Alice and a couple of additional team members slashed through the pages-long to-do list, communicating their progress via chat windows. Keith glanced through the updates periodically while he pretended not to be dwelling on Cara.

Probably he should forget about how gorgeous and tantalizing and challenging she was. He'd done nothing to reconcile his screwup, and her *back-off* sign couldn't be any larger.

A reminder beeped on his phone but he didn't need it. Today was his mom's birthday and with the time difference between here and Miami, he should catch her before she started preparing for an evening on the town. His father escorted her to the opera and dinner every year like clockwork.

She picked up on the forth ring.

"Hi, Mom. Happy birthday."

"Keith. How nice of you to call," she said coolly as if he never called, which was patently false. "Are you enjoying Turks and Caicos? I prefer Bali this time of year but Grace Bay is satisfactory for a weekend getaway, I suppose."

Cara is here, Mom. At the resort. Yes, she's still a knockout but different, too. Unexpectedly so. I have no idea what to do about her.

"I'm working," Keith said. "I'm not on vacation."

Mitchells didn't *work*; they made money as passively as possible. Neither of his parents understood his drive to break family tradition and actually get his hands dirty. The most immersing activity his dad had done in the past twenty years was browse through the prospectus of the multibillion-dollar portfolio he'd amassed as a hedge fund manager. Following in his father's footsteps was about as attractive to Keith as sucking up Florida swamp water with a straw.

A strong work ethic, the satisfaction of tangible results and the pride of making his own way—these were the things that got Keith out of bed in the morning. Not money. Money was strictly a reward for following his own path. His father had never understood that and expressed his disappointment in Keith's lack of interest in Wall Street on a routine basis.

"How's the weather?" he asked.

"Dreadful. I was just telling your father that the humidity is suffocating me."

"Did you get the gift I sent?" Alice had sent it but it was the same thing.

"Of course. It was lovely. I'd have preferred you bring it in person, but you're too busy *working*."

Keith stifled a sigh. If he recorded this conversation, he could play it back and skip the actual phone call next time. "I'll visit soon. Maybe next month after the resort opens."

Visits were to be endured. Much like the calls, but he did both with frequency because it meant something to his parents. What, he couldn't fathom. They were essentially polite strangers who shared a last name. They never discussed personal feelings or anything of substance. Such was their relationship and always had been.

"Your father is having chest pains again." His father always had chest pains because he refused to stop eating spicy food, but his mom had never met a guilt trip she didn't like to bestow on her only child. "Don't dally, or it might be too late this time."

Cara's running her own business, which I know doesn't impress you since you've never acknowledged how hard I've worked to do the same. If it didn't sound so patronizing, I'd tell her I'm proud of her.

He longed to say the words aloud, longed to talk to someone who really cared about his thoughts and dreams and disappointments.

"There's a tropical storm developing," he advised, well against his better judgment, but he'd sleep better for it. "Keep an eye on the Weather Channel. Tropical Storm Mark. It's headed northwest toward the Bahamas and could hit Miami after that as a category one."

"Oh, they couldn't forecast where a shoe was going to drop if they held it out in front of them."

"Have a nice time at the opera, Mom. Give my regards to Dad."

Keith disconnected the call and put his parents out of his mind. The loneliness the call had sparked wasn't so easily dismissed. But that was the price of his lifestyle.

Ten minutes later, Elisabeth sent him a text message about a problem with spa services, which immediately sparked an idea he would have thought of earlier if he'd been on his game. It wasn't nearly enough to balance his mental ledger, but it was a start.

Shoving away from his desk, he went in search of Cara and Mary. They were having a heated conversation at a conference table in one of the resort meeting rooms.

"Brides don't want someone picking out their flowers for them," Cara said, so sweetly he'd have thought she and Mary were lifelong friends. Except you'd need a chain saw to cut the tension in the room.

"They do if they come to Grace Bay. It's a destination wedding, not a church wedding. The couples will not be able to select everything ahead of time." Mary drummed her long nails on the table but the lilt in her island accent had elongated, giving away her irritation before she'd finished speaking.

"Honey, that's what the internet is for. Put up pictures."

"We don't have the budget for an interactive web—"

Mary glanced up when Keith cleared his throat. "I thought you were discussing the mock expo wedding. Not the resort's wedding services."

"You can't separate one from the other," Cara said with a syrupy smile at Mary. "You invited editors of bridal magazines to the expo. They're going to do a write-up of the mock wedding. Next month, an engaged woman sees the spread, thinks 'Yes, that's *exactly* what I want,' only to find out the mock wedding doesn't resemble the real thing the resort offers. How would you feel about explaining this discrepancy to Regent executives?"

Keith closed his mouth before it started gathering flies. "Excellent point."

Arms crossed, Mary shot both him and Cara a glare. "Maybe you should start working on your explanation for Regent executives about the expense of her grandiose notions."

He had a better idea. "Mary, I'd like a report detailing the resort's proposed wedding services. Work with Alice to pull the budget numbers and post the report to the document collaboration site in one hour. Cara, come with me."

Wariness crept across Cara's expression. "I'm not finished here."

"You are for now. I'll review Mary's report and we'll reconvene in the morning. Thank you both for your spirited commitment." He bit his tongue to keep from smiling at their scowls. Women and weddings. Mix the two and stand back.

Mary left to find Alice, and a quick text message to his admin explained the emergency interruption he'd just sent her way. Cara leaned back in the conference room chair and crossed her bare legs in defiance instead of standing so they could go.

"Is your macho card worn out yet?" she asked.

He didn't bother to stop the grin now that they were alone. "Not quite. I have a few days left before it expires. Come on. Or do you need me to carry you?"

She crossed her arms, which did not help his mind stay out of her cleavage since it was so nicely framed and jutting upward. "Where are we going?"

"It's a surprise."

Her mulish expression didn't change. "I'm not having dinner with you. I have a lot of work to do and apparently will be spending more of my precious time tomorrow doing your job. Unless the surprise involves wine and a bubble bath, keep it."

"It does." Smoothly, he bent down and extracted her from the chair, pulling her to her feet. "The manager of spa services needs a guinea pig with high-end tastes to evaluate the recently added staff. I immediately thought of you."

"That was a backhanded compliment if I ever heard one," she groused, but her face lit up and the sledgehammer took aim at his gut. She was inches away, close enough to get a hint of her perfume, which wound through his brain like an opiate.

One small movement forward by either of them would draw their bodies together. And his hadn't gotten the message to forget about how much he wanted to take a slow, leisurely tour of her cleavage.

"I think she mentioned champagne." He cleared the catch from his raw, burning throat. He should step back. Into the next room. The next building, before he started breaking her back-off sign into tiny little pieces.

"Lead the way."

Golden flecks in her espresso irises had him pinned. He couldn't look away. "You're not too busy?"

"For the spa? Never." Her husky voice whispered from parted lips and he was acutely aware that if there was any breaking going on, it was to his sanity.

He rocked on the ball of his foot and at the last instant moved back. Not forward. "It's this way."

His senses buzzed as they crossed the pool deck to the spa building overlooking the beach. The late-afternoon sun cast everything in shadow. It was going to be a long, long, frustrating night, he suspected.

Keith introduced Cara to the spa manager, Elisabeth, a diminutive French transplant from another Regent property in the Canaries, and turned to leave.

"Where are you going?" Cara asked.

"Back to work." As always.

Elisabeth excused herself to prepare the technicians as Cara spread a graceful hand across his chest and shoved. He took a step back to humor her.

"Not so fast, Mitchell. We have much to discuss. Besides, your tastes are just as high-end as mine."

"Are you suggesting I be a guinea pig, as well? A spa day is not on my to-do list." Neither was listening to her ream him again for his crimes. His subconscious was doing a fine job of that without additional input.

"Mine either. But here I am, doing you yet another favor. The least you can do is listen to what I have to say about the wedding services. Mary is going to make all kinds of mistakes."

That was a different kettle of fish. If she wanted to discuss her ideas, that counted as work. "Fine. I'll stay. But I'm not getting a manicure. I'll be the unobtrusive one in the corner."

"Ha. You're as unobtrusive as an elephant in a lingerie store."

Elisabeth, who had returned, broke in. "They're ready for you."

She guided Keith to a plush suede chair and settled Cara into a matching one across the aisle. Three smocked women with various instruments of torture in their hands swarmed around it, chattering to each other, to Cara, to Elisabeth, doing things to Cara's nails and face and completely ignoring him. He was content to watch, especially when one of the ladies drew off Cara's shoes and plunked her feet in a tub of soapy water.

After a few minutes of soaking, the technician began working her thumbs into the arch of Cara's bare foot and Keith was mildly ashamed of how erotic his lower half seemed to find the whole scene.

"Elisabeth." He jerked his head, indicating she should

come closer. In a low voice, he said, "Tell your girl to be careful with Cara's left ankle. She twisted it earlier today."

"Yes, sir." Elisabeth repeated the instructions to the technician, which Cara clearly overheard. She narrowed her eyes at Keith and stuck her tongue out.

"I thought you wanted to talk," he called to her.

"That was before I knew your magicians were going to melt my bones." Her eyelids drifted closed and pure bliss radiated from her body. "But I know you're busy, so listen up."

His own body bristled in response, and little licks of lust tormented him for the next thirty minutes while Cara outlined all the problems she'd identified with the previous wedding coordinator's plans, which he and Elena had approved long ago. Then she launched into an impassioned explanation of ideas involving flowers, honeymoon packages and the *pièce de résistance*—butterflies. Despite being overly fanciful, Cara was on the mark.

He would have to take all of this into consideration, along with Mary's report. Tomorrow.

The technicians finally put away their instruments and helped Cara from the chair. As she stood, she wobbled on unsteady legs. Any reasonable man would put an arm around her to keep her off the tile, and Keith prided himself on being reasonable.

She snugged up next to his torso, comfortably, which shouldn't come as a shock—their bodies knew each other. Intimately. Two years hadn't been nearly long enough to forget the curve of her waist and how beautifully it nipped in at the juncture below his palm.

Once they cleared the door of the spa, he realized how late it had gotten. The sky was in the throes of a spectacular sunset, bleeding orange, pink and yellow into the horizon in all directions. The water had darkened to deep blue and a cool breeze wafted inland across the sand.

"Nice timing, Mitchell. A girl might think you planned it this way."

A laugh scraped his dry throat. "As much as I appreciate the compliment, even I can't control nature."

She stepped out of his embrace and his side cooled much too quickly. "The spa was nice. Thanks."

"I'd like to do more."

"I just bet you would." She swept him once with an amused glance. "Is this when you were going to casually mention the late hour and suggest we grab a quick bite to eat?"

It was now. "You have to eat sometime."

"Not with you I don't." She whirled and started hobbling off but he caught her easily, backing her up against the side of the building, scant inches separating his chest from her rapidly rising and falling breasts.

She met his gaze boldly as he braced both hands against the stucco on each side of her neck. "Going somewhere, Cara?"

His body, still galvanized from watching her enjoy ministrations at the hands of another, snarled for release to plunge in.

"I have a date." She licked her lips and he nearly came apart. "And it's not with you."

A growl rumbled in his chest. "Cancel it."

"I don't want to."

Stay. I want to spend time with you. Get to know the real *you, the person you've become.*

He leaned in a centimeter and her breasts quivered as she sucked in a breath. "Sure about that? You know it's only a matter of time before I have my hands on you. Here." He traced a line down her throat and stopped short of the luscious, mounded V of her cleavage. He'd keep going in a heartbeat if she gave the slightest sign she'd welcome it.

The past, his mistakes, the emotional responses she kept

pulling from him—all of that was too complicated. But this heat between them he knew precisely how to deal with.

He pressed closer.

"Take a cold shower," she advised with raised brows. "Feels like you could use one."

His erection had obviously caught her notice. It would have been hard to miss. "Take one with me."

I don't want to be alone right now.

"Doesn't that sort of defeat the purpose?" She blinked, breaking their locked gazes. "Let's cut to the chase. I'm not interested. I can't begin to understand why you'd think otherwise."

With the slightest tilt of his hips, he nudged the soft flesh of her abdomen, and those amazing rosy lips parted in a raspy exhale that he felt all the way down to his knees.

"I'm reading between the lines."

"Keith," she breathed and lifted her chin, bringing her face to within a millimeter of his. His lungs forgot to function and he flattened both palms against the stucco to hold himself upright. "You know what's between the lines? Space. Same as what's between your hands."

She ducked under his braced arm with ease and walked away. Without limping.

Four

That night, Cara slept poorly. She'd have liked to blame it on Meredith's vampire-like schedule, but when the sun finally rose, she didn't have the heart to gripe about her sister's late-night rendezvous or her 3:00 a.m. return to their room that had sounded like a gazelle learning to ride a bike.

It wasn't Meredith's fault Cara was restless. That award went to the master of reading between the lines, dang it. Why did Keith have to be so delicious and so hard to walk away from?

She rolled from bed and wished she'd indulged in at least one glass of wine the night before to go with the hangover quality of this morning. Two cups of coffee and a shower did not improve her mood.

"Time to get up." Cara yanked the covers off the still-sleeping lump in her sister's bed.

Meredith stretched like a sated cat and blinked. "Mmm. Good morning to you, too. Any coffee left?"

"You're entirely too perky for someone who's had five hours of sleep."

"You'd be perky too after the night I had." Meredith waggled her brows. "Paolo worked at a resort in Phuket and let me tell you, Thailand must be the place to learn a few tricks, if you get my drift."

"Your drift is as subtle as a nuclear bomb," Cara said drily. "We have a lot of work to do today, and somehow I got roped into helping he-who-must-not-be-named with the mock wedding."

"Yeah. Somehow." Meredith grinned and flounced to the shower, buck naked and not at all ashamed. Of course, when you looked like a centerfold, what was there to hide?

Cara sighed and got to work on the alterations she hadn't finished yesterday thanks to the side trip to the spa. Which had been very nice indeed and had totally worked the kinks out of her ankle. She had a feeling Keith had meant the spa session as some kind of treat, despite his insistence the "services" needed testing.

So maybe both were true. It didn't matter. She needed to stop thinking about Keith and especially stop remembering the good parts of their relationship. There was no scenario in which that would end well.

She stuck the needle through the dress's fabric and focused on how this creation would transform one of her models into a beautiful bride. Eventually, a real bride might want this same dress and Cara would gladly restitch it to fit its future owner. These dresses *weren't* one-use-only, no matter what Keith tried to claim, and regardless, Cara filled a bride's critical need by helping her have the most memorable day possible.

Cara Chandler-Harris Designs filled a need, too—it gave her the sense of belonging she craved. One day, marriage would give her that. Until then, she'd sew.

When Keith texted her an hour later, the sight of his

name on her phone's screen put a sharp thrill in her midsection. Quickly, she squelched it. What was wrong with her?

"I'm going to meet Keith at the beach," Cara called to Meredith casually. "You can stay here and keep working on the dresses."

"Are you out of your mind?" Meredith stood so fast, a box of thread crashed to the floor. "I'm not missing this."

Cara strangled over a groan. "It's not a show. We're just going over the basic plan for the mock wedding. The expo starts tomorrow, and these dresses are not going to alter themselves."

"Honey, whenever you and Keith are in the same room, it's always a show." Her sister carefully folded the dress in front of her. "And I never said I wasn't going to do alterations while I was watching."

Cara let it go, mostly because she wasn't sure why she'd protested in the first place. It wasn't as if she'd wanted to be alone with Keith. The opposite was a much saner idea anyway. The buffer of Meredith would be a blessing in disguise.

When the two women reached the beach, it was teeming with people. Had she missed a memo? She could have sworn Keith had said he was short staffed and needed her help.

The wind picked up and blew Cara's hair into her mouth as she zeroed in on the tallest man present. And she'd deny to her grave that she'd noticed him the moment she'd hit the edge of the beach.

"What's all this?" she asked.

"We need to run through the ceremony." Keith waved at the crowd without glancing in Cara's direction and barked out an order to a passing member of the catering staff. "These are all the participants."

All righty then. She squared her shoulders.

"Let's get to work. You." Cara put a hand on the shoulder

of a baby-faced guy walking by. "We need white wooden chairs set up in two parallel sections on each side of the walkway leading to the gazebo. Find them. Set them up in about ten rows. Come tell me when you're done."

That got Keith's attention. His gaze swung around to zero in on her as the errand boy snapped off a "Yes, ma'am."

Keith grinned and it swirled up a hot jumble in her midsection.

"That was the sexiest thing I've ever heard uttered in a large crowd," he drawled and crossed his arms. "Do it again."

Coolly, she smiled back so he didn't guess that his appreciation affected her far more greatly than it should have. "You. Go find Mary and ask her for the preselected flowers she's so fond of. Be nice or she'll pinch the heads off just to spite me. She can get them to the beach herself or assign someone, I don't care. I just need them pronto."

"Here's where you get to be impressed with how efficient I am." With a wink, Keith sent a quick text message and pocketed his phone. "Next?"

Cara's smile grew into something a little more genuine, even though she'd devised the task with the strict intent of making Keith disappear for a minute or two while she got herself under control. "Are you actually letting me tell you what to do?"

"Until it stops being sexy." He shrugged good-naturedly. "I expect that'll take a while. Plus, I asked you to help. I have no problem if that translates into you being in charge. Feel free to order me around at will."

Keith raked her with a once-over that easily conveyed his willingness to continue that philosophy in whatever venue she chose. Heat flushed her skin and sparked at her core, where nothing should be sparking.

"Music," she murmured, calling on all her debutante blood to get the word out. If she'd learned anything from

Mama, it was how to put on a crowd face when you were anything but settled inside. "Recorded or live?"

"Recorded for now." His gaze was riveted to her lips and she felt a rush as if he'd actually bent his head, aiming his mouth toward hers.

That was the cause of her sleepless night. She'd dreamed of Keith closing that gap and kissing her as he used to, with masterful skill and mind-altering power.

Neither of them had moved but the sand beneath her feet seemed to shift, falling away at an alarming rate. It was useless to pretend she wasn't interested when both of them knew it was a lie.

"Mr. Mitchell."

They jolted and turned in unison to the speaker. One of the many groundskeepers launched into a question. Keith rattled off the answer and then turned to survey the beach, where a mock wedding was now spontaneously forming around them. But not before she caught a flash of guilt on his face.

God above, what was she doing letting such a moment draw out here in front of everyone? They both had a job to do. As if the job was the biggest issue to why that charged, simmering moment was a not-good-very-bad idea.

"You," she muttered under her breath to herself. "Get your mind out of Keith's boxer briefs and focus."

Keith must have given himself the same stern lecture because he didn't meet her eyes for the next two hours as they worked seamlessly side by side to put wedding props in place around the stationary gazebo anchored to the sand by four concrete pylons. Slowly the area took shape, but the wind kept carrying away the rose petals Mary had strewn down the aisle between the white chairs.

"Why in the world did you plan this expo in September?" Cara groused to Keith after one of the torchères lining the aisle blew over. Fortunately, it wasn't lit yet. Otherwise they'd be facing an out-of-control fire.

"September is the slowest time of year. Because of the weather," Keith said without batting an eye. "And I need the resort opened by October. So we'll deal with our friend Tropical Storm Mark and pray it veers away."

As he'd claimed very clearly last night, even Mitchell the Missile couldn't control nature.

The concern in his voice was so evident, it gave her a strange desire to make things easier for him in whatever capacity she could. "There's enough set up to run through a ceremony. Who volunteered to be the bride and groom?"

A wolfish gleam in his eyes set her spine tingling. He held out his hand. "We did. Will you do me the honor of being my stand-in bride?"

Cara fought the urge to laugh hysterically. "Might as well keep up the trend."

Always the bride, but never married. Story of her life.

When Cara took Keith's hand as if she actually intended to play Holy Matrimony with him, he barely caught the shock before it spilled into his expression.

He'd expected her to stick her nose in the air and tell him to find another bride. Because he'd been kidding.

"Are you giving the deal a thumbs-up?" he asked.

She should say no, especially considering the point of this exercise was to practice for the mock wedding scheduled for the expo later in the week. It would be hard to evaluate the process while in the middle of it.

Actually, she should say no simply because he'd already burned her once in the wedding department. And because the sensual heat sizzling the atmosphere was starting to make him sweat.

"Sure, why not?" Cara jerked her head toward the metal gazebo wrapped with blooms that had taken her and Mary forty-five minutes to arrange. "It's about time I see what all the fuss is about."

It was a not-so-subtle reminder that she hadn't gotten to participate in her own wedding, and remorse over his role in the fiasco took on a new low. But if she was making a joke, she must really be over it.

He risked a joke of his own. "Looks like you're going to get me down the aisle after all."

She smirked. "Looks like I got you to help plan the ceremony after all."

Touché. They exchanged grins, and the weight Keith had been carrying since the elevator lessened all at once. Why wedding jokes had accomplished that above anything else, he couldn't say. What had he done to deserve both her help and absolution?

They were still holding hands, not that Keith would point it out and lose the tenuous connection with a woman he definitely didn't know as well as he wanted to.

"Shall we get all our guests in order?" Keith suggested.

"You take the guests. I'll handle the music and the officiant." She let her hands slide from his and his palm grew cool.

He watched Cara corral Meredith and the pool boy attached to her sister's hip into handling the portable music system. Cara's face glowed with purpose, and the silk sleeveless blouse she wore V-ed over her chest so nicely, it was hard to tear his gaze away. With regret, he turned to handle his appointed task, also sorry he hadn't suggested testing out the honeymoon suite afterward.

But that was for the best. Probably. She'd just shut him down again and his ego was still a little bruised from last night.

In a matter of minutes, fifty or so of his employees had taken their seats and the stand-in officiant stood under the gazebo. After opening day, Regent would utilize a handful of freelance wedding officials who worked with the local resorts on a couple-by-couple basis, but for now, Cara had solicited the help of what appeared to be one of the chefs.

Cara waited for Keith at the head of the aisle, clutching a spray of flowers Mary thrust into her hands. Meredith hit Play on the recorded music and something string-laden and weepy filled the air. The wind died down a bit in apparent reverence for the occasion—and checking this particular task off his ever-growing list definitely constituted an occasion in Keith's book.

He walked down the aisle and ignored all the grinning faces aimed in his direction. No doubt they loved the opportunity to see their boss in a starring role. The price of an ill-timed and ill-conceived joke.

Cara's smile, on the other hand, hit him hard. Framed by the flowered gazebo and breathtaking ocean, she had never been more stunning. Out of nowhere, the image of her in her wedding dress popped into his head and superimposed itself over the woman several yards away.

She'd been beautiful then, too—as were the decorations she'd selected—but he vastly preferred this wedding, and not just because he'd still be single at the end of it. Maybe it was the beach, or the minimal props, but the ceremony had a much more free-form feel to it, lighter and with less expectation. Exactly as he'd envisioned for both the mock expo wedding and the long-term resort wedding services.

Cara had done an exceptional job. Not that he was surprised. Keith was good at what he did and he'd have never asked her to organize the wedding if he'd thought Cara would fail.

Okay, maybe he was a little surprised. But only over the fact that Cara had nailed this task he'd dropped on her, which hit all the right notes. In-charge Cara rocked his socks.

He joined Cara at the end of the aisle with a mental list

of small adjustments—the sand needed to be raked prior to the ceremony, the chef couldn't be the officiant in the mock wedding because he'd be otherwise occupied and Cara should definitely stop smiling at him like that.

It was messing with his ability to concentrate.

"What's got you so thrilled?" he asked brusquely. "This is all fake, you know."

"Ah, but you're wrong." She speared him with a heated glance that he couldn't have misinterpreted even if someone had blindfolded him. "I can see it on your face. This is exactly what you wanted out of the mock wedding. Which means you owe me one. And when I collect, it's going to feel very real to you indeed."

That had all sorts of interesting possibilities threaded through it and sounded distinctly opposite from her back-off mantra of last night. Asking Cara to assist with this mock wedding might go down as the best idea he'd had all week.

"Yeah?" he growled, mindful of the eyes on them. "We'll see about that."

His warning was all for show. He didn't mind one bit being at the mercy of the windblown, in-command woman by his side.

She winked and ran through a host of instructions directed at other people while Keith made more mental notes. Cara had done a great job, but nothing was ever perfect. Tweaks could and would be made constantly, even after the resort opened.

Behind them, the music abruptly cut off and the crash of waves filled the silence. Gulls dived overhead, their cries a strange but fitting complement to the scene.

The chef, whose name tag said Hans in an amusing contrast to his clear island heritage, cleared his throat. "Dearly beloved, we are gathered here today to celebrate the—"

"You can skip all that," Keith commented drily. "I do. She does. No one objects."

Cara elbowed him in the ribs. "I'm in charge here and I told him to do the whole spiel. It's not worth practicing if you skip parts. How long will the mock wedding take? Do you know? No. So shut up and listen to the vows like you wrote them yourself."

The crowd muttered their agreement so he took a cue and closed his mouth. She was right, after all.

Hans started again, droning through the ceremony verbiage, and Keith shot Cara a sidelong glance. Under his breath, he whispered, "Careful what you wish for, sweetheart."

"What's that supposed to mean?" she murmured back, and the wind blew a lock of her honey-colored hair across her lips, drawing his gaze.

It meant that he was not one to let a prime opportunity pass to take full advantage of her advice.

"Only that I'm totally on board with not skipping one single part of this ceremony." Keith waited until Hans pronounced them husband and wife and spun Cara into his arms. "Not one."

With deliberate care, he brushed the hair from her lips and replaced it with his mouth. Slowly, to give her time to get used to the idea.

Her body aligned with his and it was like a sledgehammer to the gut. Desire exploded, racing through his veins, heating his skin. It had always been hot with Cara. But not like this, out of control with fast-burning lust.

I want you, right here, right now.

Forget slow. He tightened his arms and tilted his head to find a sweeter angle. Instantly, the kiss deepened into something better suited for behind closed doors. But he couldn't stop.

She softened under his lips, so responsive that he nearly

took her to the sand so he could properly explore every inch of her. Yeah, he'd done that plenty in the past, but not with this Cara, whom he could not get enough of. New discoveries lay just out of reach and the clothes between them needed to be gone.

What had started as a way to get her into his arms without protest had boomeranged on him, detonating into a wild inferno of need.

The hoots and whistles of the crowd registered a moment later.

Cara broke away and his hands fell from her hair, which was slightly mussed from his fingers. That was as sexy as her kissing him back.

What had happened to no distractions?

Cara Chandler-Harris had happened.

Without looking at him again, Cara clapped once to get everyone's attention and reeled off another set of instructions, including a pointed reminder to Mary that she should document every step for the real thing. Cara's wits clearly hadn't been as affected by that kiss as his—he was still in a fuzzy la-la land.

He eyed Cara through the lens of a man who had just kissed a woman and wanted more. "You did a fantastic job with this run-through today. Would you shoot me if I asked for another favor?"

"Depends on what it is."

There it was. Her gaze finally reflected a bit of the unsettled ripples in his own stomach. It cheered him for some strange reason and had him reevaluating how many bruises his ego could actually take.

"Check out the honeymoon suite with me."

She'd either deck him or laugh. He knew it was too soon after the aborted kiss to try again, but with "challenge" practically tattooed across her forehead, he couldn't let it lie.

Plus, he wanted to find out what else might be different from the first time around, because he'd bet anything the changes in Cara went well below surface level.

She didn't blink. "Yes. I'd shoot you if you ask me for that favor. Try again."

He grinned. "Come on. You said it was going to feel very real after the ceremony was over. That kiss was genuine, grade-A attraction between two consenting adults. Let's get real, Cara. Real naked."

At that, she did laugh as he'd predicted, and it warmed him dangerously.

"You've got an expo to organize and I've got dresses to alter so I can launch my designs into the big leagues. That's as real as it's going to get between us. For now."

With that enigmatic parting comment, she sailed toward the main building, leaving Keith to wonder if she'd developed a fondness for playing hard to get.

The first time, he'd pursued her pretty fiercely but she'd proved easy to catch. Had that decreased her attractiveness back then more than he'd credited? Because he couldn't deny he wanted her ten times more now than he had two years ago.

And neither could he deny he'd thoroughly compromised his ability to stay focused on this job. The faster he got Cara into bed, the faster he could burn off this blinding need to figure her out. She was one target he refused to miss.

Five

Rain began pelting the window shortly after Cara escaped to her room. The drops hit the screen with an unsatisfying thud, a distinct contrast from the rhythmic showers of Houston.

She wished she'd never heard of Regent's bridal expo. If she hadn't, she'd still be holed up in her condo, blissfully unaware Keith could still knock down her defenses and blessedly certain she'd fill the yawning chasm inside with a career until she could do a relationship again.

Her lips stung from being kissed by Voldemort Mitchell, who was every inch a wizard of seduction. But the real pain crawled through her chest, and she'd had enough of that for a lifetime. Keith equaled heartbreak. Period.

Why hadn't she slapped him silly? She'd known instantly what he meant by not skipping parts, and even if she hadn't caught the drift, the heated vibe shooting in her direction had been obvious. Every second she wasted on Keith was another second she couldn't get back.

Meredith spilled into the room, laughing. She was drenched down to her underwear, evident by the outline of her bra under her blouse. It had probably been by design—Meredith had never met an exhibitionist tendency she didn't like.

Water pooled under her ruined Pradas as she squeezed out her hair. Cara frowned. Scratch that; they were *Cara's* ruined Pradas.

"When did I tell you that you could borrow my shoes?"

Meredith scrunched up her face as if attempting to recall. "When you were born? It's a sister rule. What's yours is mine and what's mine is mine, remember?"

"Whatever. Ask next time."

"As if you'd have said no or something?" She eased off the shoes and shed her wet clothes as she strode to the bathroom, unconcerned, evidently, about spreading water into the rest of the room. "And stop taking your bad mood out on me. It's not my fault you still have a thing for Keith and he's impossible to escape on a tiny little resort property."

Cara made a face at Meredith's back. "That's not why I'm in a bad mood."

The door to the bathroom shut midsentence, before Cara could insist the real problem was that she'd spent so much time helping Keith today, they were behind on alterations. The hope of gaining national attention for Cara Chandler-Harris Designs was the only thing that made being in this situation with Keith bearable. Her company was like her family and she refused to let them all down because she couldn't stop being attracted to the wrong man.

No matter. Meredith would pick up on the lie. Oh, the alterations were definitely behind, but Cara's current black mood had more to do with the unsettling realization that she hadn't slapped Keith because she'd wanted him to kiss her. The mock wedding had been fun to organize, and she'd gotten caught up in the moment. Who could resist a wedding and Keith and the ocean breeze, all wrapped up in one romantic package?

Except it wasn't her wedding and she wasn't marrying Keith. Just like the last time.

Cara stabbed a needle through the dress in front of her but couldn't get into the right spirit for alterations to wedding dresses. Once again, she'd wear one and still be single when she took it off.

But in stark contrast to last time, she *would* have a thriving business. These alterations represented something greater than the required steps before a model wore the dress down a runway—Cara had a real and lasting place to belong, which this expo was an integral part of promoting.

That was better than a wedding of her own any day. Mostly.

When Meredith exited the bathroom after the longest shower on record, she had her phone in hand. "Paolo just texted me that everyone's in the Caribbean Lounge blowing off steam. Hans threw together a buffet and Keith unlocked the liquor cabinet. Get dressed and come on."

"I'm busy." It was a little too soon to be in Keith's orbit again, especially while in the same galaxy as the rest of the staff, who'd witnessed the scorching kiss their boss had laid on her. The embarrassment over falling so heavily into the playacting hadn't quite faded yet.

"No, you're in sore need of fun, alcohol and sex. All three are within your reach, honey." Meredith slipped into a skin-colored dress that hit her midthigh and made her look as if she should be on the arm of a Grammy-nominee as he walked the red carpet. "Or you can just come eat. You can sulk later. Don't make me go by myself."

"There's zero danger of you being by yourself in that dress."

Her sister shot a treacherous smile over her shoulder. "I

brought that Balenciaga dress that you like. I'll let you wear it, even though you were so mean about the shoes earlier."

Cara's heart twisted. Meredith was a good sister and all Cara had done was snipe at her. Besides, Meredith had been oh so correct—it wasn't her fault Keith and Cara weren't a good mix. "Thanks. I'll come with you. And wear the dress."

The smirk on Meredith's face didn't faze her. Cara was used to letting her sister get her way. In their relationship, that's what love looked like.

The rain hadn't let up and it took a while to get across the resort while sharing a very small umbrella. By the time the sisters arrived, the party was in full swing.

As promised, it did indeed seem as if everyone had come. Mary sat at a four-top laughing with a few of the maids, and Holly, who still looked like a runway model even when off the clock, chatted with the services manager at a mahogany bar near the far wall.

Paolo bounded over, muscles rippling underneath a skin-tight shirt, with two drinks in hand. He handed one to Meredith with an apologetic glance at Cara's empty hand. No big deal. Cara didn't need a pool boy to bring her a drink.

Her sister sipped the frothy pink concoction and smiled the smile she used to humor people. "Thanks, I adore Cosmopolitans."

Martinis, the drier the better, were Meredith's vice of choice. She hadn't touched a drink with an umbrella since a weekend in Vegas that Meredith still refused to talk about.

"For you."

Cara whirled to face the speaker and there was he-who-must-not-be-named himself, holding a wineglass full of deep red liquid. She accepted the goblet from Keith with a nod of thanks, because her stupid heart had just tangled up her tongue too much to talk, and sipped.

God, it was an exquisite cab that swirled through her mouth like a taste of heaven.

"You're serving this to guests?" she asked when she'd stopped worshipping the wine long enough to speak. This was high-quality, exorbitantly expensive stuff, which he no doubt knew that she'd recognize.

"Only the ones in the honeymoon suite." He clinked his glass to hers. "I tried to tell you you'd appreciate checking it out with me, but your mind went straight to the gutter. Shame."

"Yeah, but I still got a glass, so..." She swallowed some more to see if it cooled her suddenly hot throat.

She hadn't *really* been jealous of Meredith's uncomplicated fling with Paolo. Not a whole lot anyway. But all at once, it seemed as though Cara might have the better deal. There was something to be said for having the attention of a man who noticed details, and Keith rarely missed one.

Maybe she should thank Meredith for goading her into joining the party instead of sulking in her room—as her sister put it—which hadn't been too far off. And sulking for what? Because a yummy man kissed her? It was time to relax and stop worrying so much about Keith messing up her plans.

The entertainment director clapped his hands and drew everyone's attention. As he was unfortunately named Mark, someone had apparently thought it appropriate to make him a paper crown with the word *Hurricane* written on it and then crossed out with a large X.

"What's that about?" Cara whispered to Keith. "Is the tropical storm the reason it's raining?"

She hadn't seen a weather report lately, but foreboding gripped her all at once. The expo couldn't go on if the storm hit the island. Could it?

Keith leaned in and his breath teased her hair, sending a quick tug through her middle. She squashed it flat. She'd gone a long time without male companionship—why was she all of a sudden having heated flashes just because a man pressed up against her?

"Why don't you let me worry about the storm?" he suggested, his voice low and sexy in her ear. "I would tell you if there was a problem."

Mark lifted the microphone from its stand. "I need some volunteers to play the resort's version of the *Newlywed Game*. Two couples. Come on down. You don't have to be a real couple, just willing to play."

Cara shot Keith a don't-you-dare look, which he intercepted with a grin. "I wouldn't dream of it. Let some of the others have a chance to pretend to be married."

Keith sank into a chair and patted the one next to him. Since he'd agreed to keep his volunteering mouth shut—and then sweetened the deal by holding up the half-empty bottle of wine—Cara settled into the front-row seat he'd designated for her.

He inclined his head, nose nearly buried in Cara's hair again. "That dress looks amazing on you, by the way."

Cara's cheeks sparked with heat and she wished she could claim it was the only hot spot on her body. "Go on. You say that to all the girls."

"You're the only one I'm talking to. Which is not an accident."

He slung an arm across the back of her chair as if this was a date or something and she thought long and hard about staring at him with disapproval until he removed it. But the borrowed dress had a low back, and Keith's sleeve brushed her skin pleasantly. It would probably draw a lot of attention if she made a big deal out of it. So she leaned against his arm and ignored all the heat being generated by his close proximity.

To the surprise of no one, Meredith and Paolo lined up on the small stage at the front of the lounge and took the seats Mark had set up on the left-hand side. Cecelia, one of the maids, and the baby-faced kid who had set up chairs for Cara on the beach hopped up on stage to take the other set of chairs.

Mark handed out dry erase tablets and markers to all the "newlyweds" and asked the wives to answer the first question about their new husbands. "Boxers or briefs?"

The contestants scrawled their answers and when Mark said "Reveal!" the wives flipped their tablets. Cara rolled her eyes at Meredith's board, which read "Neither" in flowery script with a heart over the *i*.

Paolo's dimples popped out as he flipped his board. It read "Nada."

The crowd clapped and laughed simultaneously. Cecelia and her baby-faced fake husband, who apparently weren't on intimate terms, had opposite answers, so Meredith and Paolo got a point.

"I'm surprised you allowed everyone a break," Cara murmured to Keith, tilting her head close, mostly so he could hear her over the crowd noise, but it wasn't a chore to inhale his masculine scent at the same time.

"It's hard to crack the whip twenty-four/seven when everyone's worked like dogs for days and days," Keith allowed. "We can get back to the grind tomorrow, assuming we can find enough indoor tasks to keep us busy."

It was an unexpected admission from someone like Keith, who thought the sun rose and set over the bottom line, but she covered her shock. "That's very humane of you."

Her sister and the pool boy continued to dominate and won handily, high-fiving each other as Mark pronounced them the champions. Meredith and Paolo strutted across the stage, lording their victory over the poor fake couple who clearly knew each other only in passing.

Cara, meanwhile, had drained her wineglass and for God

knew what insane reason, yelled out, "Bet you couldn't beat a real couple."

Her sister threw a glance over her shoulder. "Bet there's not one in this room. Therefore, we are champions, my friends." Meredith devolved into an obnoxious Queen number, karaoke-style, complete with upraised fingers in the classic V for Victory.

That was the last straw.

"Come on." Cara didn't even glance at Keith before she grabbed his hand and hauled him up on stage. To Meredith, she simply said, "You're going down, honey."

Thankfully, Keith hadn't protested Cara's impulsive move or she'd have looked really silly trying to drag him someplace he didn't want to go.

"You think?" Her sister smiled as if she had the secret address to a 50-percent-off sale on designer shoes. "Sit down, Paolo. Let's show them how it's done."

The crowd hooted their approval and Mark fished around for a second set of questions.

Cara risked a glance at Keith, who was watching her with amusement. "What?" she asked defensively.

"Thought you weren't interested in pretending to be a couple."

"I'm not pretending. We've seen each other naked. Should be a snap to kick the behind of the—" Cara stuck two fingers of each hand in the air to make air quotes "—champions."

"So you're not going to be happy with me if we lose, are you?"

"No. So don't lose," she advised.

With a verbal drumroll, Mark asked the first question of the wives. "What's your favorite position?"

Cara winced. Okay, she'd totally deserved that. She shook her head and wrote, "Missionary," because it was true, thank God.

Mama would have heart palpitations if she knew her daughter was flaunting her sexual preferences for an audience, but at least Cara could maintain *some* dignity.

"Reveal!" Mark yelled.

Meredith and Cara flipped their boards. The crowd laughed and Cara craned her neck to see Meredith's, which read "CEO."

Cara bit back a smile. Meredith had enough ambition to decide what to eat for dinner that night, but definitely not enough to become CEO of anything. Her sister was letting her win, the big dolt, as a peace offering for bullying Cara into coming to the bar.

Keith flipped his board, and it thankfully read "Missionary."

Paolo's board read "All of them," so Keith and Cara received the point.

Except she hardly noticed because she was picturing Keith poised over her, every inch of his delicious body bared. The things that man could do to her—

Keith cleared his throat and she blinked at him, fairly certain the wicked glint in his eye meant he knew exactly what she'd been fantasizing about. And he heartily approved.

Heat rolled over her and she squirmed against the hard chair as she envisioned what might happen if she agreed to test the honeymoon suite after the party. As a bonus, the suite might have another bottle of that awesome wine.

No. No naked after-party honeymoon suites. She was here to work, not waste time and energy on an island fling with a man who'd already had a chance to "fling" with her all he wanted and instead chose to let her watch his backside as it disappeared.

"Next question," Mark said. "Few people know this about your husband, but he's… Okay, wives, fill in the blank!"

Oh, God. What kind of question was *that*? Cara scoured her memory but came up with exactly nothing. Meredith had already scribbled down her answer, so Cara wrote the only thing that might work, and revealed her board.

It read: "A jogger." At least it was true.

But Keith had written down "A microbrewer."

"What does that even mean?" Cara demanded, too surprised to do it quietly. "A microbrewer? Of beer?"

Keith shrugged. "It's been my hobby for ten years."

Yeah, she got the not-so-subtle dig. Keith had been making his own beer throughout the period they'd been a couple. And she'd been totally oblivious.

This game was stupid. But that didn't eliminate the panicky twinge in her midsection.

Their competition had both written "Third-degree black belt" for the point. Really? Cara eyed Paolo with new respect and squashed the odd feeling that her sister knew her Caribbean fling better than Cara knew the man she'd almost married.

The next question had Cara scouting for her wineglass. "My husband and I are complete opposites when it comes to _____."

Somehow, she suspected *marriage* wouldn't go over well as an answer to a newlywed game. The last of the amazing cab went down smoothly but didn't jog her brain. What was with all these fill-in-the-blank questions? At least Mark could have supplied some choices. These questions were much harder than the ones he'd asked in the first round.

Harder, because she and Keith were virtually strangers now. Maybe they always had been. After all, she hadn't even known about his aversion to commitment until recently. *Before* she'd planned a wedding might have been a better time to learn that.

When would it have been a good time to find out he wasn't in love with her? Better yet, shouldn't she have realized that on her own? But she hadn't even realized her own feelings weren't as strong as she'd told herself. She'd have sworn she was in love with Keith, but how could she have been? She couldn't even name his hobby.

In desperation, Cara wrote "Religion." Keith was Catholic and Cara had gone to a Methodist church growing up. It was the only thing she could think of.

Keith's board said "Balancing our checkbook."

"Oh, for heaven's sake. I've told you a million times that I *do* balance my checkbook." Cara threw up her hands. "When I get my monthly statement, I enter all the transactions in my checkbook and voilà. It balances."

Or at least that was how she'd done it before, when her father subsidized the account. Now she watched every dime, but Keith didn't have to know that.

"That how you run your business, too?" he asked mildly.

"Please." Cara snorted. "I pay a CPA to deal with all of that."

With a deadpan expression, Keith tapped the board. "Like I said. Complete opposites."

Opposites in everything else important, too, like marriage, children and love. The thought rang a little false, especially since she was beginning to realize she didn't have a firm grip on all those things either. Was that why she couldn't seem to get past the wedding and become an actual wife?

"We mere mortals can't add up the contents of a full shopping cart in our heads." Cara waved a hand to encompass the rapt crowd. "Well, we can, but we wouldn't be within a few pennies like you, Mitchell."

His smile could have melted butter. "I'll take that as a compliment, both that you recall something as mundane as grocery shopping together and that you've bestowed divine status on me. Guess we *are* complete opposites when it comes to religion."

Lord Voldemort had spoken. She chuckled darkly, though at what, she had no idea.

Mark clapped his hands, oblivious to the rising tension. Cara's spine hurt from holding it so straight, but she couldn't relax.

"Last question," the emcee shouted. "Who was the first person to say 'I love you'?"

Cara's board dropped to the floor with a crash. She couldn't do this particular brand of torture anymore.

Keith smiled apologetically at his staff and followed Cara's flight from the lounge. He only hoped that she wouldn't take out his kneecaps when he caught up with her.

But he couldn't let her go, not when it was obvious how close to tears she was. This wasn't a little snit because they were losing, but something else entirely. And he had an unexplainable urge to know what had provoked her.

If it was the checkbook joke, she really needed to lighten up.

Cara dashed through the rain, surprisingly swift for someone wearing heels in a downpour. Finally, she reached the door of her room and ducked inside. Keith bolted for the threshold and put a palm to the door before she could slam it in his face. To be fair, she probably didn't realize he'd been behind her.

He eased into the room, fully prepared to be thrown out, but determined to at least make sure she was okay before leaving. "Hey."

Cara whirled. "What do you want?"

The sight of a drenched Cara punched him—hard—in the gut. Her little pink dress was plastered to her body as if it had been painted on, and she'd clearly forgotten that she wasn't wearing a bra. Tight, hard nipples poked the fabric, and it was far more erotic than if she'd stood before him completely nude. Her hair hung in damp hanks around her face as if placed there by a team of designers for the maximum sexiest effect.

"You okay?" he managed to choke out.

She wiped her eyes with the back of her hand. "Obviously not. I left because I wanted to be alone. Go away."

"Sure thing." Keith crossed his arms and leaned against the door frame. There was no way he was leaving now, not while she was still upset. And definitely not while the view was so wet and so smoking hot. "As soon as you tell me what's up. I've never known you to be so competitive as to get mad over being beaten."

"Well, that's the problem, isn't it?" she shot back, her voice wobbly and clogged with baffling undercurrents. "You don't really know me that well, do you?"

"Not nearly as well as I'd like," he admitted readily. "Hence the invitation to join me in the honeymoon suite."

She rolled her shiny eyes, and the moisture wasn't from the storm overhead, but the internal one. "You already know me that way, Mitchell."

"Do I?" Any sensible person would shut the door. It *was* raining. So he eased it closed and leaned back against it. "You haven't developed some new moves under the sheets in two years? You've started jogging. Maybe you're doing some tantric yoga, too."

Fire flashed in her gaze and all the tears dried up, which was exactly what he'd been going for. All her unexplained emotions were unsettling. Uncomfortable. Sweat broke out along his neck.

"I'm not. And for your information, I've been building a business for the last two years, not brushing up on my *Kama Sutra*." She raked him with that fiery gaze. "So what if you get me naked and it's cataclysmic. What then? What does that really tell you about me—as a person?"

"That you're someone I want to spend more time with?" he offered and pulled at his tight shirt. She was clearly fishing for something. "And God, Cara. It's like an oven in here. How do you sleep?"

"Yeah, the air conditioner is still broken. Thanks for noticing." Her sarcasm only made the neckline of his shirt more constricting. "Don't you dare use that as an excuse to try to get me into your bed."

"I wouldn't dream of it," he lied. She didn't have to know that was exactly what he'd been about to suggest.

Still off balance, Keith ran a hand through his own damp hair. He kind of hoped the fantasy in pink never figured out she looked like a model about to pose for the cover of a men's magazine—but she was killing him. In more ways than one.

He should leave. Tension crackled through the air and he only wished it was just sexual. That he could handle. But the sizzling awareness was laced with something heavy, deeper. And he wasn't sure what to do with it, not on the heels of the mind-bending kiss on the beach. Not on the heels of playing the newlywed game and recalling Cara underneath him with extreme clarity.

He glanced at the wall behind her, but it did nothing to ease the churn of warring responses beneath his skin. Maybe they should get back to the original subject.

"What's going on with you? If you took off because Meredith and her stud boy were winning, I wouldn't put too much credence into it. The only reason she knew Paolo was a black belt is because he uses that as a pickup line. He's told every available woman on this property that he's a black belt. Whether he actually is or not is another story."

The wall was a very boring beige with a framed photo of a shell hanging dead center. Who decorated these rooms— a half-blind eighty-year-old? The decor would have to be updated. Yet another detail he'd missed with his fine-toothed comb because he was too busy chasing after a woman who'd already rejected him countless times over the past couple days.

His gaze drifted to Cara's face. Who was he kidding? He couldn't stop looking at her any more than he could stop digging beneath the surface of her "not interested." Any more than he could stop wanting her.

"I didn't know he was a black belt." Cara sniffed, but her expression lost a bit of the edge she'd worn since he walked into her room.

"You're not available," he pointed out. "Are you?"

"No! Well, maybe. I don't know." She dropped onto the bed as if her legs couldn't hold her any longer and scrubbed at her cheeks with her palms. "That's what's wrong. I don't know anymore."

Defeat pulled at her expression and another unsettling wave splashed through his insides.

Talk to me, sweetheart. He wanted to say it. Meant to say it.

But he couldn't spit out the words.

Cara fingered off her sandals and while she was occupied, Keith risked sitting on the bed next to her. Bad move. Now he was close enough to touch the fantasy in pink and very far from the door, which he should be disappearing through at this moment.

Especially given that he'd just looked down from this emotionally precarious tightrope and nearly lost his balance.

She needed…something, and Keith Mitchell was probably the last person on the planet able to give it to her.

For once, he had no idea how to hit this target.

Six

He had to do something, so he reached out and enfolded her hand in his, cradling it in his lap without speaking.

Her fingers curled around his and his stomach settled. Slightly.

"You don't have to stick around and watch me fall apart," she said. "I'm sure there are plenty of other things you'd rather be doing. Go back to the party. I'll be fine."

"There's nothing I'd rather be doing than sitting here with you." Which seemed to be the God's honest truth, despite all the heaviness. Otherwise, he would have taken advantage of his close proximity to the door to make his escape, wouldn't he?

He tried to convince himself he stayed because of the challenge. But he had a feeling there was more to it than that, and the mystery of it kept him firmly rooted.

"Only because you think you're going to get lucky."

"Yeah, that's why I'm here, Cara." Frustration exploded through his chest and came out of his mouth, unchecked.

Anger he didn't have any trouble expressing. "I live to take advantage of crying, upset women. It's a total turn-on. Can you please stop assuming all I care about is sex?"

Clearly stricken, she stared at him. "I'm sorry. I didn't... Wait. You mean that's *not* all you care about?"

Keith groaned. The trap had closed so neatly, he hadn't even realized he'd set it up. And he had only himself to blame. Five minutes ago, sex *was* all he cared about. Or at least it was all he could think about. When had everything shifted around?

It made him mad enough to say exactly what was on his mind.

"Let's examine this, shall we? I'm missing a party where alcohol I'm paying for is flowing freely. It's raining and I followed you back to your room anyway. My pants are still wet." Which he'd totally forgotten about until now, but he was too worked up to recall why it was important to mention. "You're upset and in a crappy mood. I would have assumed the facts speak for themselves, but since they don't, I'll spell it out. I care about you," he said honestly, though who the hell knew where that came from. "Or I wouldn't be here."

"Oh." She processed that, a hundred unfathomable thoughts traveling across her face at warp speed. "I'm sorry I dragged you away from the party. And for being in a crappy mood. It's not your fault, by the way. I'm just questioning every life decision I've ever made and you happened to get caught in the crossfire."

"Good to know. By the way, I'm not here to stand in the way of your crisis. Question away," he offered because it was the closest thing to support he could muster. "I'll listen."

She flung herself backward on the bed, legs still dangling off the edge. Staring at the ceiling as if it held the secrets of the universe, she hefted a sigh. "How did we get all the way to the point where we were about to march down the aisle and didn't really know each other that well?"

"Uh…" *You were pregnant* clearly wasn't what she was going for. "I think the better question is why it matters so much to you. We didn't march down the aisle."

"But I would have. I don't even think I was in love with you. I convinced myself I was. But I don't *know* that I was. How could I not know?" Her fists came down hard on the bed, but it didn't seem to unload an iota of her frustration. The motion flung still-damp hair into her face, but she left it there in favor of cursing colorfully at the ceiling.

"Where is this coming from? The stupid newlywed game? That was supposed to be fun, not an opportunity to ponder the choices we made a million years ago." He couldn't help but reach out and stroke the hair from her forehead since she didn't appear to be so inclined. Plus it was an excuse to touch her…and maybe communicate something he couldn't with mere words.

"Yeah. From the game. But also from the elevator conversation. The kiss." She bit her lip. "Never mind. Scratch that last one."

His hand froze against her temple. "Not on your life. What about the kiss?"

She hesitated long enough for him to assume she wasn't going to answer. But then she rolled to face him, effectively threading his fingers through her hair. "It was just… different. I've kissed you before. Lots of times. How could it be different?"

Before he answered that, he needed a critical piece of intel. "Different better or different worse?"

"Fishing for compliments?" At his eye roll, she shrugged with a faint smile. "It wasn't worse. But it wasn't like it used to be."

That might be the best news he'd heard all day. Satisfaction flared to life and turned dangerously fast into an ache in his chest that couldn't be explained. "Maybe because it was spontaneous, without all the pressures we had the first time around?"

"Maybe."

Stroking her temple some more because he liked it and because he could, he weighed what he wanted to say versus what she probably needed to hear. This was important and he didn't want to flub it up.

"We got serious really fast. And we're at different places in our lives now. You're a business owner. I took on the biggest consulting gig of my career and it came with hefty responsibilities." Grasping at straws and totally out of his depth, he took a stab at helping her make sense of things. "Neither of us really has the luxury of a permanent relationship, and the kiss was about nothing more than being in the moment."

No. It hadn't been. That was so far from the truth, he should take it back immediately. That kiss had been about need. About exploring what had changed, what was exciting about who they were now.

Deny it, Cara. Tell me it meant something.

"That's the problem." Her mouth turned down. "A relationship is what I want. Or I did. Now I don't think I do."

"What do you want?" He was clearly so bad at this, so bad at reading her, he should win a Terrible Person in a Crisis award.

"My whole life I've wanted to have a big wedding and be blissfully happy as Mrs. Someone. And then you left." She speared him through the heart with a baleful glance and went on without even giving him an opportunity to counter the offense. "I told myself no more pining for what obviously isn't meant to be and put my head down to make something of Cara Chandler-Harris Designs. When I looked up, I had a wedding dress business instead of a husband.

And that's probably what should have happened. During the last few days, I realized I don't even know what love is."

Misery pulled at her expression, dampening her eyes, and it was so painful, Keith cupped her face with his palms, forcing her to look at him. "Who does? You think Meredith and Paolo are in love and that's why she knows the answers to a few inane questions? Love isn't all it's cracked up to be."

Love probably didn't even exist. It had never touched his existence in any form or fashion. But the greeting card industry would have the entire world believing in it if it had its way. So what did he know?

"Obviously." She made a face. "It's just hard. I thought I was trying to get over you, and instead I got a great big wake-up call that I have no idea what a relationship should be. Now what am I supposed to do?"

"Sounds like you need a hot and heavy tropical island fling with someone who knows how to treat you right," he suggested with an eyebrow lift. "No pressure. No wedding bells in the future. It would be nothing but two consenting adults having some fun."

Which was not so coincidentally what he needed, too, more than he could possibly explain to her. Or himself. That's why he preferred to keep things temporary and easy—because he wasn't good at anything else.

"That would be great, except Paolo seems pretty happy with my sister."

"Ouch." It took every ounce of his considerable stamina to utter that one word without sounding pathetic.

She eyed him. "I'll take your words of wisdom under advisement, okay? Thanks for hanging out with me, but I'm beat and I just need to shut my eyes in a tomorrow-is-another-day kind of thing."

He'd been dismissed. Soundly. "Get some sleep. I'll be around."

Keith let himself out and cursed the fates that had seen fit to strand him on an island with a woman he wanted more than his next breath but couldn't seem to get naked.

Somehow he'd managed to have an emotionally charged conversation and gotten through it without having a heart attack. And he had the distinct impression he'd also managed to give Cara the support she'd needed without taking a thing for himself.

What was she *doing* to him?

He dashed through the rain to the other building and went to his room instead of back to the party. He preferred being alone anyway, didn't he?

When Cara opened her eyes, she was shocked to note the clock read 7:00 a.m.

The lump in the next bed had appeared sometime during the night. Cara hadn't even heard Meredith come in. Either her sister had learned to enter a hotel room at something less than the force of a tornado, or Cara had been more exhausted than she'd realized. She'd slept the whole night through without waking once.

After the kiss and Keith being all understanding and strong and spread out over her bed like the best possible thing she could have ordered from room service, she'd been convinced the combination would result in a sleepless night of tossing and turning.

Apparently not.

She rolled from the bed and peeked out the window in the off chance it had stopped raining. It hadn't. She rolled her twinging ankle. Not too sore today. Maybe it would be fun to jog on the beach in the rain. At least the odds of running into Keith were slim.

She was still downhearted to discover all her hopes and dreams were twisted up. And she had no crystal ball to help her sort out what her real goals were. What they should be. Keith would only make her confusion worse.

He met up with her ten yards outside her door.

"Run with me?" he asked casually as if everything was cool between them.

And really, wasn't it? As he'd said, neither of them was in a good place for a relationship. He knew she was an emotional mess and hadn't fled screaming into the night. Nor had he tried to take advantage of her while she'd been conflicted and upset.

The invitation to slide beneath the sheets with him had been quite clear. But he'd never pressed her, choosing to let the invitation stand without being obnoxious about it.

Keith had been very gentlemanly last night, all things considered. He deserved a break.

"Sure. I'd like to run with you."

To his credit, he didn't make a wisecrack.

They ran in silence through the downpour. The wet sand proved a little more treacherous than Cara had expected so she concentrated on fighting the elements instead of worrying about the mistakes of the past or the nebulous future.

It was a downright therapeutic experience.

After two miles down the beach and two miles back, they slowed near the bridal bower where they'd promised to love, honor and cherish in the fake wedding.

"What's on your agenda for today?" Cara asked, suddenly reluctant to end what had been a nice way to start the day. Rain notwithstanding.

And to be honest, she couldn't get last night's conversation out of her mind. If he wasn't interested only in sex, what *was* he interested in?

"I'm personally inspecting each hotel room. If yours is any indication, they're not ready for public consumption, and the majority of the guests are due tomorrow for the start of the expo."

"That's a big task, isn't it?" There had to be over five hundred rooms on the resort grounds, and her building still didn't have a working elevator.

He smiled slightly. "All my tasks are huge. Staving off Tropical Storm Mark being the insurmountable one."

She'd been trying to convince herself the rain was normal for this time of year and nothing to worry about, but something about his tone struck her. "We're going to get hit, aren't we?"

Keith swiped rain off his face in a deliberate gesture. "I think you should revise that to present tense instead of future."

The sound of dismay rose up in Cara's throat before she could stop it. "What? Can we weather the storm here on the island? I mean, is it safe?"

Lord above, they were on an island during a tropical storm. Every hurricane documentary she'd ever watched on the Weather Channel flashed through her mind in full color, including what 120-mile-an-hour winds could do to a building, not to mention the flooding.

Why hadn't they evacuated the island when there was still a chance of getting out?

"Safer than the rickety huts the island residents live in. The brunt of the storm is still a hundred miles away and may still miss us in the end. We should be fine here on the west side of the island. Maybe we'll lose power for a few hours." He shrugged. "The show must go on."

He seemed nonchalant about it, so Cara tried to relax. After all, he was the one with the NOAA app. There must not be imminent danger, right? She chewed on a fingernail and immediately yanked it out of her mouth. Destroying her manicure would not cause the storm to veer away. She'd have to find another way to de-stress.

"Let me help you inspect the rooms," she volunteered impulsively.

There was no way Cara could sit around and nervously wait to be battered by a tropical storm. Meredith could stay in the hotel room and do alterations all day if the weather was only going to get worse.

He eyeballed her. "Don't you have stuff to do?"

"Yeah, but I'm the boss." She liked the sound of that. It was the first time she'd ever thought of herself as such. But when you signed all the checks, what other title could you give yourself? "That means I can order my lackeys to do the work while I…go do other work."

"I'll take all the help I can get, then. Meet me in the lobby in forty-five minutes?"

"Sure." Plenty of time. It wasn't as if she planned to get all dressed up to tramp around in the rain. She might not even take a shower.

She ended up just changing clothes and shoving a packaged muffin into her mouth for breakfast. Her sister groused about being forced to do slave labor while Cara jetted off to hang out with Keith and then drank her coffee with a sulky pout. But by the time Cara was ready to leave, Meredith had a sewing kit in her hand.

Cara hid a smile. The reason her design business had grown so successful so fast was because she genuinely valued the place she'd created for herself—and the other girls in her employ. Meredith included. It was the best kind of pseudo-family because they'd all chosen to be in it.

"I'll be back later," Cara said and ducked back out into the rain, where she thoroughly squashed the little voice inside that was asking what in the hell she thought she was doing running off and leaving both her family and her responsibilities. And for what? To help Keith *work*?

Keith flashed a smile when he caught sight of her walking toward him in the lobby. Her borrowed flip-flops squeaked on the marble tile, but he didn't even glance down. He kept his attention squarely on her face, and that killer smile lit up her insides. She sighed. Maybe her impulsive offer was a veiled attempt to hang out in Keith's presence in hopes he'd give her a little more insight into his thoughts. There wasn't a law against it.

She'd almost married him but hardly understood his basic motivations. It was far past time to change that.

He handed her an electronic tablet.

"What's this?" She glanced at it. Holy cow, the screen displayed a fifty-item-long checklist.

"Each room has to pass with at least forty-eight of these, but none of the problems can be in the top ten." Keith tapped the screen. "Only 100 percent in the top ten will do. As you inspect a room, enter the room number at the top and then use the stylus to hit the check box for each item."

"This is very…involved." It would take an hour to inspect one room. Maybe instead of running herself ragged doing a job she really didn't have time for, she should just admit she wanted to get to know the Keith Mitchell from last night. Who he'd been. Who he was now. What he hoped for the future.

"Regent hired me to turn this resort around. Rooms were rated the lowest for the last five years on customer surveys."

"You should have at least ten people doing this job if you plan to finish today."

"That's probably true. But I don't trust anyone else to meet my high standards."

Yet he trusted her. Her insides exploded with warmth and she was pathetically grateful to have signed up for this exhausting task. "Where should we start?"

He pointed upward, eyes on his own tablet as he tapped a few times. "This tower. We'll go to the top floor and work our way down, you on one side of the hall, me on the other."

Though she didn't have a very clear picture of what she'd intended this morning's activities to look like, that sounded like the exact opposite of it. "You mean we're inspecting separately? I thought we'd do it together."

The taps stopped abruptly and Keith's gaze swung up to meet hers, the caramel in his eyes wickedly decadent. "You do realize we're inspecting hotel rooms. Empty rooms. With beds. Right?"

Answering heat rose up in her middle, flushing outward. "Of course I realize that. Are you worried I'll take advantage of you, sugar? I'll keep my hands to myself."

She *so* shouldn't be flirting with him. It was dangerous and would give him the wrong idea. Unfortunately, she wasn't sure any longer what idea was the right one.

He chuckled and it rolled through her. "We'll get this task completed much faster if you're in a totally separate room, trust me."

They worked on their respective rooms for an hour or two until Cara thought she could do the whole process in her sleep. Art on the walls. Check. Shower curtain present and accounted for. Check. Air conditioner operational. Check.

That one hurt. Every room so far had a functional air conditioner. By the twentieth room, she had a bone to pick with the man in charge around here. Plus, doing all of this alone was boring.

"What's the deal, Mitchell?" she demanded as she poked her head into the last room she'd seen him disappear into. Not that she'd paid attention or anything.

Keith exited the bathroom, tablet in hand, and good gravy—the man exuded something she couldn't tear her gaze from. He'd shed his suit jacket and rolled up the sleeves on his button-down shirt, letting sinewy forearms speak to what the rest of his body looked like.

"The deal about what?" he asked.

Her mood veered into dangerous territory. Keith was not part of the plan. Wanting him was not part of the plan.

Of course, the biggest problem was she had no plan. And confusion was not something she did well.

"All of these rooms have air conditioners. How come I'm staying in the one room on the whole property where it's broken?"

"If I recall, you told me not to use that as an excuse to get you into my bed." He crossed his arms, tucking the tablet under one. "I didn't."

"Move me to one of these rooms." She mirrored his stance and leaned a shoulder against the door frame, prepared to be as obstinate as Keith until the cows came home. "This one looks good."

"These rooms are all intended for expo guests. I can't put them in the tower with the broken elevator."

She scowled. "But it's okay for the help to be in the other tower?"

His quick grin put a flutter in her tummy. And that was not cool.

"You won't write an article about the elevator or lack of air-conditioning in a bridal magazine. I need the guests to be wowed. You will accomplish that with amazing wedding dresses. I will accomplish that by ensuring every last one of these rooms is up to par for the VIPs arriving tomorrow."

Somehow she'd crossed the threshold and met Keith in the middle. "*Your* room is in this tower."

"Yep." He slid a sizzling once-over down the length of her body and the unspoken message was pretty clear—he would gladly share his room with her, but it was the only one available in this tower. And she'd already declined.

Without checking her strength, she poked a finger in the middle of his chest. "Stop being so logical."

God, he was so tall when she wasn't wearing heels. And the chest under her finger was hard with well-defined muscles she remembered well. It took an enormous amount of will to keep the pad of her finger in one place instead of tracing the plane of his torso south until she hit the six-pack abs he surely still had.

Why couldn't she? He wouldn't stop her. In fact, he would probably encourage it.

He glanced down at her finger. "Thought you were keeping your hands to yourself. Did you find something you wanted to touch bad enough to break your self-imposed rule?"

Just as she flexed to snatch back her hand, he captured her palm with his own, holding hers tight against his pectoral and yeah, it was still hard as stone. His heart thudded against her hand, speeding up as she glanced at his lips. They'd felt amazing when he kissed her, and it didn't matter how hard she'd tried to forget, she couldn't.

"It was more of a guideline than an actual rule. Also an example of you being too logical." She should go back to the room she'd been inspecting. The checklist was only about half-complete and...

"Sure you want me to stop being logical?" he asked softly. "Logic has its benefits. For example, we're in a hotel room where a newly married couple will eventually stay. It would be a shame if the bed didn't hold up to a vigorous round of honeymoon sex. Logically, I should ensure this resort gets high marks on all aspects of Regent's destination wedding services."

"That's very um...logical." Apparently her brain had now completely deserted her. Because she definitely didn't want to go anywhere and definitely didn't think it was a good idea to stay.

He dipped his head, lips hovering near hers, then he turned slightly to murmur in her ear in a hot tease. "I'm glad you agree."

His nose nuzzled her ear and through no fault of her own, her head swiveled, causing his lips to collide with her neck. She arched involuntarily at the pleasurable contact.

Never at a loss, he molded his mouth to her skin expertly, finding the perfect hollow to lave. It sent a shower of sparks along her throat, and she moaned.

Seeking fingers gripped her face and he guided her chin toward him. His mouth claimed hers, swallowing her moan, and when his arms snaked around her waist, he hefted her against his solid frame.

Her body ignited. He kissed her with tightly wound control but the hint of abandon was there, just below the surface. He'd let his control drop the moment she said so, and devoured her with carnal pleasure until she cried out under the onslaught.

Yes, this was *definitely* what she'd intended when volunteering for this Herculean task. One telling comment yesterday—*I care about you*—had possibly changed the course of their future.

She wanted to explore it, wanted to find that place she belonged, that place she'd thought she found with him two years ago. What might be possible now that hadn't been back then? In the past few days, she felt as if she'd learned more about Keith than she had in the entire six months they'd been together before. She wanted more, wanted him.

She wanted to know what love looked like—*felt* like—in a relationship. She wanted to know what love felt like in *their* relationship. True love, not the pale shadow of affection they'd held for each other before.

The kiss deepened and Keith drenched her senses with his hard masculine body and powerful, purposeful hands. She inhaled him. He shifted a knee between her legs, and the rough friction sparked at her core. Hot and thick desire billowed over her skin, scorching her from the inside out.

Keith's phone beeped, startling her and effectively breaking the mood. How had she gotten so lost in him so fast? They were both in the middle of the biggest projects of their respective careers and all she could think about was exploring the depths of the man in charge.

Pulling back, she peered up at him. "Do you need to get that?"

"Wasn't planning on it." He made a noise of disgust. "Guess I will now."

She smiled at his consternation. "We can pick this up again later."

His wolfish smile put the exclamation point on it. "That was always going to happen. I was thinking we could pick it up again now *and* later."

Clarity rushed in to fill the space where the saturation of Keith had been a moment ago.

She made a face. "Despite the logic in testing *all* aspects of the room, we both have a lot of work to do today. Besides, if we really wanted to do it right, we'd have to test the bed in every room."

"Funny, I was thinking the same thing." Keith glanced at his phone and spit out the filthiest curse in his vocabulary.

He uttered that word in her presence only when something really bad had happened. "What's going on?"

Seven

Now that Cara had put the brakes on what would have surely turned into a naked free-for-all, Keith was having a hard time getting his body to understand playtime was over.

And over in a big way.

He glanced at the message on his phone again in a poor attempt to reorient. Instead of siphoning the blood from his lower half and returning it to his brain—where it needed to be—all his phone did was infuriate him further. The news hadn't changed.

"Looks like we're inspecting these rooms for no reason," he explained and ungritted his teeth. "Tropical Storm Mark has shut down Providenciales Airport."

As if this project needed another complication.

"What does that mean? The expo is canceled?" Worry crinkled the corners of Cara's eyes.

He'd prefer it if her gaze was still full of come-hither. He blew out his frustration in a heavy sigh and tapped a quick message to Elena, the resort manager, on his phone.

"No way. Well…I don't know. But we have to assume the airport will be reopened in a few hours. And if it is, we have to be prepared for the expo to go on as scheduled."

Which vastly increased his mile-long to-do list. Additional staff members should have arrived today, all of whom had critical roles in preparing for a wide range of expo elements.

Was it five o'clock yet? Hell, the rapid deterioration of Keith's mood and the expo might call for tequila shots in the middle of the day regardless of his rules against drinking on the job.

The interruption and subsequent issues were both nasty reminders that he wasn't on vacation with Cara, free to seduce her into having sex on the beach, skinny-dipping in the hot tub or taking a long shower together. The only water in their future was pouring down from the sky.

It was unsettling to realize he resented the gargantuan pile of tasks standing between him and what he wanted. Turning this resort into a premier wedding destination was his job, and the number of zeroes Regent had tacked on to the end of his paycheck made it well worth his while. But for the first time in his professional life, what he wanted had nothing to do with the job.

Frustrated beyond all belief, he sent another text to Alice, instructing her to call a meeting with the core management team. Everyone would look to him for leadership in the wake of the airport closures and imminent storm, and he couldn't fail them.

"I've got to finish these rooms and then run to a meeting," he said instead of laying Cara on the bed as he'd planned.

Cara picked up her tablet from the dresser where she'd dropped it earlier. "I take it we won't be picking things up later?"

There was no way he'd have time for Cara later—she

deserved more than a fifteen-minute quickie. *He* deserved more than that.

Well, there was one way. According to Cara's philosophy, being the boss meant you could order your employees to do extra work. Perhaps it was time to delegate a few things.

"If I can plow through the most critical issues, I'll text you, maybe around nine. Come to my room and have a drink. Don't be late," he advised.

"Or what?" she shot back.

"Or I'll come looking for you and you will lose one article of clothing for every minute it takes me to find you."

She laughed throatily. "Are you trying to get me there on time or convince me I'd rather be tardy?"

"Go." He pushed her gently in the direction of the door. "Finish the rooms on your side, and for God's sake, let me do mine without you entering any more of your air-conditioner grievances onto the record."

They parted and he didn't stop checking off items on the inspection list until Alice texted him that everyone was in the staff meeting room in the main building. He dashed through the rain, and spent the afternoon having terse conversations about fun concepts like contingency plans, insurance claims and flood preparation.

It took a supreme act of will to remain focused, especially when he'd rather be drowning his sorrows in Cara. Elena ordered food to be brought in at some point and Keith ate without tasting it, one ear on Mary as she talked through ideas for how to move the expo indoors. The remainder of his attention stayed fixed to his computer screen, where a constantly refreshing radar image tracked Mark.

The good news: the tropical storm hadn't been upgraded to a hurricane.

The bad news: it was still a tropical storm and the airport hadn't been reopened.

Alice typed up notes and split the tasks amongst the senior management. Keith's list contained exactly the same number as everyone else's because at the end of the day, he didn't have the heart to foist more work on his staff just because he had a selfish desire to get an old flame between the sheets.

No one left the little meeting room and Keith didn't look up until nearly ten o'clock. Wind howled outside, occasionally gripping solid objects and flinging them against the side of the building. The storm had slowed the moment it hit land and battered the island for hours.

The airport remained closed indefinitely and Keith's doubled workload had decreased by two items in two hours. The long evening loomed, promising to be lonely and stressful, but only because he'd hoped to have other plans. Most days, stress couldn't touch him because he lived and breathed his work and liked it that way.

Elena plopped into the next chair and put her head in her hands, groaning.

"Yeah," Keith commiserated. "Tell me about it."

"It's that definition of insanity. You know, doing the same thing over and over again and expecting different results? I look at the agenda for the expo, and every time I think I'm going to see a magic solution that will allow us to kick it off tomorrow as planned."

"There's no magic. Just hours upon hours of hard work for zero payoff." Normally, he'd sugarcoat a comment like that at least a little bit, but he was out of both sugar and patience.

Elena frowned. "That's unacceptable."

And that was typically Keith's line. An unwillingness to fail coupled with hard-core will got him through the day.

"You're right. There will be a payoff. Eventually." It was just hard to see it right this minute through the red haze of professional and personal roadblocks. "I don't know what's wrong with me."

"You've been putting in twelve- and sixteen-hour days for weeks," Elena said mildly. "Take a break. The storm is going to do what it's going to do and no spreadsheet in existence will change that. Let's reconvene in the morning, assuming any of the resort is left standing around us."

His grin felt a little flat but it was genuine. That's why he'd handpicked Elena Moore—she had a pragmatism he appreciated. Especially when all he really wanted to do was text Cara and see if she'd still meet him for a drink in his room.

"That's a great idea." Without hesitation, he grabbed his phone and typed a message.

He hit Send, stood and gathered his laptop and other stuff, which had somehow become strewn across the table.

If Cara wasn't already asleep, he'd get a chance to blow off some of his personal frustration. The professional frustration would have to wait until dawn.

Like a teenager, he held his phone in his hand, screen up, so he'd see the return text from Cara the moment it arrived.

Nothing.

Maybe she was making a point, refusing to answer because it was way past nine o'clock and he'd made such a big deal about punctuality.

He dashed to his room without an umbrella. The wind nearly knocked him sideways, but he finally got a hand on the door and pushed his way inside, already soaking wet.

Cara would be soaking wet too by the time she got to his room—if he could entice her out of her snit.

That put the cap on it. She'd be wet, sexy and all the things he'd been fantasizing about since last night.

Once he got off the elevator and into his room, he texted her again.

Weary all of a sudden, he slumped on the love seat to

wait for Cara, too tired to pretend he wanted only the carnal pleasures to be had in her arms, when in truth, he'd be happy if she'd just be with him awhile. As a business owner, surely she'd understand his drive to be self-made—no family gravy train required—and would also be sympathetic to his failures. She didn't look to him for strategy, results, dollar signs, fill in the blank.

He needed her tonight—for more than sex.

How strange was *that*?

By ten forty-five that knock on the door hadn't come. She wasn't going to show, leaving him to decide whether he had the energy left to hunt her down.

Cara spun on her toe to pace in the other direction, phone clutched in her hand so tightly, the screen might be permanently damaged. The room was unfortunately too small to unload the high level of anxiety and frustration coursing through her blood.

"That carpet is going to start crying before too long," Meredith commented without looking up from her tablet, where she was watching *Bridget Jones* for the four hundredth time. "Why are you still here? Keith texted you like twenty minutes ago."

"I can't do it."

She couldn't physically move toward the door. Couldn't text him back. Couldn't make a decision to save her life. This was it, the line in the sand, and she had no idea what would happen if she stepped over it.

This bout of indecision had started the moment she left Keith earlier and then had grown to something monstrous as the day dragged on. Part of her had hoped Keith would be too busy to meet up so she could avoid the line as long as possible. Regardless, Meredith had bossed Cara into a slinky thong and matching bra, then forcibly shoved her arms into a low-cut sundress.

It was fine. Keith might not even call.

Then her phone had beeped and flipped her into panic mode instantly.

"Can't do what? Let a hot man make you feel amazing?" Meredith rolled her eyes. "You're certifiable."

She was. "I am not."

Anyone who would open themselves up to being crushed again, who'd decided she wanted to see what love felt like in a relationship where that wasn't on offer, could easily be labeled crazy. Anyone who would pass up the opportunity to be with a man who'd made it clear he wanted her, trusted her and of all things *cared* about her was crazy times two.

The problem was she didn't know which one this summons would lead to. And she couldn't say the same about her feelings toward Keith, not 100 percent. After all, she'd thought she loved him before, only to find out nothing was as she'd told herself. And she certainly didn't trust him. Which left two consenting adults having an island fling with no pressures and no promises.

Or did it?

Cara moaned and sank to the floor. "He told me he cares about me in the same breath as saying neither of us has the luxury of a relationship right now. What does that mean? Maybe he'd be open to it later? Or was it just to get me into bed?"

"Asking the wrong person."

"Well, I can't ask Keith. He's the one who got me all confused in the first place."

She would have sworn she had it all figured out before coming to Grace Bay. Cara Chandler-Harris Designs was a business she'd created to get over Keith. And as a result, she'd found something she loved. Something she was good at. Something that fulfilled her aching soul.

But she'd never expected it to take the place of a relationship. She'd never expected Keith to come back in her life and show her she didn't know diddly-squat about what was supposed to happen after the "I-dos."

She'd never expected to want to learn with Keith by her side.

Her sister snorted. "What in the world is there to be confused about?"

"What's going to happen next?" Keith wasn't marriage material. But then what if she wasn't either? "What if I sleep with him and we end up with completely different ideas about where our relationship is—"

"Oh, honey, you're going about this all wrong." Meredith ditched her tablet and put a hand to her chin as if about to impart sage advice. "Stop being such a girl. You are woman, hear you roar. Get that man naked and horizontal and use him all up. Then after he's rested, do it again. Do your gender proud and take what you want."

Cara's mouth twisted into a wry smile. "Is that the secret?"

"There's no secret. You're thinking about this too much. Don't let the past ruin what you can have now. And really don't let the future mess up the present. That hasn't even happened yet."

"Because you're such a relationship expert?" That wasn't fair and it had more to do with how closemouthed her sister always was about her own love life, or lack thereof. Meredith's interaction with men started and ended in the bedroom, but that didn't give Cara an excuse to be mean.

She started to apologize but her sister cut her off.

"No." A shadow passed over Meredith's face. "Because I'm an expert in messing them up. That's how I know what not to do."

According to Meredith, obsessing about the plan fell squarely in the category of What Not to Do. And maybe her sister was right. Cara bit her lip.

Cara's design business filled her with purpose and gave

her a level of satisfaction she'd never known. Maybe it wasn't such a bad thing to take that and run…straight to Keith. This was Grace Bay, not Houston, and Cara could do whatever she wanted. Be whomever she wanted. If Cara Chandler-Harris could start her own business, she could have an island fling with her ex, too.

No plan needed.

Then, when it was over, *she* could walk away. The possibility of making that choice was empowering. What did she have to lose, really?

Meredith jerked her head at the door. "Get going and pray he's not already passed out from boredom."

Cara took a deep breath. She *could* do this. Or at least she could knock on Keith's door. One step at a time.

Tap, tap, tap.

Keith woke instantly from his uncomfortable catnap on the love seat, heart tripping. The light knock that had roused him could be only one person—Cara.

He yanked open the door and eyed the fully dressed woman on the other side. "You're late. That means you lose an article of clothing for every minute."

His already-surging blood pumped faster as he surveyed her. She was indeed wet. But not wet enough.

"I seem to recall you said you'd come looking for me," she said primly and stood her umbrella against the outside wall. "Which you did not."

"Now who's being logical?" He held out his hand and when she took it, he pulled her inside the room, where he'd lowered the lights. Soft jazz music, which he'd switched on earlier before he fell asleep, played in the background. If she'd warned him of her imminent arrival, he could have done a little more to set the mood.

Of course, it would help if she'd tell him what sort of mood to set. A woman's extreme tardiness usually didn't bode well when a drink invitation clearly came with benefits.

"Nice," she commented as she followed him into the room. "Being the boss has its privileges."

Small talk didn't scream "I'm into you" either.

She sank gracefully into a leather chair near the lounge table, pointedly ignoring the love seat, where they could have both easily fit. And could have indulged in a little foreplay.

Which might have been the point. But if she wasn't here to pick up where they'd left off earlier this morning, why *was* she here?

"I didn't think you were coming."

Now, why had he opened that can of worms? Obviously, if she'd dropped him butt-first on a Tilt-a-Whirl she couldn't have thrown him more off balance than she had with her late arrival.

Cara cleared her throat. "I didn't think I was coming either. But I'm here now."

Despite the ambiguity, he could roll with that. Something loosened in his chest. She *was* here and that was enough. If it led to more, great. If not, that was okay, too.

For the first time in their relationship, he genuinely wanted to spend time with her, talk to her, hear her opinions and—

God, what was *wrong* with him?

He poured her a glass of wine from the same label she'd enjoyed last night and handed it to her, then took the other chair, suddenly feeling oddly as if they were on a first date.

And maybe they kind of were. At least it was a first date between Keith and this new woman Cara had become. A first date after wiping the slate clean of all their disastrous history, including Keith's mistakes. Perhaps she'd come to that conclusion as well—hence the distance.

She'd earned the right to be romanced, no matter how many times they'd seen each other naked in the past.

"I'm curious about something." He sipped wine to set the conversational mood, which would serve to put her at ease. "What do you hope to get from this expo? Professionally?"

Surprise flew into her expression. "Exposure, of course."

He grinned in spite of the strange tension between them. "I realize that. I mean, what are your goals? Fifteen percent increase in orders? By when? What's the measure of your cost investment versus payoff? That sort of thing."

"Why do you want to know?"

Her tone sounded the opposite of someone letting their guard down.

"Because I'm interested in you," he blurted out. Too touchy-feely and now he felt as if he'd stepped in quicksand. *Backpedal.* "And on the off chance the expo is canceled, I'd like to know what your losses will be."

Better. Keep it about work. That he understood.

"I don't need you to cover them, if that's where you're headed."

"No, that wasn't my intent at all." He downed half his wine in hopes it would get his brain and tongue in sync or at least dull his wits enough to not care how badly he was botching this.

Maybe he should shut up and kiss her. They'd never had problems communicating *that* way. But the vibe was so weird, he hesitated. Besides, he'd told her to stop assuming all he cared about was sex—and somehow they were at a place where that remained true, so he should practice what he preached.

After a deep breath, he tried again. "Businesses intrigue me. The flow of capital, margins, profit-loss statements. Spreadsheets are my crack. It's why I like consulting, because I can dig into what makes a company live and breathe from a ten-thousand-foot view. When we dated before, our common interests were always other things. Now we have something new in common. I want to talk to you about it."

The tension melted from her face. "Keith, that's the sweetest thing you've ever said to me."

"Uh…what?" He watched her as she set her glass down on the table, gaze squarely on him. And it was noticeably warmer. Then she rose and skirted the table to lean over and kiss him soundly on the lips.

He was too busy trying to not stare down her still-damp dress to kiss her back, but then she touched his cheek in a brief caress and thoroughly ensnared him with the expression on her face. He couldn't look away.

"You basically said that you see me as an equal. That's the best compliment you could have given me. Thank you." She settled into the love seat instead of returning to her chair and swirled her fingertips across the next cushion in blatant invitation.

That was some magic wine he'd selected. He switched seats gladly, still clueless how his neurotic love of entrepreneurship had somehow shifted the mood.

"The truth is," she drawled, "I don't have good projections for this expo. I have enough of a marketing background to know that exposure is king, but difficult to quantify. I'd love to have some solid numbers, but it's hard to be the CEO, CFO, chief marketing officer and actually get around to designing dresses at the same time."

"I'll help you," he offered instantly, surreptitiously inhaling her exotic perfume. "It'll be fun. Really."

Exotic with enough of Cara laced through it to thoroughly intoxicate him. He couldn't remember a blessed thing about what kind of perfume she'd worn before. Because he'd never noticed it. Not like this, as if it was part of the full, potent package of the woman.

She rolled her eyes without malice. "Only you would call

that fun. It's an interesting proposition. I'd kill for your expertise, but in lieu of that, I'd pay for it. Name your price."

"No strings attached." And he meant it. "I insist. It'll be a thank-you for helping me out earlier."

It was the least he could do, and it made him pathetically grateful to have a concrete way to repay her for organizing the mock wedding. And for helping with the room inventory. And for her freely given forgiveness, which he hadn't realized would come to mean so much.

"Wow. If I'd have known that would be the reward, I'd have volunteered to clean the oven with my tongue." She slid a glance down his torso. "But I can't let you do it for free. I insist on tit for tat. If you won't take money, what other form of barter could we possibly cook up?"

Instantly, the strange first-date, why-was-she-here vibe vanished and everything fell into place.

"I'm sure we could come up with something," he murmured and reached up to finger a lock of her curling, damp hair. "But I owe you. Not the other way around. After all, you're the one who had to dash through the rain to get here."

"No problem." She smiled. "It was worth it."

"Yeah?" The thought warmed him enormously.

Placing a delicate palm against his thigh, she leaned in, peering up through lowered lashes. "Totally. You have air-conditioning."

He bit back a snort. "Yes, among other luxuries. Let me show you."

Before she could open her smart mouth again, he tipped her chin up and laid his lips on hers. Her soft sigh bled through him, energizing him.

The long, stressful day melted away as he fell into her. Her soft lips firmed and she came alive, hands in his hair, body snugged against his. Hot spikes of desire exploded in his groin and he groaned.

It had been a while. Even longer since he'd had a woman

in his arms who intrigued him as much as this one. Their bodies knew each other intimately, but the nuances of this new Cara bled into the experience, heightening it. Heating it. What other new things would he uncover?

She pulled his shirt from his pants and her fingertips slid along his sensitized back, dipping lower. His lungs contracted and his brain went fuzzy.

"Wait." He drew back but Cara's kiss-stung lips and mussed hair called to him. He resisted diving back in. Barely.

I want to love you like you deserve. Like I should have the first time.

He dropped to his knees between her legs and eagerly she scooted forward, aiming for his mouth, as if to kiss him again. Oh no, not this time. He held up a palm to stop her and gently leaned her back, ensuring she rested comfortably against the couch cushions. He kissed her throat, working his way down until he hit fabric.

"Let me," he murmured and drew down the shoulder straps of her sleeveless dress and bra, baring her breasts.

Gorgeous. Her nipples peaked under his gaze and he swallowed back the urge to spout poetry. As if he even knew any, especially a verse good enough to describe how magnificent the sight of half-dressed Cara was.

"I could look at you for hours." But he wanted to touch, so he traced the lines of her uncovered torso a bit more reverently than he'd intended, but oh well. As he enjoyed himself, he worshipped her with his gaze.

She watched him, a hint of curiosity in her expression. As if she couldn't quite figure out what he meant to accomplish, which unsettled him. Had he never made it all about her in the past? Their physical relationship had been satisfying for them both. Hadn't it?

It didn't matter. She'd come to him tonight and regard-

Eight

Rain beat against the window, melding with the jazz music to create a rhythmic, sensual tempo that seemed to infuse Cara's blood. Or maybe that was the heat in Keith's expression as he swept her with another gaze full of promise and wicked intent.

When she'd knocked on the door, she'd expected to have a nice evening with Keith that included a satisfying round of intimacy. In the past, he'd proved to be an energetic, generous bed partner. They got naked, it was hot, they both climaxed and that was it—why should it be any different this time? One island fling coming up.

And then he'd changed it all up by starting this couch seduction. Keith didn't do slow, or at least he never had before. And that's when she got the first inkling this evening wasn't going to be anything like she'd expected.

Without warning, Keith lowered his head to her breast and swirled his tongue across her flesh, then latched on to suck with quick little pulls. Breath whooshed from her lungs, her back arching involuntarily to meet his lips. Her nipple drove deeper in his mouth, his teeth scraping at her sensitized breast, and she moaned.

Thick, dense heat gathered at her core and spun outward, enflaming her skin.

He switched to her other nipple, laving it sensuously as if he had all the time in the world, while she fought to keep from sliding to the floor in a puddle of sensation. His palms gripped her rib cage, jutting her breasts forward. He licked and sucked, alternating as he pleased, while she squirmed, head lolling back against the cushions until she could hardly breathe, hardly think.

Moans spurted from her lips, and nonsensical phrases floated through her mind. Shouldn't she be reaching for him, to pleasure him in kind?

Her leaden arms refused to move and sensation swamped her. She had no idea her breasts were such an erogenous zone, but then no man had ever expended so much effort demonstrating it to her.

As often as Keith commented how much she'd changed in two years, he'd seemed pretty much like the same guy. Until tonight.

He raised his head, gaze hot with unfulfilled longing and mysterious intent. With a gentle lift of her bottom, he pulled off her dress in an impressive one-handed move and threw it over his shoulder. Rocking forward on his knees, he bent and aimed for the juncture of her thighs.

What was he doing? He couldn't…he'd always respected her discom—

White-hot sparks exploded at her core as he put his mouth over her center, nibbling her through her panties.

She almost bucked off the cushion. Firm hands to her hips held her in place against the couch as he tongued her. He had to stop. This wasn't…she couldn't…and then the exquisite torture ratcheted up a notch as his strong fingertips slid beneath the string of her thong to grip her rear and shove her more firmly against his mouth. His tongue tunneled under the fabric to find her bare flesh, and his light touch teased her in a place no man's fingers had ever teased.

It was too much. And oh so amazing.

Hands in his hair, she held on as he flung her into the heavens. Again and again, he drove his tongue against her nub, then deep in her core, and back to where he started. Bright pinpoints of light blurred her vision, and the cresting wave broke over her in a thick flood of release.

Panting, she scrabbled for purchase against Keith's shoulders, desperate to hold on to *something*. As her body cooled and her heart rate slowed, her mind decided to start functioning again.

And it was turning over the fact that while it had always been good with Keith, it hadn't been like *that*.

When she could speak, she eyed him. "What was that all about?"

His eyebrows shot up and his satisfied smile widened. "Well, I hoped it would be fairly obvious. Do you need a repeat, so you can figure it out? Because I'd be happy to help."

Her lips involuntarily curved up in response. "You know what I mean. That was not standard operating procedure between us."

He shrugged and picked up one of her feet to unbuckle her stiletto, still grinning as if he had plenty more where that came from. "We had busy lives in Houston. We didn't live together. It was hard to justify taking my time when I always had a twelve- or fourteen-hour day ahead of me."

The shoe slid from her foot and he started rubbing the arch, which felt so amazing, she groaned. "Because tomorrow isn't going to be a backbreaker of a day?"

"No. Hear that?" He tilted his head to the window, where rain lashed at the pane and wind whined through palm trees. "That's the sound of a storm giving me all the time in the world to do exactly as I please. I've got all night and a strong interest in getting…creative with how I spend it."

Her tummy began humming. Her mama had raised her right and there were some things a lady didn't do. Intimacy was something to cherish, something to create with the right person, and she'd never slept with a man she couldn't imagine being with forever.

But this wasn't her mama's island fling. It wasn't as if Cara had a true aversion to being adventurous—she'd just never had the right opportunity. There were limits to what you could realistically do and then look someone in the face every morning for the rest of your life.

But tonight wasn't about the rest of her life. And she was safe with Keith. What better opportunity was there to take what she wanted and use him all up, as Meredith would say.

It would make it that much easier to walk away afterward.

With renewed interest, she cocked her head. "That sounds promising. Tell me more."

His wicked grin curled her toes as he swept her with a pointed once-over. "Remember your answer to the newly-wed game about your favorite position?"

"Missionary works," she shot back. "What's wrong with that?"

"Nothing." He kissed her foot and moved to her ankle with little butterfly caresses of his lips that teased and excited at the same time. "But there are so many more we can try."

The idea took root and blossomed. But there was one small factor she couldn't figure out. "Why now? What's the occasion?"

They'd certainly never had such a conversation before.

Her other shoe hit the floor and Keith draped one leg over his shoulder, then bent the other one toward her torso, opening her up to his hot perusal. She let him roll with it and got a delicious little thrill for her effort.

"You're a businesswoman now. Independent. I cannot stress enough what a huge turn-on that is."

Oh my. So designing a few wedding gowns had suddenly cast her into a whole new level of hotness?

The thought was fascinating. He wasn't turned on by her sexy lingerie—he'd barely noticed it. No shade of lipstick or hair color could have given her the slightest edge. Instead, something intangible beneath her skin had brought about this new realm of possibility. The best part? It would never fade because it was internal.

The fact that he found her sexier because of her accomplishments was turning her on, too, picking up the remnants of her earlier orgasm and fanning the flames. There was entirely too much talking going on, and it was totally her fault. But choosing to be adventurous and doing it were two different things.

Before she could decide what to do first, he turned his unshaven jaw into her thigh and abraded her skin lightly, then sucked. It was slightly painful but thoroughly thrilling, and the answering tugs at her core shocked her at their intensity.

As he edged closer to her panties, he left a trail of light marks in his wake. When his lips hit the fabric, he glanced up through his lashes. "I've always wanted to do that."

"Is that how this works?" she asked, her voice catching over the tangle of stimulation in her throat. "We just do whatever we want?"

"Yes." He nodded succinctly. "Take charge of your pleasure, Cara. I insist. Be in control. I will not complain."

Emboldened by his frank instructions, she rolled her hips, brushing her panties against his jaw. "Do that again, but without the thong."

His gaze heated. "Liked that, did you?"

Without another word, he hooked the strings of her panties and yanked them off, resettling between her thighs, but unlike the first time, gentleness didn't seem to be a part of the agenda.

He gripped her hips, pulled her to the edge of the couch and pushed her thighs apart. His tongue raked her still-sensitive nub and she gasped, bowing up. Then he slid two fingers into her and twisted. The eruption of heat nearly made her black out.

She swallowed a very unladylike curse, hips swiveling with a mind of their own as he shoved her to the edge of desire. And beyond. The release rocketed through her, encompassing her whole body.

With the aftershocks still gripping her, Keith murmured, "You know what's really good? Me inside you before you've fully come down."

This could be *better*? Half-blind, she sat up—how, she didn't know when all her bones had disappeared—and clawed at Keith's shirt, popping buttons as she stripped him out of it.

He pulled his arms from the fabric, and the motion propelled her off the love seat and into his lap. She took it as a sign to lock lips and lost herself in the dark, sizzling splendor of his kiss.

His strong, amazing lips. The things they'd done to her. The things they were *still* doing. He tasted of wine and earthiness, and it was exquisite.

She pulled off his pants, and in her urgency got the legs all tangled up. He was no help, grappling with one side while she yanked on the other. Finally, her questing hands found bare flesh and she stroked every inch she touched.

Keith's head tipped back and he groaned. Her lips curved up, surprising her. It was heady to cause a man so controlled and so big and so masculine to feel pleasure.

"Now," she said and pushed him back against the carpet, then mounted him.

Wordlessly, he held up two fingers with a foil packet caught between them. Yes, of course he'd be on top of that. She shoved aside the reminder that they of all people shouldn't take any chances and paused as he put on the condom.

Thighs wide, she guided his body until everything clicked and he filled her instantly. Oh, yes, that *was* good. Still sensitized, still damp, the additional friction and pressure nearly set her off again.

Throwing her own head back in ecstasy, she found a rhythm that got a guttural sound of approval from Keith. Wantonly, she glanced down at him spread out underneath her like an offering to a goddess, and the power of it shot through her.

He reached up to touch her and she shook her head, lacing her fingers with his to pin them to the carpet. Despite knowing that he could break free any moment, she reveled in the ability to command a 190-pound man covered in sinewy muscles.

His eyes shut in apparent pleasure as she changed the angle again, driving her hips harder, and all of it coalesced into a bright, hot ball at their joined bodies. Nonsense words flowed from her throat as the orgasm built and exploded in an epicenter of ripples.

Totally sapped, she collapsed on Keith's chest as he cried out with his own release. His arms came around her, binding her tightly to him as he spent himself.

Chests heaving together, they lay torso to torso. She couldn't have moved if the hotel room caught fire.

"That," Keith huffed, "was un-freaking-believable."

It had been. Keith never talked like that, but she agreed—no other term could describe it.

"And then some."

But only because Keith had encouraged her to spread her wings. Only because he'd told her how hot it was. Only because this was a fling and nothing more.

The thought made her a little sad all at once. Why couldn't sex between them be adventurous and fulfilling and wonderful while they were a couple?

Well, because it didn't work that way, obviously. Either it could be tender and meaningful or it could be a smoking-hot fling. And honestly, it hadn't been all that tender the first time around, when she'd thought they were in love.

"As much as I enjoyed the floor, I'm a little carpet burned," Keith murmured and stroked her hair. "Shall we move to the bed?"

Cheek to his pectoral muscle, she listened to his heart rate slow. Did that mean he was good and rested already? "I've got another round in me."

He groaned and it was not one of anticipation. "Dawn is going to come much sooner than I'd like and I'm afraid storm cleanup is going to be brutal. What if we just go to sleep?"

Sleep? Here? That was the opposite of a good idea. As if doused by a bucket of cold water, sense returned to her brain. Rolling off Keith carefully, she scouted around for her dress, found it and yanked it over her head without taking the extra time to don her bra and panties.

"I, ah…think I'll head back to my room."

Still naked and apparently not interested in fixing that, Keith sat up, muscles bunching and flexing. Dang it if he wasn't the sexiest male on the planet, with or without clothes. Why was she leaving again?

"Your room doesn't have an air conditioner," he reminded her. "Stay. I'd like to see your face in the morning."

Oh yeah. *That* was why. "No, it's better we keep this expectation free. Sleepovers are like the gateway. It starts feeling like we're a couple again and neither of us has the *luxury* of that."

Wincing at her catty tone, she gathered all her things and headed for the door before he could say anything. "Thanks, Mitchell. That was amazing. See you tomorrow."

The storm nearly blew her sideways, dousing her instantly. As she dashed through the rain to the other tower—because in her panic she'd fled without her umbrella—she had to admit that part of her wished they did have the luxury of more and it was something they both wanted.

They'd tried a just-starting-to-date relationship. They'd tried being an engaged couple. They'd tried hot, no holds barred and no strings.

And against all good reason, she wanted to know what it would be like with Keith if they were in love. If birth control wasn't so critical... But it *was* critical, because she couldn't trust him with anything other than her body. It didn't matter if he cared about her or had other interests besides sex, because she couldn't let him hurt her again.

She sighed as she mounted the stairs to her room, dripping water and despondency all over the place. Maybe no strings got easier. She'd have to try harder to not care that Keith's expression had resembled granite when he'd watched her leave.

Cara Chandler-Harris Designs would never walk out on her, never disappoint her. What did she need with a man long-term anyway?

Keith let Cara go and spent the night watching the weather radar on an endless loop. It mirrored the chaos in his head perfectly.

Too restless to sleep, he prowled around the suite looking for something to punch, because he feared that was the only way he'd expel the black mood he'd fallen into when Cara had waltzed out the door.

It was for the best. She was absolutely right. They weren't in a relationship. Sleepovers weren't a good idea. When the storm passed, Keith would be overloaded with revised expo plans and Cara would be in the way. She knew that, had made herself scarce, and he should completely respect and appreciate it.

But all he could think about was how he'd yearned to slide into sleep with her sated body nestled against his, breathing in sync.

Disgusted and furious for no reason, he took a long shower and forced himself to crawl into bed, where he listened to the wind howl and caught snatches of shut-eye, only to bolt awake because he'd dreamed Cara had come back, blubbering apologies and begging him to let her stay. But it was only the crack of branches outside or the tap of rain against the window that, in his delirium, he'd mistaken for her.

Dawn brought with it an even blacker mood.

Overnight, the storm whirled out into the interior of the Caribbean to wreak havoc with Cuba and Grand Cayman. The resort hadn't lost power, which Regent executives would be quite pleased to note since Keith had insisted on installing top-of-the-line generators and storm-proof wiring.

But the pool resembled tree limb soup with a generous garnish of dirt and leaves. The permanent wedding gazebo was gone—the storm had even ripped away the concrete moorings, then filled the holes with sand. A new one would have to be ordered and reanchored, but obviously better and differently.

The door to the sports equipment shed hung drunkenly from one hinge and the floor sat underneath two inches of water. Fortunately, the kayaks, surfboards and other gear seemed no worse for wear. They were supposed to get wet, after all.

The outdoor bar was weatherproof, or it was supposed to be. Scrapes marred the surface as if the wind had dragged tree limbs across it. The bar would have to be refinished, and the list went on and on. Alice scurried after him as he barked out orders and observations. Eventually, they organized resources and the challenges began to look a little more doable.

Sometime around midmorning, Keith holed up in his office to respond to email. Coffee and a solid plan had improved his mood. When Cara knocked on the open door, he even managed a smile.

"Got a minute?" she asked and leaned on the doorjamb.

He nodded and let the image of Cara's naked body astride his flash through his mind because he wanted to and because it was still powerful. What had started out as a method to make sure she had an amazing experience had somehow morphed into the best sex of his life.

"What's up?" He cleared his throat, though it was pretty useless since the huskiness in his voice was due to the raging erection he'd just given himself with a simple memory.

"I was curious about the expo. What are the plans?"

Dry Cara wasn't any less sexy and alluring than a wet Cara. She appeared well rested, as if sleep had come easily to her, and today's dress hugged the curves he'd eagerly reacquainted himself with last night.

"The airport is scheduled to reopen tomorrow morning. So we'll go on, albeit late." He sat back in his chair and wished they could have had this conversation over breakfast. Because she'd stayed with him overnight. Pathetic. Why was he torturing himself with fanciful scenarios? "I'm sending out the revised schedule to all the expo guests and vendors now. You're on the email distribution list."

"The resort doesn't seem too worse for wear. Have you got a good handle on the cleanup?"

He shrugged. "Elena's got it. She's corralling the

groundskeepers as we speak and we'll have to adjust a few of the events. But we've got a promising start."

"That's good to hear." Cara flowed across the threshold and shut the door behind her with a wicked gleam in her eye. "Hope you'll pardon the interruption then."

Before he could get a word in edgewise, she rounded the desk and climbed into his lap.

Hungrily, she fused her lips to his and kissed him open-mouthed, tongue sliding against his. Rough and wild, she savored him and he groaned under her commanding offensive.

His body instantly responded, spreading heat and fire outward from his already primed erection to encompass every organ. Her fingers worked his buttons clumsily until she apparently gave up and ripped the fabric wide to slide her hands along his torso, around the sides and up his back. Everything she touched leaped under her palms, crackling with energy.

Then she dipped into his pants to curve his shaft into her fisted hand. He pulsed and nearly lost complete control.

"Wait," he bit out. "I…wasn't expecting you and—"

"It's okay." She pulled a wrapped condom from inside her bra. "A gift from Meredith."

Breath he hadn't realized he'd been holding whooshed out. Thankfully, Cara got the necessity of being careful. No ties this time. "I really, really like your sister."

Cara grinned. "I'll tell her you said so. Later. I want you to take me right here on your desk. Now," she commanded.

Sweeter words had never been spoken. Quickly, he stood with Cara in his arms and situated her on the desk, thighs spread wide. He stepped between them and yanked her dress and bra down in one motion. Her gorgeous breasts spilled free and he shoved one between his teeth.

She thrust against his mouth, moaning, and he shut his eyes at the perfection of her taste.

"I want you naked," she rasped, and her lithe fingers undid his pants, dropping them to the floor. Her hand closed around him for the second time but nothing hindered her movement, and his breath hitched as she stroked him.

This hot little morning quickie was about to be very over if she kept doing that.

To distract her, he stripped off her dress and threw it... somewhere and then she was spread out on his desk wearing nothing at all, so achingly beautiful it hurt his chest to look at her.

I need you. Right now. Later. Tomorrow. Maybe longer than that.

His fingers shook as he rolled on the condom. From need. From emotions he couldn't name. From the sheer desire this woman evoked. He bent one of her legs to open her farther but she smiled wickedly and shook her head.

"Not like this." She flipped over on her stomach, arching her back and glancing over her shoulder at him like a naughty fantasy come to life. "Like this."

Legs spread wide in invitation, she jiggled her rear. His eyelids slammed closed involuntarily and he forced them open because no way was he missing a moment of this visual delight.

"Keith, hurry. Take me now and make me come like you did last night."

Groaning, he slid into her slowly, relishing the tight heat. But she was having none of that. Impatiently, she rolled her hips, drawing him deeper, and her little cries inflamed him with urgency.

Gripping her hips, he filled her again and again until she went rigid and then convulsed around him, squeezing a shattering climax from the depths of his soul.

His midsection contracted as he emptied himself, leaving nothing behind. Almost unable to stand, he braced his arms against the desk, one on each side of the amazing woman before him. Cheek to the blotter, she closed her eyes and let a blissful, smug smile bloom.

She was thoroughly enjoying the liberties he'd insisted she take. Good. He was, too.

It hit him like a two-by-four to the head—their affair wasn't so great this time around just because she was so hot and ready and taking charge, but because they were coming together as equals. He'd never had that before.

When he thought he could move without collapsing to the floor in a jellified heap, he bent forward and laid his lips against her temple in a long kiss. "Maybe next time we'll make it to the bed."

I want you close to me while you dream.

"Been there, done that. No thanks. Next on my list is the hot tub out on your balcony."

Disappointment flared but he shoved it back. He was getting exactly what he'd asked for—what was there to be disappointed about?

"Done. Come by tonight." The last thing he needed was to spend another sleepless night after Cara left, but he was apparently incapable of saying no.

He helped Cara get dressed and drew on his ruined shirt. She pecked him on the cheek in what he assumed was good-bye and then dived in for a long, lingering kiss full of sensual promise that he couldn't have stepped away from if a category five hurricane hit.

Who could blame him for spitting out yes after yes? This new Cara blew his mind, in so many ways. And the more he tried to convince himself it was strictly sexual, the less he believed it.

This was a dangerous game to be playing in the midst of the rescheduled expo. Perhaps he should focus on that and not on this impossible dynamic between them. But as Cara's sexy backside disappeared through the door and

Keith contemplated how he'd get past Alice with the buttons hanging by threads from his shirt, he had a pretty good idea a hot tub was in his future.

Nine

The promised email was indeed in Cara's inbox when she returned to her room from Keith's office, not at all ashamed to have just experienced an amazing orgasm on the boss's desk with his staff milling around outside the door.

Cornering him in his lair had been the most daring thing she'd ever done. But she knew he wouldn't have shoved her out the door. It was part of what made this fling so great—she didn't have to wonder where she stood with Keith. Didn't have to worry he'd leave her again because she planned to ensure this relationship stayed fun and non-permanent, as he'd specified.

It was perfect.

And he'd never find out she'd cried herself to sleep last night, longing for it not to feel as if she'd sold her soul to the devil for a company with her name on it and an earth-shattering carnal affair with someone she'd probably never see again after the expo finished.

The expo's new schedule called for the bridal fashion

show on the second day, which was perfect. She and Meredith would be able to make the final alterations today and tomorrow, no problem…assuming Cara stayed out of Keith's office, that was.

Humming to cover a tightness in her throat she couldn't explain, Cara gathered the models and Meredith to go over the revised schedule for the next couple of days. She answered the understandable questions from the girls about accommodations and rescheduled return flights—Regent was footing the bill for any and all additional fees, a classy move that as a business owner without an unlimited expense fund, Cara appreciated.

Since she did have a business to run and her return to the States had been delayed, Cara sent the models off to relax and assigned Meredith the task of assessing the beach pavilion. If it had been damaged, they'd need a venue change or, barring that, an understanding of what might need to be adjusted in the fashion show itself.

Then she spent a much-needed hour going through some accounting paperwork and paying a few bills. While she was online, an email popped into her inbox containing messages sent to her via the contact form on her website.

Two requests for more information. Cara picked up her cell phone immediately and dialed the first potential customer. The bride-to-be answered, a rarity as she usually had to play phone tag for a few days. Cara spent several minutes chatting with the woman about her upcoming wedding, hoping to put Yvette, the prospective customer, at ease.

This was one of her favorite parts of being a dress designer. The brides were always so eager to talk to *anyone* about what was sure to be the best day of their lives and Cara loved to hear every last detail, especially because she got a good, clear sense of what kind of person the woman was. It helped her visualize the perfect dress. Plus, Cara loved weddings period.

"The theme of your wedding sounds almost ethereal," Cara commented after several minutes of prodding Yvette about the minutest details, even down to the favors. "I see you as the star of your own fairy tale, with a long train, lace bodice and sweetheart neckline. Stark white because you'll want to stand out against the off-white lilies."

Yvette sighed happily. "That sounds lovely. I knew you were the right one to create my dress when I saw that all your designs had princess names."

Cara smiled at Yvette's enthusiasm. "Was there a particular dress you liked in the online portfolio?"

Despite having nailed the high-level specifics a moment ago, much more went into the design than the train and color. They'd work through the details for several weeks before Cara picked up her shears.

"All of them. But I want something no one else has. A one-of-a-kind exclusive."

"Absolutely. That's no problem." Exclusive dresses took longer because Cara didn't have a set pattern, but any bride who asked for one never minded the wait. Or the cost.

True love paid the bills, but brides who wanted to keep up with other Houston brides put Cara in the black very early on.

Cara asked a few more follow-up questions and verified Yvette's email address in order to send design mockups once Cara created them. She ended the call and realized she hadn't once thought about her own halted wedding, nor felt the accompanying tug of sadness.

That was a vast improvement over the majority of the other calls she'd conducted in the course of the past eighteen months. It was a small triumph and she reveled in it for a moment.

She'd moved past it, once and for all. This business was hers and no one could take it away. Oddly, Keith had helped her begin viewing herself as a businesswoman, independent and in charge of her destiny. If she hadn't splashed head-first into this fling with him, no plan, no pressure, would she have gotten to this place?

It was a very interesting thought. Apparently Meredith was far smarter about matters of the heart than Cara had credited.

The second request for information listed a man's name as the contact—Nick Anderson. Interesting. Cara dialed the referenced phone number, wondering if she'd be discussing a bride's dress with the groom instead. There was always the unlikely possibility of one of her dresses ending up in a drag-queen revue. Either would be okay as long as the check cleared and her name was spelled right on any recommendations.

The call connected. "Ever After. Nick Anderson speaking."

Cara's tongue went numb. Ever After? As in the boutique retail outlet specializing in high-end wedding dresses—*that* Ever After?

"Um." Cara cleared her throat. "This is Cara Chandler-Harris. I'm a wedding dress designer. You requested that I contact you through my website."

"Yes, I did." His voice warmed. "That was fast. I only did so a couple of hours ago. I'm unexpectedly planning to be at the Regent Resorts Bridal Expo in Grace Bay tomorrow and hoped to meet with you. Are you still participating?"

"I… Yes, of course. I'm already here actually."

"Great. The storm delay caused a shuffle on our end, which is why I'm now attending, so I thought I'd verify."

"Right." Cara had been reduced to monosyllables. Not an auspicious start to…whatever this was. "What is the purpose of the meeting, if I may ask?"

"Well, it's a little preliminary, but our focus at Ever After is changing. We'd like to discuss the possibility of featuring your dresses in our stores. I saw your name on the vendor list for the Expo and since I'd never heard of you, I looked up your work. I'm very impressed."

The phone slipped from Cara's hand and she scrambled to pick it up. "Thank you," she squawked, her heart galloping a mile a minute.

Tropical storm Mark's trajectory over the island had proved to be a blessing in disguise.

"Seems like fate that we'll be in the same place this week. I hope you'll be able to give me a few minutes of your time."

"I wouldn't miss it."

Cara ended the call and sat there, dazed, for a moment. Then she leaped to her feet.

Keith. She had to tell him.

She couldn't wait to see that killer smile bloom when she announced the news. Oh, sure, the deal with Ever After could fall through, but still. Someone with real clout in the wedding industry praised her designs and wanted to meet with her. As a potential business partner.

The meeting alone made Cara Chandler-Harris Designs real in a way that she hadn't experienced yet. Up until now, it had almost felt like a hobby that happened to net her some cash and afforded her a fun way to do it. But Ever After Boutiques was the big time, exactly the kind of attention she'd hoped to attract by participating in the expo.

Keith would congratulate her and say he was proud. Then he'd tell her it was sexy that she'd made a career out of her design business.

Laughing like a loon, she dashed through the pool area, nearly running smack into Meredith.

"Whoa." Her sister put up her hands, tottering back on her stilettos until she regained her balance. "Where's the fire?"

"Oh, I have the best news." Breathless, she started to

skirt Meredith, hoping Keith was still in his office. Okay, that was probably not a very good locale for a conversation, actually…

"Well?" With a cheeky grin, Meredith jammed a hand on her hip. And waited.

Eyes wide, Cara stared at her. "Well, what?"

"Don't make me beg. What is it?"

It finally dawned on her. Meredith thought Cara had been looking for *her* to share the news. "Oh. I was actually on my way—"

She swallowed the rest before she admitted out loud that she'd wanted to share this triumph with Keith first. Before her sister, who was also her best friend. And her assistant. "Never mind."

"Never mind you're not going to tell me? That's not fair. You got me all excited for nothing."

Cara rolled her eyes. "It's not that big of a deal," she lied. The last thing she wanted was to hurt her sister's feelings. "I just got word of a potential proposition for my dresses that I need to discuss with Keith. Because he offered to advise me on my business plan."

That last part may have come out a little too rushed, but it *was* true. And it was better than admitting she'd never even once thought of telling Meredith.

"Uh-huh." A knowing light glinted in Meredith's gaze. "You've got it bad, sister."

The joy of having someone who could read her so well. Cara sighed. "I do not."

That was such a lie she couldn't even keep a straight face as she delivered it.

As wake-up calls went, it was not pleasant. When exactly had she fallen off the sex-and-nothing-else wagon?

Well, she should climb back on, stat.

Hooking arms with Meredith, she reversed course and returned with her sister to their room, chatting up the call with Nick Anderson. Keith would never find out she'd accidentally started thinking of him as someone to share things with.

She deliberately stayed away from Keith the rest of the day. Fortuitous, since she made significant progress on the critical tasks for the fashion show in two days. She also got a lot of practice at squelching the ache inside that she feared meant she missed Keith.

At nine o'clock, the expected text message from the man in question arrived, inviting her to his room. Period. No further explanation, as if he knew she'd come running when he called.

Yeah, so he was correct and sticking her tongue out at the phone didn't make the fact that she'd been sitting here yearning to see him any less true.

Cara borrowed Meredith's bikini, which roughly resembled three postage stamps attached with string, figuring she wouldn't have it on longer than about five minutes, and belted a trench coat over it.

Keith tossed his head back against the fiberglass edge of the hot tub, eyes closed as he struggled to drag oxygen into his starved lungs. Cara splashed to her own recovery spot a few feet away, likely as depleted as he was.

The value of high-powered water jets and a daring spirit could not be exaggerated.

"You're amazing," he murmured without opening his eyes. "I didn't really think you'd go for that last suggestion."

"That'll teach you to bluff," she said, her voice low and seductive with a ragged edge that spoke to how vigorously she'd proved that particular point.

"I wasn't bluffing. Just really, really hopeful." And he'd been really, really rewarded.

More splashing alerted him that Cara was on the move.

He forced an eye open to glimpse her climbing out of the hot tub. "Where are you going? We just got started."

Why was she always so eager to disappear? Was his company that objectionable when he wasn't naked?

She chuckled. "I think twice was enough for tonight. Busy day tomorrow."

"Wait." He captured her hand before she could take another step and lost his train of thought for a moment. Water rolled from her bare body, running from her hair in long trails down her torso. One drop hung from a pert nipple, begging for his tongue, and he hardened all over again.

Simply looking at her hurt, way down on the inside where it couldn't be salved.

He should let her leave. The expo would begin in the morning and Regent executives would be on the property before nine. Everything had to go off without a hitch, and his attention to the minutest detail couldn't be more critical.

"Stay and have a drink instead. One glass of wine. You'll sleep better, I promise."

Don't leave. Not this time. If he could only put his finger on why it mattered so much to him, *he'd* sure sleep a lot better.

"That's not what we're doing here. Right?" A line appeared between her eyebrows as she pulled her hand from his. "That's what you said. No pressure, no relationship."

"Oh, come on." He flashed a quick grin, though it was a little forced. Somehow her constant and immediate exits seemed to be driven from a mixed-up view of his expectations. "No pressure isn't the same as no conversation. We can hang out and talk. That's part of what's making sex so great between us, don't you think? All the nonnaked time we've had thus far?"

In what world did it make sense that he was arguing with her about staying for a *drink* instead of trying to sweet-talk her clothes off? But here they were, in the alternate uni-

verse of Grace Bay, where Cara eagerly bared her body—
which he fully appreciated—but balked at anything else.

"I do like your wine." Indecision rippled across her expression. "One drink?"

"Or two. Who's counting?"

"I don't have any clothes."

As if that was a good argument against it. But his still-
scrambled brain couldn't latch on to a good enough argument for it.

Stay. Because you want to. Because you want more.

But what if he reached out and she slammed him down?
Or worse, thought "more" was code for a white picket fence
and another diamond ring?

A drink was all he could reasonably offer until…what?
He had no idea, but he did know he couldn't let her go this
time.

Muscles protesting, he climbed to his feet and exited the
hot tub to wrap her in a giant towel before she could flee
again. "Let me dry you off and you can borrow a shirt. Stop
being difficult and relax."

She stood still while he swiped her radiant skin with the
terry cloth, but contrary to what he'd expected, she didn't
avert her eyes. Oh no, she watched him unashamedly, gaze
fastened squarely on the erection he couldn't hide.

He should have gotten dressed first, obviously, if he really meant to have a drink, but this was one test of wills
he did not intend to lose.

Finally, he got her dry and clad in one of his white
button-downs, which did not decrease her attractiveness
quotient in the slightest. But he bit his tongue, donned his
own clothes and poured her a glass of wine.

One glance at his phone was enough—twenty text
messages and an ungodly number of emails. Pointedly, he
switched it off. What could ten more minutes of being in-
communicado hurt?

She swallowed a hefty third of her wine as if intending to set the record for fastest drink between lovers.

Or she was trying to dull her senses to make it easier to spend time with him?

"I don't know how to do this," she blurted out before he'd even gotten comfortably settled next to her on the love seat.

He contemplated whether he should pretend to misunderstand or deflect with a joke. The climate felt precarious, as if he'd frighten her away if he messed up and said the wrong thing. "If it makes you feel better, I'm not sure either."

Nothing about this rekindled affair felt the same as it had the first time. Or as he'd expected it to be the second time. He'd spent his adulthood fending off money-grubbing women who cared only about the lavish lifestyle he could provide them, and somewhere along the way forgot that some people actually got something out of relationships. Companionship, maybe.

"Why does it have to be so hard?" Her fingers gripped the stem of her wineglass in what looked like a fair attempt to break it in half. "I can't find the middle ground. This is supposed to be an unemotional pleasure romp, right?"

Something rasped in her voice, a hint of sentiment that pinged inside him strangely. "You mean it's not?"

Say no. Please say something that can help me make sense of all this.

She met his gaze unflinchingly, and he couldn't break eye contact. Didn't want to. God, why was she so heartbreakingly beautiful in his shirt and with her damp hair?

"No," she whispered. "I'm afraid I'm not one of those girls who can love 'em and leave 'em."

"Well, that's easily fixed." He laughed, a little awed at how tender it came out. He wouldn't call *tender* a particular skill of his. "Don't leave."

Now, how hard was that? He should have opened with it.

"Actually, I was thinking about axing the 'love' part."

Keith went cold and then hot. No, that was definitely ice sliding down his spine. *That* was why he hadn't bared his soul from the outset. None of this had a handy spreadsheet for reference or a concrete result set.

"Now, that would be a downright shame. Reconsider."

When he picked up her hand and held it between his, she didn't pull away this time, and he greedily latched on to the small sign that he hadn't irrevocably messed up yet.

"What would you have me do, Keith?" she implored him. "I'm trying to stick to the rules, but it turns out I can't sleep with you and then forget about you the rest of the day."

She thought about him? That pleased him enormously. "I don't see what's wrong with that."

Misery tugged her mouth downward, and that hurt in a whole different way.

"I got some news today. Really good news. I wanted to share it with you."

The long pause stretched.

"But you didn't," he prompted and started to get an inkling of what was troubling her. "Is that what this is all about? You're afraid I'll feel like you're pressuring me if you tell me personal things?"

In the course of fending off women he felt nothing for other than a mild sense of affection, he'd also forgotten that relationships were about giving another person something, too. A warm shoulder. Support. Encouragement.

If he could do that with anyone, it would be with this new Cara who no longer wanted to be Mrs. Someone. The aspiring trophy wife of two years ago had completely vanished.

The thought of being there for her beyond the expo wasn't as scary as he might have supposed. Still no pressure or wedding bells. But *something*. They could define it as they went along.

"It wasn't even personal news. It was about my design business."

This was like pulling teeth without anesthesia, and he'd lost track of whom it was hurting the most.

"Cara, look at me." When she complied, eyes swimming with unshed tears, it was more like a full-on evisceration than a simple tooth extraction. "I want you to talk to me. I'm the one who asked you to stay. I'm the one who wants—"

"You're not listening to me!" And then she did yank her hand from his, tears running angrily down her face. "*I'm* the one feeling pressured. I don't want to stay. *Me*. I don't know how to do this because it's confusing. Sex and intimacy and emotions are all tied together, and what we're doing makes me think I want a relationship. I start to believe in the possibilities. And then I remember."

She remembered that I said no permanent relationship. The blank wasn't difficult to fill.

Lost in her own thoughts, she stared into the empty wineglass cupped in her palms and the silence convicted him.

"I'm sorry."

It was the most freely given apology he'd ever uttered. Because he'd pushed her into a type of relationship she couldn't handle out of pure selfishness. For once, he needed to get his head out of his rear end and pay attention to what this amazing woman wanted from him. Regardless of how uncomfortable it was.

"I know. You already apologized and I'm over it. But it doesn't make everything go away. There are still consequences."

He shook his head. "I already apologized?"

"For leaving me. But that's what it always comes down to. I start to believe and then I remember. I can't trust you."

The bomb exploded in his midsection with a sickening squelch. None of this was about the parameters of their current relationship or lack thereof but about the sins of the past. Sins he couldn't absolve. It was a target he'd missed two years ago and couldn't reverse time to correct.

Where did that leave them?

Ten

Cara shivered and nearly fell off the love seat in shock when Keith crossed to a wicker chest in the corner to retrieve a blanket. Without a word, he covered her with the navy chenille throw and returned to his seat next to her, but with a pointed foot of couch between them.

Contemplatively, he watched her. "What can I do, Cara?"

His voice washed through her, settling some of the swirl this impossible, ridiculous conversation had churned up. "There's nothing to do. It doesn't matter. We were never going to see each other again after the expo. Why does any of this change that?"

"It's not right to leave things this way."

Of course he hadn't argued the point about whether they'd see each other again.

"Because you can't stand to lose the bed-buddy benefits?" she shot back.

Ha. They hadn't made it anywhere near the bed. By design. It had become symbolic for her. No bed equaled no relationship.

"Because I hurt you," he responded quietly.

Sighing, she tucked her feet up under the blanket, but it didn't provide nearly the barrier she needed against the tension she'd foolishly introduced first by staying, and second, by not keeping her stupid mouth shut. She should have downed a glass of Keith's expensive wine and kissed him goodbye fifteen minutes ago, as she'd planned.

"Yeah. Well, there's no way around that. That's the point. I forgave you for hurting me, but I can't forget. Then you come around and you're all strong and gorgeous and telling me you see me as a success and that I'm sexier for it. We make love and I *do* forget. I hate it."

"So, here's a thought. You're not really over it," he suggested and threaded his fingers through her hair to stroke her temple, as if they were a couple who touched each other affectionately. "Let's work on that."

Together? She glanced at him, too surprised by the offer to even address the affectionate part. "What, like it's a project?"

"It's a problem. This is how I deal with problems. Head-on."

The smirk popped onto her face before she could stop it. "Not always. In my experience, you take off. It's easier to not deal with it."

To his credit, he waited without comment for her to fully process what had automatically come out of her mouth. The silence stretched, deafening her, and she had to fill it. "Okay, yeah. I get it. You're here now and that was a long time ago."

When had he become someone who stayed? She'd been too busy being the one to leave to notice.

"I'm here now," he repeated. "It's a do-over."

"But we can't really do it over, Keith. I've lost so much

in the last two years, things I can't get back. And right, wrong or otherwise, inside where I can't erase it, your name is all over it."

Her voice broke and she fought back the brimming anguish that seemed to bubble up from nowhere, but honestly, it was always there just behind her rib cage, lurking. Waiting for her to stop pushing it away.

God, he was right. She wasn't really over what had happened. Cara Chandler-Harris Designs had been a form of therapy and it had been a godsend, but running her own business hadn't fixed anything. Bandaged it more than anything, and ripping off the haphazardly applied strip had left a raw, gaping wound.

Stiffening, he sighed and rubbed the back of his neck. "I thought we talked about this and you agreed we were better off not getting married."

"Yes!" she snapped. "Because I can't trust you. Because you left me to deal with everything by myself. I'm thrilled we didn't get married if that's the kind of man you are."

He didn't flinch and God Almighty she didn't want to respect him for taking whatever she dished out. But it happened all the same.

"Isn't that the point of not being over it?" he asked more gently than she would have thought him capable of. "Deep down, you're still mad because I walked away from our wedding."

Is *that* what he thought she wasn't over? Agape, she stared at him for a moment, but he didn't seem to catch how very far off base he'd veered.

"Are you that dense? I lost a *baby*, Keith. My future child. Then you walked away. I was expecting to grieve together. To process, with you holding my hand and telling me everything was going to be okay."

"Cara... I..." A dark shadow passed through his expression and he clamped his lips into a thin line. Without a word, he slid his palm into hers, squeezing tight. Painfully tight, but she barely registered the pain when it couldn't compete with the ache in her chest.

He'd reached out. Finally.

Eyes closed, he sat frozen, anguish playing across his features. Speechless. Keith's silver tongue had deserted him, and it touched her more profoundly than anything else he could have done or said.

This was clearly difficult for him. But he was here and it encouraged her to go on, to spill the blackness inside that had become frighteningly real, very fast.

"The pregnancy was an accident. But I wanted that baby," she began slowly, sorting her thoughts as they came to her. "Then it was gone. Well, not really gone. They don't tell you that. Instead of going to Aruba on our honeymoon, I got to have a D & C."

"What is that?"

"It's...not something I care to relive." She shuddered and Keith pulled the blanket up higher around her shoulders with his free hand. "Look it up later if you think you can handle it."

With a small growl of warning, Keith tipped her chin up to force her to look him in the eye. "You handled it. By yourself. I'd like to think I'm at least as strong as you. Tell me. I want to know what happened."

The fire in his expression rendered her as speechless as he'd been mere moments ago. A strange flutter in her midsection scared her because it felt a bit like panic. *Panic.* If he'd morphed into a man she could lean on, who wouldn't desert her to deal with the horrors of a miscarriage aftermath by herself, did that mean she could trust him this time?

How would she know?

There was only one way to find out. "I think I need more wine for this."

Instantly, he complied, filling her glass nearly to the brim. And then he listened without interrupting as she told the unvarnished tale of the day before the wedding when she'd felt shuddery and nauseated but assumed it was nerves until the bleeding started. He didn't butt in when she mentioned how Meredith had sat with her through the interminably long wait in the doctor's office until the miscarriage was confirmed.

And then Cara described how she silently carried the knowledge that the pregnancy had terminated through the rehearsal dinner, smiling woodenly while friends and family toasted the couple, but slowly fading on the inside. Over the past two years, she'd often wondered if he'd picked up on the vibe because he'd been so quiet that night.

But in retrospect, he'd probably been dreading the ceremony and mentally preparing himself to enter into a union with a woman he didn't want to marry.

In the cold light of the current conversation, she realized he had been there for her in the simple fact of being willing to marry her. Had she failed to give him enough credit for that? It couldn't have been an easy decision to make or to carry out.

Coupled with his solid presence tonight, she just didn't know what to make of the still-present flutter that felt a lot less like panic now and more like anticipation.

Over half of her glass of wine remained, but she abbreviated the story of the day after the abandoned wedding. Some details were too much to repeat, but judging by the increased pressure on her hand and the bleakness in Keith's gaze, she'd given him enough of an idea what happened during a D & C to make the point.

When she stopped talking, Keith pulled her against his chest and held her fiercely, wordlessly. But no words were necessary to absorb the strength he'd offered her.

The cleansing meant everything to her.

* * *

Keith held Cara for as long as she let him and when she pulled away, it seemed as good a time as any to switch to scotch. Because he sorely needed something stout to blunt the seething mess in his stomach.

When he'd convinced her to stay, he'd envisioned a slow, languorous dive into the kind of lovemaking they'd thus far been unable to indulge in due to Cara's vanishing acts. That was the "more" he'd hoped for, not gut-wrenching emotional knots he had no idea how to untie.

The small bar in the corner of his suite provided a good cover for his shaking hands. Cara hadn't pulled many punches, that was for sure. On the second try, he clunked ice into the highball and splashed amber liquor over it, then took a healthy swallow.

Fortified, he turned back to Cara and leaned a hip against the bar, hoping it didn't look as if he was holding himself up.

He'd started this descent the moment he spied Cara across the room at the Dragonfly back in Houston. Now he had to see it through with no map and a broad field of quicksand in all directions.

"I don't know how to do this part either," he confessed.

Mostly because he had no idea what he was trying to hit. There were no goals, no tangible checklists or a specific solution to a particular problem. He had no skill set for relationships or any training, which was one of the many reasons he tried to avoid them.

Cara, as always, had turned that upside down. No matter what kind of parameters he put around their island fling, the emotional depths had been set up long ago and couldn't be sidestepped.

Besides, he owed her for messing up two years ago, owed her for jumping into this rekindled affair willingly and without censor, and most of all, he owed her for her unconditional forgiveness.

"I'm not sitting over here with a scorecard," she said. "I'd be the last person to tell you if you were doing it wrong."

He poured a second glass of scotch and opted to return to the couch. Cara's small smile bolstered him. Not a lot but enough. "I… Thank you for telling me about the miscarriage."

"Really?" She pursed her lips in confusion. "I can't honestly say what I was expecting your reaction to be, but that was not it."

He couldn't have said what his reaction should be either. But he had to man up and admit the truth. Or at least the part he could actually verbalize.

"I spent two years completely unaware you'd really been pregnant. And I've spent the last few days thinking about how I messed up." And working through the guilt. "I spent zero time thinking about how the miscarriage happened, what you must have gone through. I'm sorry."

Her strength astounded him. While he'd been admiring her business savvy and letting her cross his eyes with her new adventurous spirit, she'd actually been quietly amazing from the beginning. In his haste to escape the noose he'd created for himself, he'd missed it.

And in his haste to get her to stay tonight, he'd created an impossible internal quagmire. While processing her surprisingly calm recitation of the events, one thing had clearly risen to the surface—she'd been pregnant with a child. *His* child.

It had never been real before.

There in the low light of the temporary suite where he'd been staying for the duration of a temporary job, where he'd made love to a woman under the guise of a temporary affair, the baby became real—and just as temporary.

Something he could describe only as sadness filled him,

hitching his lungs. For the first time in his life, he mourned the necessity of temporary.

"It's okay." Her hand on his thigh was warm and reassuring. "You've had a lot to process. And you're here now. That means a lot to me."

Yes, he was here. But he sensed she needed so much more than his largely mute presence. How much longer would she put up with his inability to say the right words, to reach out and express his own feelings?

This had gotten far too complicated and he had no solution.

"Cara…" *I can't do this.*

The silence stretched and grew painful. He shifted uncomfortably, a little sick with the discovery that he wished he could be the man she deserved—but not only was he not, he couldn't be. Furthermore, she didn't trust him and he didn't blame her. What were they really doing here but resolving her issues so she could say goodbye with a clear conscience?

"I get that this is hard for you, Keith." Her espresso-colored eyes tracked his, carrying no condemnation, no expectation. Just understanding.

It nearly undid him.

"Do you really?" It came out all wrong, accusatory and harsh, but he couldn't have changed it, not with all the ups and downs and the ache at the back of his throat.

He looked away.

"Yes," she answered calmly. "I may not have known you very well back in Houston, but the reason for that is because you never let me in. I mean, I know that you grew up on Long Island and your dad worked on Wall Street. You went to Penn State and got a degree in international business. But those are just surface-level things by intention. It's not a mystery to me that you're the strong, silent type when it comes to intimacy."

She cupped his jaw and guided his face up to meet her gaze.

"It's okay," she repeated. "I meant what I said. You're here and that's enough. I'm not asking you to bare your soul."

Stricken, he stared at her, falling into her empathy with an ocean of relief swimming in his chest. She was giving him a pass and he was pathetically grateful enough to take it.

And then she sealed it with a soft kiss. Her lips rested on his and there was nothing but pure compassion in it.

"Come with me," she instructed and stood, holding out her hand.

He took it, thoroughly intrigued when she led him to the bedroom. There, she undressed him carefully and threw back the covers on the king-size bed he'd slept in alone since arriving in Grace Bay.

"We've got a long day tomorrow and we need to get some sleep." She patted the mattress. "Lie down."

She was putting him to bed. It nearly made him laugh, but it caught on the lump in his throat. "Yes, ma'am."

She was about to leave. Again.

The moment he slid under the sheet, she unbuttoned the borrowed shirt and dropped it to the floor. And then joined him, burrowing under the covers to snuggle up next to him, warm and comfortable.

"You're staying?" he asked needlessly, but in his surprise, thought it was worth the clarification.

"This is where you are," she explained simply and laid her head against his shoulder as if she belonged there. "I want to be with you. Turn off the lamp and stop talking."

But once it was dark, suddenly he couldn't shut off the swirl of unexpressed commotion in his head. The longer he stayed silent, the worse it grew.

"You know why I don't babble on about all my inner-most thoughts, right?" he blurted out.

"You're a guy," Cara responded sleepily and kissed his throat.

Yes, but…it was a flimsy excuse and his DNA wasn't the real reason. Normally, he'd let it go at that but she'd been so accepting, so easy to be with. So forthcoming about her own struggles. Somehow it loosened his vocal cords. "It's because of my mother."

"Isn't it always?"

He laughed and the heaviness inside melted away. "Yeah. It wasn't okay to talk about how something made me feel. She would cut me off, change the subject. Mitchells don't talk to each other about anything except money. It's what makes the Mitchell world go 'round. Money is a tangible reward for your effort and it's the only thing that lasts."

According to George and Judith Mitchell, anyway.

"Is that how you feel about money, too?"

"Money is a by-product of success. I like the things it buys but I get more satisfaction out of seeing what I've done with this property than seeing my bank balance grow. That's the difference between my father and me. His success was measured in zeroes. It was almost like play money to him. So what if he lost a million or so dollars of a customer's money? He got a commission regardless." Unrepentant anger swept up from Keith's gut to inflame his chest. "He was so furious I didn't want to follow in his footsteps. But I didn't want money to rule me."

And he didn't want a trophy wife either, one who cared only about money, cared only about Keith's ability to earn it. Like his mother. If Keith decided to chuck it all to go live in a fishing village in the Philippines, he could and no grasping, money-grubbing woman would ever stand in his way.

In talking this through, he got the one thing he'd always

wanted from his mother but never received—someone to simply listen to him. His arms tightened around Cara and she slipped one sexy leg between his, but instead of feeling like an invitation to physical intimacy, it was all about growing closer emotionally.

He kissed her forehead. "That was probably more than you wanted to know."

"On the contrary," she corrected softly, "it was exactly what I wanted to know. I like you, Keith Mitchell. Now that I've glimpsed who you really are inside."

His lips curled up in a genuine gratified smile. She'd gotten him to share without intruding into an area he wasn't comfortable with. It was nice. "I like you, too."

Drifting in the silence, he blessed the storm that had brought them together.

The morning dawned through the floor-to-ceiling glass, nearly blinding Keith. So he shut his eyes and held the sleeping woman still tangled around him as if she couldn't get close enough.

Her firm breasts were pressed against his side, nipples rubbing his skin with every breath he took. And the more they rubbed, the faster his lungs pumped. Last night had been about something other than sex, and that had been great. A totally different experience from any he'd ever had with a woman.

But this morning, all bets were off.

They were in bed—naked—and he wanted to connect with Cara more than he wanted his heart to beat. She'd unlocked all sorts of raw, primal emotions inside and he wanted to grab on to them, before they faded.

Nudging her legs apart, he slid his thigh between them, tight against her sex. He tipped up her chin and kissed her awake. She arched against him languidly and kissed him back, slow and deep.

He was so hot and hard and ready for her, he couldn't wait. Poised at the entrance to heaven, he groaned, savoring the sensations, contemplating how slow he could reasonably take this before he came apart.

Suddenly, she broke the kiss and angled her body away from his. "Condom," she murmured.

The reminder shocked him. How could he have almost forgotten? Hadn't they both gone through enough anguish from the first pregnancy? They didn't need another one.

So why was he thinking about what it might be like if they weren't worried about an accidental pregnancy? If they had the kind of relationship where birth control wasn't a consideration?

What was he *doing* to himself? That was crazy talk, and a little misplaced sadness that nothing in his life lasted longer than a few weeks was not a good enough reason to go off the deep end.

He fumbled around on the nightstand until he found a foil packet and rolled on the barrier quickly. Satisfied, she wiggled back into place and made short work of setting off fireworks behind his eyes.

As he sank into her, spiraling into oblivion, the rawness inside blossomed into something huge and real and so perfect, there should be a whole aisle at the greeting card store devoted to it.

He just wished he knew what the aisle would be labeled. Happy Temporary Fling Day didn't have the right ring.

Finally, they heaved from bed at half past seven, a good hour later than he should have gotten up. But he wouldn't have missed that round of good-morning sex for any price. Saucily, Cara paraded around in his unbuttoned shirt and he almost blurted out an invitation to take a real vacation with him after the expo—with limited luggage, a lot of water and no cell phone.

But he didn't. If things went well, they'd both be very busy very shortly.

Before he lost his mind, he shooed her out the door with a kiss and a heartfelt "See you later." She took half a step and his hand shot out to snag hers before she could fully leave. "Stay with me again tonight."

Surprise danced around in her expression but she nodded. "Okay."

Her concession gave him perma-grin. She'd stayed last night and it had ended up being unexpectedly amazing. Maybe he could do "more" after all. Maybe they both could.

Checking his text messages wiped the smile from his face in an instant. Elena had sent him a list of items that needed attention before nine o'clock, the witching hour. Regent executives would be arriving from the airport on the dot and the resort was not ready for prime time.

While he'd been lost in his little bubble with Cara, the show had come to a screeching halt. For crying out loud. Was he the only one around here who could make decisions?

Cursing, he stabbed Elena's number and when she answered, he barked, "Talk to me."

"Where have you been?" she demanded. "I sent you like ten emails and normally you respond within a few minutes. It's like you dropped off the face of the earth."

Close. He'd dropped off the face of the resort and it was unacceptable to have left things hanging. This was his job, his reason for being in Grace Bay. Cara wasn't.

"Give me fifteen minutes and I'll meet you in the lobby. Bring able bodies and sharp minds."

Keith threw himself in the shower and scrubbed all traces of hot tubs, hot honey brunettes and intimacy from his body. He wished he could say the same about his head. Because Cara was firmly in it and no admonishment in existence could remove the memories from his mind.

He crossed the Regent emblem in the lobby in thirteen minutes.

Elena, dressed in a crisp Regent uniform, hair smoothed into a bun, waited by the front desk. Staff buzzed around the lobby, similarly dressed, attending to various duties with a heightened sense of urgency.

Regent Resorts at Grace Bay was open for business.

Keith dived in. Instead of diminishing, the list of problems grew exponentially as he began investigating.

"Pool furniture." He pointed at two uniforms. "Spread it out and make it look like we didn't lose so many pieces in the storm."

They scurried off. Keith grabbed a handful of groundskeepers. "Retrim the palm trees. They still look like they were hit by a tropical storm."

Elena rolled her eyes. "I think the executives are going to have to understand the property *was* just hit by a tropical storm."

"No. They will understand this is the premier wedding destination resort on the planet and tropical storms do not interfere with an engaged couple's plans when they stay at a Regent property."

Keith Mitchell might not control the weather but he controlled his destiny, and it was not going down in flames because he'd stumbled and fallen into the eye of Cara's whirlwind.

He sent the resort's limo to the airport to retrieve the executives and put the fear of God into the rest of the staff. True to his nickname, Mitchell the Missile's heat-seeking radar found even the smallest unearthed issues and addressed them. A general on the battlefield couldn't hold a candle to Keith's natural skill with both organization and delegation.

When the limo rolled to the curb with the executive team inside, the resort was not in the shape it should have been.

But it would be. Better the executive team see the mended seams instead of the expo guests, who would begin arriving at noon.

Keith had three hours to pull off a miracle—and convince Regent's executives to continue their faith in his ability to turn around this disaster in the making. Adrenaline pumped through his body, fueling his blood and making it sing. This was his hour of glory and he'd worked fiendishly for months to earn it.

Ronald Schmidt, the CEO of Regent, emerged first, hand outstretched for Keith to shake.

"Welcome," Keith said to the team at large and spent the next hour as a personal tour guide to Regent's entire C-suite. Simultaneously, he fielded messages from Alice and Elena and responded with a barrage of instructions as they flawlessly walked on water in Keith's stead.

At the end of the tour, Ronald shook his head with a small smile. "I don't know how you did it, Mitchell. This place is indeed the jewel you insisted it could be, even with the added complication of an unanticipated storm. Your reputation is well-founded."

"Thank you, sir." Keith inclined his head and slipped a hand in his pocket to still his yet-again vibrating phone. Interruptions could wait for a couple of minutes, especially if Ronald had more to say.

"I was going to wait until after the expo to discuss the terms of your contract, but it's clear I don't need to. As you know, the continuation clause was contingent on how you performed with this property."

"Yes, I'm aware." Tingling at the base of Keith's spine swept upward and he clamped down on it. This was no time to let euphoria interfere with what might quickly turn into a negotiation over Keith's future.

"You'll have a contract extension in your inbox within two days for the remaining fifteen Caribbean resorts. And let's bump up your rate. A million a property. We can discuss specifics whenever you're ready."

Ronald shook Keith's hand and waved to include the rest of the team. "We're all looking forward to the expo. I'm sure it will be a grand show."

"Unparalleled. I hope you enjoy your stay with Regent Resorts at Grace Bay." Keith motioned to the bellboys standing at attention behind him. "Let us show you to your rooms."

Yet another mark of distinction—treating the men who signed the paycheck of every employee here like guests. The service philosophies Keith and Elena had infused into the staff culture would catapult Regent to the top of the luxury vacation heap.

And Keith had just been granted the opportunity to do it again—fifteen more times.

It was everything he'd dreamed of when he went into consulting. It was the perfect culmination of his effort to make it on his own over the past decade. The perfect job. He could do his thing and move on; no roots, no relationships with employees...or anyone else.

Temporary ruled his life for a reason. It was what he did best. He didn't know how to do anything *but* temporary. He yearned for the next challenge, the next job that would take him someplace new, and balked at the kind of "more" Cara deserved. What could a man like that really offer her?

Nothing. He couldn't ask her to take an extended vacation. Or even a short one. He couldn't be there for her as she needed, emotionally or physically. And he hadn't even been very good at it in the first place, despite the pass she'd given him. If he'd had more practice at developing relationships, or even the skill set to try, that would be one thing. But he preferred being alone because it was easier than figuring out how to tap into an emotional center he probably couldn't ever reach.

It was a good thing he'd planned for their liaison to be finite from the beginning.

A good thing, he repeated, and wished it actually felt that way.

Eleven

Cara watched frisky sandpipers chase each other on the beach and smiled when the lead bird let herself be caught. It was worth it sometimes to slow down long enough to notice something unexpected and wonderful in the one chasing you.

Keith had revealed some pretty spectacular depths over the past few days, climaxing in the midnight soul-baring conversation. She'd had no idea he was capable of such understanding and strength—and maybe he hadn't been the first time. But he certainly was now.

Maybe the events of two years ago, and everything since, needed to happen in order to get them both to a better place. Which wasn't necessarily together. This was supposed to be a burn-off-the-excess-heat fling in the background of their real lives. The expo should be the most significant thing on *both* their minds.

Unfortunately, it wasn't, at least not in her case.

Turning her gaze back to the statuesque models in white

parading down the makeshift runaway, Cara nodded in response to Meredith's question, though she hadn't actually heard it. The original canvas tent pavilion had been dismantled in advance of Tropical Storm Mark, but unfortunately it had been stored in a nonwaterproof shed. It had suffered severe water damage, forcing the fashion show to take place on the beach.

As long as tomorrow's weather mirrored the calm, balmy conditions of today, the show would still be the centerpiece of the expo.

Meredith noted something on her legal pad and shot Cara a smirk. "Do me a favor and smack me if I ever walk around with such a dreamy smile on my face."

"That'll never happen," Cara promised without missing a beat. "Because only Keith could produce such a smile and you can't have him."

Her sister lifted a brow. "Oh my. I thought you were all dopey-faced over the meeting with the Ever After guy and planned to rib you about it mercilessly. But this is a much more fun development."

The meeting with Nick Anderson was slated for tomorrow, after the fashion show, and if all went according to plan, her design business would leap ahead of everything she'd ever hoped for. It *should* have been the reason for a dopey smile. Not that she was agreeing there was anything dopey about her expression.

Cara's cheeks heated. "Shut up. You're the one who encouraged me to get Keith naked. What did you think was going to happen?"

"I thought you were going to achieve some much-needed stress relief." Meredith yelled at one of the models to watch her train and tilted her head toward Cara as if about to impart a secret. "Maybe some closure. I did not think you were going to fall head over heels again for he-who-must-not-be-named."

"Head over heels is a bit of an overstatement." Wasn't it? Just because she'd slept in his bed didn't mean she'd gone off the deep end and started imagining a future where none existed. "He's different this time, that's all."

She wished it was easier to articulate how she felt about Keith. If she could say it to anyone, it would be Meredith, regardless of her sister's inclination to give her grief. But the only certainty in this situation was that Keith still confused her…and she still couldn't imagine trusting him enough to put his engagement ring on her finger again. He'd done very little to regain that trust.

"I think it's you who's different," her sister commented wryly. "I still remember what you said to me after your first date with him. Do you?"

Of course she did. It had come back to haunt her often enough. "I said I was going to marry him."

A premature statement to be sure since she'd only just met him. But he'd been exactly what she wanted in a husband. Successful, handsome, attentive.

Correction. What she'd *thought* she wanted in a husband. The past two years taught her the folly in her wish list. She needed a mate with the ability to stick with her through the bumps, as well as the actual desire to be a husband. Oh, and most critical—she wanted a husband who loved her and one she loved back unquestionably.

"Yep. You were really focused on getting married. Every guy you met got the Husband Test. Your man Mitchell was the first one to pass."

That was uncomfortably true. Had she forced their relationship because of her goals instead of letting their feelings evolve naturally? Her throat tightened.

Of course she had—that's how they'd gotten engaged and almost married without really knowing each other. Or being in love. They'd *both* let the pregnancy cloud their judgment. "Yeah. What's your point?"

"You haven't said a word about getting married in two years," Meredith said quietly. "That's what's different. You seem a lot less fixated on the outcome and more into the experience of the moment. It looks really good on you and in the long run will probably be a lot better for your state of mind. That's all I meant."

Cara mulled that over the rest of the day, studiously avoiding Keith as she'd done yesterday, but for a different reason this time. Yesterday, she'd still been lying to herself about whether she thought of Keith as her lover in every sense of the word. Today she knew it was too late to stop that train—and too impossible to be near him without blurting out everything on her mind.

Her sister's revelations weighed on her heavily. Meredith thought Cara was doing the right thing by falling head over heels into Keith without worrying about whether he'd marry her or not. It was exactly what this affair was supposed to be about.

And on the surface, it was. At least as far as everyone else knew. The problem lay underneath, where Cara had discovered marriage wasn't her ultimate goal after all. She wanted that and more, far more. She wanted that man Keith had been last night when he held her hand as she talked through the difficult aftermath of the miscarriage. She wanted the man who encouraged her to take her pleasure and thought it was sexy that she ran her own business.

She wanted that man to love her. And she feared a rolling stone like Keith would never be capable of that even if she gave him twenty years to get there. This was a short affair, made possible only by these special circumstances.

When Keith texted her that night, she almost didn't go. But she'd missed him and the two brief glimpses she'd gotten of him across the property as he strode off to do some Consulting Wizard task hadn't been enough to sate her.

Plus she couldn't quite get the hot tub off her mind. She should enjoy her fling to the fullest, right?

In the end, she threw on his shirt without any underwear because she liked the feel of it against her bare skin and wore the trench coat over it. A similar look had benefited her greatly last night. But when she got to Keith's room and used the key he'd given her to let herself in, he was hunched over his laptop, an open longneck beer in his left hand as he pecked at the keyboard with his right.

He glanced up but didn't otherwise move from his spot at the table, where it appeared he'd been for some time. "I'm almost finished here. Give me a minute."

The tired smile he aimed in her direction melted the ice she'd scarcely been aware surrounded her heart.

"You look like a man in sore need of a shoulder rub," she said instead of a flirty comment designed to get him away from the computer. Which she had no doubt would have worked but wasn't what he needed.

"I'm in sore need of you, period," he muttered to his laptop screen.

She stood behind him and kneaded the knots in his neck and shoulder muscles while he read a report with multicolored graphs and pie charts.

"That feels amazing." Ditching his beer, Keith groaned and leaned into her fingers, head tipped back slightly. "I didn't know my neck hurt so bad until you started doing that."

His head rested between her breasts and his lashes fluttered closed, and it was so sexy she couldn't help herself. Screw work. "Would you like me to find out what else needs attention? I'd be happy to take inventory. And yes, I mean that exactly the way it sounds," she added in case he was too tired to connect the dots.

He chuckled and reached up to still her hands, taking them into his. Instantly, he twisted her into his lap and his mouth fused to hers before she could squeal. And then she couldn't think over the pounding of her pulse as Keith's mouth drained her of everything but pleasure.

Later, she lay draped across his bed, debating whether he'd fully recovered well enough to seduce him into round two, when he cleared his throat.

"You never told me your good news."

She rolled to face him and bent up a leg casually, as if they often hung out naked and talked.

"I didn't?" she hedged. No, she hadn't. Because the intimacy they'd fallen into last night had been about the past. Necessary to heal, but not necessary to continue their affair. They still weren't a couple who shared stuff.

"Tell me." His earnest caramel gaze latched on to hers and wouldn't let go. "Unless it makes you uncomfortable. I don't want to push you into something you're not ready for."

Her heart stumbled over a beat. *He* didn't want to push *her*?

Was it possible that she was the problem in this equation? That her confusion and refusal to trust him had somehow jeopardized whatever relationship might be possible?

No. The issues were his. He didn't want a relationship and that made it irrelevant to him that she did.

"It's nothing." She shrugged, embarrassed all of a sudden to have even mentioned it, especially since it wasn't a done deal yet. "A buyer for a small boutique in Houston contacted me about selling my dresses in their stores. It's not set in stone. We're in the opening stages of discussion."

"That's great!" His effusiveness set her back teeth on edge for some reason. "I'm proud of you. That's an amazing offer and you should have told me earlier so I could order champagne."

"Save the champagne for when I close the deal," she advised and eyed him. "What's with the overly enthusiastic support?"

"I got some good news of my own today." His expression brightened and he propped his head up on his hand. "Regent extended my contract. It was contingent on the board's assessment of this property and they were so pleased with what they saw today, they offered the extension on the spot. It's two years and fifteen more Caribbean properties."

"That's…great," she said in an unintentional echo of his sentiment. But her chest had slowly frozen over as his meaning sank in and she couldn't come up with anything better.

He nodded, oblivious to her turmoil. "It's what I've been working toward my entire professional life. To show I've made it on my own merits. This is the pinnacle."

Two years. Fifteen properties. She didn't have to be a math genius to put two and two together. Keith wasn't coming back to Houston after the expo. He'd be working his magic on other Regent resorts as he'd done with Grace Bay. And she'd seen enough of his daily responsibilities to fully understand her place in his bed had come about only because of the storm. Without the lull in activity, he'd probably have continued to be too busy to make a move in her direction.

It took every ounce of her upbringing to smile and kiss his cheek. "I'm happy for you. Seems like we're both getting what we've always wanted."

It was a lie—she wanted Keith. Of course she did. All the dodging and convincing herself otherwise, all of it was a lie. And now every last shred of hope she might have gathered at the corners of her heart had been lost.

She'd tried to convince herself Cara Chandler-Harris Designs was enough. It was a business she'd built without her father's money, without any man's help, and it was hers. But it wasn't a substitute for the love of a man, a life partner she could share all the ups and downs with. It wasn't a business she'd built to get over Keith because there hadn't been anything to get over other than disappointment that he hadn't fallen in line with her fierce determination to get married.

And she knew for sure she hadn't been in love with him before because she absolutely was now and there was no comparison.

She wanted Keith but he didn't want her. There was no worse sound in Keith's mind than the clang of wedding bells.

The ache in her heart hurt in a massively different way than it had two years ago. Because she had to let Keith go instead of holding on to him to achieve her own selfish goals.

She'd gotten her wish. This was what being in love with Keith was like and it was the harshest lesson of all—sometimes love felt an awful lot like sacrifice.

Keith cleared his dry throat. He was oversharing again. He felt it in the chaste, emotionless kiss to the cheek she'd bestowed on him, could feel it in her posture, in the atmosphere.

It had started the moment he began talking. She'd slowly withdrawn, as if she wasn't really on board with staying overnight and wished he'd shut up so she could leave, even though she'd agreed this morning to stay.

Why had she said yes if she didn't want to? Disappointment lodged in his esophagus and he couldn't swallow it away. He'd been looking forward to seeing her all day. They'd have some downtime, just the two of them, when he could really savor the professional coup he'd scored today.

He'd been entertaining the notion of asking her if she'd come with him. Just to the next assignment. Just for a couple of days. A week, tops. She could sew some dresses during the day and be waiting when he returned to their room at night. No anxiety-filled, interminably long minutes as he waited for her to respond—or not—to his text message at the end of a stressful day. She'd just be there.

A sharp pull in his chest was bittersweet and he feared he'd fallen into a hole he'd never climb out of. The way he felt about Cara…it wasn't going to go away. It wasn't a slight sense of affection as he'd had the first time. This was something else, something powerful. It might be this elusive thing called love that neither of them could define.

Whatever it was, he was screwing it up.

Stupid to think she'd magically gotten over feeling pressured. The only way that would happen was if he *stopped pressuring* her.

"So why does it sound like you're the opposite of happy?" *Way to drop it, Mitchell.* Obviously he couldn't let it ride.

"I'm…tired. That's all."

So tired she couldn't muster the energy to be a little more inventive with her excuses? "Is it really so difficult to spend time with me that you'd rather be anywhere else but here?"

Her gaze snapped to his. "I wouldn't be here if I didn't want to be."

Frustrated, he vised his pounding temples between his thumb and middle finger. There was no set procedure for this conversation, but he wanted to get the best results. So he kept trying. "Then what's wrong? This contract is a big deal to me. I hoped you'd be a little more…congratulatory."

"Congratulations, Keith. It's an amazing accomplishment." She said it so sincerely, he did a double take.

"Uh, thanks. Why does it feel like I'm in the middle of a fight and you forgot to show up?"

She laughed but it rang a little hollow, ratcheting up the tension. "Because this is not a fight. We're not a couple. Therefore there's nothing to get upset over."

Fine lines around her taut mouth betrayed it as the lie he knew it was. Because he was upset too but he had no idea why. He'd like to chalk it up to stress over the expo, but it was bigger than that. They were having *some* kind of relationship. One that had evolved into something he barely knew what to do with, but that didn't make it any less real.

"What am I missing here, Cara? Saying we're not a couple is equivalent to reeling in a sea bass and then claiming you weren't fishing. Why is your line in the water if you're not trying to catch a fish?"

"God Almighty. Seriously?" Finally, she seemed to have a little more going on under the surface than she'd let on. "My line is in the water all right and it has been since we met. I've never made any secret out of the fact that I want to get married and it's also not a mystery why I'd never walk down the aisle again with *you*. Since you like fishing metaphors so much, here's mine. I'm throwing you back, sugar. Swim away and watch out for those hooks next time."

"Is this still about you not trusting me?" He rolled to his stomach, suddenly feeling exposed. "What else do I have to do? I've apologized. I've listened. I've put my mouth on your—"

"Don't be crass. This is not about trust. You can't have it both ways, Keith. Either you're in this to marry me or it's temporary. Which is it?"

A weight dropped onto his shoulders, pushing him down further with each passing moment. Who was pressuring whom here? "Who said it had to be one or the other? I thought we were having a grown-up relationship, where we enjoyed each other's company and focused on our careers."

He was losing his grip, losing his mind. Why had he tried to do this when he was so ill-equipped?

"What's that supposed to mean?" Her voice shook slightly. "Grown-ups don't want a ring on their finger?"

"No, only women who can't earn their own way. Who can't stand to be alone. I thought you were different."

It had all been a lie. She was still an aspiring trophy wife

hiding behind a business that got her into the middle of as
many weddings as possible.

The disenchantment was harsh and quick. And it hurt.
How could it hurt?

She visibly shrank in on herself. "Is that what you think?
That marriage is only something a woman would want if
she can't be on her own? You think I want nothing more
than to be an…an *appendage*?"

She was twisting his words, making him out to be the
bad guy.

"I thought you were a woman who took charge. Who
was my equal, strong and fiercely independent."

If any woman could have been his match, it was that
Cara. He'd wanted more with that Cara, thought he might
have figured out how to be what that Cara needed.

But she'd vanished inside an immature girl who still
dreamed of being Mrs. Someone, instead of a woman who
took a setback like being left at the altar and turned it into
a successful business. A woman with strength and determination could handle someone like Keith, who was bound
to mess up, bound to look for that next challenge. A woman
like that could understand him.

He and Cara weren't even in the same book, let alone
on the same page.

"And I thought you were a man who didn't see the value
in something with only one purpose," she countered quietly, apparently still determined to pretend she wasn't as
pissed off and frustrated as he was. "Like a wedding dress.
Or frosting. I have more than one use. I'm good for more
than just sex."

He shook his head and a half laugh escaped, though he
found nothing funny about this fight that wasn't a fight because they weren't a couple. Maybe she really *wasn't* upset.
Maybe she'd figured out that she didn't want "more" with

him a long time ago and was perfectly fine with tossing him back once the expo was over.

He was fine with that, too. It was what he'd planned all along. Or at least it was what he'd planned before he actually got Cara into his bed. And before he'd gotten the contract extension. And before this conversation had started, during which he'd discovered Cara had no intention of continuing their relationship in any way, shape or form.

She'd mixed up everything.

And on second thought, he wasn't fine with any of it.

"But that's exactly my point, Cara. I don't think of you as having only one use. When you lick off the frosting, you still have cake. You're my cake, or at least I thought you were. I want you to be cake, not a mess that needs frosting to hide all the flaws. You have substance. That's what I see in you, that's what's so attractive about you."

How could she not be upset? Didn't she see how wrong marriage was for them—for anyone who valued making their own way—but how right two independent, career-minded people could be together? That's what he wanted. Right now. With the Cara he'd met since coming to Grace Bay.

"That's precious. You want to have your cake and eat it, too." She tossed her head and flopped onto her back, apparently feeling the opposite of exposed. "These metaphors are ridiculous. For once, just say what you're feeling. Or is that too hard?"

"Cara, please." She was taunting him, hitting below the belt for some unknown reason. He'd confessed to having difficulty in expressing his emotions and she was throwing it back in his face. "I'm feeling like we're not even talking the same language. You said after the newlywed game that you didn't think you wanted a relationship. Have you changed your mind? Instead of metaphors, why don't *you* say what you really mean."

"What, like I should tell you thanks but no thanks for calling me a mess and accusing me of using frosting to cover my flaws? Because that's what I really wanted to say. Or better yet, maybe I should say I don't want to get married just so I can hide a multitude of shortcomings underneath a name change."

"Then why *do* you want to get married?"

"Because, Keith." She sat up on her haunches, so thoroughly composed he wanted to rattle her just to make sure she was still breathing. "Cake is great by itself but frosting makes it so much better. I wish you could see that."

"I've lost track of what frosting is supposed to represent." Hence the reason for all the metaphors—neither of them could seem to lay it all on the line. "It would be so much easier if you'd just flat out tell me what you want me to hear."

She nodded slowly, her face blank. "After the newlywed game, I was confused. But you've helped me figure it out. I want to get married because I'm so in love with a man, and he's so in love with me, that we both have a desperate need to share everything. A bed, a house, a life, a family. Even names."

Oddly, that sounded…not so horrifying. But before he could fully process the revelation, she smiled tremulously and one tear fell.

"And that's not going to happen with you," she concluded. "So here we are, having an island fling, no pressure, no wedding bells. Stop me if you hear something that doesn't jibe."

She wanted to get married. But not to him.

So apparently *he* was the only one with difficulty in laying it all on the line. And the only one with difficulty in the parameters of their relationship, such as it was. He'd been developing all these feelings and she…hadn't. How in the hell had that happened?

Twelve

The moment of Cara's triumph had arrived.

The wedding dress fashion show, which was the highlight of the expo, would start in seventeen minutes. Cara Chandler-Harris Designs would meet the world's elite wedding professionals with a splash, yards from the pristine beach. A balmy breeze played with the white fabric sheets hanging from metal frames, which served as a makeshift barrier to separate the audience from backstage.

Every one of the brides radiated with a *je ne sais quoi* that brought to mind romance and beauty and a touch of pageantry. Cara's eyes prickled with unshed tears. Tears meant the dresses were perfect, selected with each model's attributes in mind, altered with precision.

Or it just meant she'd fallen in love with the wrong man and it sucked.

What had she expected it to be like? Moonlight and roses and a breathtaking marriage proposal by the sea?

No, actually, she'd expected it to end exactly as it had.

Badly. Because in her heart of hearts, she'd known it was going to end. But at least she'd done the right thing and pushed him away. It certainly hadn't been hard—he'd already been halfway out the door to his next resort, gleeful to turn around yet another failing wedding destination with his superhuman efforts. All the wedding and marriage talk had just been icing on the cake of his departure from her life. Like last time. Like always.

"Sand in your eye?" Meredith murmured and poked her head around the sheet to survey the audience.

"I'm fine." When Cara returned to their room last night, dry-eyed and numb, her sister hadn't so much as lifted an eyebrow, and hadn't asked any pointed questions. For that, Cara couldn't begin to express her gratitude.

It was the only reason she'd spilled everything to her sister. Every last horrible detail.

"That's good. But if you can't do this, no one would notice the hole in the lineup." Meredith nodded at Cara's dress, her gaze chock-full of sympathy. "We have five other designs to show. It's enough."

How did her sister always know the right thing to say?

"Bless you, honey. But Mulan is the first dress I designed because I wanted to, not because I had an order. It's my best work." She bit her lip and struggled not to take the easy out. "I need to wear it and I need to participate in my own show. People will love it."

More therapy. Obviously she required a lot. But she had a burning need to prove something to herself, and walking down a runway in a wedding dress somehow had become part of it.

Music piped through the sound system, and one by one the girls paraded down the runway, twirled, paused to a barrage of applause and returned to the backstage area. Cara went last.

Her smile was genuine.

She'd come full circle. Cara Chandler-Harris Designs had started as a way to get her through. And it would continue to provide her satisfaction and purpose. Nothing had changed, other than the fact that Cara could finally accept the truth.

She was always the bride, but never married. And that was okay.

Weddings were fun and she got to participate in the centerpiece of every one—the dress.

And before she'd come to Grace Bay, Cara had let the glamour and romance of the event itself seduce her into forgetting that "I do" wasn't the end of the wedding but the beginning of a marriage.

Flashes around the perimeter from professional cameras burst in rapid succession. Photographs. Of her dresses. These were magazine photographers and wedding bloggers capturing her designs to show to their readers. Which might lead to more customers.

At the end of the runway, she pivoted and held the pose to thunderous applause. Lord above, they were clapping for *her* dress. And *her* design. And Cara herself. It was heady and gratifying and fulfilling.

It flooded her all at once.

This is what Keith had meant by being cake. This feeling, this sense of accomplishment, this being in the essence of something she'd created from nothing. He'd encouraged her to forget about the frosting and focus on the substance underneath.

Cara Chandler-Harris Designs wasn't a business; it was an extension of Cara, a manifestation of her wedding dreams. Those dreams would live forever, caught in visions of silk and lace.

Marriage wasn't the most important thing she could do in her life.

The realization was freeing in a way she'd never expected. During this time in Grace Bay, she'd liked that Keith saw her as an equal, but she'd never quite figured out that to him, marriage meant inequality.

That was an aspect of the man she loved that she'd never known before. No wonder he'd fled from their first wedding. In a misguided way, he probably thought he was doing her a favor. And really, he had, in so many ways.

Keith's dark head rose above the crowd, catching in her peripheral vision as she walked back up the runway to the head of the stage, where the other girls stood in various poses. He hung back, arms crossed, watching her with a slightly hooded expression. But he couldn't have hidden his six-three frame, not in a crowd. Not from her.

Her heart recognized him instantly.

They'd parted last night in complete agreement—their island fling was over. He'd go his way, she'd go hers. But she seemed to be the only one unhappy about it.

After the show ended, Cara turned to follow Meredith and the other girls back to their rooms. The dresses should go back into airtight bags as soon as possible, especially because Cara had a feeling she might be selling all of them very shortly.

"Ms. Chandler-Harris?"

Cara turned to the male speaker, an elegantly dressed man in his midthirties who obviously knew his way around a stylist and wasn't afraid to be seen shopping at Bloomingdale's. His name placard read Nick Anderson—Buyer for Ever After Boutiques.

She swallowed a great big ball of sudden nerves. "Mr. Anderson. How lovely to meet you. I've spent many hours in your boutiques."

"Checking out the competition?" he asked with an innocuous smile as they shook hands.

"Daydreaming," she corrected graciously. "That's what

we both sell, right? A bride's dreams, plucked from her mind and brought to life in fabric."

Hooking arms with Mr. Anderson, she walked with him along the beach and spun the tale of a woman who loved being a bride so much, she'd created wedding dress after wedding dress to celebrate that bright, brief moment when all eyes were on the most beautiful woman in the room.

And when it was Nick Anderson's turn to talk, he smiled. "You've hooked me. What will it take to get your designs in my stores?"

"Well, my stars. You flatter me," Cara drawled to cover the hitch in her throat. And she only wished it was because she'd just been handed a golden opportunity.

But that was secondary to the intense desire to leap into Keith's embrace and tell him she'd done it. She wanted him to kiss her and say how proud he was.

Instead, she smiled through the twinge pulling at her heart. "Let's get down to business, shall we, Mr. Anderson?"

Keith watched Cara stroll off with a man entirely too well put together to be trusted. And she was still wearing her long white dress. It was the same one she'd been wearing that first day, when he'd accosted her in the pavilion during the fashion show run-through—on purpose because he'd wanted to catch her off guard.

Of course, he'd been the one flattened.

She'd been just as stunning then as she was now and always had been. The white dress with the high collar and clean lines only heightened her lush beauty, as if she'd been born to wear that exact dress as she walked down the aisle toward a besotted groom. They'd promise to love each other forever and the poor dimwit would whisk her away to a honeymoon at a resort like this one, where they'd hardly venture out of their suite because they were too wrapped up in each other.

Maybe her groom wouldn't be this too-carefully dressed expo guest, but she'd marry someone eventually.

Jealously—big, green and ugly—flared in Keith's gut, and he did not care for it any more than the sharp longing and utter confusion Cara had provoked the moment she'd stepped out on that stage.

"Still got my eyes on you, Mitchell."

Keith whirled. Meredith stood behind him, tapping one stiletto against the sand, which should have been impossible but the laws of physics apparently didn't apply in the Chandler-Harris world.

"Great," he growled. "You can watch me get back to work."

The mock wedding was scheduled to round out the day's events, and the crew still needed to tear down the runway from the fashion show before the chairs could be set up. A sunset wedding starring a couple of actors would put the cherry on top of the resort's launch.

Without Cara's help, he had a suspicion it wouldn't go as well as the run-through. Mary would do her best but the resort still hadn't hired a full-time wedding coordinator.

Thoughtfully, he eyed Meredith. "Since you apparently have nothing better to do than hang out with me, how about giving me a hand?"

"Are you out of your mind?" She laughed. "I wouldn't help you if you were the last man on earth. Besides, I have a strict policy that I only help men who can repay me with sex, and I have a feeling that wouldn't go over so well."

"I'm pretty sure Cara wouldn't mind," he shot back without thinking and then cursed.

He might as well have come right out and admitted she'd messed him up. That he'd lain awake last night for hours trying to understand why he'd gotten exactly what he'd asked for—a short-lived affair, no pressure, no wedding bells—and he was miserable.

Not only was he miserable, Cara had already moved on, apparently, to someone who made her laugh as they strolled on the beach, arm in arm. So why would Cara care whom he slept with, even if it was her sister?

He never should have let even that much slip. This wasn't a random drive-by. Meredith wanted something and she was smarter than nearly everyone gave her credit for. He'd never figured out why she hid it behind overblown sex appeal.

"Oh, I'm pretty sure she would mind. But I have a feeling you'd mind even more. Why are you standing here talking to me instead of going after her, anyway?" Meredith hit her head with the heel of her hand as if she'd just remembered something important. "That's right, you're an idiot."

"Thanks, I appreciate your assessment," he commented drily. "Is this your way of buttering me up before you get to the real point of this ambush?"

Meredith flashed him a smug grin. "Don't tell Cara, but I've always liked you. For her, I mean. You'd drive me to homicide in under four seconds flat."

"The feeling is mutual." God help the man who fell in love with Meredith. He'd have to be made of sterner stuff than Keith.

Thankfully, he'd picked the right sister from the start. Cara was the only woman he'd ever considered an equal, the only woman capable of getting him to talk about his feelings—however brief of a discussion that had ended up being. The only woman who'd ever triggered such strange rawness in his chest.

And she was the only woman he'd ever tried to be there for when she needed him. Fat lot of appreciation he'd gotten for that.

"Since we agree we wouldn't touch each other with a

ten-foot pole, how about you stop being such a weenie about the woman you do want? Please tell me you're not going to mess it up with Cara *again*."

"You should be reading the riot act to your sister. *I'm* not the one messing it up." They'd had something perfectly fine that worked for both of them. Why couldn't their relationship continue as is, no pressure, just two people who liked spending time together? Cara's insistence on being Mrs. Mitchell or nothing had ruined it all. Ruined the fledging feelings that Keith could barely admit to himself, let alone to her.

"You're impossible. How do you think I know that's not true? I *did* talk to Cara. She let you go because she didn't want to force you into another unwanted trip down the aisle."

He snorted unevenly, guilt crowding into his lungs. "Cara couldn't have done that at gunpoint."

"Exactly. And given what happened the first time, can you blame her for not wanting to introduce any more *accidents* into the mix?" Meredith's laser-sharp gaze tore through his flesh to pierce his heart. "She gave you up, despite being madly in love with you, because she didn't want to unintentionally trap you into marriage. Happy with yourself, Mitchell?"

Keith's knees turned to jelly. "She's in love with me? Why didn't she say anything?"

The notion planted itself in his chest and spread. Cara was in love with him. For real, this time. She wouldn't have told Meredith if it wasn't true.

Meredith shook her head with a grunt of disgust. "I take it back. I don't like you. You're a moron and Cara can do much better. You deserve to spend the rest of your life alone. Good luck with that."

Mahogany hair flying, Meredith turned her back on

Keith and stomped off through a sea of wedding professionals socializing on the beach.

Keith's gaze lit on Cara and her friend as they stood talking near the shoreline. Their faces fuzzed under his scrutiny and his own face superimposed itself over that of the man standing by the woman Keith had held in his arms last night. The woman he'd walked away from once again because he couldn't do what she wanted.

No, he'd refused to do what she wanted. Refused to even consider the possibility that marriage could be something other than a cold union designed to give a woman a life of luxury. Maybe it was like that with some people. Maybe it would have been that way with the Cara he'd almost married the first time.

But everything was different now. *She* was different. And he'd skipped right over the possibility that marriage could be something else. Cara had never even given him a chance to figure out what their relationship could be, just waltzed out the door and didn't even bother to tell him something so important as the fact that she'd fallen in love with him.

And hearing it from Meredith instead of Cara was unacceptable. She owed him an explanation for how she'd figured out something so monumental.

Suddenly he had a perverse need to hear it from Cara's own lips.

"Mr. Mitchell." One of the groundskeepers launched into a question about the mock wedding setup that Keith barely heard.

"Excuse me." Keith stepped around the uniformed man, leaving him hanging midsentence, and strode across the sand with nary a thought for his best Italian shoes.

He crashed Cara's little party with the same amount of remorse—none.

"Keith Mitchell." He stuck his hand out and sized up the

man as they shook. He was too pretty, too well dressed and too short for Cara.

And their conversation was over.

"Come with me, Cara," Keith said shortly and drank in the luminous vision in white, so beautiful, his lungs hitched.

"I'm a little busy," she responded just as shortly. "Can't it wait?"

No. It couldn't. And he was this close to picking her up and throwing her over his shoulder to take her somewhere private so she could explain *right now* why she could tell Meredith about her feelings but not Keith. He wanted to hear her say she loved him and then he could figure out what to do about it.

That's when he actually read the guy's name tag. The word *buyer* leaped out and whacked him upside the head. This must be the source of Cara's good news. And he'd intruded like a jealous lover.

Well…he kind of was a jealous lover. And he deserved every bit of the heat in Cara's glare.

"It can wait." Keith nodded to the man who was likely offering Cara the business proposition she'd mentioned. "Sorry I intruded. Cara, text me when you're free. Meet me in my office."

"Sure. See you later," she said and shifted her gaze pointedly. *Go away.* It wasn't hard to interpret.

Morosely, Keith cooled his heels in his office for a solid thirty minutes, holding his phone like a lifeline, shaking it occasionally. Still no text messages.

But he did get three phone calls from Mary asking his opinion about the mock wedding setup and all Keith could tell her was to use her best judgment. Mary's return comment summed it up.

"You should keep Cara around permanently. That woman knows brides."

She did. And she knew that she wanted to be one. Keith had bad-mouthed marriage for the past week, so of course she'd bailed on him. Yeah, he *was* a moron. Cara hadn't told him she'd fallen in love because he hadn't given her any reason to.

Just as he hadn't given her any reason to meet him in his office. She wasn't coming. And he couldn't blame her.

If he hoped to salvage anything from this debacle he'd made of their relationship, he needed to go big or go home. It was time to turn around the one thing he'd resisted thus far—himself. Mitchell the Missile had a very worthy target to hit.

And if he wanted to hear from Cara's lips that she loved him, he probably needed to admit he'd fallen in love with her, too. Out loud. To her.

The revelation would probably shock her as much as it had shocked him.

Cara perched on the white wooden folding chair in the first row, where the groom's family would normally sit if this were a real wedding. But since the bride and groom were actually actors Mary had hired to perform for the expo guests, Cara didn't think anyone would mind if she grabbed a good seat.

She loved weddings. No doubt about it.

Her island fling with Keith had given her back the ability to see a wedding for what it was—a celebration of love and commitment between two people who wanted to be together. She'd never settle for anything less and if it meant she'd never experience a walk down the aisle, that was the price of holding out for love.

Still clad in Mulan, Cara carefully crossed her legs so she wouldn't rip a seam. She should have gone back to her room and changed, but she couldn't bear to take it off yet. The dress had become symbolic of the growth in Cara

Chandler-Harris Designs, of her own growth. And it was her dress and she liked wearing it.

Music piped through the sound system and the bride floated down the sand aisle, barefoot, exactly as Cara had suggested to Mary. When the bride reached her groom, the minister, also an actor, began the ceremony.

"Dearly beloved…" The minister droned through the first bit and then said, "If anyone objects to this union, speak now or forever hold your peace."

"I object."

Keith's voice cut through the balmy sunset atmosphere. Cara whirled and there he was, waltzing up the aisle as if he owned it. He halted at the first row, gaze on Cara.

Everyone else's gaze was on him. Yummy Interrupting Man had struck again.

"On what grounds?" the minister asked on cue, as if this was part of the script.

"On the grounds that every wedding should unite two people who are in love with each other," Keith said but not to the minister. His melty caramel eyes held fast to Cara. "The bride and groom don't qualify."

"What are you doing?" Cara whispered.

"What I should have done two years ago," he said at normal volume because obviously all the expo guests should be included in a discussion about their ill-fated history. "And last night. Instead of walking away, I'm in the middle of a wedding. Where you want me."

The power of speech nearly deserted her but she managed to keep her composure. Somehow. What was he up to?

Warily, she swept him with a bored once-over. "Well, sugar, that's mighty nice but if I recall, your Speedy Gonzales shoes make quite an impression, especially at weddings."

"That's why I took them off." He lifted one bare foot for emphasis. "I'm not going anywhere."

Her heart stumbled and erratic beats throbbed in her throat as she finally caught up. He'd interrupted the wedding to make a specific point, but he was sure taking his sweet time in getting there. "What's this all about?"

Had he crashed the mock wedding because she hadn't responded to the royal summons to his office? Unlikely. The fashion show had been her crowning achievement and this was his. Keith Mitchell had turned Regent Resorts into a premier wedding destination and the mock wedding should be the highlight of it.

Why was he ruining it?

Keith skirted the chairs and knelt by her feet. Almost as if—

No! He wasn't about to sweep her up in some sort of sham proposal strictly as part of the show. He wouldn't dare.

Then he took her hand, his gaze swimming with earnestness and something else she couldn't place, couldn't fathom, and she couldn't look away.

"I have trouble expressing myself," he said. "I like that you don't force me to dredge up what's inside. But you deserve more. I want to give you more. I want to stop pretending temporary is all I can do instead of sticking around and figuring out how to say what I'm feeling."

Sincerity resonated in every word out of his mouth. Oh, this was real. So achingly, wonderfully real.

A hum in her tummy spun outward to sweep across her skin with a delicious heat. "So temporary *isn't* all you can do?"

He shook his head. "Not anymore. I want to give you everything your heart desires. No matter what it is. Losing you is unacceptable. Because I love you."

The crowd murmured and sighed as all the blood drained from her head and white stars burst behind her eyes. "What?"

"It's for real." His voice dipped, laced with all sorts of emotions. "I'm sorry it took external forces to get me to realize it."

"Meredith told you what I said, didn't she?" Sisters. Can't live with them, can't shoot them. "That…blabber-mouth."

Of course, her interfering sister's conversation with Keith had prompted all of this so maybe it wasn't so bad that Meredith couldn't keep her fat mouth shut.

Keith nodded once. "I'd like to hear it from you, though. That's what I wanted to talk to you about earlier."

Oh my. Stubbornness had nearly cost her everything. Fortunately, Keith wasn't one to sit around and wait for life to happen. She heaved a happy sigh. "Yeah, I'm afraid it's true. I do love you. But I can't believe that's what it took to get you on your knees."

"It didn't. When I saw you in that dress, that's when it clicked. I want to marry you and be there for you every moment of every day for the rest of our lives."

Her chest squeezed and she forgot to breathe. *Marriage.* Keith was talking about marriage. Obviously he'd been out in the sun too long. "That's crazy, Keith. It's just a dress."

"That's where you're wrong. It's special because it's *you* in the dress. Be my bride, but not just for one day. Every day."

Her heart lightened all at once. He really and truly got her. For so long, she'd yearned to wrap herself in the experience of getting married, to put on the dress as if it held some mystical power. But eventually, you had to take it off and start the marriage.

And there was no one she'd rather do it with than this man, who'd crashed a fake wedding to turn their relationship into something real, who encouraged her to be his equal, who'd told her to grab what she wanted. And she wanted Keith Mitchell.

KAT CANTRELL 189

"Cara, I want to share everything with you. Houses, names, futures. Say you'll marry me."

She held the hand of the man she'd sworn to never trust, to never let crush her again, to never be in the presence of while wearing a wedding dress. Looked as if the answer was easy.

"Yes."

Epilogue

Dawn burst through the floor-to-ceiling glass in the honeymoon suite and the pristine beach spread out in both directions as far as the eye could see. Cara snuggled up against Keith's warm body and watched the sun rise over Aruba from their bed.

"I don't think I'll ever get tired of this view," she commented. "It doesn't seem to matter that I've seen it every morning for two months straight. It never gets old."

"I agree, Mrs. Mitchell," Keith murmured, his gaze on Cara and not the panoramic scene outside their room. "You are definitely the best thing in the world to wake up to every morning."

Was it possible for your heart to actually burst from happiness? She hoped not. "Ha. That's not what you said yesterday. I believe your exact words were, 'Stop that or you'll make me late for the third day in a row.'"

Her husband laughed. "Yeah, I guess I did say that. And you did not stop if I recall."

Cara shrugged. "Sorry. That's what you get when you bring a girl to a resort in Aruba and then insist on working the whole time."

She liked to think of it as fate that the next resort on Regent's turnaround agenda was located in Aruba, the same island she and Keith had selected for their canceled honeymoon two years ago. But they'd made it to the altar, and the honeymoon, this time.

"It's my job," he said, and not the least bit apologetically. "Which you encouraged me to take right away, I'll remind you. I wanted to take some time off but you were worried Regent would amend the contract."

Yeah, that *was* her fault. The day after the expo concluded, Keith had marched Cara down the sand aisle and married her in a real wedding on the beach in Grace Bay, with no ring, no influential guests and no fanfare. But there'd been plenty of love and a desperate desire to be united in matrimony. It had been the most romantic thing that had ever happened to her.

She'd repaid him by insisting he start immediately at the next resort. Because he loved his job and she loved him. Of course, when her husband's job promised to take them to fifteen different versions of paradise over two years, it was a little hard to complain about much of anything.

"Yes, the contract. That was the reason." She kissed him soundly and shoved him out of bed. "Go to work. I'll be here later."

Keith grinned. "Be naked when I get back."

"Maybe." She pretended to contemplate but it was pretty much a sure thing. "I have to finish Yvette's dress but then I might be available."

Keith made short work of getting dressed in a delicious dark suit that she couldn't wait to strip him out of at the end of the day. "Now who's the workaholic? I thought Meredith was taking over more of the business since you're in bou-tiques and have more orders than you can handle?"

Cara had asked Meredith to be a full partner and even offered to change the name to Chandler-Harris Designs, but her sister had pointed out that she was the only Chandler-Harris around and until Meredith could afford to buy into the company, Cara's name should remain.

"She is. But the company is still mine."

"That's my bride." Keith blew her a kiss and went to ter-rorize the resort staff.

Yes, Cara was a bride…and a wife and a business owner. Instead of replacing one with another, she'd gotten it all, thanks to her perfect husband who had made her life com-plete.

* * * * *

HIS BRIDE
IN PARADISE

JOANNA NEIL

CHAPTER ONE

'I CAN'T believe my luck,' Alyssa said excitedly, cradling the phone close to her ear. 'The house is magnificent, Carys, and it's right next to the ocean.'

'Mmm...that's exactly how I imagined it,' her cousin answered. 'So you managed to find the place all right? How's it all going for you?' On the other end of the line, Carys's voice held a note of eager anticipation.

Alyssa smiled at her enthusiastic tone. Carys lived on the mainland in Florida, some sixty or seventy miles away from here, and she was keen to know everything that was going on.

'Oh, it was easy enough,' Alyssa said. 'The taxi driver dropped me off. Apparently everyone around here knows the Blakeley property.' She adjusted the fluffy bath towel around her damp body. She'd not long come from the shower and had been sitting for a few minutes by the dressing table, blowdrying her long hair so that the mass of chestnut-coloured curls gleamed softly in the lamplight. 'I'm doing just fine,' she added. 'It's lovely here. You wouldn't believe how beautiful it is.'

She left the dresser and went to settle down on the luxurious softness of the large divan bed, stretching out her long, slender limbs. 'I only arrived here a couple of hours ago, so I haven't really had time to look around, but the house is perfect. There are double glass doors everywhere, even in the bedrooms, and when you step out onto the deck you look out over the Atlantic Ocean. It's fantastic, Carys…it's so incredibly blue.'

A faint breeze wafted in through the open veranda doors, and glancing there from across the room Alyssa could see the branches of the palm trees swaying gently against the skyline of the setting sun. Birds called to one another, sleepy in the warm evening air. 'I'm sitting here now, and I can hear the waves breaking on the shore.'

'It sounds heavenly.'

'Mmm, it is.' Alyssa couldn't believe her change in fortune. Within a few weeks she'd gone from enduring a bleak, desperately unhappy situation back in the UK to finding herself in this idyllic haven on a sand-fringed island in the Bahamas. 'I keep thinking that any minute now someone will come along and pinch me and tell me it's all a dream.'

Carys chuckled. 'No, I think it's really happening. Is Ross there with you? I know he was keen to help you get settled in.'

'No. He rang to tell me he'd be along a little later. He had a meeting with the director so that they could iron out a few things before filming starts tomorrow.'

Alyssa stopped to listen for a moment as a faint creaking sound caught her attention, like a footfall on the steps leading to the deck. Was someone walking around outside? Could it be that there was a change of plan and Ross was coming home earlier than expected? Then one of the voile curtains fluttered on a light current of air, distracting her, and she shook her head. Ross had stressed the importance of the meeting. It must have been the door that was creaking, that would be it.

'Well, he'll make sure that everything goes smoothly for you, I'm sure,' Carys murmured. 'You can put all your troubles behind you now, and forget about your awful ex. I've known Ross for ages, and he has a heart of gold. He'll take good care of you. I know he was besotted with you from the moment he set eyes on you.'

Alyssa sat up against the pillows. 'Oh, no…surely that can't be true… At least, I hope it isn't.' Ross knew how she felt. She'd come here to get away from all the mess that relationships involved, clutching at the chance Ross had given her to make her escape. This was her sanctuary.

Her work back in the UK had proved to be a stumbling block, too, and she'd reluctantly decided to put what had once been a promising medical career temporarily on hold. At least, she hoped it was only a relatively short-term move. In the end, things had proved too much for her, and she'd had to accept that she needed to take time out to recover from the burnout that had crept up on her and caught her unawares.

Somehow, she had to try to get herself back together again and she was pinning her hopes on the healing qualities of these next few months. As to the rest…

'I've finished with romance,' she said, her tone quiet and restrained. 'I'm done with all that.'

'So you say.' Carys laughed. 'Anyway, your ex is finally out of the picture, so with a bit of luck you can relax now and look forward to a few months of sheer luxury and self-indulgence.'

'Well, of course,' Alyssa answered, tongue in cheek. 'How could I not enjoy all this? I've got it made, haven't

I? Nothing much to do but enjoy the sunshine and surf and thank my lucky stars. I'll take money and all these rich trappings over love any time. Who wouldn't?'

'Sure you will,' Carys murmured drily. She knew full well that Alyssa was joking. 'Look, I have to go. I'll call you again. You take care. Love you.'

'And you.'

Alyssa cut the call and put down the phone, listening once more as the creaking grew louder. *Was* someone or something out there? It couldn't be Ross, surely? He'd said he would be delayed for at least an hour. Frowning, she went over to the doors and stepped out onto the deck.

A white ibis caught her attention in the distance, wandering along the shoreline, dipping his long red bill into the shallows in search of any tasty morsels that might have been washed up by the sea. She watched him for a moment or two.

'We see those birds quite often around here,' a male voice said, catching her completely unawares. The deep, resonant tones smoothed over her, making her swivel around in startled surprise.

The man moved from the shelter of the open sitting-room door and came to stand just a couple of feet away from her. He leaned negligently against the rail, making himself completely at home.

'Who—who are you…? What are you doing here?' She stared at him, shocked, wide-eyed, a little afraid and uncertain as to what to do. She was completely alone out here. He was at least six feet tall, long limbed, broad shouldered, definitely a force to be reckoned with.

She quickly thought through her options. The neighbours were too distant to hear if she were to shout out, and for an instant she floundered, before self-preservation took hold. Maybe he *was* a neighbour, and she was simply jumping to conclusions. Just because he was standing on Ross's veranda, it didn't have to mean he was some kind of would-be felon...did it?

'I was originally planning on helping myself to a cool drink and something to eat,' he answered with a faint shrug. 'I thought the place was empty, but then I heard a woman's voice and thought maybe I'd better find out who was here.'

His glance travelled over her, gliding along the creamy slope of her bare shoulders, moving down across the brief white towel that clung to her curves and coming to linger for a while on the golden expanse of her shapely legs. His gaze shifted downwards. Her feet were bare, her toenails painted a delicate shade of pink, and there were tiny gemstones embedded in the pearly nail varnish. A faint smile touched his mouth. 'I certainly hadn't expected to find anyone quite so lovely here to greet me.'

Alyssa felt warm colour invade her cheeks and her fingers tightened on the towel, clutching it to her breasts. He seemed to be quite at ease here, yet he still hadn't explained who he was.

'Well, whoever you are, you shouldn't be here,' she said. What kind of person would have the gall to calmly walk in and help himself to a drink? Ross had insisted she would have the place to herself. Her green eyes flashed a warning. 'You'd better go before I call the police.'

Belatedly, she remembered that she'd left her phone on the bedside table. Could she sidle back into the room and dial the number without alerting him to her actions? Hardly. Still, a bit of bravado wouldn't come amiss, would it?

He'd made no attempt to move. 'I can't think why you're still standing there,' she said in a terse voice. 'I meant what I said.'

'Yes, I realise that... I just don't think it's a very good idea.'

'Of course you don't. You wouldn't, would you? Even so...' She took a couple of steps backwards into the bedroom, not taking her eyes off him for a second. The smooth, Italian-tiled floor was cool beneath her feet, soothing to her ragged nerves. Her heart was pounding, her pulse thumping out an erratic beat.

He didn't look the least bit put out. He was dressed in cool, expensive-looking chinos and a loose cotton shirt. His hair was dark, the perfect styling framing an angular face, but it was his eyes that held her most of all... They were narrowed on her now, grey, like the sea on a stormy night, and compelling, a hint of something unknown glimmering in their depths as he studied her.

Slowly, he pushed himself away from the rail and began to move towards her, and her insides lurched in fearful acknowledgement. Instinctively, she recognised that this was a man who knew what he wanted and who was used to getting his own way. He wasn't going anywhere, and it certainly didn't look as though he intended to heed her warning.

She felt behind her for the mobile phone on the bedside table.

'As I said, I really wouldn't advise you do that,' he murmured, his gaze following her actions. 'You might find yourself having to explain to them what exactly you're doing in my house.'

Her jaw dropped a fraction. '*Your* house?' She frowned, then shot him a steely glance. 'No...no, that can't be right. You're the intruder, not me. I'll tell them so.'

There was a glint in his dark eyes. 'Okay, let's get this straight—I'm Connor Blakeley, and this has actually been my home for a number of years. My brother lives here too, from time to time, but it's a fact that it's my name on the deeds of the property.' He studied her. 'So, would you like to tell me who you are and what you're doing here?' His mouth moved in a wry smile. 'Or perhaps I can hazard a guess. This is bound to be something to do with Ross. You must be his latest girl-friend.'

She stiffened. He made it sound as though there had been a stream of them. Deciding to ignore his comment, she shook her head so that her bright curls tumbled about her shoulders. This man had to be an imposter, surely? Doubts were beginning to creep in, but she said cautiously, 'Connor's away for the next six months. Ross told me so. His brother's in Florida, helping to organise a new medical emergency unit over there.'

He nodded briefly. 'That was true. Unfortunately an urgent situation occurred right here in the Bahamas, and I was asked to come back and take over the accident and emergency department at the hospital. So I'll be working here and at the same time I'll be keeping an eye on the Florida unit from a distance.'

Her indrawn breath was sharp and audible. What he said sounded plausible enough. Could it be that she'd made a mistake in doubting him? He did look a bit like Ross, now she came to think of it.

Carefully, she replaced the phone on the table and

straightened up. Now what was she to do? Her cheeks burned with colour. How could she have ended up in such a humiliating situation? Hadn't she put up with enough of those back in England? This was meant to have been a fresh start, and now it looked as though her expectations of spending a relaxed, trouble-free few months out here were being rapidly consigned to the rubbish bin.

She lifted her chin, determined to pull herself together. It was a setback, that was all. Somehow she would sort this out and find herself another place to stay. She just had to hope that the cost wouldn't be way beyond her means. It had only been Ross's conviction that she could stay in this house rent-free that had persuaded her she could afford to come out here in the first place.

'I'm really sorry,' she said. 'I'd no idea... I wasn't expecting anyone else to be here tonight.' She hesitated, drawing in a calming breath. 'I'm Alyssa Morgan. Your brother invited me to stay here.'

'Was he planning on staying here with you?'

She frowned. 'Not with me, exactly. He said he would take the upper-floor accommodation, and I could have the downstairs apartment.' She looked across the room to where her suitcases stood against the louvred doors of the wardrobe. She hadn't even had time to unpack. 'But, of course, it's all changed now. I'll get my things together and find somewhere else to stay.'

'At this time of the evening?' He raised a dark brow. 'Even supposing you could find anywhere at such short notice, I couldn't let you do that. I've a feeling that an attractive young woman alone in the city would be far too great a temptation for some of our, shall we say, less civilised, male citizens?'

She straightened her shoulders. 'I can take care of myself.'

His glance moved over her. 'Really?'

His obvious disbelief stung. She felt his dark gaze linger on her slender curves, and she hugged the towel to herself in a defensive gesture. With so much pale golden skin on display she felt she was at a distinct disadvantage. 'Anyway, I should get dressed,' she said, with as much dignity as she could muster. 'If you wouldn't mind…?'

He nodded. 'Of course.' He started to walk across the room but stopped by the door to look back and say, 'You seem a bit flushed. Perhaps I could get you an iced drink and maybe something to eat? Or have you already had supper?'

Her eyes widened. She wasn't expecting such generosity, given the circumstances, and it only made her feel worse, after the way she'd spoken to him. 'No…um…I haven't had time… I only arrived here a short time ago, and I was feeling hot and dusty after the flight and so on, so I decided to have a shower before I did anything else. Ross and I were going to have supper when…' She broke off, then added, 'He had to go to a meeting.'

'Hmm.' Connor was frowning as he looked at the suitcases. 'I take it from your accent that you're English. Is that right? Did you and Ross meet over in the UK? I know he was over there scouting for talent for his latest film project.'

'Yes, we did.' Connor was American-English, she knew, as his father had been born in the United States and his mother was from London. 'We…uh…have a mutual friend over in Florida…my cousin, Carys…and she suggested he look me up.'

'Oh, yes. I know Carys.' He made a faint smile as he
studied her. 'I expect Ross was glad he took the time
to follow up on that.' He started to turn back towards
the door. 'Well, maybe I'll make a start on preparing
some food and then Ross can join us when he gets here.'

'I… Yes, that would be good. Thank you.' Her head
was reeling. How on earth would Ross react on finding that his brother was here? One way or another, he
was in for something of a shock.

Connor left the room and Alyssa pulled in a deep
breath. It wasn't the best way for her to have met
Connor, was it? She'd heard quite a bit about him from
Ross, and her overall impression was that Ross was a
little in awe of his older brother. Now that she'd met
him, she could certainly understand why. There was
that quality about him, something that suggested he
would always be in complete control of any situation,
that nothing would faze him. Everything about him underlined that. He was supple and lithe, his body honed
with latent energy, and a calm, inherent sense of authority oozed from every pore.

She dressed quickly, choosing a pale blue cotton
dress with narrow straps, cool enough for the warmth
of the evening. It wasn't much in the way of a defence,
but at least being fully dressed made her feel more in
command of herself.

A few minutes later she walked into the kitchen and
found Connor busy at the table, adding tomato paste
and grated cheese to a large pizza base. He looked up
as she entered the room. 'You look fresh and cool,' he
murmured. 'That colour suits you.'

'Thank you.'

'Sit down,' he said, waving her to a chair by the pale

oak table. 'Would you like mushrooms with this? And peppers?'

'Yes, please.' She nodded, watching as he deftly cut and sliced mushrooms and then sprinkled them over the cheese.

She glanced around. From here, by the deep, broad window, she could look out over the ocean, and closer to home there was what seemed to be a small kitchen garden just beyond the veranda. The light outside was fading now, but solar lamps sent a golden glow over a variety of vegetables and a small grove of trees laden with plump, ripe oranges.

She turned her attention back to the kitchen. 'You have a beautiful home,' she said. The kitchen was full of state-of-the-art equipment, along with a tiled island bar and glass shelving that housed colourful ceramics and delicately sculpted vases.

'Thanks.' He smiled. 'I must admit I'm pleased with it. When I moved here I wanted a house where I would be able to relax and shrug off the cares of the day, and this seemed to be the perfect place in an idyllic setting…a small piece of paradise, if you like. I sit out on the deck of an evening and watch the waves breaking on the shore. It's very relaxing, especially if you like to watch wildlife, as I do. You sometimes see herons and egrets around here, and there might even be a golden plover that appears from time to time.'

'It sounds idyllic.'

'It is.' He slid the pizza into the hot oven and came over to the table, picking up a jug of iced juice. 'Would you like a drink? I can get you something stronger if you prefer.'

'Thanks…orange juice will be fine.' She made a

face. 'I'm not used to this heat. I seem to have been thirsty ever since I arrived here.'

His mouth curved. 'You get used to it after a while. I have air-conditioning, but sometimes I prefer to throw open all the doors and windows and let the sea air in.'

'Yes, I can understand that. I think I would, too.' She sipped the cold juice, pausing to rest the glass momentarily against her throat to cool her heated skin. His glance followed her movements, but his eyes were dark and unreadable.

'So, you and Ross must be working together on his new film, I suppose?' he commented. He poured himself a glass of juice and took a long swallow, looking at her over the rim. 'He and I haven't talked much about the casting, but I can see why he must have wanted to bring you over here. I imagine you're very photogenic. And I guess you must have auditioned well.'

'Um…that's not exactly what happened,' she murmured. She frowned. He obviously had the wrong idea, if he was assuming she was an actress. 'I'm really not expecting to have anything to do with the filming as such.'

'Ah…that's interesting.' He shot her an assessing glance. 'Still, he must think a lot of you, to have brought you over here and set you up in the family home. After all, you can't have known each other very long.'

Alyssa put down her glass, her mouth firming into a straight line. 'Um…I don't know, but…I think you must have the wrong idea. I get the impression that you've put two and two together and made five.'

'Have I?' His mouth tilted in disbelief. 'I may have some of the facts wrong, but in essence I know my brother pretty well, and this wouldn't be the first time he's fallen for a young woman and gone out of his way to throw the world at her feet.' There was a gleam in his eyes. 'Unfortunately for him, this time he wasn't expecting me to turn up out of the blue. I can see how that might make things a bit difficult.'

She stood up. 'You know, on second thoughts, I don't think this arrangement is going to work out after all. I think I'll go with my original plan and find somewhere else to stay.'

She started to move away from the table, but he caught hold of her, his fingers curving around her bare arm. 'Please don't do that, Alyssa, it's really not a good idea.'

'Maybe so, but that's my worry, not yours.'

She tried to pull away from him, but he simply drew her closer to him, so that her soft curves brushed against his long body. 'I'm afraid it's very much my problem,' he said, 'since my brother has seen fit to install you under my roof.'

'You make me sound as though I'm a package to be parcelled up by your brother and shipped wherever the fancy takes him,' she said in a terse voice. 'That's not only insulting, it's downright chauvinistic. Where have you been living these last thirty or so years? It's obvious to me that your mind-set is stuck somewhere in the last century.'

He laughed. It wasn't what she was expecting, and anger and frustration rose up in her like mercury shooting up a gauge on a blazing hot day. 'You'd better let me go right now,' she said, 'or I swear you won't like the consequences.' When he didn't release her, she started to bring her knee up, ready to deliver a crippling blow, and he swiftly turned her round so that his arms encased her from behind. Frustratingly, she was locked into his embrace, her spine resting against his taut, masculine frame.

'Of course I'll let you go,' he murmured, 'if you promise me that you won't try to leave before morning. I apologise if I've been jumping to conclusions. I've been assuming that Ross is behaving in his usual hedonistic manner, but I have to admit you're very different from what I might have expected. You're not at all like his usual choice of women.'

'Is that so?' She was rigid in his arms, still seething with indignation.

'I didn't mean to offend you,' he said. 'Honestly. I'm trying to explain. Look at it from my point of view. I had no idea that he was bringing anyone home. He usually tells me. So why didn't he do that if everything was open and above board? For all he knew, I might have arranged for a friend to stay here while I was away. That's why we always tell each other about our plans.'

'Perhaps he acted on impulse and meant to tell you later.' Her body relaxed a fraction.

'Yes, I suppose that could be it.' He nodded, and his cheek lightly brushed hers. His hold on her eased a little, and it seemed to Alyssa's heightened senses that it became much more like a caress. She felt his warm breath fall softly on the back of her neck, and his arm brushed the rounded swell of her breast as he held her to him. It was unintentional, she was sure, but the heated contact ricocheted through her body, bringing with it a shocking, bone-melting response. She closed her eyes, breathing deeply. How could she be reacting this way? She didn't even know him. It was unthinkable.

Clearly there was something wrong with her. Jetlag, probably. She needed to break free from him, but the warmth of those encircling arms and the gentleness of that embrace had taken her completely by surprise. It seemed like such a long time since anyone had held her in such an intimate way and, worryingly, she was discovering that she liked it.

'I'll find somewhere else to stay first thing in the morning,' she said.

Slowly, almost reluctantly, he released her. 'You don't need to do that. You're Ross's guest, and therefore mine, too. I wouldn't dream of having you go elsewhere. Please stay. I'd like you to stay.'

'I'll think about it.' She dithered for a moment. She wanted to walk out of the room, but as she stood there, undecided, she glanced towards the oven, conscious of the appetising smell of melting cheese and sizzling herbs and tomato permeating the air. She hadn't realised until now how hungry she was…her last meal had been virtually a snack on the plane journey over here.

He looked at her, his head tilted on one side, a faint smile playing around his mouth. 'You're hungry,' he said. 'It's no wonder you're feeling a little fractious. Sit down and we'll eat. Things always seem better on a full stomach.'

Annoyed by her own weakness, she did as he suggested and went back to the chair. Maybe he was right, and circumstances had combined to throw her off balance. A long plane journey, a change of surroundings and the appearance of the proverbial tall, dark stranger had certainly knocked her for six. Her heart was racing as though she'd run a marathon, and the world seemed to be spinning around her ever so slightly. She felt decidedly odd.

There was a noise from across the room and they both turned as the kitchen door opened and Ross came in.

'What on earth…? Connor, what are you doing here? Aren't you supposed to be in Florida?' He was tall, like his brother, with dark hair and the same angular jaw, but Ross had more homely, lived-in features, and generally there was a happy-go-lucky, almost boyish air about him. 'You said you'd be away for several months.'

'I did, but there was a change of plan. It turns out I'm going to be working here, on the island, for the most part.'

'So you'll be staying here.' It was a matter-of-fact statement. Then Ross added, 'I've arranged for Alyssa to have the ground-floor apartment. I'd no idea you would be coming back so soon.'

Connor nodded. 'Yes, she told me. That's okay. That arrangement can still stand. It just means that you'll have to stay at your place near the film studio. That won't be a problem for you, will it?'

Ross's grey-blue eyes narrowed. 'I guess not.' He looked at his brother as though he suspected him of some devious ploy.

'Good. So now that's all sorted, perhaps we can sit down together and enjoy a meal.'

Connor took the pizza from the oven, and Alyssa said quietly, 'Is there anything I can do to help? I could set the table for you, if you like.'

'Thanks. That would be great. There's a bowl of salad in the fridge. You could put that out, too, if you would.'

'Okay.'

They worked together, while Ross went to freshen

up. 'So, if you're not involved with the filming, what will you be doing all day while Ross is at work?' Connor asked. 'Is this meant to be a holiday for you, or a sight-seeing trip, or something like that?'

Alyssa smiled. 'It's nothing like that. I'm going to be working as a medic on the film set. Apparently, the company Ross usually calls on to provide that service is tied up with other projects right now, so when he found out that I was looking for work, he asked me if I'd like to take it on.'

Connor's dark brows lifted. 'You're a nurse?'

She shook her head. 'I'm a doctor. I've worked in the same line as you, accident and emergency, so I should be able to deal with any problems that arise if stunts go wrong, and so on.' She smiled. 'Though, hopefully, that won't happen. Mostly, it'll be a case of handing out headache and sunburn medication, I expect.'

'So now you've managed to surprise me all over again.' Connor stared at her for a moment or two, before starting to slice the pizza into triangular wedges. 'Now I understand what you meant when you told your friend that there would be nothing much to do but enjoy the sunshine and the surf and thank your lucky stars.'

She frowned, sending him a fleeting glance. 'You heard me talking to Carys on the phone?'

He nodded. 'I didn't know it was Carys, but I heard some of the conversation you were having. I came out onto the deck and I couldn't help but hear what you were saying.' He paused as he checked the filter on the coffee pot.

'The only part that bothered me was when you added that you'd take money and all the trappings over love any time.' His gaze meshed with hers. 'I don't know

what your plans are, but perhaps I should warn you to
tread carefully there. I wouldn't want to see my brother
hurt. He has his faults, but he's family and I care about
him very much.'

Once again this evening she felt hot colour rise in
her cheeks. No wonder he'd been so edgy with her from
the beginning. He'd heard what she said and had drawn
his own conclusions.

'It was just a joke,' she said. 'The sort of throw-away
remark we all make from time to time. It didn't mean
anything.'

'Maybe so.' He acknowledged that with a wry smile,
but she noticed the warmth didn't reach his dark eyes.
'But the warning stands... I've always looked out for
my brother, and I see no reason to stop doing that.'

'Even though he's a grown man who owns a successful film company? Don't you trust him to make
his own decisions?'

'Of course I do...to a certain extent. But Ross is a
fool where women are concerned. He's made a few mistakes over the years that have cost him dearly. I don't
want to see that happen again.'

'And I'm obviously the scarlet woman whose talons
cut deep?' She sent him a scornful look.

'You've come all the way from the UK to be with
him.' His mouth twisted. 'I don't blame you for that.
Who would turn down the chance of living a life of
luxury on this beautiful island? But I'm inclined to be
cautious all the same.'

Clearly he wasn't going to believe she was on the
level. Alyssa opened her mouth to make an answering
retort, but Ross came back into the kitchen just then,

and she concentrated instead on carefully laying out the cutlery on the table.

'I'm starving,' Ross said, eyeing the food with a ravenous eye. 'This looks good.'

She smiled at him, handing him a plate, and took her seat at the table. She didn't need to say anything more to Connor. They simply looked at one another, and that glance spoke volumes. They both knew exactly where they stood. He didn't trust her an inch and for her part she was ultra-wary of him. The battle lines were drawn.

CHAPTER TWO

'ARE we all clear for this shot?' Ross was talking to the cameraman, making sure that every detail was covered. They were standing just a few yards away from Alyssa, and she could hear every word that was being said. It was fascinating, she'd discovered, to watch a film being put together. In principle, Ross was the producer, but she'd learned that he also had a hand in directing the films.

'Let's start off by letting the audience see the coral reef in the distance,' Ross said quietly, 'and the sheer drop to the sea. Then we can gradually move to the background of the pine forest and sweep down to a view of the lake, so that we see the sun shining on the surface.'

The cameraman nodded, and Ross went on, 'Lastly, I want you to bring in the bridge over the main road and try to give us an impression of the sheer height and majesty of it all. We'll tie all that in with atmospheric music and build up to a crescendo.'

'Okay. And that's where we cut to the car chase?'

'That's right. As soon as that comes to an end, we'll go straight into the stunt scene.'

'You want the lorry to come into the picture from the east? I'll need a clear signal for that.'

'Yes. I'll let you know as soon as the driver starts up the engine.'

'Okay.'

Alyssa watched all the activity around her with interest. The actors who would be needed for the next scene were standing around, chatting to one another, languid in the heat of the sun as they waited to be called. Everyone wanted to see how the stunt would go. The technicians had planned it down to the last detail, and there had been several rehearsals, but now it was time for the real thing, and the stuntman, Alex, was in position on the bridge, a lone, dark figure against the protective rail.

Ross came over to her. He was in prime form, bubbling with energy and totally enthusiastic about the way things were going. 'I'm going to be tied up with this for the next hour or so,' he told her, 'but I thought we might have lunch later at the new restaurant that's opened up in town…Benvenuto. It's down by the marina. They do some great dishes there. I think you'll like it.'

'Sounds great. I'll look forward to it.' Alyssa smiled at him and on the spur of the moment he wrapped his arms around her and kissed her soundly on the lips.

'Me, too.'

'Oh.' She was startled by the fervour that went into that kiss. 'What was that for?'

He grinned. 'I really appreciate what you've done here for us these last few weeks. Everyone says you've been brilliant, helping with everything from toothache to blistered toes. And I love the way you've looked over the script and offered advice on the medical stuff. Even if they're just a minor part of the film, it's important we get the hospital scenes right. And in the restaurant, when the man keels over, we needed to know how a doctor would respond.'

'Let's hope that won't be necessary at the restaurant today.' She laughed. 'It'll be great to sit and enjoy a meal in peace and quiet after all the goings-on on set.'

'Yeah, too right.' He gave her a final hug before letting her go. Then he hurried over to the lorry driver to give some final instructions.

'Going by the looks of things, it seems you and Ross are getting closer every day.' There was an edge to Connor's voice, and Alyssa looked at him in surprise as he came to stand beside her. His jaw was faintly clenched as though he was holding himself in restraint. He was wearing stone-coloured trousers and a casual, open-necked shirt, and he looked cool in the heat of the day.

'Hello, Connor,' she greeted him in a light tone, trying to counteract his disapproval. 'I wasn't expecting to see you here. I imagined you would be at work.' In fact, she'd seen very little of him these last few weeks, considering that they shared the same house, but she guessed he started work early at the hospital and he often came home late. Occasionally, he'd gone over to Florida to oversee his other project. Perhaps he'd been going out of an evening, too, once his shift ended.

As to his comment about her and Ross…she simply wasn't going to answer him. He was obviously hung up on the situation, so why make matters worse? It bothered her, though, that he had seen that kiss. How would she ever be able to convince him that there was nothing going on between her and his brother after that?

'It's my day off,' he said, 'so I thought I'd come and see how things were going here. Apparently the filming's on schedule so far.' His dark gaze moved over her. 'And I wondered how you were getting on. Has it been the quiet, relaxing time you expected?'

'Not exactly,' she murmured. 'But, then, I've been making something of an effort to get to grips with the job from the start.'

'Yes, so I heard.' A glimmer of respect flickered in the depths of his eyes. 'Ross has been singing your praises for days now. Apparently, you've made yourself known to everyone on set and managed to get a medical history from each one of them. He's very impressed with the way you've been handling things.'

Alyssa shrugged lightly, inadvertently loosening one of the thin straps of her broderie-anglaise top, so that it slid down the lightly tanned, silky smooth slope of her shoulder. 'It's what I'm paid to do, and the job is exactly what I thought it would be. I made it my business to get to know as much as I could about everyone beforehand so that I would have a good idea what I'm dealing with.'

'Very commendable.' Before she could remedy the offending strap, he reached out and hooked a finger beneath the cotton, carefully sliding it back into place. His touch trailed over her bare flesh like the slow lick of flame, causing an unexpected, feverish response to cascade through her, heating her blood and quickening her pulse. 'There,' he murmured. 'You're all neat and tidy once more.'

'I…um…have you…have you been to see every one of Ross's films being made?' she asked, disconcerted by his action and lifting a hand to push back the curls from her hot face. The movement lifted her brief top and exposed a small portion of her bare midriff, pale gold above the waistband of her dark jeans. His glance flicked downwards and lingered there for a while.

'I…uh…' He sounded distracted for a moment and then he cleared his throat. 'Most of them. I like to keep up with what's going on in the film world from time to time. Even though he's my brother, I must say Ross's work is good. He's had some notable successes. He deserves them because he works hard and pays a lot of attention to detail.'

She nodded. 'I've noticed that, too. He's been worrying about this morning's stunt, though. The timing has to be perfect. The stuntman has to jump from the bridge onto the moving lorry to escape from his pursuers, and he has to do it at exactly the right moment. They've even worked out how to make sure the lorry will be going at a certain speed when he jumps.'

He nodded. 'I guess that's what you might expect with these action adventure films. There always has to be something spectacular going on. After all, that's what the audience pays to see.'

Ross gave the signal for the camera recording to begin, and they turned to watch the proceedings. Around them, the buzz of conversation came to a halt and everyone's gaze was riveted to the scene about to take place. A lorry began to gradually pick up speed on the main road, which had been temporarily cleared of traffic while filming took place. The stuntman abandoned a wrecked car on the bridge and ran, chased determinedly by burly men who looked as though they meant business…nasty business. Coming to the concrete bulwark, he glanced around as though his character was trying to assimilate his options in double quick time.

With nowhere to go, and his pursuers gaining ground with every second that passed, he sprang up onto the guard-rail, remained poised for a moment, and then, as the men snapped at his heels, he leapt from the bridge.

The landing was perfect. He balanced, feet apart on top of the moving lorry, but a moment later a shocked gasp went up as the onlookers took in what happened next. Somehow Alex's foot twisted beneath him and the momentum of the still moving lorry flipped him onto his back, causing him to topple to the ground.

Alyssa was already on the move as it was happening, grabbing her medical equipment and racing towards the road where Alex was lying on the grass verge, groaning in agony. Her heart began to pound against the wall of her chest. This was the last thing she had expected. They'd been working so hard to make sure that nothing could go wrong. She had even checked him over to make sure that he was in prime physical condition before he attempted the feat.

'Alex, can you tell me where it hurts?' She quickly knelt down beside him, looking at him in concern.

'It's my back,' he said, his face contorted with pain. 'I think I caught it on the side of the lorry as I went over. I thought I felt something crack.'

The thought of the damage that might have been done to his spine made her sick with fear. All those old feelings of dread that she'd experienced back in the UK came flooding back to her, but she knew she had to get a grip on her emotions for her patient's sake. Small beads of perspiration broke out on her brow.

'Okay,' she said, disguising her inner fears with an

air of confidence, 'try not to worry. We'll soon have you feeling more comfortable.' She dialled emergency services, calling for an ambulance and warning them of a suspected spinal injury, and then she turned to Alex once more. 'I just need to check you over to see what the damage is.' All the colour had drained from his face, but at least he was still conscious and able to talk to her. That was perhaps a good sign, but she'd seen the way he'd fallen, and it didn't bode well.

'I can't believe I…could have messed up like that,' Alex said in a taut, strained voice. 'I thought…I thought it was going to be okay…' He broke off, and small beads of perspiration broke out on his brow.

'Are you in a lot of pain?' she asked. 'On a scale of one to ten?'

'Twelve,' he said, squeezing his eyes closed and pushing the word out through his teeth.

'All right.' Her head was swimming—the shock of this awful event was beginning to crowd in on her, but she made a huge effort to cast her feelings to one side. 'I'll give you something to take that away, just as soon as I've done a preliminary examination. Try not to move. It's very important that you stay still.'

She made a brief but thorough check of his injuries and noted his blood pressure and pulse, before injecting him with a painkiller. 'I need to put a collar around your neck to immobilise it and make sure there'll be no further damage.'

Alex didn't answer her. His strength seemed to be ebbing away, and she realised that he might be slipping into neurogenic shock through a combination of pressure on the spinal cord and possible internal bleeding.

A wave of panic swept through her. It was down to her to get him through this. What if she couldn't do it?

'Would you like some help?' Connor came over to her, and she guessed he'd been standing by, waiting to see if he was needed.

'Yes, that would be great, thanks.' Alyssa sent him a fleeting glance. His expression was serious, but he was calm, and his long, lean body was poised and ready for action. If only she could experience some of that inner composure. She said quietly, 'His blood pressure and pulse are both dropping rapidly, so I'm going to try to stabilise him with intravenous fluids.'

It was a very disturbing situation. When she tested his reflexes, Alex wasn't aware of any sensation in his legs and that was tremendously worrying, because it meant the eventual outcome could be disastrous. It was possible the damage was so great that Alex might never walk again.

She dashed those thoughts from her mind and breathed deeply to try to overcome the chaotic beat of her heart, concentrating on doing what she could for her patient. It was down to her to bring about the best outcome possible for him and the responsibility weighed heavily on her. 'I want to get a rigid collar around his neck…that's all important…and we must give him oxygen.'

He nodded. 'I'll do that for you.' He knelt down and supported Alex's neck while Alyssa carefully fixed the protective collar in place. Then he placed the oxygen mask over their patient's nose and mouth and started to squeeze the oxygen bag rhythmically. All the time, Alyssa was aware that Alex was slipping into unconsciousness.

She sucked in her breath. 'His heart rate is way too low. I'm going to give him atropine and have the defibrillator standing by, just in case.' Simply, if the heart didn't pump blood around his body effectively, her patient would die, but the atropine should help to increase the heart rate.

She quickly prepared the syringe while Connor continued with the oxygen. 'Okay,' she murmured, 'let's see if that will bring him round.' While they waited for the drug to work, Alyssa placed pads on Alex's chest and connected him to the portable defibrillator.

'It's not happening—the heart rate's not picking up enough,' Connor observed with a frown a short time later. 'Maybe it's time to deliver a shock to the heart.'

She nodded and set the machine to the correct rate and current. 'Stay clear of him while I do that.'

Connor moved back a little, and both of them waited. For a second or two, nothing happened, and Alyssa's mouth became painfully dry, the breath catching in her throat. She realised she was praying silently. This had to work.

Then there was a faint bleep, and the display on the defibrillator began to show a normal heart rhythm. She breathed a sigh of relief. The rate was still slow, but at least he was out of the woods for the moment.

The ambulance arrived as she and Connor continued the struggle to regulate Alex's blood pressure. The paramedics greeted Connor as a friend, as if they'd known him for a long time, and then they listened as Alyssa quickly brought them up to date with what was going on.

'I'm very worried about any injury to his back,' she said quietly, 'so we need to take great care when we move him. We'll help you to get him onto a spinal board.'

She and Connor knelt with one of the paramedics alongside Alex's still form, each one ready to lift and gently roll him on his side towards them on Alyssa's command. 'Okay, let's do it…three…two…one…go.'

The second paramedic slid the board underneath Alex, and then they carefully rolled him onto his back once more.

'That was well done.' Alyssa stood back as the paramedics strapped him securely in place and lifted him on to a trolley stretcher. Alex was still not speaking and she was dreadfully afraid his condition was deteriorating fast. 'I'll go with him to the hospital.'

'Okay.' The paramedic nodded and turned to Connor. 'Will you be coming along, too?'

'Yes. I'll follow in my car.'

Alyssa watched as they trundled Alex towards the ambulance, and saw, out of the corner of her eye, that Ross was hovering nearby. Seeing that she had finished working on her patient for the time being, he hurried over to her.

'Is he going to be all right? I couldn't believe what I was seeing. It's my worst nightmare.' The lively, boyish young man he'd been just a short time ago had disappeared completely. He looked haggard, devastated by what had happened.

'We'll know more after they've done tests at the hospital.' She laid a hand on his arm, wanting to comfort him. 'It wasn't your fault, Ross. All stunts carry danger, you know that. It was plain bad luck.'

'Even so, I feel terrible about it.' His face was ashen. 'Maybe I shouldn't have been directing today, but Dan had to be somewhere else, so I had to step in. I know he wanted to be here for this scene. Maybe it was an omen...'

'Ross, you mustn't blame yourself. No one could have foreseen what happened.'

His shoulders sagged. 'I don't know...I thought I had everything covered...' He pulled himself together, straightening up. 'I want to go to the hospital to be with him, but I have to get in touch with his wife, and stay here and talk to the police, and try to explain what went wrong. There will be all sorts of questions, accident reports, insurance forms to be dealt with... I'm going to be sifting through all that over the next few hours, but tell him we'll take care of his family and see to anything that he needs, will you? Anything he wants, he just has to ask.'

'I'll tell him.'

'Thanks. I'll come along to see him just as soon as I can.'

'Of course.'

She gave him a reassuring hug and then turned back to the ambulance. Connor was standing by the open doors, supervising Alex's transfer.

'It looks as though Ross isn't taking it too well,' he murmured.

'No, he isn't. He feels responsible.' She glanced at him. He looked concerned as he watched his brother brace himself and walk towards a uniformed officer. 'Do you want to stay with him while he talks to the police and so on?'

He shook his head. 'No, I think I can probably be of more use at the hospital. I'm sure Ross will cope once he's over the initial shock.'

'Maybe. Let's hope so.' She frowned, rubbing absently at her temple, where a pulse had begun to throb.

He studied her, his grey eyes narrowing. 'Are you all right? You've gone very pale all of a sudden.'

'I'll be fine. It's just a bit of a headache starting.' She had to admit to herself, though, that now her role as an immediate response medic was complete, she wasn't feeling good at all. She'd taken this job feeling pretty certain that nothing like this would ever happen. When it had, despite all the odds, she'd found herself acting purely on instinct, following the basic tenets of medical care in the way that she'd been taught, in a way that had become second nature to her.

Now, to her dismay, the adrenaline that had kept her going through those initial moments was draining away and in the aftermath she was shaking inside. She was experiencing those same feelings of dread, of exhaustion and nervous tension that had started to overwhelm her when she had been working in emergency back home. A feeling of nausea washed over her.

She climbed into the ambulance and seated herself beside Alex, closing her eyes for a brief moment as though that would shut out the memories. He reminded her so much of that patient she'd treated back in the UK. They were about the same age, the same build, with dark hair and pain-filled eyes that haunted her, and both had fallen...

The paramedic closed the doors, bringing her back to the present with a jolt, and within a few seconds they were on their way, siren blaring, to the hospital.

Connor met them at the ambulance bay. 'Welcome to Coral Cay Hospital,' he murmured, reaching out to help Alyssa step down from the vehicle. His grip was firm and the hand at her elbow was reassuringly supportive. 'Our trauma team is all ready and waiting for the patient. They'll take good care of him, you'll see.'

Oddly, she was glad he had decided to come here with her. 'Yes, I'm sure they will.' By all accounts, the hospital had a good reputation and Alex would be in safe hands.

The registrar was already walking by the side of the trolley as the paramedics wheeled Alex into the emergency unit, and Alyssa went with them, ready to talk to the doctor about his condition.

'We'll do a thorough neurological examination,' the registrar told her. 'And then we'll get a CT scan done so that we can find out exactly what's going on.' He glanced at Connor. 'Do you know how we can get in touch with any of his relatives?'

Connor nodded. 'You don't need to worry about that, Jack. My brother's already spoken to Alex's wife. He rang to tell me on the car phone when I was on my way over here. She's going to make arrangements for someone to look after the children while she comes to be with him.'

'That's good.' They'd reached the trauma bay by now, and Jack started on his examination of the patient. Alyssa and Connor took turns to tell him what had happened and describe the treatment they had given Alex.

'You did everything you could,' the registrar said, 'but there's nothing more you can do here. Why don't you two go and get a cup of coffee, and I'll let you know as soon as the scans are finished? I know how concerned you must be, but I promise I'll keep you in the loop.'

'Okay. Thanks. We'll get out of your way.' Alyssa

glanced at Alex, who was connected to monitors that bleeped and flashed and underlined the fact that he was in a distressing condition.

'I can hardly believe this is happening,' she said under her breath as she walked away with Connor.

He nodded. 'It's hard to take in.' He sent her an oblique glance. 'Are you okay? You don't look quite right.'

'I'm fine,' she lied.

'Hmm. I suppose all this must come as a shock when you imagined the job would involve nothing more than having to deal with a few minor ailments or lacerations.' He led the way along the corridor and showed her to his office, pushing open the door and ushering her inside, his hand resting lightly on the small of her back. It was strangely comforting, that warmth of human contact.

'Please…take a seat.' He waved her to a chair by the desk, and then flicked a switch on the coffee machine that stood on a table in a corner of the room.

She looked around. The office had been furnished with infinite care, from the seagrass-coloured carpet that added a quiet dignity over all, to the elegantly up-holstered leather armchairs that would provide comfort and ease to anxious relatives, keen to know the details of any treatment their loved ones would need. There was a leather couch, too, set against one wall, adding a feeling of opulence to the whole.

To one side of the room there was a mahogany book-case, filled with leather bound medical books, and in front of the large window was a highly polished desk made of the same rich, dark mahogany. This was topped with a burgundy leather desk mat and beautiful accessories, which included a brass pen-holder and an intricately designed brass paperweight.

'You're still look very white-faced,' he remarked as he set out two cups and saucers and began to pour coffee. 'It's not just that you're worried about Alex, is it? I can't help thinking there's something more.' He hesitated for a moment. 'Shall I get you some painkillers for the headache?'

She shook her head. 'Like I said, I'll be fine.'

He slid a cup towards her. 'Would you like cream and sugar with that?'

'Please.' She nodded, and he slid a tray containing a cream jug and sugar bowl onto the desk beside her. The bowl was filled with amber-coloured chips of rock sugar that gleamed softly in the sunlight and gave off a pleasing aroma of dark molasses.

Connor sat down, leaning back in his black leather chair, eyeing her over the rim of his cup. 'Something's definitely not right,' he said. 'What is it? You did all you possibly could for Alex, so it can't be that. Does it have something to do with the reason you're not working back in the UK?'

Her eyes widened and her heart missed a beat. 'Why would you think that?'

He shrugged. 'A few stray connections linking up in my mind. It's odd that you would leave the place where you did your training and where you worked for several years and give it all up to come halfway across the world. I can't help thinking something must have gone wrong. It's not as though you could afford to travel the world and simply take time out.'

She raised a brow. 'How do you know all that? Have you been talking to Ross?'

He smiled. 'Of course. He talks about you every opportunity he gets.'

'Oh, dear.' She brooded on that for a moment or two. She'd never given Ross the slightest encouragement to think of her as anything more than a friend, but somewhere along the way he must have started pinning his hopes on something more developing between them. Judging by what Connor was saying, she would have to put a stop to it, and sooner rather than later.

He was watching her as she thought things through. 'He thinks the world of you and would do anything for you, but we both know that you don't really feel the same way about him, don't we?'

She stiffened. 'I like Ross. I think he's a wonderful person.' She didn't appreciate the faintly challenging note in Connor's tone. It annoyed her that he should imply she had come here with an ulterior motive.

'Yes, he is…' Connor agreed, 'but that still doesn't explain why you abandoned everything to come out here with him.'

She sipped her coffee, giving herself time to gain a little more composure. 'You think I was sick of working for a living and gave up on it to follow him, don't you?'

'Isn't that a possibility?' He studied her thoughtfully. 'The idea of coming to a sun-soaked island where you could relax and forget your cares must have had huge appeal.'

She smiled briefly. 'Of course it did. But you're forgetting…in my case I'm actually here to work. Ross gave me the opportunity to try something new and I jumped at it. I don't see anything wrong with that. Do you?' Her chin lifted and a hint of defiance shimmered in her green eyes.

'When you put it that way, no…of course not.' His glance wandered over her face, lingering on the perfect curve of her mouth, the fullness of her lips made moist by the coffee and accentuated by the inviting, cherry-red lipstick she was wearing. After a moment or two he pulled himself up and shook his head as though to clear it. 'I dare say a lot of people would envy you being able to simply take off and leave everything behind.'

'I guess so.' She might have said more, but his pager went off just then, and he frowned as he checked the text message. 'Jack Somers has finished the preliminary tests. We can go and talk to him now.'

'That's good.' Her stomach muscles tightened in nervous expectation.

They went to find the registrar in his office. 'I have the CT scans here,' he said, bringing up the films on his computer screen. 'You'll see there are a couple of fractured vertebrae and there's a lot of inflammation around that area.'

Connor winced. 'It'll mean an operation, then?'

Jack nodded. 'I'm afraid so.' He glanced at Alyssa. 'We'll get him prepped for surgery as soon as possible, maybe within the hour. The surgeon will stabilise the spine with metal rods and screws and do what he can to ease the pressure on the spinal cord. Unfortunately, it'll be some time before we know what the outcome will be regarding him regaining any movement in his legs. There's so much swelling that it's hard to see exactly what damage has been done.'

'I appreciate that. Thanks for letting us know.' Alyssa was saddened, looking at those films. How would Alex take the news, having been an active, athletic man? He was in his prime, with a young family to support, and it grieved her to think of how this would affect them.

Connor added his thanks and they left the office, going over to the trauma room where Alex was being tended by two specialist nurses. Alyssa spoke to them and watched for a while as they set up drips and programmed the medication pump. He was still unresponsive, but he was being well looked after, she felt sure.

There was nothing more they could do there and she went with Connor to the car park a few minutes later.

'Time's slipping by faster than I imagined,' he said, looking briefly at the gold watch on his wrist. 'Maybe we should go and get some lunch and come back later to see how he's doing once the operation is over.' He glanced at her. 'We could go to Benvenuto, if you like. It would be a shame to let Ross's lunch reservations go to waste, don't you think?'

'I don't know. I…' His offer caught her unawares. Until that moment she hadn't even realised she was hungry, but now he mentioned it there was a definite hollow feeling in her stomach. Even so, it made her feel uncomfortable to think of deserting Ross and going out to lunch with Connor instead. 'Is there no chance he could join us? Perhaps I should give him a call…'

'I already did that.' They had reached his car, a low-slung, highly polished sports model, and now he pulled open the passenger door and waited for her to slide onto the leather upholstered seat. 'I spoke to him while you were talking to the nurses. He agreed it would be a shame to let the booking go to waste.'

'Oh, I see.' She frowned. 'I suppose he's still busy dealing with the accident reports? Did he say how it was going?'

'He's still talking to the insurers and working on his report. Then at some point he'll have to meet with the director and work out how they can reschedule the filming. Everything's been put on hold for the next couple of days. Everybody's too upset to go on right now. He's spoken to Alex's wife, and arranged for a car to take her to the hospital.'

'I'm glad he did that.'

Connor slid into the driver's seat and set the car in motion, while Alyssa sat back, thankful for the air-conditioning on such a hot day. Connor had a light touch on the controls and it seemed as though the car was a dream to handle, smooth and responsive, covering the miles with ease. If it hadn't been for her worries, the journey to the marina would have been soothing and a delight to savour.

Instead, she tried to take her mind off things by looking out of the window at the landscape of hills clad with pine forest, which soon receded into the distance and changed to a vista of lush orange groves and thriving banana plantations.

'We're almost there,' Connor said a little later, pointing out the blue waters of the marina in the distance. 'I expect the place will be quite busy at this time of the day, but Ross reserved a table on the terrace, so we'll be in the best spot and able to look out over the yacht basin.'

'That sounds great.' She made a face. 'I'm actually starving. I hadn't realised it was so long since breakfast.'

'Hmm. I'm not surprised.' He looked her over and smiled. 'I doubt you can really give what you have to eat the term "breakfast". Fruit juice and a small bowl of cereal is more like a quick snack, I'd say.'

She looked at him in astonishment as he drove into the restaurant car park. 'What do you mean? How do you know what I eat?'

He slipped the car into a parking space and cut the engine. 'I've seen you from the upper deck—you often go out onto the terrace to eat first thing in the morning, don't you? You're a lot like me in that. I like to be out in the fresh air so that I can take stock of my surroundings and, like you, I drink freshly squeezed orange juice. It makes me feel good first thing in the morning. Though how you can expect to last for long on what you eat is beyond me.'

He came around to the passenger side of the car and opened the door for her. She frowned. 'I usually take a break mid-morning and catch up with a bun or a croissant,' she said in a rueful tone. 'Of course, with everything going on the way it did today, that didn't happen.'

'You should enjoy the food here all the more, then.' He locked the car and laid a hand on the small of her back, leading her into the restaurant.

Alyssa was glad of the coolness of the interior. His casual, gentle touch felt very much like a caress to her heightened senses, and the heat it generated seemed to suffuse her whole body.

A waiter showed them to their table out on the terrace, and once again the heat of the sun beat down on Alyssa's bare arms. Her cheeks felt flushed and Connor must have noticed because he said softly, 'At least we'll be in the shade of that palm tree. There's a faint breeze sifting through the branches—couldn't be better.'

'It's lovely here.' She sat down and absorbed the

beauty of her surroundings for a while until gradually she felt herself begin to relax. On one side there was the marina, with an assortment of yachts bobbing gently on the water, and on the other there was the sweep of the beach, with a magnificent stretch of soft, white sand and a backdrop of low scrub and palm trees.

In the distance, the coastline changed yet again, becoming rocky, with jagged inlets, peninsulas and lagoons. There, the trees were different, smaller, and she could just about make out their twisting trunks and branches laden with sprays of yellow flowers. 'Are those the logwood trees I've been hearing about?' she asked, and he nodded.

'That's right.'

'I heard the wood yields a rich, deep reddish-purple dye,' she said. 'I've seen some lovely silk garments that were coloured with it.'

'Yes, it's used quite widely hereabouts. The flowers give great honey, too, so I guess it's a useful tree all round.'

The waiter handed them menus, and they were silent for a moment, studying them. Connor ordered a bottle of wine.

'I can't make up my mind what to choose,' Alyssa said after a while. 'Everything looks mouth-wateringly good to me.'

'I thought I might start with conch chowder and follow it with shrimp Alfredo and marinara-flavoured pasta,' he murmured. 'They do those dishes particularly well here.'

'Hmm…I think I'll go along with that, too.' She smiled and laid down her menu.

The waiter took their orders, and Connor poured her a glass of wine and asked about her family back home.

'Do you have any relatives in the UK? I know you have your cousin Carys in Florida.'

'My parents are living in London at the moment,' she told him. 'I don't have any brothers or sisters.'

He frowned. 'I imagine they must miss you, the more so since you're an only child.'

'Possibly.' She thought about that for a moment or two. 'But they're really quite busy... My mother runs a boutique and my father is a businessman, a director of an electronics company. I don't think they'll really have time to worry about what I'm getting up to. And of course I've lived away from home for a number of years, since I qualified as a doctor.'

'Hmm...that sounds like quite a...sterile...relationship.' He studied her for a while, pausing the conversation as the waiter brought a tureen of chowder to the table and began to ladle it into bowls.

Alyssa tasted her creamy soup and mulled over Connor's remark. 'I don't know about that,' she said. 'It was always that way, for as long as I can remember. In my teenage years I was what people called a latch-key kid, coming home to an empty house because my parents worked late. I didn't mind back then. In fact, I never thought much about it. I learned to fend for myself, and there were always friends that I could be with, so I wasn't lonely.'

He'd hit on something, though, the way he'd described her relationship with her family. Her eyes were troubled as she thought it over. Sometimes she'd missed that intimacy of family closeness that her friends had seemed to take for granted, especially when her career had started falling apart and her love life had taken a dive. She hadn't felt able to share her innermost secrets, even with her best friends, but it would have been good to be able to turn to family in her hour of need.

She told him a little about her mother's fashionable boutique, and how she would try on the latest designs and try to persuade her mother that she could be a good advert for the shop by wearing the beautiful creations.

'She didn't fall for that one very often, unfortunately.' She smiled, and hesitated while the waiter cleared away the first course. 'Do your parents live close by?' she asked.

He nodded. 'Reasonably so. They live in the Bahamas, but on different islands. I see them quite often, but never actually together. They divorced some years ago and my father remarried recently.'

'I'm sorry.' She frowned. 'It must have been hard for you to cope with that…for Ross, too.'

'Yes. It was difficult for Ross, especially. He was about eleven at the time, and very impressionable. Of course, you grow up hoping that your parents will stay together for ever, and when it doesn't work out that way you struggle to come to terms with all the fallout.'

'I understand how that must be a problem.' Her gaze was sympathetic. 'I've been lucky, I suppose, in that my parents are still together.'

The main course arrived, and they were quiet for a while, savouring the delicate flavours of pasta and shrimp, and then they both marvelled at the way the chef had brought his magic touch to the ingredients. The pasta was made with tomatoes, garlic and herbs, and was particularly good.

'I can see why this place is so popular,' Alyssa murmured, spearing a shrimp with her fork and raising it to her lips. 'This is delicious.' She loved the flavour of the Alfredo sauce, made from a blend of white sauce and cream cheese.

Connor watched her, his glance following the gentle sweep of her hand and hovering around the full curve of her mouth. He topped up her glass with wine, a light, fruity complement to the superb food.

'It is,' he agreed softly. 'But, you know, there are lots of good experiences to be had on our island. Sightseeing, sailing, maybe even exploring the coral reefs…though I expect you know all about those.' He lifted his glass and swallowed some of the clear liquid. 'Have you had time to look around and get to know the place?'

She shook her head, causing the bright curls to quiver and drift against her shoulders. 'Not yet, unfortunately. Ross wanted to show me around, but he's been very busy with the film, and for my part I'm still trying to get settled in and find my way around my new job. I dare say there will be time to do all those other things before too long. I have a couple more months on my contract here, so there's no hurry.'

'I could take you anywhere you wanted to go,' he suggested. 'It would be a shame to miss out on any of the delights of this beautiful island, don't you think?' His voice was silky smooth, reassuringly pleasant and somehow intimate at the same time.

'I…uh…yes, I suppose so.' Alarm bells started to ring inside her head. His offer was tempting, but why was he offering to show her around? He'd made it quite plain where they stood, on two sides of a dividing line, with Ross in between. 'Um…it's great of you to offer, but you really don't have to put yourself out.' She returned his gaze. 'I'm sure Ross will be free soon enough to take me out and about, and even if he isn't, I can manage some sightseeing by myself.'

'But that wouldn't be quite as enjoyable, I think.' He leaned back in his chair as the waiter came to clear the table and take their order for dessert. He handed her the menu. 'What's your fancy? There are all sorts of dishes flavoured with coconut—as you might imagine, with the number of palm trees around—or bananas, of course. Or maybe you prefer chocolate?'

'Do you know, I think I'd like to try the crêpes Suzette. Have you tried them?'

'I have. They're a good choice. I think I'll join you. One of their specialties here is to bring them to the table and flame them in Curaçao and Grand Marnier and then top them with luscious, sweet, dark cherries.' He smiled and gave the order to the waiter, then offered to top up her wine glass once more.

She covered the glass with her hand. 'No more for me, thanks. I need to keep a clear head.'

'Why do you have to do that? You're not on duty any more, are you? Filming has stopped for a couple of days, so you can relax for a while. Why not take the opportunity to ease back from work and being on your guard?' His dark eyes seemed to glint as he spoke, but it might have been a trick of the light. 'Because you are on your guard, aren't you?' he murmured.

With him, yes, she'd been constantly on her guard, ever since the moment they'd first met. He knew it, and she couldn't help but feel he was tormenting her with the knowledge.

'I've always found it best to keep an eye on what's

going on all around,' she said quietly. She'd been caught unawares with James, her ex-boyfriend, and she was determined nothing like that was ever going to happen again.

'Hmm…I wonder why?' His eyes narrowed on her, but she didn't answer him.

Instead, she took an interest in the dessert dish that the waiter prepared with a flourish before placing it in front of her. She dipped in a spoon and tasted the mix of flavours. The crêpe Suzette was hot, with a melt-in-the-mouth sauce, and the smooth, cold ice cream served with it was a delicious contrast. Connor watched her for a moment, as though he was fascinated by her absorption with the food.

'We both have some free time outside work,' he murmured, 'so perhaps you could think again about us spending it together… Maybe we could take a trip on a glass-bottomed boat so that you can see the coral close at hand. Would you like that?'

'I'm sure it would be a delightful experience,' she said softly, and he lifted a dark brow in expectation until she added, 'but somehow I don't think it would be right for you and me to be together too much outside work.'

'You don't?' He studied her thoughtfully, taking time to taste his dessert. 'Why is that? Are you afraid Ross might be concerned about what you're doing?'

'Not exactly…but I'm a bit puzzled. After all, if you really think there's something going on between us, it's a bit strange that you would think of asking me out.' She finished off her dessert and laid down her spoon, resting her hand on the table alongside her wine glass and running the tips of her fingers over the delicate stem.

He shrugged. 'I heard you say that you were through

with romance, so maybe I'm taking that statement at face value. In that case, why should it be a problem for Ross if you and I were to spend some time together?' He reached for her hand, taking it into his palm and brushing his thumb lightly over her smooth skin. Her heart began to thump heavily.

'I'd like to spend time with you, Alyssa, and get to know you better.'

'Like I said, I don't think that would be a very good idea.' Her voice was husky, drowned out by the thunder of the blood in her veins as his fingers travelled along her wrist in a subtle caress. 'I...uh...I'm not looking for any kind of involvement right now.'

'That's all right. Neither am I. Things don't have to get serious. I'm not looking for commitment.' His mouth made a wry curve. 'After the mess my parents made of things, that's the last thing I'm looking for.' His gaze meshed with hers. 'But we could have a good time all the same, you and I...no strings.'

She made a faint smile. 'That sounds...interesting,' she murmured, the breath catching in her throat. Her heart had switched into overdrive now, the beat building up to a crescendo as his fingers gently massaged the back of her hand and his thumb made tantalising circles over her wrist. 'Only...' She pulled in a deep breath. 'Only I have the feeling you're not being quite straight with me. I did mean what I said. I'm not looking for any kind of attachment right now, strings or no strings.'

She carefully extracted her hand from his. 'I'm sorry if that messes with your plans.'

He frowned. 'Not at all. It was just a suggestion, and I don't want to upset you in any way.' His glance drifted over her. 'Can you blame me for trying? You're a beautiful young woman, and I'd surely need to have ice water in my veins if I wasn't interested in you.'

She swallowed hard. 'I'm flattered, I think, but my answer's still the same, I'm afraid. I'd sooner keep things the way they are.'

'As you please, of course.' He smiled. 'Though that's not to say I won't keep trying.'

He signalled to the waiter to bring coffee, and for the rest of their time at the restaurant he was charm itself, talking to her about the island, the people and places that made up its exotic appeal. He backed off from making any more overtures and she tried to relax a little.

She didn't believe for one minute that he was interested in her for her own sake. No matter what he said, he was acting purely in his brother's interests. He thought she was involved with him in some way, and he wanted to break it up, even if it meant taking her on himself. If Ross were to be hurt in the process, then so be it, because in his mind she was the dangerous one here.

He believed she had the power to ruin his brother's happiness, and he meant to put a stop to that by any means possible. She would be as wary of Connor as she would be of a stalking tiger.

CHAPTER THREE

'I CAN'T believe we've had such a difficult day.' Ross waited while Alyssa stopped to pick up the local newspaper that lay on the porch, tossed there by the delivery boy earlier in the afternoon.

Ross followed her along the hallway and into the spacious living room. 'Do you mind if I open the doors onto the veranda?'

'Please do. Open every one you come across.' She shrugged off her light cotton jacket and kicked off her shoes. It was early evening and she was looking forward to sitting out on the deck for a while. 'I'll fix us a drink. Would you like hot or cold?'

'Cold, definitely. All I want to do is to sprawl in a chair and wind down for half an hour or so.' He ran a hand through his dark hair, leaving it dishevelled and giving him a distinctly youthful appearance.

Alyssa looked at the newspaper, scanning the headlines, and winced. 'It says here there was an accident on the highway this morning. I wonder if Connor had to deal with that? I expect he must have, unless the casualties were flown to the mainland.'

The standard of driving out here could be atrocious, she'd discovered, with people speeding and driving recklessly, or overloading their vehicles to the point where they were dangerous. According to the news report, this latest crash was as the result of a motorcyclist weaving through lanes of moving traffic.

'He most probably did,' Ross said. 'In fact, he might have been called out to go to the scene—he does regular stints as an on-call first attender. The emergency services want him there if the injuries are very serious and it's something the paramedics can't deal with on their own.' He frowned. 'I'll give him a ring,' Ross said, 'if that's all right with you? I think I heard him moving about upstairs. I want to speak to him, anyway, to see how things are going, so I expect he'll want to come down here for a while.'

She nodded. 'That's okay. I'd better set out three glasses and some sandwiches.' She didn't feel that she had much choice but to see Connor, given that she was living in his house rent-free for the duration of her contract. To object would simply be churlish, wouldn't it? Her head was aching already, though, and the last thing she needed was to be on her guard around Connor.

He walked out on to the veranda a few minutes later, bringing with him a basket of fruit. 'For you,' he told Alyssa. 'I thought you might like to sample some of the fruits of our island.'

'Wow, that's quite an assortment,' she said in an appreciative tone, gazing down at the beautifully arranged wicker basket. 'There must be almost a dozen different types of fruit in here. Thank you for this.' She was impressed. Among them there were mangoes, papaya and green sugar apples, along with pears and a large, golden pineapple. 'I don't know what I've done to deserve this.'

'You didn't have to do anything at all. Think of it as a delayed welcome-to-the-island present, if you like.'

'I will. Thanks.' She was thoughtful for a moment or two. 'Perhaps I ought to take something like this along to the hospital when I go to see Alex.'

'He already has one.' Connor's expression became sombre. 'I had one made up for him and took it in to him this morning. He's not really very interested in anything, though, at the moment. He's very depressed.'

'I suppose it doesn't help that he's not able to move much at the moment, but at least the operation went well,' Alyssa murmured. 'It's just a question of taking time to heal now, isn't it? And he'll have physiotherapy, of course, once he's up to it.' She sent Connor a fleeting glance. 'I'm surprised you found the time to look in on him if the evening paper is anything to go by. It looks as though you had to deal with a nasty traffic accident.'

He pulled a face. 'Yes, it was pretty bad. There were a few people involved, with some severe fractures, and the motorcyclist is in a very worrying condition. He went into cardiac arrest at the scene, but we managed to pull him through and get his heart started again. It's touch and go for him at the moment.'

'I'm sorry.' She frowned. 'It's a difficult job. You do what you can to patch people up, but the downside is that some of them don't make it.' Working in the emergency unit back in the UK, she had seen more than her fair share of traumatic injuries. Dealing with them day in and day out had become more than she could handle, especially when things hadn't gone well for the patient. She'd tried her utmost to help them, but occasionally fate had been against her, and that had been really hard to take.

She put down the basket of fruit in the kitchen and carried a tray out onto the deck, where they sat around on wicker chairs by a glass-topped table. She'd made up a jug of iced fruit juice and put out plates alongside a selection of sandwiches.

'Help yourselves,' she said, coming to sit down in one of the chairs. She reached for one of the filled glasses, then leaned back and stretched out her long, bare legs. Her cool, cotton skirt draped itself just above her knees. 'Mmm…this is good,' she murmured, taking a long swallow. She held the glass against her hot forehead, letting the coolness soothe her aching head.

'It looks as though you've had a difficult day, too,' Connor remarked, pulling up a chair beside her. He wore light-coloured trousers that moulded themselves to his strong thighs, and a short-sleeved shirt that was open at the neck to reveal an expanse of lightly tanned throat. His arms were strong, well muscled, the forearms covered with a light sprinkling of dark hair. For some inexplicable reason his overwhelmingly masculine presence disturbed her, and she quickly looked away.

'You name it, everything went wrong today,' she murmured wearily. 'First of all part of the prefabricated set collapsed, causing some minor injuries, and then there was a problem with some of the actors getting sick. They'd been out to breakfast early this morning and were violently ill a few hours later—gastroenteritis, I think. I gave them rehydration salts and sent them home.'

'So now we're going to be even further behind schedule,' Ross put in. 'Tempers were fraying and everyone was in a bad mood…all except Alyssa, that is.' He smiled as he looked at her. 'Somehow she managed to stay serene and patient through it all. She's a very calming influence all round.'

He sat down in a chair opposite them, by the rail on the veranda, close to the shrubbery where bougainvillea bloomed, its glorious, deep pink, paper-thin flowers bright in the sunshine. They had been planted all around the property, between showy hibiscus and the pretty, trumpet-like yellow allamanda flowers.

'We managed to keep most of the film footage where Alex did the stunt scene, which was a relief.' He frowned. 'That sounds awful, me talking like that, doesn't it, seeing how ill he is, but it could have set us back really badly. As it is, that's one worry at least off our minds.'

'Are you having problems, then?' Connor asked. 'Apart from the scenery collapsing, I mean.' He made a wry smile.

'Like Alyssa said…you name it. Nothing's going right. It's as though the whole thing is jinxed. Everything that can go wrong is going wrong. Next thing you know, we'll not be able to shoot tomorrow because there'll be a hitch with the outdoor schedule we've set up.'

'Hmm…' Connor appeared to be turning things over in his head. 'That reminds me, I had a call from Dan a short time ago. He's been trying to get hold of you but your mobile was switched off, or something.'

Ross frowned, and checked his phone. 'Wouldn't you credit it?' he said with a grimace. 'Battery's flat.'

Connor acknowledged that with a slight inclination of his head. 'Actually, he said he wanted to meet up with you at the studio. He just got in today from Florida and he wants to talk to you about the filming. He said he'll be at the studio for another couple of hours.'

Ross sighed. 'I guess that puts paid to my evening of relaxation.' He took a couple of sandwiches from the plate and stood up. 'Thanks for these, Alyssa,' he said. 'It looks as though I'll have to eat them on the move.'

Alyssa watched him go, and then looked at Connor with narrowed eyes. 'Was it really essential that he had to go over there right now? Surely a phone call would have done?'

Connor lifted his shoulders in a negligent fashion. 'I'm just the messenger,' he said. 'Far be it from me to interfere with the day-to-day work of the producer and the director.'

She looked at him from under her dark lashes. There was a smile hovering around his mouth and she didn't trust him an inch. She had the strongest feeling that he had manoeuvred the situation so Ross didn't get to spend the evening with her.

Her own phone rang just then, and she excused herself for a while, going into the living room to answer it. 'It's Carys,' she told Connor, as she glanced at the name displayed on the screen. 'Help yourself to sandwiches and salad, and there are cheese and biscuits in the kitchen if you want them.'

'Thanks.'

She handed him the evening paper, and left him to look over the headlines while she went to speak to Carys.

Some ten minutes later she went back out onto the deck, the headache considerably worse, and her mood decidedly fractious.

Connor sent her a sideways glance. 'It doesn't look as though your cousin managed to cheer you up,' he commented. 'Just the opposite, I'd say.'

She gave him a tight-lipped smile. 'She was just giving me the news from back home. She's in touch with friends over there, and they help her keep up with the latest gossip.'

'It wasn't good news, though, judging from your expression.'

'Nothing bad. My parents are as busy as ever. Apparently my father is thinking of expanding the business, and my mother has a fashion show coming up in the next couple of weeks, where she'll be able to parade some of the latest styles she has on sale.'

'That's good, isn't it?'

'I guess so.' It would perhaps explain why they hadn't had time to return her calls or answer her emails.

'Is there something more? You seem tense.'

'Nothing important,' she said. She wasn't going to tell him about James, her ex. He'd been asking after her, apparently, wanting to know how he might get in touch. That was the last thing she wanted.

She sat down and drank more of the fruit juice. 'It's another niggling headache,' she told him when he continued to subject her to a brooding stare. 'I suppose I need to learn to relax a bit more and not let things get to me so easily.'

'That would be sensible, if you could take your own advice.' He gave her a faint smile, adding on a thoughtful note, 'You could try some of the local bush medicine. That might do the trick. Do you know about the tamarind tree?'

She shook her head.

He looked around. 'See that tree over there…?' He pointed to a tree a short distance away. It had attractive leaves that billowed in the slight breeze, and there were large, reddish-coloured seedpods hanging in clusters from the branches. She nodded.

'The natives call it the jumbie plant,' he said. 'It's another name for the tamarind. You collect the leaves and boil them up in water, and then let the mixture infuse for a while. When it's cool, you drink the brew. It's supposed to make you feel much better.'

'Hmm. That sounds interesting.' She frowned. 'I wonder if it works.'

He chuckled. 'Then again, you could save yourself all that bother and just take a couple of aspirin.'

She laughed with him, and he said quietly, 'Why don't we take a stroll on the beach for a while? It might help to make you feel better. You're probably just wound up after a stressful day.'

'Yes, you could be right about that.' A walk on the beach sounded inviting, and before she gave the matter any more thought she found herself nodding. 'Okay. I think I'd enjoy a walk in the fresh air.'

She went to fetch her sandals from the sitting room, but draped the straps over her fingers as she walked barefoot along the white sand. The sun was beginning to set, casting a golden glow over the horizon, and the wading birds had come down to the shore, getting in a last meal before they retired for the night. Close by, humming birds flitted among the yellow elder flowers, sipping the nectar, and the sweet smell of frangipani filled the air. It was a magical time and Alyssa began to relax, watching the waves break on the shore, leaving behind small ribbons of white foam.

'I love this time of the day,' Connor said softly. 'Everything seems so peaceful and I find all the cares of the day begin to seep away. There's something very calming about coming down here to watch the ocean roll over the sand.'

'Mmm...that's true. I think it's because it's so steadfast. We're busy running around chasing our tails, but the forces of nature stay the same throughout, the ocean ebbs and flows and day follows night, come what may.'

They walked along the shoreline, and Alyssa felt the warm wash of water bathe her feet. Connor joined her, going barefoot by her side, so that their feet left prints in the damp sand.

As they moved further along the beach, he reached for her hand, enclosing her fingers in his palm, and at the same time he put a finger to his mouth, indicating that they should fall silent. Then he pointed ahead and she saw what he was focusing on. It was a bird, standing almost two feet high, black with a white underbelly and a large, orange bill.

'What is he?' she whispered. 'I wish I knew more about the wildlife out here.'

'He's an American oystercatcher,' he said softly, 'looking for clams or mussels, I expect. The birds migrate here in the late summer, but I've not seen any around here for a while. I think this one's a juvenile, judging from the black tip of his bill.'

'It's fascinating to see it,' she whispered back, standing still so as not to cause any disturbance that would make the bird fly off. 'I've seen so many gorgeous tropical species since I've been here.'

He smiled, drawing her close and sliding his arm around her. 'I guessed you were interested in nature from that first day. That's why I wanted to bring you down here. I know you've been busy of an evening, with one thing and another, and you haven't had time to venture very far.' His hand rested on the curve of her hip, warm, coaxing, inviting her to lean into him, to nestle into the shelter of his long body.

She was sorely tempted to do that. Here on the balmy Caribbean shore, with the sun low in the sky and nothing but the intermittent call of birds to fill the air, anything was possible. And yet it was strange that she should feel this way, considering that she was cautious now about getting close to any man. With Connor, though, everything seemed different. He confused her and set her at war within herself.

Now, as he held her with gentle, natural intimacy, she felt mesmerised by him, as though it would be the simplest thing in the world to turn in his arms and give herself up to the sheer joy of his caresses. It was what she wanted, and that was bewildering because it was as though her mind and her body were totally unconnected, her body responding to his embrace with a will of its own.

His touch was smooth, gentle, gliding over her body with infinite care. His hand trailed a path over the swell of her hip, along her waist, enticing her to him with persuasive, hypnotic ease.

She looked up into his eyes. They were dark, engrossed in her, his smile reflected in the shimmering depths. Slowly, his head bent towards her and she knew what he was about to do and for the life of her she had no will to stop it. He was going to kiss her, and it would be everything she dreamed it would be, and a whole new world would open up for her...a world with Connor at its centre.

How could that be? She gave herself a mental shake

and put up a hand, flat against his chest. 'I can't,' she said softly. 'I just can't.'

'Alyssa…' Her name was a gentle sigh on his lips. 'You and I could be so good together. There's a chemistry between us…you know it and I know it. What would be the harm?'

'It's not right. It doesn't feel right. And besides, there's Ross… I can't do that to him.'

She felt as though she was taking Ross's name in vain, but Ross was the only safeguard she had. No matter that there wasn't anything between them, it was enough that Connor would have to think twice about what he was doing. Through all this, he had his brother's interests at heart.

'You don't want him,' he said huskily. 'You've been overwhelmed by the chance he gave you to come out here. Who wouldn't be? But if you're honest with yourself, you'll see that you want what he can give you… the kudos of being with a film producer, with a wealthy man, a man who can make all your cares disappear.'

His hand stroked along the length of her spine, a slow sweep of silk that made her insides quiver and fired up her blood so that her pulse throbbed and her heart hammered against her rib cage.

'You and I are a lot alike, though you may not see it right now. Think about it. We could make a go of it, have a good time, with no commitment on either side. It'll be fun, you'll see, if only you're brave enough to give it a try.'

She shook her head and took a step away from him. 'No, Connor,' she said. 'Forget it. It isn't going to happen.'

She swivelled around and started to walk back along

the beach. She'd been badly hurt back home by James, who had sworn that he loved her, wanted her, needed her, and it had all ended in disaster.

She wasn't going to let that happen all over again, especially with a man who was only playing games with her heart.

CHAPTER FOUR

'HEY, look at you…you're absolutely gorgeous!' Ross exclaimed, his grey-blue eyes lighting up as Alyssa came out onto the deck. He gave a low whistle. 'You are fantastic.'

She gave him an uncertain smile. 'Well…thank you, but it's just a cocktail dress. I wasn't sure what I should wear for our evening out. Is this a bit over the top for a few drinks at a bar, do you think?'

'No way. But I can see I shall have to be on my guard—you'll turn the head of every man in the place.'

She made a wry smile. 'That's not exactly what I had in mind.' Ross was full of enthusiasm, and didn't seem to have noticed her worried expression. 'I just wanted to pick out something that's a little dressy to go along with the nature of the place and yet casual enough for an evening with friends.' She frowned. 'Now I'm not so sure I've made the right choice.'

'You have, believe me.' A soft, thudding sound caught their attention and they turned to see Connor climbing the steps onto the deck. 'Tell her, Connor,' Ross said. 'You must have heard what we were saying. Tell her she looks great.'

Connor was already looking at her, his eyes widening a fraction, but he didn't say anything for a second or two. He'd just arrived home from the hospital, and she could see by his expression that it had been a difficult day for him. There were lines of strain around his eyes and mouth, lending his strong features a trace of vulnerability.

He dragged his gaze away from her and nodded. 'You've pitched it just right,' he said at last. 'I'm assuming Ross is taking you to the Reef?'

'That's right.' Perversely, she didn't know whether to be disappointed or thankful that he'd made no other comment about how she looked. She was wearing a dress that faithfully followed the outline of her curves, an off-the-shoulder style, with a lightly beaded top and a skirt that finished just above her knees. 'We're having a get-together for the cast and crew, a sort of half-time rallying call. After everything that has gone wrong lately, Ross felt we needed some kind of pick-me-up.'

Connor nodded, coming to lean negligently against the rail. He looked good, dressed in pristine, dark trousers and a mid-blue linen shirt. 'Sounds good to me, but I'm not sure this is the best time to be going.'

She frowned. 'Why not? I don't know what you mean.'

'There's a storm brewing.' He looked up into the cloud-laden sky. 'I can feel it in the air. The heat was oppressive earlier, and now there's a change in the atmosphere. The wind's building up.'

Ross shook his head. 'It's a beautiful evening. There's just a bit of a breeze, that's all, and there have been no warnings issued. Anyway, we'll only be out for two or three hours. We all have to work in the morning.'

'Even so…' Connor stood his ground.

Alyssa sent Ross a troubled glance. 'It's not too late for us to cancel, is it, just to be sure?' For some reason she trusted Connor's judgement, and if he was cautious, perhaps they ought to take his concerns seriously. 'We could ring round and let everyone know, couldn't we? We can easily arrange a different date.'

'It's too late for that, I think,' Ross said. 'Some people will already be there. Besides, I don't think there's anything to worry about. The wind's coming in off the sea, it's true, and it feels a little chillier than we're used to, but it'll be fine, I'm sure. We might get a heavy rainstorm, but it should blow over fairly quickly.'

'Okay...' There was a hint of doubt in her voice. 'If you think so.' She looked at Connor, but he made no further comment. He was watching her, his gaze brooding, and she wondered if he was thinking about the day's events. 'Would you like me to get you some coffee, Connor? You look as though you could do with a cup.'

'Thanks. That would be good.' His gaze travelled to the mass of coppery curls that framed her face, lighting on the beaded clips that held her hair back and then dipping down to the silver necklace at her throat. For a moment she thought he was going to say something more but he stayed silent, and she turned to go into the kitchen. Both men followed her.

'Have you had a bad day?' she asked Connor as she switched on the coffee maker and set out mugs on the island bar. 'You look weary.'

He frowned. 'Let's just say, I've known better. I lost a patient today...a road-accident victim.'

Her green eyes clouded with compassion. 'I'm so sorry.' Despite her ambivalent feelings about him, Alyssa was torn by the tinge of raw emotion she saw on his face. She knew what it felt like to come home after a particularly bad day at the hospital.

Seeing those same feelings echoed in Connor's demeanour made her want to go to him and put her arms around him to offer sympathy and support. But after what had happened on the beach the other day, she had to steel herself to keep some distance between them.

He pressed his lips together briefly. 'We did everything we could, but it was hopeless from the start, really. His injuries were too severe, and he'd lost a lot of blood.'

She nodded, understanding what he was going through. 'You try to tell yourself you've given your best, but it doesn't help when the outcome is bad, does it? That awful sense of loss is always going to be there.' She sent him a quick glance. 'Was it the motorcyclist from the other day? You said he had multiple injuries.'

'No, fortunately he's recovering after surgery. It'll be a long job, but he's on the mend.' He accepted the mug of coffee she offered him and took a slow, satisfying sip. 'It's the same with Alex. He's recovering, but he has a long path ahead of him.'

'Yes, I realised that when I went to see him at lunchtime.' She recalled Alex's mixed feelings, pleasure at having visitors, and frustration with his situation. 'He wants to walk, but the signals from his brain are not getting to his legs properly and so he's finding it very difficult. It may be that the spinal cord is badly bruised and perhaps things will improve with time.'

'We're doing what we can for his family, in the meantime,' Ross said. 'There will be an insurance payout, but until that's finalised we're making sure that they can pay their rent and put food on the table.'

She smiled at him and laid her hand on his in acknowledgement. 'That must be a huge relief for him.'

'It is.' He returned her smile and squeezed her hand. 'It's one less pressure on him, anyway.'

'So how have things gone for you this week?' Connor dragged his gaze from where her hand was engulfed in Ross's larger one, and looked Alyssa in the eyes. 'Have you managed to steer clear of any major casualties?'

'It's been good.' Conscious of his narrow-eyed scrutiny, she carefully extricated her hand. 'I haven't had to do much at all, except to soak up the sun while I've watched the film being made. I'm looking forward to spending a few more weeks doing that.'

'Hmm.' Connor studied her thoughtfully. 'Doesn't it ever bother you, the fact that you have great medical skills at your fingertips and yet you're not using them? You showed your expertise when you worked on Alex. Doesn't it ever occur to you that you're wasting years of expensive medical training by opting out?'

She sucked in a sharp breath. He'd delivered a thrust that had gone directly to her heart. She hadn't been expecting it, and the way he'd said it, in such a straightforward, matter-of-fact way, somehow made it seem all the worse.

'I don't see it that way. I felt I needed a change of direction.' There was a faint quiver in her voice. 'I'm doing what's right for me at the moment.' She shook her head. 'I don't expect you to understand.'

Ross wrapped his arms around her. 'Don't let my brother get to you. He's sometimes very blunt and doesn't realise how he might hit a nerve.' Glaring at Connor, he said in a terse voice, 'You shouldn't judge Alyssa that way. You don't know her well enough.'

'Obviously not.' Connor's gaze darkened as Ross kissed Alyssa lightly on the temple and hugged her close. He straightened up and moved away from the worktop. 'I'm going up to my apartment to take a shower. Enjoy your evening…if you still insist on going. Just take care, and make sure you watch out for any warning signs. You might find you need to stay at the bar until things settle down.'

'I doubt that'll be necessary,' Ross answered. 'We'll be home by ten-thirty at the latest, because we have to get an early start tomorrow. We're shooting the scenes that take place at sunrise.'

Connor acknowledged that with a nod and left the room, but Ross kept his arms around Alyssa for a moment or two longer.

She looked up at him. 'Could he be right? I mean…'

'You worry too much. We get used to these tropical storms around here.' He smiled and dropped a gentle kiss on her mouth. 'You should try to relax a little.'

She sent him a cautious glance. 'Ross…you know Connor has the wrong idea about you and me, don't you? He thinks we're involved with one another, and it doesn't help when he sees you hold me this way. It's bound to make him think there's something going on.'

Ross sighed. 'Yeah, I know.' He looked into her eyes. 'And there isn't anything between us, is there? Not on your part, right?'

Alyssa frowned. She had to deal with this, once and for all. Ross had to understand the way she felt. 'You know how I feel, don't you? We're friends, Ross…great friends, but that's all. I can't think of you any other way. Besides, after the way my ex treated me, I'm not even going to think of getting involved again. It's just too painful. I'm sorry.'

'I know.' He ran a hand down her bare arm, his expression filled with sympathy and understanding. 'As for Connor, I know he has the wrong idea about you and me, but that annoys me. He's my big brother and he's always looked out for me since I was small, but it's time he realised I can make my own decisions for good or bad.' He laid a finger beneath her chin. 'I can't resist tormenting him a little, just to teach him a lesson. You're a good person and he shouldn't let his prejudices rule him.'

She shook her head. 'Even so, I want you to stop. It isn't helping and I don't like him getting the wrong impression.'

'Okay.' He slowly released her. 'I'm not promising anything, but I'll try.'

They left for the Reef Bar a short time later, and met up with friends in the lounge area where doors had been opened onto a covered terrace to let in the fresh evening air.

The atmosphere was boisterous and happy, with heavy beat music coming from a group of men playing drums, cowbells and whistles, along with a brass section made up of horns, trumpets, trombones and tuba. It was lively and very loud so that Alyssa had almost to shout to make herself heard.

'I'll get you a drink,' Ross said. 'What will you have? They do all sorts of cocktails here.'

She studied the list, written up on a board at the side of the bar. 'Hmm…let me see… Tequila Sunset sounds good…a mix of vodka and Cointreau…and so does Yellow Bird.' That was made from a herbal liqueur called Galliano and added rum. She mulled things over. 'But I think I'll go with Brown Skin Girl.' It was a mix of rum with crème de cocoa, cranberry and orange juice, and when Ross handed it to her it was in a wide-rimmed cocktail glass filled with ice and topped with a cherry.

'Mmm…this is delicious,' she told him, taking a sip. She noticed he wasn't drinking anything alcoholic, probably because he would be driving later. It didn't seem to spoil his fun, though, because he joined in with the general chatter, laughter and dancing, pulling her out onto the wooden dance floor to move to the rhythm of the Caribbean.

They danced and chatted with members of the film crew and cast, and the time passed so quickly that Alyssa was taken by surprise when it was time to leave.

'Do you want to stay on?' Ross asked. 'I could arrange a lift, or a taxi, for you.'

'No, don't do that. I'll go home with you,' she told him, and together they went to say their goodbyes to everyone.

'I've had a wonderful time,' she murmured, as they left the bar a short time later.

'So have I.' He pushed open the side door that led on to the car park, and for the first time that day Alyssa felt the chill of the breeze on her bare arms. She shivered a little, and Ross put his arm around her to warm her. Looking about her, she noticed the branches of a nearby casuarina tree shaking wildly in the breeze, its thin, needle-like leaves tossed about with casual ease.

'It's going to rain,' Ross said, looking at the leaden sky. He frowned. 'Let's get to the car before it starts.'

His car was a sleek silver saloon, and Alyssa was

glad to slip into the passenger seat as his prediction came true. Her bare arms were already wet and within a few seconds the initial individual raindrops had turned into a lashing downpour. She could hear it beating down on the roof of the car.

'Do you think we ought to follow Connor's advice and stay at the bar until the storm passes over?' she asked, looking out of the window at the growing turbulence all around. The wind had become almost violent in nature, and there was a noise, an ominous sound in the background, that she couldn't quite fathom.

Ross frowned. 'That could mean we're stuck here for hours,' he said. 'We're only about twenty minutes' drive away from home, so we could probably make it back before things get too bad.'

'I suppose so.' She wasn't convinced, and she was still worried about that loud, booming sound she could hear, even from within the relatively safe interior of the car. She saw that the Reef's bartenders were beginning to close the doors and draw the shutters over the windows. 'What's that noise I can hear? Do you know?'

'It's probably the sea,' he answered. 'The danger from these tropical storms isn't to do with the wind so much as the sea. It gets whipped up and the waves build up and the water starts to encroach on the land. Any inlets or streams quickly get swollen with flood water.'

'That doesn't sound too good.'

'No. But we're some distance from the ocean here, so we probably don't need to worry too much.'

A thought struck her, and her brows drew together in a frown. 'But we're right next to the sea back at the house. Doesn't that mean Connor's in danger?' The fact that he might be in trouble made her want to rush back right away.

Ross shook his head. 'We're on the leeward side of the island, so we're relatively sheltered there. And the trees and shrubs tend to act as a windbreak. We're on quite a raised plot, too, which is why you can look out over the sea from there. Connor will be all right.'

She was relieved. 'That's something, at least.' She wasn't happy about going on but, then, she wasn't used to life on the island, whereas Ross had lived here most of his life. She'd follow his lead.

He started up the car and they headed out along the road towards the main highway. Alyssa was apprehensive, watching the branches of the trees that lined their route sway dangerously in the wind. Some of the less sturdy ones would lose their branches if things became much worse, she felt sure.

Ross turned the car onto a quiet, rural road. 'This should be the safer option, I think,' he murmured. 'It's less open to crosswinds.'

She nodded, following his logic, but she was cautious about the tall trees that stood like menacing sentinels on either side of the road. The sky was ominously dark, and the trees appeared as black figures against the skyline, their branches dipping and swooping in a frightening way.

There was a sudden creaking and a crashing sound as one of the smaller trees seemed to uproot itself and she stared at it in horror as it started to fall across their path. Ross was quick to take evasive action, turning the steering wheel vigorously and driving towards the opposite side of the road, but Alyssa had the dreadful feeling that it was too late. Her stomach clenched in fear as a massive branch fell across the front of the car, smashing into them. At the same time the car came to a sudden stop as Ross slammed on the brakes.

Alyssa instinctively bent her head and covered her face with her arms as the thick windscreen glass groaned and shattered. Small pieces of laminated glass fell over her, but as the car shuddered to a halt, she gradually came to realise that, apart from some possible bruising from the emergency braking, she was all right. She wasn't hurt. She sat up, brushing blunt fragments of glass from her hair, and turned to look at Ross.

What she saw left her rigid with shock. Some of the tree's branches had speared the windscreen, coming through on the driver's side, and Ross was slumped over the wheel. There was a gash to the side of his head, and even in the darkness she could see that blood was trickling from it down his cheek.

Heart thumping, she felt for a pulse at his wrist. It was beating, an erratic kind of rhythm, but it was there and he was still alive. She sighed with relief, but it was short-lived. What would she do if his condition began to deteriorate? How would she cope?

'Ross, can you hear me? Can you talk to me?'

He mumbled something, and she tried again. 'I need to know if you're hurt anywhere other than your head,' she said slowly. 'Talk to me, Ross.'

Somehow, she was going to have to get them out of this mess, but for now she couldn't think what to do. It wouldn't be wise to move him, because he might have sustained a whiplash injury or worse when the branch had struck him. She flipped on the car's interior light and looked around to see if there was anything she could use to make a neck collar that would prevent him from sustaining any more damage.

In the back seat of the car she saw a newspaper, quickly leaned over to get it and began to roll it with trembling hands into a serviceable, tight wad. There was some tape in the glove compartment, and she used this to secure it around his neck. Then she gently eased him back in the seat so that the headrest supported his head. Blood oozed from his wound and he started to retch.

She searched in her handbag and found some tissues. They weren't much use, but they would help to contain things a bit if he was sick.

She breathed deeply and tried to pull herself together. Foraging in her handbag once more, she found her mobile phone and dialled the emergency services' number, only to discover that there was no signal. Dismayed, she thought through her options. Judging from what had happened to her, the ambulance and rescue services would probably be overrun with calls right now. She'd heard about the nature of these storms and could only imagine the damage that would have been caused to property, especially in the poorer areas.

She sat back in her seat and fought to stem the tide of panic that ran through her. The front of the car was completely destroyed, rendering the car out of action, even if she'd had the strength to move the tree.

She had never felt so completely alone. On a dark, stormy night she was stranded on a lonely road in the middle of nowhere, in a strange country, and for a second or two she felt a wave of panic wash through her. Her heart was thumping wildly. If only Connor was here. He would know what to do.

Only he wasn't here, and he was way too sensible to

ever have risked coming out on a night like this. Would he even know that they were in trouble?

All she could do was to sit things out and wait for the storm to abate. They were off the road, as far as she could see, so they should be safe from any traffic at least. It seemed that when he'd seen what was about to happen, Ross had swerved onto a verge on the opposite side of the road. The tree was a worry, though, a danger to other road users.

'Ross, how are you doing? Are you able to talk to me? Please try to answer me.' Somehow she had to get him to respond.

He mumbled something once more, words that she couldn't make out, but at least it meant he was semi-conscious. He didn't appear to have any other wounds, just the nasty gash on his head.

She didn't know how long she sat there, but lights suddenly dazzled her, coming from straight ahead. Was it another motorist heading towards them? She had to warn the driver about the fallen tree blocking his path. Ought she to stop whoever it was and ask for help? At least he might help them to get to a hospital.

The other car was still some distance away so she might yet be able to catch the driver's attention. She reached over and switched on the lights, flashing them on and off several times. Then she pushed open the passenger door and tried to step out into the road.

The force of the billowing, gusty wind almost knocked her over and she fought desperately to keep her balance, holding onto the car door. In the gloom she saw that the other driver had stopped and was getting out of his vehicle.

'What on earth are you doing? Get back inside the

car.' It was Connor's voice and she was so stunned to see and hear him that she stayed where she was and stared at him, wide-eyed and open-mouthed.

'In the car,' he said again, taking her by the arm and urging her back inside. Making sure she was securely settled in her seat, he came and sat in the back of the vehicle.

He must have been shocked by what he'd seen as he'd driven towards them, but he steeled himself now to reach forward and examine his brother, quickly assessing the damage.

Alyssa struggled to gain control of herself. Relief had washed over her when she'd seen him, but now the enormity of the situation was bearing down on her. Her heart beat a staccato rhythm. 'He has a head injury,' she told him, 'but he's semi-conscious. I've been trying to talk to him, to keep him awake.'

He nodded. 'We'll have to get him to the hospital. It's not too far from here.'

'I wanted to do that, but I knew, from the size of it, that I wouldn't be able to shift that tree on my own.'

'Of course you couldn't.' He studied her, his expression taut. 'Are you all right? Are you hurt in any way?'

She shook her head. 'I'm fine,' she said.

'Are you sure?' He reached out and touched her cheek as though he would physically check her out. 'You were shaking when I first got here.'

'Really, I'm okay.' She frowned. 'What are you doing here, anyway? How did you know we needed help or where to find us?' That had to be the only reason he was out here on a night like this. He'd come specially to find them.

'When you didn't come home when I expected you

I tried to call both of you on your mobiles. I guessed there was no signal, which made me all the more concerned. But I managed to get through to the Reef Bar on a landline, and the bartender told me you had left there almost an hour previously. I was worried.' His expression tightened. 'I didn't like to think what might have happened to you.'

'So you came to find us.' Thank goodness he had cared enough to do that. The brothers might have their differences from time to time, but Connor's loyalty was unshakeable. She frowned. 'You took a big risk coming out here, knowing what conditions were like.'

'I had to find out what had happened. Anyway, I have a solid, four-wheel drive that I keep for times like these. I assumed Ross would have avoided the main highway.'

He looked around. 'Okay, you stay here. I'm going to try to move the tree to make things safer for anyone else who comes this way. Then I need to get Ross out of here.'

'I'm coming with you.' She'd already started to slide out of the car, and when he started to object, she said quickly, 'You'll need help.'

Perhaps he could see from the determined tilt of her chin that there was no point in arguing with her. 'Make sure you keep hold of something at all times,' he said.

They set to work. Between them they attempted to pull the tree from the car, battling all the while against the raging storm. Rain drove into Alyssa, drenching her, and the wind took her breath away.

'Here, give me your hand,' Connor said when he was satisfied the road was clear. 'I'll help you back to the car.' She did as he asked and they huddled together against the driving force of the wind.

'Sit back in the car while I move Ross,' he said, but she shook her head.

'I'll give you a hand. We don't know if he has any other injuries, and we need to be as careful as possible,' she warned him. 'I'll hold the door open for you.'

He pressed his lips together. 'All right… But, as before, make sure you keep hold of the car, or me, at all times.'

'Okay.'

He went around to the driver's side and slowly, carefully, eased Ross over his shoulder in a fireman's lift. Alyssa helped to keep Ross's body from twisting or jerking in any way, and between them they managed to transfer him to the back of Connor's car. Even in the darkness she could see it was a top-spec model. There was no time to dwell on that, though. The gale howled all around them, whipping the branches like a maddened beast. Alyssa's teeth started to chatter.

Connor made sure that his brother was securely fastened into his seat, and covered him with a blanket that he retrieved from the boot of the car. Alyssa went to sit beside Ross, talking to him the whole time, trying to get him to answer her. Connor took off his jacket and draped it over her.

'But you'll need it,' she protested.

He gave her a wry look. 'I think right now you need it more than I do.'

He went around to the boot of the vehicle once more and came back a moment later to hand her a first-aid kit. 'There are dressings in there, and bags in case he's sick.' He frowned. 'He's badly concussed.'

Then he slid into the driver's seat and started the engine. The car purred into action and a moment or two later heat began to waft around Alyssa as he engaged climate control. It was one small comfort after what they'd been through. Very soon they were on their way to the hospital.

They'd gone a mile or so, and had emerged from the leafy lane to turn on to a road leading to a small settlement area. A creek ran alongside a cluster of wooden houses, and Alyssa guessed it had burst its banks and flooded the area, because the land all around was awash with water. She could see the moon glinting on the surface ripples. Flimsy roofs had been torn off the wooden outhouses, and here and there doors were missing.

She peered through the gloom. Even with such conditions causing havoc all around them, a group of people huddled in the wide, covered entrance to what she guessed was an old, brick schoolhouse. One of them, a man in his thirties, she guessed, started to wave frantically, trying to get them to stop.

Connor carefully drew the vehicle to a halt, glancing at Ross in the back. 'Are you still with us, Ross?' he asked.

Ross mumbled a reply. His eyes were closed and he seemed oblivious to what was going on. Alyssa had covered the gash on his head but the dressing was soaked with blood.

Connor wound down his window a little. 'What's the problem?' he asked.

'It's my little girl—she was swallowed up by the creek—it swept her away and she nearly drowned. We rescued her, but we can't get her to breathe—she needs to go to hospital. Can you help us?'

Alyssa wondered what the child was doing up at this time of night. Whatever the reason, it was a horren-

dous situation these people had found themselves in—
she doubted that any of them had transport that would
withstand the journey to the hospital.

She glanced at Ross, wondering if she dared leave
him, because Connor was already climbing out of the
vehicle to go and see what he could do to help. 'I'm
a doctor,' he told the distraught man. 'I'll see what I
can do.'

Now that she focussed more clearly, Alyssa could
make out a small figure lying in the covered porch.
The child couldn't be much more than five years old,
she guessed.

Connor knelt down beside the girl and checked her
breathing and her pulse. Then he looked in her mouth
for any obstruction and made a finger sweep search.
Alyssa guessed he found something because he shook
the debris free of his hand and started to press down on
her chest, with steady, rhythmic movements.

Alyssa made up her mind what she had to do.
Turning to Ross, she said urgently, 'I'm sorry, Ross,
but I have to go. I won't be long, but I think Connor
might need some help. I promise I'll be back with you
in a few minutes.'

Keeping her head down, she struggled through the
storm to get to Connor. Hands reached for her, and the
small assembly drew her into the relative safety of the
archway.

She knelt down beside Connor. 'What can I do?'
she asked.

'Take over from me. I'll go and get the oxygen kit
from my car.'

'Okay.' She took his place, going on with the CPR,
while Connor searched in the boot for his medical kit.

The little girl wasn't moving. She was deathly white, her lips taking on a bluish tinge, and Alyssa's heart turned over with dread. How could this happen to such a small, helpless child?

'Can you do anything for her?' the father pleaded. 'She isn't breathing, is she?' His voice broke. 'We were having a birthday celebration. That's why she was up so late. But then she wandered outside...'

Connor returned and straight away checked the little girl's pulse. 'It's very faint, but she's still with us...' He looked down at her frail form. 'Just a little more effort, sweetheart. Breathe for me. Try to fill your lungs, you must breathe.'

He placed the mask over her face and then looked up at the child's father. 'What's her name?'

'Bijou. It means "jewel".'

Connor smiled. 'That's a lovely name.' Then he turned back to the child and said softly, 'Breathe for me, Bijou. You can do it, I know you can.'

Alyssa watched him. He cared so much that this tiny girl should live. He wasn't going to give up on her while there was the remotest chance, and she desperately wanted him to succeed. She was numb inside, scared about what might happen, but she went on with the CPR without interruption as Connor rhythmically squeezed the oxygen bag.

Bijou suddenly spluttered, turning her head to one side and dislodging the mask. She coughed and seemed to choke, and then after a second or two she tried desperately to suck air into her lungs. When she settled once more, Connor held the mask over her nose and mouth. 'That's it. Good girl. Take your time. Breathe in...that's it, nice and deep.'

Alyssa smiled, overcome with joy. 'She's going to be all right.' She glanced up at the parents. 'We must take her to hospital all the same, to make sure everything's as it should be.' There could be some irritant after-effects of having water in her lungs, and the hospital would be the best place to make sure she received the right support.

Connor agreed. 'We can take her, along with one parent. I'm sorry, but I've no room for any more because my brother's injured and I have to take him to hospital. Who will it be?'

'I'll go with her.' The child's mother stepped forward. Her face was drained of colour, etched with the strain of seeing her daughter struggle for life. 'Thank you so much for what you've done. I don't know what to say. I can't thank you enough.'

Bijou's father joined in. 'Yes, yes…a thousand thanks. We owe you so much. Thank you.'

The small crowd of people helped them back to the car. The little girl was very cold but they managed to find a blanket for her, and Alyssa removed her wet dress and carefully wrapped her up warmly before placing her beside her mother in the back of the car.

Both she and Connor checked on Ross. He was still quiet, sitting with his eyes closed, occasionally retching.

Alyssa was glad of the warmth of the car once more. Connor drove carefully, looking ahead for signs of trouble but keeping on a steady path towards the hospital. It was hard to believe the evening had turned out so badly.

'We're here. Let's get everyone inside.'

Alyssa looked around, startled to find that they were at Coral Cay Hospital already. Her mind had wandered, thinking about Connor's calm, assured actions as he'd battled to save the small child, and how careful he'd been to make sure his brother came to no harm. She didn't like to dwell on either outcome if he hadn't turned up when he had.

He made his report to the on-duty registrar, and Bijou was whisked away to the paediatric ward. The registrar spoke soothingly to the child's mother. 'We'll make sure she's thoroughly warm and then we'll examine her to be certain there's no ongoing damage,' he said. 'She may need a chest X-ray and antibiotics, or possibly even medication to stop any spasm of the airways. That can sometimes happen a few hours after the event, so we'll keep her in for observation.'

Ross was wheeled to a treatment bay, where one of the emergency doctors started to check him over, looking for signs of neurological damage. 'We'll get the wound cleaned up and apply a fresh dressing,' he told Connor. 'He'll probably be glad of some painkillers, too. Leave him with us for a while.'

He looked Connor over and then glanced at Alyssa. 'You both look as though you could do with getting out of those wet clothes. We could find you some fresh scrubs to wear and then maybe you'd like to warm up from the inside. Our cafeteria is still open.'

'That sounds good to me. Hot soup would be just the thing.' Connor sent Alyssa a questioning glance, and she nodded, her mind somewhere else, watching the small girl being wheeled away.

It was beginning to dawn on her how close she had come to seeing a child die. The thought hit her like a hammer blow, leaving a heavy, aching feeling in the pit of her stomach. She felt faint. She didn't know how to handle the emotions that rippled through her like a shock wave.

Connor held out his hand to her. 'I'll show you where you can change,' he murmured. He gave her a sideways glance, a questioning look in his eyes.

She nodded, unable to answer him just then. The events of the night were beginning to crowd in on her and she had an overwhelming feeling that she was about to cry. The responsibility of being a doctor was awesome, and she didn't think she could cope with it for much longer.

He showed her to a room where she could dress in private, and handed her a large, white towel and a set of scrubs.

'Thanks.'

He left her, again with that thoughtful, musing glance, and once she was alone she stared at herself in the mirror that had been fixed to the wall.

She looked a mess. Her dress clung to her, and her hair had reverted to a mass of unruly curls, the way it did whenever it was wet. Connor, on the other hand, had looked as good as ever, with his shirt plastered to his chest and a damp sheen outlining his angular features. He was strong and capable, and she didn't know how she would have managed without him.

She removed her dress and towelled herself dry then put on the hospital scrubs, loose-fitting cotton trousers and a short-sleeved top. As for her hair, she did what she could with the towel and then used the hot-air machine next to the sink to get rid of the worst of the damp.

There was a comb in her handbag, and she ran it through her curls, restoring as much order as was possible. A smear of colour on her full lips made the final

touch, and she braced herself to go and meet with
Connor once more.

'Are you feeling a bit better?' he asked, and she nodded.

'Yes, thanks.'

'Good. I had some food brought down from the cafeteria. It's all set up in my office. I thought it might be
a bit more private in there. You don't feel much like
company, do you?'

'No, you're right. I don't.' She tried a smile. 'That
was thoughtful of you.'

He led the way to his office, putting an arm around
her waist, the flat of his hand splayed out over her rib
cage. 'Here we are. Do you want to take a seat on the
couch? You might be more comfy there.'

She sat down on the luxurious leather couch, and
he brought a tray over to the small table in front of her.
A coffee pot and cups had already been set out there,
along with cream and sugar, but on the tray there was
a small tureen of soup, together with bowls and an assortment of bread rolls. He lifted the lid from the tureen,
and the appetising aroma of chicken and vegetables
filled the air.

'This will warm you through and through,' he said,
ladling the rich mixture into the bowls. Then he came
to sit beside her and for a few minutes they sat in silence, appreciating the food and waiting while the hot
soup helped to make the chill of the night disappear
from their bones.

'You seemed very upset after we treated the little
girl,' he said when she finally laid down her spoon.
'Perhaps the events of the night were beginning to catch
up with you. You must have been shocked by what hap-

pened, with the tree coming down and everything that followed.'

She nodded. 'I was. You don't realise it so much at the time, but afterwards it comes home to you.'

'And looking after the child was the clincher, perhaps?' He opened up a box from the tray and produced a couple of glazed fruit tarts for dessert, gloriously exotic, with small slivers of strawberries, kumquats and kiwi, topped with raspberries and blueberries.

'I suppose so.' She accepted the tart he offered, but didn't begin to eat. He obviously wanted to know what had happened to suddenly make her become so emotional, and perhaps she owed it to him to tell him the truth after the way he'd risked everything to come and find her and Ross.

'The thing is, I don't seem to deal very well with those kinds of situations any more.' She frowned. 'That's a bad thing for a doctor to say, isn't it?' When he didn't answer, she pressed her lips together briefly and went on, 'I worked in emergency back in the UK, and for a time everything was fine. I was good at my job and people respected me. I always did what I could to make sure I pulled people through and helped them back on their feet.'

She hesitated, lost in thought for a moment or two, and Connor began to pour coffee, sliding a cup across the table towards her. 'Go on, please…you were saying you worked in emergency…'

'Yes. Then, one day I witnessed an accident. I was there when it happened, sitting at a table in an open-air café, watching the traffic go by. A man was at work, up a ladder, painting the window frames of the building next door to the café. His wife and children were sitting at the table next to me, talking to him as he worked, enjoying a light snack. It was a beautiful summer day and they seemed such a lovely, happy family. I think they'd been out on a shopping trip and had come to the café especially to see him. Every now and again he would stop what he was doing to pass a comment or two.'

She thought back to that time and a vivid picture filled her mind, blanking out everything else.

She sipped the coffee and realised that her hand was shaking so badly that Connor reached out to cup her hand in his, holding it steady and keeping the coffee from spilling over. 'It's all right, I have you,' he murmured. 'Are you able to go on?'

She nodded and pulled in a deep breath. 'He was in his early thirties, I think. Perhaps it was because I saw it happen that it made such an impact on me. Usually, in emergency, we see people as they come in to hospital. We treat them, patch them up, and we don't really get deeply involved in their lives and relationships, do we? We can be a little bit impartial.' She frowned. 'Does that sound bad? I mean, we do care, but...'

'I know what you mean,' Connor said. 'We don't know them when we're treating them. It's only afterwards, when they're recovering, that we begin to feel the impact.' He looked into her eyes. 'Did something happen to this man?'

She nodded again, swallowing hard. 'The café was situated on a bend in the road. All of a sudden a car came around the bend, going way too fast, and mounted the pavement. It crashed into the ladder and took out part of the wall of the building. The young man fell and went through the windscreen.' She closed her eyes briefly.

Connor helped her to put her cup down on the table. 'That must have been awful,' he said quietly.

'Yes, it was.' She clasped her fingers together in her lap. 'The driver escaped with just a broken arm and whiplash, plus a few cuts and bruises. I did what I could for both of them, but the decorator suffered a head wound and arterial bleeding. I managed to stop it and I tried to stabilise him on his journey to hospital. I even thought he might stand a chance…but it turned out that he was bleeding internally, and we couldn't do anything to stop it. The…the damage was too great.' Her eyes filled with tears.

He wrapped his arms around her. 'Here, let me hold you. I think maybe you need to let this all out. Have you never talked to anyone about this before now? I mean, properly talked about it, about how much it upset you? I get the feeling you haven't.'

She shook her head, taking up his invitation and nestling against him, letting the tears slowly trickle down her cheeks. There'd been no one she could talk to, no one who would really understand how she felt. 'No one had any idea what it felt like.'

Her parents had frowned, alarmed to hear about what had happened, but they had soon forgotten about it and moved on. To them, it was a moment of conversation. And James… James hadn't been able to understand why she wasn't able to shake off the images. 'Put it behind you,' he'd said. 'You deal with injured people every day. You'll get over it.'

It was expected of her that she would carry on. And she had, for a long time, until one day it had all become too much for her. There had been too many critically ill patients and she had found it more and more difficult to go on. Soon after that, Ross had stepped into her life.

Connor comforted her, his hand gently stroking her back, her arm, as she wept into his shirt. She felt secure in his embrace, as though he was sheltering her from the world. He didn't say anything but waited patiently until she became still, until she managed to pull herself together and started to dash the wetness from her eyes.

'I'm sorry,' she said, straightening up. She shouldn't be burdening him with her problems. Why would he care? 'I know I should be stronger. I despise myself for being so weak.'

'You shouldn't worry about that. Take your time. Take a few deep breaths and you'll start to feel better.'

She nodded, sitting up and sweeping her fingers across her cheeks to clear away any remaining dampness. Then there was a knock at the door of the office and the registrar came in. Alyssa picked up her coffee cup, holding it in both hands to enjoy the warmth, and she sat with her head down, absorbed in her own thoughts. She didn't want to face anyone right now.

'Your brother is coming round,' the registrar told Connor. He smiled. 'I thought you'd like to know. He's going to be okay.'

'That's great news. Thanks. I'll be along to see him in a minute.'

'Okay.' The registrar left the room, and Connor turned to face her once more.

'I'm glad Ross is recovering,' she said.

'So am I.' He pushed the fruit tart towards her. 'Eat it,' he said. 'They're delicious. I think you need something tasty and exotic right now.'

'They look wonderful, almost too good to eat, don't

they?' She looked up at him, suddenly concerned. 'I shouldn't have loaded all my troubles onto you. I'm sorry about that. And anyway, you have other things on your mind. I know he's going to be okay, but even so Ross needs...'

'It sounds as though he's going to be absolutely fine. I expect they'll keep him under observation for a few hours, maybe overnight, and then let him go.' He dipped a spoon into his tart and tasted the fruit. 'Mmm...fantastic.' She had the feeling he was eating in order to encourage her to do the same.

She followed his cue and started to eat. When they had both finished, he stood up and said, 'I'm going to see how my brother is doing. Do you want to stay here for a while and relax with another cup of coffee?'

'No, thank you. That was really good, but I'm full up now. I'll go with you.'

'Okay.'

They left the room together. Connor made no mention of what had gone before, and she couldn't help wondering what he thought about what she'd said. She wished she'd never given in to her feelings that way. How could she represent her profession when she was emotionally vulnerable and clearly unfit to practise? He must think she was weak and not fit to be a doctor. Wouldn't he have even more reason for doubting her now?

CHAPTER FIVE

'HAVE I called at a bad time? It sounds as though you're a bit breathless, or in a hurry, maybe? Are you getting ready for work?' On the other end of the line, Carys was keen to know what Alyssa was up to, and Alyssa paused for a moment, peering into her wardrobe and taking stock of the situation.

'I'm trying to decide what I should wear for a trip into the mangrove swamps.'

'The mangroves?' Her cousin was intrigued. 'That sounds interesting. What's that all about? Anyway, I'd have thought jeans and a light top would do the trick.'

'Yes, you're probably right.' Alyssa reached into the wardrobe and drew out a pair of white jeans and held them in front of her while she looked in the mirror. 'We're filming there later today, and I need to look okay because…guess what…' She paused for effect. 'I'm going to be on film! Can you believe it? I've been roped in as one of the extras.'

'Wow! And here I was worrying they were working you too hard!'

Alyssa laughed. 'Of course I'll be there in my medical capacity, too. But with any luck everyone will be fine and I'll be able to sit back and enjoy the ride.'

'It sounds great. I'd love to be there with you…' Her voice sounded wistful. 'Maybe we could meet up one weekend? I could come over and visit you, if you like.'

'Oh, Carys, that would be great. How about next weekend?' She chatted with Carys for a little longer and then hurried to get ready for the day ahead. The sun was out in its full glory this morning, and the sky was a tranquil blue. It was all so different from a couple of days ago when the storm had wreaked havoc over the island.

Since filming had been stopped for a couple of days, she'd been out with the teams that had been hastily set up to help clear up after the devastation, and at times she'd found herself working alongside Connor, when he'd been able to grab a few hours away from work.

Today, though, everything was serene as usual. The palm trees swayed gently in the breeze, and bordering the beach everything was rich with vibrant life. From the open doors of her bedroom Alyssa could see the pretty pink flowers of the oleander, and on the veranda itself there was a terracotta pot filled with the flamboyant orange and yellow blooms of poinciana. Just looking at them made her feel cheerful.

Strangely, since that evening when Connor had held her in his arms, she'd felt an odd sense of release. She didn't understand it at all. But it was definitely there, this lightening of spirit.

'Are you about ready to be off, then?' Ross came into the kitchen as she was doing a last-minute bit of tidying up. He'd been staying with his brother in the apartment upstairs for the last couple of days, as Connor insisted on keeping an eye on him while he was recovering from concussion. 'I wish I was coming with you as we planned, but I suppose Connor's right—the company's insurance people would have all sorts of problems with that.'

'I think it's probably best if you stay at home and rest up for a few days more,' Alyssa told him. 'You certainly look better today than you have done these last couple of days.' Apart from a dressing on his head wound, he seemed to be in reasonably good shape. He'd had an ongoing headache since the accident and some slightly blurred vision, but he'd finished taking painkillers now, and that was hopefully a good sign.

'I'd still rather I was going with you on this trip. I hate sitting back and leaving everything to other people.'

'That's because you simply don't know how to delegate,' she said with a laugh. 'Dan *is* the director, you know. You have to let him handle things.'

'Hmmph. Maybe.' He was in a grumpy mood, and that wasn't like him at all.

She patted his hand. 'Take some time out to lie back in the hammock,' she told him, pointing to the canvas that was strung up outside between two palm trees. 'It'll do you the world of good.'

'Yeah, right. Anyway, I'm sorry I won't be able to take you to meet up with the cast and crew—Connor has a day off, though, and he said he'll take you, so there won't be any need for you to call a taxi.'

'Yes, he mentioned it to me last night,' she said as she stacked crockery into the dishwasher. She'd been surprised by his offer. 'I really didn't want to put him out—he leads such a busy life and I'd have thought he'd welcome the chance to stay home and do nothing for a change. He even had to go out somewhere this morning. I heard his car start up as I was thinking about getting out of bed.'

Ross nodded. 'He went to see my father. He rang up this morning, complaining of stomach pains, and said he didn't want to call his own doctor.'

She frowned. 'I'm sorry to hear that. Do you think it's something serious?'

He shook his head. 'The beginnings of an ulcer, probably. I expect Connor will give him some tablets. I don't think it helps that my father's constantly at odds with our stepmother—his second wife. She's turned out to be a feisty individual. But, then, his judgement was never very good where women are concerned. He had an affair while he was married to our mother—not a great move, because she divorced him after she found out.' He was quiet for a moment or two, thinking about that. 'We were still quite young when it happened…I think I was about eleven.'

He pulled a face. 'So we became part of a divided family, going from one parent to the other throughout the year. And, of course, after the divorce my father became very attractive to other women who liked the idea of his wealth and the lifestyle it could bring them. I was upset, I remember. I wanted my parents to stay together, and I wanted to protect my mother from being hurt, but I didn't know how. So I poured out my worries to my big brother, and he tried to find ways to make me feel better…when all the time he must have been going through it, too.'

She tried to imagine how Connor must have felt, being torn by the disruption to family life and suddenly worrying about his little brother's well-being. She frowned. 'I can't begin to guess what that must have been like. It must have been so difficult for both of you.'

No wonder Connor was so protective of his brother even now. Back then, being some three years older than Ross, he must have taken it upon himself to shield him from any upsets that might come along. Her heart went out to those young boys struggling to come to terms with the break-up of their family.

'Yeah.' Ross absently massaged his brow with his fingers. 'It was hard when we were young, but that's all in the past now.'

'Is it?' She wasn't so sure about that. 'These things probably leave scars of some sort or another.'

'Well, you could be right. I suppose it was bound to leave some kind of legacy, and we were both at an impressionable age. That must be the reason Connor avoids getting deeply involved with anyone. If things start getting too close for comfort, he tends to bail out. And according to him I go after all the wrong kinds of women.' He made a faint smile.

'He's probably right—I've had a few near misses over the years. I tend to be too trusting, I suspect, and then I realise too late that some women are wowed by the prospect of being with a film producer. I'm just me, but they see me as something else.' He sighed. 'I guess all the upheaval in our lives was bound to affect us in some way.'

She thought about that when Ross left a few minutes later. It wasn't really a surprise to learn that Connor was reluctant to get involved in relationships in any meaningful way. There had been rumours amongst the cast and crew and people she'd spoken to at the hospital about women who'd loved and lost him. They'd been keen for something more to develop out of the relationship with Connor, but in each case apparently he'd chosen that time to gently engineer a parting of the ways.

But she didn't want to dwell on any of that right now. Thinking about Connor only left her confused and distracted. So, instead, she carried on with her chores, wiping down the work surfaces and making sure that everything was spick and span.

Connor arrived back at the house a few minutes later as she was watering the houseplants.

'Is everything all right?' she asked, checking the soil around the base of a fern. He looked ready for the day, dressed in casual clothes, dark trousers and a crisp linen shirt that was open at the neck. He glowed with health, and his keys dangled from his fingers as though he was ready to be on the move again. He was full of vibrant energy, and she resisted an urge to put her arms around him and slow him down. 'Ross told me your father wasn't well…he said he thought it might be a stomach ulcer.'

He nodded. 'I think he'll be okay. At least he seems to be feeling much better now. I gave him some tablets and told him I would speak to his doctor to arrange for tests to be done. There could be a bacterial cause, but he's suffered from ulcers before, and I don't think the atmosphere at home helps. I expect Ross told you about that?'

'A little.' She put away the watering can and turned to face him properly. 'It sounds as though your father and stepmother have a fairly volatile relationship.'

He shrugged. 'Well, you know what they say…he made his bed, now he has to lie in it.'

She frowned. 'You don't seem particularly sympathetic.' Maybe that wasn't altogether unexpected, given the circumstances. 'Ross mentioned that you went through quite a bit of upheaval when your parents split up.'

'Yes, we did, but these things happen. You learn to be philosophical about it in the end. Anyway, I expect they're happy enough. Some people enjoy living life on the edge.'

'Hmm. That wouldn't do for me.' She wondered how much of what he said was bravado. After all, that fourteen-year-old boy, shielding his brother from upset, was very much still part of the man.

'Or me.' He looked around and saw her bag on the table. 'So, are you about ready to leave?'

'I am.' She smiled at him. 'I'm looking forward to this trip. Though I do have a few misgivings. I hope we don't…' She frowned as a sudden thought struck her. 'I mean…we're not likely to come across any nasty creatures, are we? Like crocodiles, maybe? I'm not sure quite how I'd cope with them.'

He laughed. 'No, nothing like that. You'll be quite safe. It's really very tame out there. You might see a few crabs scuttling about in the water, but that's about as dangerous as it gets.' He studied her thoughtfully. 'How are you on the water? Do you think you'll get on all right in a kayak?'

She pondered on that for a moment or two. 'Um… actually, I don't know… I imagine I'll be okay. I've been in a rowboat before, and I can swim, if that's what you're asking.'

He smiled. 'I don't think swimming will be necessary. If by some remote chance you manage to overturn the boat, you'll be able to stand up in the water. It's not very deep.'

'Hmm. That's all right, then.' Her shoulders relaxed as relief washed over her. 'But I was hoping I wouldn't be on my own. These are two-man boats we'll be using, aren't they?' She walked with him to the door.

'That's right. But you'll be with me, so you shouldn't have any problems.'

Her eyes widened. 'You mean...you're coming along on the trip?' Her pulse leapt in response to the unexpected news. 'I didn't realise—I thought you were simply taking me to the meeting point.'

'Oh, no. I'm definitely along for the ride.' His gaze meshed with hers. 'I wouldn't miss out on the opportunity to spend the day with you, would I?'

Warm colour flushed her cheeks. He wanted to be with her?

'And besides,' he went on, 'as one of the partners in the company I've always thought it a good idea to see how things are going with the filming. I need to take an interest and have some say in what goes on.'

Her jaw dropped. 'You're a partner? I didn't know. Ross never said...'

'Did he not? Ah, well...' He opened the passenger door of his car and waited for her to be comfortably seated. 'I helped to set up the company with Ross some years back, but I'm more of a silent partner, so to speak. I'm so busy at the hospital that I don't have time for anything more.'

'I wondered how it was that you came to see the filming whenever you had the chance.' She looked at him as though she was seeing him for the first time.

'What was it that made you get into film production? It's a long way from medicine.'

'True.' He gave it some thought as he started up the car. 'We've always been interested in films—as boys we went to see all the latest blockbusters, and Ross had a knack for seeing how scenes were set up or how things could have been done better. For myself, I thought there was a brilliant opportunity for basing production on these islands. There's a whole lot of glamour and excitement here, all the things that filmgoers want to enjoy.'

'It's not everyone who has the money to contemplate starting such an enterprise. Were you just fortunate that way?'

'I guess so.' He drove along the coast road for a while, so that the vista of the deep blue ocean washing up onto an unbroken stretch of white sand stayed with them along the way. 'My grandfather made a good deal of money from exporting fruit, and he set up a trust fund for us. My father runs a financial consultancy business, and I learned from him how to invest any money I managed to save.' His mouth curved. 'I did pretty well out of it, all things considered.'

'So it seems.' Her eyes were wide with admiration. He'd done more than well. 'I suppose Ross must have done much the same.'

'Yes, he did.' Connor sent her a brief, sideways look. 'Where is he, anyway? I thought he would have been around to see you off.'

'He was. He came down to the apartment for a while, but then he took himself off back upstairs. I think he's feeling a little out of sorts.'

'Poor Ross.' His mouth made a crooked line. 'He hates it when I get to spend time with you.'

'No…no, it isn't that.' She shook her head to emphasise the point. 'He just hates to be away from the filming.'

'Sure he does. He'll get over it soon enough.' Connor was still smiling as he turned the car onto the main highway.

Alyssa sank back in her seat, deep in thought, contemplating the day ahead. Was it true, what he'd said earlier? Was that really why Connor had decided to come along today, because he wanted to be with her? After the way she'd opened up to him the other evening about her failures as a doctor, she hadn't expected him to be at all interested in her. After all, how could he have any respect for her when she didn't respect herself? But now…despite her misgivings about getting involved with him, she couldn't deny that the idea of spending time with him made her insides tingle.

Still, doubt crept in once more. Ever since her ex-boyfriend had let her down and proved untrustworthy, she'd had a problem taking things at face value. Was it actually the company business Connor was most concerned with today? And his reaction to Ross's grumpiness had been a little strange, too. Was he simply taking the opportunity to keep them apart whenever possible? It was all very puzzling.

'Here we are. This is the meeting point,' Connor murmured a few minutes later, and she quickly brought her attention back to the present. They had arrived at a coastal stretch of the island, where a brackish creek flowed into the sea, and people were already beginning to gather by the water's edge. Sliding out of the car, Alyssa went with Connor to join them.

All around everything was green, rich with lush vegetation, and an overhang of densely populated, leafy trees countered the heat of the sun.

They exchanged greetings with everyone who was taking part in the filming, relaxing for a while ahead of the day's events. Then the director stepped forward and spoke to them all for a few minutes, cast and extras, about the course the filming was to take. Dan was a well-built man, florid and exuberant, with brown hair that had been bleached by the sun.

'Okay folks, listen up,' he said. 'You'll be going through the mangrove swamps at a leisurely pace. Try to forget that the camera is on you. You need to be as natural as possible. Take in the scenery all around you as if you're on a pleasure trip. Our leading man will be trying to blend in like one of the tourists, and his major activity won't start until we reach the cave system, so you've no need to be anticipating anything untoward. Is that all clear?'

He looked around, and everyone nodded. 'Good. We'll be heading for the landing point—just follow the lead kayak and ignore the cameras. From there you'll take the boardwalk to the cavern system and the beach, and that's where your part ends. You'll have lunch there. It's all laid on.'

A small cheer went up. 'I hope you've provided something for us to drink,' one bright spark piped up. 'Something of the alcoholic variety would be good.' There were a few more cheers in support.

'Yes, yes, it's all arranged. Along with a bus to take you home again.' Dan clapped his hands together. 'Okay, shall we get on? Time's wasting, and the light's perfect right now. I don't want to lose it.'

Alyssa gazed around her. The mangrove swamp was

a truly magnificent sight. Huge trees seemed to walk on the water, their gnarled, tangled roots above the surface and below. Everything was verdant, bustling with life, and through the canopy the sun glinted down on the salt creek.

Connor helped her into their kayak. They were seated one behind the other, with Alyssa at the back, and slowly they edged out into the water, dipping their paddles in unison.

As they moved deeper into the swamp, she was overwhelmed by the serenity of the place. 'It's beautiful here, so peaceful,' she murmured. 'I wasn't expecting that, but it's perfect.' Birds called to one another, darting from tree to tree or gliding leisurely on the wind currents. And when she looked into the forest on either side she saw glimpses of broad-leaved ferns and, here and there, flowers, delicate, beautiful blooms in bright colours. 'They're orchids, aren't they?' she said quietly, her voice full of awe.

'Yes, that's right.' Connor stowed his paddle for a while, allowing them to drift and take in their surroundings, and Alyssa followed his example. 'They grow wild out here,' he said, 'in small pockets in the trunks of the trees or in crevices in the rocks.'

'Somehow I didn't imagine there would be flowers. It's all so lovely, it's breathtaking.'

Connor smiled. 'I thought you'd like it here. It's something we have in common, don't we…a love of nature? Ross and I often came here when we were teenagers, kayaking through the lagoons. I really appreciated it when we moved from Florida and came to live here. I loved everything about the islands. There's so much variety.'

They paddled idly through the water, passing by billowing seagrass and oyster beds, where molluscs had fastened themselves to the underwater tree roots.

They chuckled as a sandpiper teetered along the bank, in his distinctive wobbling gait, his tail bobbing up and down while he searched for titbits with his orange, pointed bill. And a few minutes later they were startled by the sudden loud call of a green heron that came to settle on the opposite bank.

'That's a bonus for us,' Connor said softly. 'You don't usually see them in the daytime, unless they're hungry or feeding their young.'

Once again they stopped paddling and remained still for a while, following the bird's movements as it picked out insects one by one and then dropped them in the water to attract any passing fish. Then, as soon as he spied his prey, he swooped, triumphant.

Soon, perhaps too soon, Alyssa thought, they reached the landing point, and tied up the kayak, stepping out onto the wooden boardwalk. On either side of them the mangrove forest became a thick, green wall of leaves and branches.

Connor put his arm around her. 'I'm glad you agreed to come along today,' he said quietly. 'I wasn't sure, after the night of the storm, whether you'd still be up for it. Those winds can be scary and they leave a wide trail of damage behind them, one way and another.'

'With people, as well as property, you mean?' She tried not to think about that arm that circled her shoulders and protected her from any stray, encroaching branch as they walked along. 'I was just so glad you came to find us that night. I don't know what I'd have done without you.'

'You'd have found a way to get him to hospital, even if it meant waiting for the next driver to come along. I was fortunate in that I found you first.'

'Yes.' She smiled up at him. 'Thank you for what you did, anyway. I was so impressed by the way you saved that little girl.'

'Ah…that was a joint operation, I think. And by all accounts, she's doing well now.'

'I'm glad about that.' She frowned. 'But what will happen about all the damage to their village? They looked like poor people, so even though things have been cleared up, it might be difficult for them to get the repairs started. I heard of other villages, too, where there were a few slight injuries and property was wrecked.'

'Yes, that's true. A number of settlements were hit, and people need help, but we've organised workers to go on with the clearing-up process.' He hugged her briefly. 'I thought it was great how you pitched in to help. Anyway, at the end of filming we'll give a gala dinner and invite people to donate to the fund we're setting up to help with rebuilding.'

She looked at him with renewed respect. 'By "we" you mean you and Ross?'

He nodded. 'We couldn't just stand by and do nothing.'

'No. I think it's great, what you're proposing.'

They walked along the pathway to a sheltered area of the rock-strewn beach, where the cast and crew were assembling for a picnic lunch. To Alyssa's surprise, someone had set up a gas-fired barbecue beneath the palm trees and a chef dressed in traditional white jacket and dark trousers was there, already busy preparing food. The cameraman turned his attention to the inlets and caves some distance away where the film action was taking place.

Connor found a patch of smooth, white sand a little apart from the crowd, shaded by the branches of a tropical sea grape tree. He sat down, reaching for her hand and pulled her down beside him. The fruits of the tree hung down in clusters above them, purplish-red in colour, as though inviting someone to pick and eat them.

'Mmm...something smells good.' Alyssa's mouth was beginning to water as the appetising aroma of chicken and barbecue ribs filled the air. 'I was expecting something like sandwiches, definitely not hot food.'

'We aim to please.' Connor smiled, and just then a couple of catering staff came around with plates, inviting people to help themselves.

Alyssa was handed a plate and Connor helped her to pick out a selection of crab cakes, served with tangy zucchini and cucumber coleslaw, along with smoked chicken wings and conch fritters. These were served with a spicy dipping sauce, and there was rice and salad to complete the dish.

A table had been set up in the shade of a cavern, where wine bottles were chilling on a bed of ice, and Connor went to fill two glasses with sparkling white wine. He came and sat beside her once more and she realised he'd brought the bottle with him, along with a bucket of ice.

'I think,' Alyssa murmured, after a while, leaning back against a sun-warmed rock, 'this is what I came here for—to the Bahamas, I mean... Sun, sand and sea, and the most delicious food ever.' There had been a wonderful selection of fruit for dessert, a perfect accompaniment to the meal. 'I sometimes think I must have died and gone to heaven.'

Connor laughed. 'Heaven here on earth, perhaps,' he murmured, filling up her glass once more. 'You might as well relax, because we're free for the rest of the afternoon, as the man said.'

She nodded dreamily as she sipped her wine. 'I will. You don't need to encourage me. I can't think of anything I'd rather be doing.'

'You can't?' He moved closer, his hand coming to rest on the soft curve of her hip, and she cautiously set her glass down on a nearby flat rock.

'Connor, I...'

'Maybe I could help you with a few ideas.' He dropped a kiss onto her unsuspecting lips and murmured softly, 'Mmm...you taste of spice and summer fruit...pineapple, I think, and plump, juicy peaches, luscious...just like you.'

She gazed up at him, eyes widening, her lips parting in startled awareness after that dreamy, soft-as-thistledown kiss, while her whole body had begun to fizz with heightened expectation. He'd kissed her just once, and to her shame she wanted more. She wanted to feel his lips on hers all over again and his hands to stroke along the length of her body.

'I...uh...'

'You...uh...need me to show you how to let go of your worries and enjoy being cosseted, don't you?' he said with a smile. 'I can do that, Alyssa. I can make you feel good about yourself. Let me show you...'

He kissed her again, slowly, thoroughly, his hand splayed out over her rib cage, warm, tender, inviting her to lean into the protective curve of his body. And she was sorely tempted. More than anything, she wanted to feel his long body next to hers, to have him hold her and to have him transport her to some magical, sensational world where nothing mattered but the two of them and their slow, sweet exploration of each other.

But something in her resisted, some faint vestige of self-preservation managed to rise above his sensual onslaught. So, instead, she shifted in his arms and even before she pressed the flat of her hand against his rib cage, he had come to realise that all wasn't well.

'What's wrong, Alyssa?' he murmured. His cheek brushed hers, teasing her with his closeness, his lips so near, yet so far, and to her dismay she felt her resistance crumbling at the first hurdle.

'Connor, I…uh…I don't think this is a good idea.'

'Are you sure about that?' he demurred softly. 'That's a great shame because, you know, I'd really like to kiss you again.' His head lowered, his mouth coming dangerously close to hers. 'Why don't you want me to kiss you?'

She made a soft groan. 'I do…but I can't let it happen. I can't get involved. Besides, there are way too many people around. It wouldn't be right. It wouldn't feel right.'

'Should we talk about conflicting signals here?' He gave her a rueful smile. 'Anyway, nobody's taking any notice of us. We're in the shade, away from where all the action is. And they'll be gone soon. The bus will be taking them back in a few minutes.'

'Won't we be on that bus with them?'

He shook his head. 'I've a boat waiting to take us back to the meeting point. I thought you might like to spend some more time here. Was I wrong about that?'

She shook her head. 'No, I love it here.'

'But you don't want to be here with me, is that it?' His features darkened, something bleak flickering in the depths of his eyes. 'Are you still hankering after my brother?'

'No, you have it all wrong, Connor. You don't understand.'

'No, I don't.' He sat up and wrapped his arms around his knees. 'Perhaps you should explain it to me.'

She pulled in a deep breath. 'You said I was giving conflicting signals, and perhaps you were right about that. I like being with you, I can't deny it. But you have to know, one of the reasons I came to the island was because I was in a relationship with someone and it all went wrong.' She swallowed. 'I thought we had something going for us, but it fell apart, and in the end I felt I needed to get away from my ex. He hurt me, and I don't think I'm ready for the dating scene again.'

'I'm sorry he hurt you,' he said softly. 'But it doesn't have to be like that with us. I'm not looking for anything heavy. I told you once before, I don't want commitment, Alyssa, but you and I could have fun together. What would be wrong in that? I like being with you. You're gentle, kind, fun to be with…intelligent… I look forward to seeing you, and whenever I'm with you I want to hold you close and cover you with kisses. Is that so wrong? I get the feeling you like being with me, too.'

'I do. But when it comes down to it, you're talking about sex,' she said in a flat voice. She shook her head. 'I don't go in for meaningless relationships, Connor. I don't sleep around, and I couldn't accept the kind of situation you're suggesting. Besides, maybe things start off that way, leisurely, friendly, no strings attached, but sooner or later, more often than not, the situation begins to change, and someone gets hurt.'

'Like you and your ex?' His glance skimmed over her, tracing a line over her taut features. 'Do you want to tell me what happened?'

She moved her shoulders in an awkward gesture. 'We were together for a couple of years.' She sucked air into her lungs. 'It started off as a mutual friendship and grew into something more as time went by. But then I found I was working more and more hours in A and E as I specialised, while he was left with time on his hands. He worked at the hospital, doing research, and his was more or less a nine to five kind of job. I think he grew tired of waiting for me to finish my shifts, and sometimes, when we had something planned, I had to let him down because I couldn't leave my patients in the lurch.'

She frowned. 'I think we might have made a go of things, all the same, but then I started to suffer from burnout. I needed someone to talk to, but suddenly he wasn't there for me. He didn't seem to understand. And for my part I began to wonder what kind of man he was if I couldn't count on his support when I needed him.'

'So you broke up with him?'

Her mouth turned down at the corners. 'Not then, not right away. We talked things through and decided to try to put things right…only perhaps I was trying a little bit harder than he was. I went over to his flat early one day, planning to surprise him with a special dinner for his birthday and tickets to a concert…but I found he was already celebrating, with a girl from his research department.'

He sucked air into his lungs. 'I'm sorry. That must

have come as a killer blow.' His eyes had darkened, his gaze moving over her.

'Yes, it was.' She lifted her chin. 'I suppose you imagine that's par for the course, the kind of thing that happens sooner or later when two people get together.'

He shook his head. 'I'm thinking the man was a fool for playing around when he could have you as his girlfriend.'

She pulled a face. 'Perhaps, deep down, he didn't believe in commitment. Like you.'

'Ouch!' He winced. 'I suppose I deserved that. But the truth is, up to now I've never met anyone that I wanted to commit to. It's not much of a defence, I know.'

He looked so deflated that she couldn't help but smile. 'Shall we just agree to enjoy the rest of the time we have here on the beach? There's more wine in the bottle—I notice you haven't been drinking much—and then I'll look forward to a ride in that boat you said you have waiting.' She frowned as a thought crossed her mind. 'It isn't a rowboat, is it? I really don't fancy paddling my way home along the coast, not after all that delicious food and wine.'

'Oh, it definitely isn't a rowing boat,' he said with a chuckle. 'It has a motor, and a cabin with a galley...as well as all the mod cons that a girl like you might like.'

'I guess that's all right, then. Everything for a girl like me...' What kind of girl did he think she was? She gave him a teasing smile. 'You seem to know me pretty well—but, then, you must have had me more or less sussed out when we first met and you decided I was after Ross for my own mercenary reasons.'

'Ah, but that was way back...an age ago,' he protested, his brows lifting. 'Are you going to keep on holding that against me?'

'Oh, yes,' she said, a glimmer in her green eyes. 'You're definitely not off the hook, by a long way.'

He held a hand to his chest as though she'd wounded him deeply, and she smiled and sipped the wine he poured for her.

The moment had passed when he would have held her close and kissed her, and she mourned its passing. But it was for the best that she'd held him at bay, wasn't it? It didn't feel too good right now, but she'd get over it soon enough. She hoped.

CHAPTER SIX

'THAT'S a really nasty sunburn you have, Ryan.' Alyssa examined the cameraman's back and shoulders, and frowned. 'How did you manage to get yourself into such a state? Your skin is very red and it's peeling, so there's a risk of infection if it's not treated.'

Ryan winced. 'I was stupid, I know. I didn't think a couple of hours out in the sun without my shirt would hurt. Only we stayed on the beach longer than I expected, and I fell asleep on my front while the others were messing about in the sea.' He moved his hands in a helpless gesture. 'I never knew sunburn could hurt so much. I've been feeling really light-headed and sick.'

'Second-degree burns can be very painful.' She went over to the sink and rinsed a cloth with cold water, giving it to him to hold over his forehead. 'That should cool you down a bit and help take away the sick feeling.'

She checked her medicine cupboard for silver sulfadiazine ointment and used the sterile applicator to spread a thick layer of the cream over the damaged skin. 'This is an antibiotic ointment, to prevent infection,' she told him. 'You'll need to come in every day for the next two or three days so that I can treat you. But I'll put a dressing on the shoulder for you, in the meantime… that's looks to be the worst bit of all.'

'Thanks, Alyssa. You're a gem. It's beginning to feel easier already.'

She smiled. 'It's the coolness, I expect. It's very soothing, but you can help yourself by drinking plenty of fluids—not alcohol but lots of water, juices and so on, over the next day or so to prevent dehydration. And make sure you wear a shirt at all times to keep the area covered.'

'Okay. Thanks again.' He left a few minutes later, clutching a prescription for ibuprofen, to help him deal with the pain.

'Another satisfied customer?' Connor put his head round the door of her makeshift surgery as she was washing her hands at the sink. The company had provided a mobile unit for her, complete with desk, couch and everything that she would need.

'I hope so. He had a nasty sunburn.'

'It must have been serious if you were using that,' he said, watching her replace the lid on the tub of ointment. 'The natives around here use something natural…gamalamee.'

She sent him a puzzled look. 'I can't say I've ever heard of it.'

'No? It's a bush medicine—the bark of the gumbo limbo tree, or gamalamee, as they call it hereabouts, cut into strips and boiled. When it's cool, they place the strips on the burn to soothe the skin and help it heal.' He smiled. 'It's sometimes known as the tourist tree.'

'Really?' She lifted a brow. 'Why's that?'

'Because the red bark peels, just like the skin of the unfortunate tourists.'

She chuckled. 'I can never be sure whether or not you're teasing me,' she said.

'Not at all. It's quite true. They say it helps a lot with sunburn.' He peered inside her fridge and lifted out a jug of orange juice. 'Is it okay if I help myself?'

'Of course. Glasses are in the cupboard on the wall.'

'Thanks.' He was still smiling as he poured juice for himself and offered a glass to Alyssa. 'It's also true that it's one of the main ingredients in a bush tea called Twenty-One-Gun Salute.' His eyes took on a devilish gleam. 'It's said to be a great aphrodisiac.'

'Hmm. I think maybe we'd best not go there,' she said with a laugh.

'Perhaps you're right. Anyway, you look cool and fresh,' he said, looking her over as she accepted the cold drink. She was wearing a short-sleeved blouse and a loose-fitting skirt that floated lightly around her legs as she walked. 'It's in the high eighties out there.'

'So you've come in here to escape the heat?'

He nodded, taking a long swig from his glass. 'It's my lunch break. I had to go and visit my father to see how he was doing, and this place was on my way back to the hospital, so I thought I'd stop by and see how you were doing.'

'Everything's going fairly well here, up to now, I think. How's your father doing?'

'He's fine. The tests showed some ulceration, nothing more serious than that, and he has medication to clear it up.' He studied her. 'So what's new here?'

She tasted the refreshing juice and took a long swallow. 'Ross is back on site—he looks fit and well, so it seems he's completely over the injury to his head. He's

so much back on form that he's getting in Dan's way,
I think.'

He chuckled. 'Is he?'

She nodded, giving a faint smile. 'He was talking to
Dan about needing to find a stand-in for Alex. There's
a water-skiing stunt coming up and they need to get it
sorted quickly. Anyway, he told Dan he wants to do
the stunt himself.'

He frowned. 'So soon after a head injury? That's
definitely not on.'

'Well, everyone seems to think Dan will agree to it.
That's the talk around here today. The thing with this
job is that people tend to drop in here and I get to hear
all the gossip. They confide all their niggling worries
and problems in me.'

'Well, I can see why they might want to do that. I notice that Ross, in particular, calls in on you fairly often.'

'And how would you know that?'

'As you say, people gossip. They know that he's besotted with you. I only have to walk on the set and people are ready to help me catch up on the news.'

She absorbed that while he finished his drink and
glanced at his watch. 'Perhaps I should be getting
back—' He broke off as someone knocked on the door,
and then Ross came in, supporting one of the stage-
hands, who appeared to be ill. He was also limping
badly, and leaning on Ross as best he could.

'Bring him over to the couch,' Alyssa said quickly.
She recognised the young man as one of the workers
who had helped with the clean-up after the storm a
few days ago. She'd stood alongside him in the flooded
area of a small settlement and piled debris onto a waiting truck.

'What's wrong, Lewis?' she asked. 'How can I help?'

'It's my foot,' he said, struggling for breath. 'The pain is really bad.' He was shivering, too, and looked as though he might pass out at any moment. This couldn't simply be a problem with his foot, she realised. The man was sick.

'Shall I take off his shoe and sock?' Ross asked, when the man was settled on the couch. She nodded.

'Please. I need to take a look.' She put on a pair of latex gloves and examined the badly swollen area around Lewis's ankle and part of his foot. 'This is very red and angry-looking,' she told him. There were blisters all around the area, as well as bruising beneath the skin, but in the centre there was an area of dead tissue. 'Have you any idea how this happened? Did you graze your ankle at any time?'

Lewis nodded, sinking back against the pillows of the couch. A thin film of sweat beaded his brow, yet his body was racked with cold tremors. 'I caught it on a rock some days ago. It was nothing really, but after the storm it really started to get bad.'

Alyssa reached for her stethoscope and listened to his chest. His lungs were rasping, and when she took his blood pressure she discovered that it was dangerously low.

'Okay, Lewis, I want you to lie back for a while and rest, and I'm going to give you some oxygen to help with your breathing.' She placed an oxygen mask over his nose and mouth and connected it to an oxygen cylinder. 'Take it easy for a while,' she said. 'I'm going to have a word with Dr Blakeley, if that's all right with you.'

He nodded and closed his eyes, and she turned

quickly to Ross. 'Would you get him something to drink while I talk to Connor for a moment?' she asked.

'Of course. He's really ill, isn't he?' he said, under his breath.

'I think so, yes. It's good that you brought him to me.'

She glanced at Connor, whose expression was sober as he checked the results on the blood-pressure monitor. 'His pulse is very high,' she murmured, moving away from the couch so that Lewis couldn't hear what was being said. 'And combined with the low blood pressure, I believe he's going into shock. I think we should get him to hospital right away.'

Connor nodded. 'He's dehydrated. Can we get an intravenous line in? And I think it would be wise to give him a strong broad-spectrum antibiotic. We're looking at sepsis here, and we need to act quickly.'

'Yes, I think you're right about that.' It looked as though Lewis's whole body was inflamed by some sort of infection. 'I'll see to it.'

She'd recognised straight away that it was a grave situation, and for a moment or two she felt the familiar rapid increase in her heartbeat and the knot in the pit of her stomach. Somehow, though, having Connor close by made her feel much stronger, and his presence was reassuring, helping her through this. After a while her hands became steadier and she started to think more clearly.

She said thoughtfully, 'But what could have caused the wound to flare up like that? What kind of organism are we dealing with here? Something waterborne? I know he was standing in flood water next to me the other day, and his legs were bare.' She shook her head. 'I've never seen anything quite like it before. There's an area of dead skin that will need surgical debridement.'

'It could be Vibrio,' Connor said. 'Sometimes after tropical storms it blooms quite profusely in flood water. Molluscs feed on poisonous plankton, and the bacteria can be passed on to people, either through being eaten, if the shellfish aren't prepared properly, boiled, and so on, or they thrive in water and can infect wounds, which is what I think might have happened in this case.'

'And it's more dangerous this way?'

He nodded. 'Extremely so. Lewis is already in a bad way, near to collapse. I think we should take him to hospital now—we can go in my car. It'll be quicker than waiting for an ambulance.'

'Okay. I'll get him ready.'

She set up an intravenous line in Lewis's arm to remedy the dehydration and try to restore the balance of his blood pressure and heart rate, and at the same time she explained to him that they needed to get him to hospital. 'They'll do blood tests and make sure you get the right antibiotic to deal with the infection,' she told him. 'In the meantime, I'm going to inject you with the strongest one I have, and that should help to stop it in its tracks.'

Between them, Ross and Connor helped him out to the car, while Alyssa held the fluid bag of normal saline aloft.

She sat with him in the back of the car while Connor started up the engine. 'Thanks for your help, Ross,' she said, giving him a light wave before the car moved away. Ross was subdued, shocked, she guessed, by what was happening. 'Try not to worry. We'll take care of him.'

Once they arrived at the hospital Connor went into action, hooking Lewis up to a cardiac monitor and checking his vital signs once more. Then he took samples of his blood for testing.

'His breathing's pretty bad,' he said, turning to Alyssa, who was looking on. 'I suspect there's a lot of inflammation there, so I'm going to put him on corticosteroids to try to reduce it. And as soon as I get the test results back, I'll give him electrolytes to restore the acid balance of his blood.' He frowned and turned to the nurse who was assisting him. 'We'll put him on a vasopressor drug and see if that will bring up his blood pressure some more. It's still dangerously low.'

'Okay, I'll get things ready for you.'

A porter took the samples over to the lab and Connor called for a surgeon to come and look at Lewis's wound.

'All we can do now is wait for the results to come through,' Connor told Alyssa some time later. 'It shouldn't take too long for some of the simpler ones to come back from the lab, but he won't be able to go to surgery until we have his condition stabilised.' He glanced at her, taking in her worried expression. 'How are you holding up? Are you okay? I know these situations are worrying for you.'

'I'm all right.' She frowned. 'It's very strange, but for the first time in a couple of years I haven't had that awful, prolonged sick feeling in my stomach when I've had to deal with an emergency. It was there, but it was over very quickly. I can't explain it.' She looked at him. He was so calm, so thorough in everything he did, reliable, capable…everything she dreamed of being.

'Perhaps it was because you were with me,' she murmured as the thought dawned on her. 'I can't think of any other reason why I should feel this way. But around you I feel more secure somehow.'

'Then I'll have to arrange it so that I'm with you more often,' he said with a smile. He wrapped his arms around her and gave her a hug, but it was over almost as soon as it had begun and she mourned the loss of that comforting embrace.

He was called away a few minutes later to deal with another patient, but he urged Alyssa to go and wait in his office. 'I'll come and find you as soon as I have anything for you. I know you're concerned about Lewis. Help yourself to coffee, or whatever. Make yourself at home.'

'I will, thanks.'

She went to his office and made coffee, as he'd suggested, and then sat down to glance through some magazines she found on a low table. She was too anxious about what was happening to Lewis, though, to be able to concentrate for long, and restlessness soon overcame her. She stood up and went to stare out of the window at the fig tree that provided shade in a corner of the landscaped gardens. Everything about Connor's place of work, including the area outside, was designed to be luxurious and peaceful, to put people at their ease.

She turned away and looked around the room. In a corner, on top of a mahogany filing cabinet, she found a child's toy, a lightweight, wooden horse and cart. The wheels on the cart turned when she gently spun them. On the seat of the cart there was a jointed, carved figure of a little girl. Engrossed in the beautiful simplicity of the toy, she took a moment to react when Connor came into the room.

'Oh, you've discovered my secret hobby,' he said, his mouth curving. 'I wasn't sure whether or not to paint it. Do you think it might look better?'

'You made this?' Her eyes widened. 'No, you should leave it. I think it's perfect as it is. I love this sort of thing—in fact, I was just thinking that I'd like to buy something hand-crafted to send home to my mother.' She looked at him with real admiration. 'So this is your hobby?'

'One of them,' he said, nodding. 'The wood's particularly easy to carve. It comes from the gamalamee I was telling you about. It's a kind of balsa wood, so it's really easy to work with. I thought I'd give this toy to the little girl who was nearly drowned. Apparently she lost her doll in the flood—I thought this might help to make up for it.' He frowned. 'What do you think? I wondered if perhaps it's not girly enough?'

She went over to him and laid her hand on his arm, looking up into his eyes. 'Oh, Connor, she'll absolutely love it. I think that's a wonderful idea.' It was such a thoughtful gesture that it brought a lump to her throat and she wanted to reach up and kiss him...and for a moment or two she was poised on the edge of doing just that. But even as she warred within herself, his arms went around her and he dropped a kiss lightly on her mouth.

'I'm glad you think so,' he murmured.

Flustered, she stayed where she was for the time being, not stirring but watching him, her lips gently parted, stunned by the intimate gesture and desperate for him to sear her mouth with flame once again.

'If you go on looking at me like that,' he warned softly, 'there'll be nothing for it except to kiss you all over again.'

'Um...' She pulled herself together and gave herself a mental shake. What on earth was she thinking? For a second or two she'd been reckless enough to think of throwing caution to the wind and basking in the shelter of his arms. That would have been sheer madness. He would lead her along the same path as all his other conquests and then disentangle himself when he judged things were liable to get out of hand. And she could see them getting out of hand very quickly.

'Did you…?' She tried to collect her thoughts. 'Did you have some news about Lewis? You seem to have been gone for ages.'

'Sorry about that. Yes…' He slowly released her. 'I had some of the results back and added some more drugs to his list of medication. His blood pressure's up a little, so that's a sign things are moving in the right direction, but his heart rate is still very fast. He's not out of the woods yet by a long way. And we need to get that infection under control.'

'I suppose it's something, at least, that his condition isn't getting any worse.'

'Yes. Anyway, he'll be admitted to one of the wards, and another doctor will go on with his treatment.'

He glanced briefly at the wooden cart and then turned back to her. 'How do you feel about going to the market in town to look for that gift you mentioned? My shift's finished so I could take you there, if you like… unless you have to get back for some reason? I can't see that either of us will do any good by staying here any longer—we'll be leaving Lewis in good hands.'

She nodded. 'The filming was due to finish over an hour ago, so I'm through for the day.' She smiled at him. 'I think I'd like that. Thanks.'

They left the hospital a few minutes later after she'd taken a quick look at Lewis to see how he was doing.

He was sleeping and his wife was at his bedside. 'I'll leave you two alone,' Alyssa murmured, laying a comforting hand on the woman's shoulder.

'Thank you—both of you—for taking care of him and bringing him here,' the woman said.

'You're welcome. We're very concerned that he should get better.'

They made their way to the car park and set off for the market. It was a short ride away, a bustling place filled with wooden stalls where all kinds of wares were set out. Nearby was an open square bordered with bars and cafés and dotted around with tables and chairs where people could sit to eat and drink. In the middle of the square a traditional steel band was playing. The whole atmosphere was lively and entertaining, and Alyssa felt her spirits lifting.

'I love this market,' she told Connor as they walked around. 'There are so many lovely hand-crafted items for sale—I don't know how on earth I'm going to choose what to buy.'

'It's true, they're very big on straw crafts here—handbags, hats, and souvenirs. It depends what you're looking for... Something for your mother, you said?'

'That's right. It's her birthday next week, on Saturday, so I thought I might get her something personal.' There were jewellery stalls full of wonderful necklaces and bracelets made from beads or seeds polished to a high gloss, and some were made of oyster pearls. They stood for a while, watching a woman thread glass beads on to a wire and fashion it into a pretty spiral bracelet.

'She makes it look so easy,' Alyssa said, 'but some of the necklaces she made are very intricate. My mother bought me something similar for my birthday last year…' She smiled. 'It was funny, because her birthday was a week earlier than mine and I'd bought her a bracelet that would have gone with it perfectly. She said it gave her the inspiration for my present.'

'You like jewellery?'

She laughed. 'I do. Show me a woman who doesn't.'

'Well, yes…' He smiled. 'But I meant, you like beaded necklaces?'

'Oh, yes. I sort of collect them. I see something pretty like that, and I can scarcely resist buying it.'

They wandered around the stalls, checking out the goods, and in the end Alyssa chose a handbag made from woven palm leaves and decorated with coloured beads. 'I think my mother will like that,' she said. 'It's lined with silk, and there's a purse to match.'

'She must look forward to hearing from you, I expect,' Connor said. 'After all, you've been here for some time now, and you're a long way from home.'

'Maybe. I don't really know about that,' Alyssa answered, a fleeting expression of sadness moving over her features. 'I've tried calling her a few times, but she's usually out—I think she's been especially busy lately, putting together a collection for her boutique.'

'What about your father? Have you spoken to him?'

'A couple of times. He's been away a lot, checking on different subsidiaries of the company, so I've tended to leave email messages instead of phoning these last couple of weeks. That way they get back to me whenever they can.'

He put his arm around her and drew her close. 'I wonder if they know how much you need them to be there for you,' he said softly.

She stared at him, her green eyes troubled. How did

he know? It was something she'd tried to keep to herself, this feeling of disconnection from her family. Was he so perceptive that he saw through the outer shell to her inner being?

'I'm a grown woman,' she said. 'They know I'm independent and they probably respect me for it.'

'Maybe.' His arm was reassuringly steady around her, and his hand lightly cupped her shoulder. 'Let's go and get a cold drink and listen to the band for a while.'

'Okay. Just for a half an hour or so, and then I should get back.'

They walked over to the cobbled square and sat at a wooden bench table under the shade of a parasol. A waiter took their order for drinks and Connor ordered a platter of sandwiches. When it arrived a few minutes later Alyssa's eyes grew large. It looked surprisingly appetising.

'I was expecting straightforward bread with a filling,' she said, 'but these look delicious.' Among the sandwiches to choose from there were chicken and bacon with mayonnaise, cheese and sun-dried tomato with a herb dressing, and surrounding it all was a bed of crispy, fresh salad. 'This is wonderful.'

They ate, and drank, and listened to the music, watching as men carried two support struts and a cane into the centre of the square. Then supple limbo dancers dipped and dived, moving around to the heavy beat of the music and taking it in turns to bend beneath the horizontal cane, which was gradually lowered to within a few inches of the ground. The crowd whooped and cheered in delight.

When the show finished, Alyssa glanced at her watch. 'I ought to go back,' she said on a reluctant note.

'Do you have to?'

'I'm afraid so. I've arranged to see Ross later on, back at the house. He said he wanted to talk to me… about the filming, I think. He's very taken up with how it's all going. And he seems to be obsessed with taking on this water-skiing stunt.' She frowned. 'Has he done this sort of thing before?'

Connor nodded. 'He's pretty good at all kinds of water sports.' His mouth made a wry curve. 'I think that's how he managed to hook up with quite a few young women—they were very impressed with his prowess…as well as his six-pack.'

'Oh, dear. Even so, even if he's quite skilled, I still wish he wouldn't do it. I wish Dan had put his foot down and refused to let him take it on.'

She frowned. 'Apparently the scene in the film calls for a race across the water, and I can't help but worry about it. All sorts of things could go wrong—there are bound to be other people and boats on the water, and he could be turned off course by the swell from other boats—not to mention that he's just recovered from a nasty head injury.'

She looked earnestly at Connor. 'Can't you persuade him not to do it? He might listen to you.'

'I can try, but I doubt if he'll take any notice.' His eyes glittered. 'I suspect he's only doing it because he wants to try to impress you. He thinks the world of you.'

'But that's the last thing I want,' she protested, appalled at the thought. 'I hate to think of him risking life and limb for the cameras.'

'Because you care for him, don't you?' Connor's features were in shadow as the sun dipped behind a backdrop of trees. 'You can't bear the thought of him being hurt.'

'Of course I care for him… I think the world of him. He helped me when I was down and encouraged me to come over here—how can I ignore all that now and watch him put himself at risk? He's your brother, don't you want to steer him away from doing anything reckless?'

'There are a lot of things I want,' Connor said darkly, his eyes glinting with some unfathomable emotion. 'And my brother's well-being is one of them. But there are also times when being my brother's keeper can be a bit like wielding a double-edged sword.'

She wasn't quite sure what he meant by that, but she had the feeling that she was at the root of his brooding manner. Was there an inherent rivalry between the brothers that he'd tried to suppress, or was he merely concerned by Ross's apparent foolhardiness?

Either way, she didn't want to be the cause of any dissension between them. What could she do to keep this from happening?

CHAPTER SEVEN

'WELL, there's a sight for sore eyes.' Connor's voice sounded close by and Alyssa woke with a start. She'd been dozing in the hammock outside in the sunshine, and as she looked around, the hammock swayed gently with her movements.

Connor looked as though he was on top form, long, lithe, energetic, dressed in dark trousers and a linen shirt that showed the flat line of his stomach and emphasised his perfect physique.

'I was just... I didn't expect to fall asleep,' she murmured, her voice husky from the heat. It was still before noon, after all, though she glanced at her watch to make sure she hadn't been sleeping for too long. 'I just came out here to take the air for half an hour or so, and before I knew it I must have been well away.'

'Mmm. Perhaps you needed the rest. You looked so beautifully relaxed, it seemed a pity I had to wake you.' His gaze swept along the length of her, coming to rest on the expanse of her bare thigh, which must have been exposed when she'd wriggled into a more comfortable position. Flustered, she tried to cover herself by quickly tugging down the skirt of her dress.

He pulled a wry face. 'That is such a shame,' he

mused on a reflective note, 'I could have stood here and watched you for hours.'

Hot colour ran along her cheekbones. 'You said you had to wake me? Is something wrong?' She sat up, still a bit groggy from sleep, and readied herself to swing down from the hammock. It was the weekend, so there was no work for her to be worrying about, and she wondered what could possibly be the problem.

'Is this to do with Ross? He was going to pick up his new car this morning. He said he would bring it over here to show me…has the deal fallen through somehow?' Ross's car had been a write-off after the accident on the night of the storm, but he'd quickly set about organising a replacement.

Connor shook his head. 'No, it's nothing like that. Your cousin rang…Carys. You left your phone out on the deck, so I answered it for you in case it was anything urgent. She said she's getting an earlier plane and wonders if you could meet her at the airport—she should be arriving in about an hour.' He frowned. 'I'd offer to take you but I have to leave for the hospital around that time. I'm on call with the emergency services this afternoon.'

'Oh, that's all right, don't worry about it. Thanks, anyway. I have my little runabout and I'm sure I'll manage to find my way to the airport, even without sat-nav.' She smiled. 'You know Carys, don't you? Ross said you and he were her neighbours when you lived in Florida, though I expect you were all youngsters back then.'

He nodded. 'We've kept in touch with the family over the years—and we both still go back there quite often.'

'So you'll both probably enjoy seeing her again. Oh, wow… It's great that she's managed to get an earlier flight. I wasn't expecting her to arrive until this evening, but now we'll have a bit more time together. She'll be going back late tomorrow evening.' She pulled in a quick breath. 'I ought to go and give her a ring.'

She went to get down from the hammock, but it started to swing from side to side and she hesitated for a second or two.

'Here, let me help you.' Connor reached for her, his strong arms sliding around her waist and bringing her up close to him. As he lifted her down her soft curves brushed against the length of his hard body, and a whole host of wild and wonderful feelings started up inside her. Blood pumped through her veins with lightning force as she found herself being drawn into his firm embrace, and her whole body was suddenly vibrant with thrilling sensation.

Her feet finally touched the ground, but he went on holding her, and she realised she was in no hurry at all to move away from him. He was tall and strong, impressively masculine, and his powerful arms were locked around her in a way that had every nerve ending clamouring for attention. Delicious tremors shimmered through her. Her breasts were softly crushed against his long, tautly muscled frame, and his strong thighs were pressuring hers, so that a flood of heat began to pool in the pit of her abdomen.

He eased her against him, his hands gently caressing her, gliding along the length of her spine and over the swell of her hips, stirring up a firestorm of heat inside her. Then he bent his head towards her, and she knew that in the very next moment he was going to kiss her. Her heart began to tap out an erratic rhythm, and elation rose up in her. All she could think about was her desperate need to feel his lips on hers.

She didn't have to wait long for her wish to be granted. In the next instant his mouth covered hers, gently coaxing, teasing her lips apart so that in a heartbeat she yielded to the sweet, tender onslaught. Her body was supple, fired up with need, and she moulded herself to him, wanting this moment to never end. Out of the blue, it dawned on her that she'd never felt this way before, never wanted any man the way she wanted him.

'Sweet, sweet girl,' he murmured, nuzzling her throat and trailing a line of flame all the way down to the creamy slope of her shoulder. 'What am I to do? I can't resist you. I'm heady with wanting you, Alyssa. It feels as though I'm drunk and off balance.'

That was how she felt, too, as though her world had been tilted off its axis and she was spinning out of control. It was a strange, breathtaking feeling, and for once in her life she didn't know how to handle things.

She didn't have much time to think about it, though. His head dipped down and in the next moment his lips brushed over the smooth swell of her breasts where they escaped the confines of her lace-edged bra. His kisses were gossamer-light, thrilling her through and through until her whole body tingled with feverish pleasure.

'Heaven knows,' he said in a roughened voice, 'I've tried to keep from doing this, from getting close to you, but it's just too much…it's virtually impossible. You tantalise me…every time I see you, I'm lost…'

His breathing was ragged, his gaze absorbed as his hands moved over her, making a slow, sensual exploration of her rounded curves. Alyssa revelled in his touch. Under the golden blaze of this idyllic island sun everything was perfection and she wanted this moment to last for ever. But she didn't understand what was happening to her. Why did she feel this way? Wasn't it madness to let this go on? Things could very soon get out of hand…

Perhaps she'd been out in the sun too long and the heat had affected her way of thinking. Hadn't he said that all he wanted was a fun, no-strings kind of affair? Was that what she wanted? Would that really be such a bad option? At least she would have him to herself for just a short while.

'I don't know what's happening to me,' she said huskily. 'I've never felt this way before…'

'I know. It's the same for me,' he murmured, his voice rough around the edges. 'I think you've cast a spell on me. I can scarcely think straight when I'm around you.' He gently lifted her hand and placed it over his heart. 'See what you do to me? I don't understand it, no other woman has ever made me feel quite like this before.'

His heart was thudding heavily, a chaotic, thundering rhythm, and she felt its beat ricochet along her arm. Had she really made him feel this way, his emotions raging out of control, just as was happening with her? A short burst of elation spiralled inside her, until she realised her thoughts were taking a hazardous course. Should she stop this right now, or was it already too late? Her heart and mind were at war with one another.

Then the roar of a car's engine sounded in the distance, breaking the spell, and Connor half turned to glance in the direction of the road. 'I guess that must be Ross, coming to show off his new car,' he said on a soft sigh. He ran his hands over her arms. 'Perhaps I should have known I wouldn't get you all to myself for very long.' He lowered his head towards her and kissed her tenderly on the lips. 'Just one more kiss to keep me going…then I'll have that to remember when I'm at work.'

She wound her arms around his neck and kissed him in return. What would it hurt to give way to her feelings just this once?

They drew apart as a car swung onto the driveway of the property. Ross parked by the side of the house and cut the engine.

'What are you two up to?' he said in a suspicious voice, looking them over as he walked towards them. 'You're getting very close all of a sudden, aren't you? Is there something going on that I should know about?'

'You know everything there is to know,' Connor murmured, sliding an arm lightly around Alyssa's waist. He looked at the shiny, metallic grey convertible on the driveway. 'So this is the new dream machine…very nice. From the way you roared in here, I guess you've already put it through its paces.'

Ross smiled, nodding. 'It purrs like a kitten, and the acceleration is so smooth.' He turned to Alyssa. 'I'll have to take you for a spin in it. You'll love it with the top down and the feel of the wind in your hair. Couldn't be better.' He checked his watch. 'How about now? There's no time like the present.'

'Sorry, but I have to get ready to go and meet Carys at the airport,' she said. 'Perhaps some other time.'

He frowned. 'I could take you there—it's no problem. It's a two plus two seater, so there's room for Carys in the back. She's only a slim slip of a girl, so she should manage okay with a small amount of leg room.' His mouth quirked. 'That's the thing with sports cars… they're built for speed, not space.'

Alyssa thought it over. 'Are you sure you don't mind

taking me? It would help as you know the roads better than I do. But I should warn you—I might have to hang around for a while if her plane comes in late. And the journey's more than just a short trip, you know. It will take at least half an hour for us to get there.'

'Or twenty minutes in my new baby.' He gave her a beaming smile.

'Are you planning on writing off this car before you've even had a chance to run it in?' Connor was frowning. 'You'll have Alyssa in the passenger seat— if you're going to drive like a maniac she'll do better to drive herself.'

'Oh, but he wouldn't do that,' Alyssa put in quickly, 'would you, Ross?'

'Of course not, sweetheart.' Ross turned to Connor. 'As if I would do anything to put her at risk. Believe in me, brother. I'll bring her back safe and sound.'

'You'd better. The problem is, I know you too well.' Connor's expression was serious. 'I've been wondering if that knock on your head didn't set off your wild streak, especially after you started to talk about doing the water-ski stunt. You're meant to be the film producer, not the stuntman. The company doesn't insure you to put yourself in the frame.'

Ross reached out and patted him on the shoulder. 'You worry too much, bro. It'll all be fine, you'll see.'

'Hmm.' Connor was still frowning. 'It had better be. Remember, you have Alyssa to think about—you don't need to be showing off in front of her—she already knows who you are.'

Ross laughed. 'I'll take care of her, I promise.' He looked curiously at his brother. 'Is this a protective instinct coming out in you? I guess I have competition.'

He made a crooked smile. 'Still, she already knows you don't have any staying power. I warned her about you and your reputation a long while ago.'

'I'll just bet you did.' Connor's dark eyes glinted, flint-sharp.

Alyssa decided it was time to interrupt. 'Look, you need to put your differences to one side for a while, both of you. And there's no competition going on here. I'm not looking to get involved with anyone. I've been there and it wasn't good, and I'm not likely to be trying it again any time soon, especially with a man who thinks he's the next James Bond and another who thinks the dating game is just that—a game.' Those few minutes in Connor's arms had been a mistake, she could see it now. Why would he think of her differently compared to any of the women who had gone before? She was deluding herself if she thought otherwise, wasn't she?

She was frowning now, and both men were looking at her with alert expressions. She glanced at her watch. 'And I really think I should be setting off or I'll be late. I'll go and get my bag.'

A short time later she slid into the passenger seat of Ross's convertible and watched him set the sat-nav. 'Okay, we're off,' he said, and the engine growled into life. She glanced at him. 'Just kidding,' he murmured. 'Connor's watching, and I wanted to make him sweat.'

'You're such a child,' she scolded. 'Behave yourself, for heaven's sake.' She turned to look at Connor, who was standing by the house, his features taut, his body rigid. She waved, and mouthed silently, 'See you later.'

Ross shot the car along the road, gathering speed until they had left the isolated property behind them. Only then did he slow down and turn to look at her in triumph. 'That gave him something to think about, didn't it?'

'That doesn't even deserve an answer,' she said, flicking him a cool glance. 'You need to grow up, Ross.'

'Yeah, I know. I will.' He slid the car onto the main highway. 'I wouldn't take any risks with you. He ought to know that.' He shot her a quick look. 'But I think you must have crept under his skin somehow and found a soft spot. He's definitely hot and bothered where you're concerned.'

'I doubt it,' she murmured. 'Anyway, could we talk about something else?'

'Sore point, eh?' He smiled. 'Sure. So what do you think of my new beauty? She even has cameras to help with parking. You just switch on the screen on the dash, press "camera", and away you go.'

Alyssa was suitably impressed, and Ross pointed out all the finer features of the car while they drove along. Traffic was building up on the roads, as might have been expected this close to midday, but Ross stayed calm and headed towards the road junction ahead. He glanced in his rear-view mirror.

'Some people are unbelievable,' he murmured, and Alyssa pulled down her courtesy mirror to see what was going on behind them.

A driver in a white saloon was weaving in and out of traffic, as though he was determined to get to the junction ahead of anyone else. He was a young man, in his early twenties, Alyssa guessed.

'He'll end up causing all kinds of mayhem, the way he's going,' Ross murmured. 'I don't see why he can't just...' He let out a mild curse as, without warning, the driver pulled out into the far lane to overtake and then swung back in front of him.

Ross touched his brakes, conscious all the time of the cars closing the gap behind him. 'Now, why on earth would he do something like that?' he murmured, frowning.

'He's obviously in a hurry.'

Too much so, because in the next minute the driver shot across the junction and there was an almighty crash and the awful sound of grinding metal as he ran straight into a car that was already travelling towards the middle of the road.

Alyssa's heart seemed to turn over. 'Oh, no... Stop the car, Ross,' she said in a shocked voice. 'Is there anywhere you can pull over? I need to go and see if anyone needs help.' It didn't look good. The left side of the other vehicle, a black coupé, had caved in, and the white saloon had lost its front end.

'I can't pull over. I'm completely boxed in,' Ross answered, searching around for a solution. 'The way people drive out here can be awful at times. I'm sorry you had to see this.' He stopped the car next to the crashed cars, and Alyssa slid out of the passenger seat. All the other traffic had come to a standstill and car horns were blaring.

'I don't suppose you have a first-aid box in the car, do you?' she asked, reaching into her bag for her phone as she pushed open the passenger door.

'I do. Connor tells me I always have to be prepared. I'll get it for you.' He stepped out of the car.

'Thanks.' Fumbling around in her bag, she pulled a face. 'I left my phone back at the house. Will you call for an ambulance?'

'Of course. I'm already on it.' He took the first-aid box from the boot of his car and handed it to her, then pulled out his mobile phone and began to punch in numbers.

Alyssa went over to the black car. At first glance that appeared to be the one where there was likely to be the most damage to the occupants.

The woman driver was bleeding badly from a chest wound and appeared to be in deep shock, though she managed to give her name. 'My name is Raeni,' she said. 'My children—' She broke off, struggling to breathe.

Alyssa glanced in the back of the car. There were two children there, a boy and a girl, aged about ten and eight, both white faced and crying quietly. 'Mama's bleeding,' the boy said in a panicked tone, his face crumpling. 'She's bleeding.' The children were very distressed by the sight of the blood.

'I know, but we're going to look after her.' As far as she could tell, neither of the children was injured, but it was clear they were very badly shaken.

'He came out of nowhere,' Raeni managed to say, gasping between each word. 'I don't know what he—' She was very agitated. 'My children—'

'They're all right,' Alyssa assured the woman. 'Try not to upset yourself. Help's on the way.' She took a dressing pad from the first-aid kit. 'I'm going to put this dressing pad against your chest. Perhaps you could hold it there to help stem the bleeding. I have to go and check on the people in the other car, but I promise I'll be back in a minute or two.'

The woman nodded, and Alyssa hurried over to the white saloon. She found the young man slumped over the wheel, but he was still conscious and able to answer Alyssa when she spoke to him. He said his name was Malik. He was alert but breathless, and complained of abdominal pain. There were some cuts on his forearm, too, but nothing that appeared major.

'Try to stay still, Malik,' Alyssa said softly. 'The ambulance will be here soon.' She wished she could give him oxygen, but without her medical equipment she was severely hampered. Added to that, she couldn't split herself two ways and had to decide which person needed attention most of all. She opted to go to the woman in the black car. She was losing blood fairly rapidly and her condition could deteriorate at any moment.

Ross came over to her. 'Can I do anything to help?'

'Yes, please,' she said in a low voice. 'Will you stay with Malik while I see to the other driver? Perhaps you could put a couple of dressings on his arm.' She gave him some dressings and a bandage from the first-aid kit. 'Try to keep him calm, if you can. If he gets agitated it will make his breathing worse.'

'I can do that. Don't worry. I'll stay with him.'

Alyssa went back to the black car but was alarmed to find that Raeni was by now unconscious and the dressing pad was soaked through with her blood. She quickly felt for the pulse at her wrist, but to her dismay it was barely discernible.

She was stunned by what had happened, and it was the worst kind of situation she could have had to face. If Raeni's heart stopped, or was at a virtual standstill, no oxygen would flow around her body, and she would be brain dead within a very short time unless something was done to save her. What could she do? Where was the ambulance? The thought that she was the only one who could help this woman weighed heavily on her. Was she up to it?

Turning to the children, she said softly, 'I need you to go and sit with my friend for a little while so that I can look after your mother. Will you do that for me? I promise I'll take care of her.'

She bit her lip as she made that promise. Would she be able to save their mother? She shook off the negative thought. She *had* to save her. She couldn't bear the thought of these two innocent children being left motherless.

They tried to object but under her gentle insistence they gradually gave way and she quickly helped them out of the car. Ross gave her a concerned glance. He seemed to understand that she didn't want them to see what she had to do and said, 'Don't worry, they'll be fine with me.'

Alyssa went back to Raeni. Acting on instinct, she lowered the back of the driver's seat so that she was lying as flat as possible. Then she opened the woman's blouse and checked the wound. What she saw almost made her gasp out loud. It was nasty, deep, wide and gaping. How on earth could she bring her through this? She was so badly injured, there was hardly any chance of her being able to pull through.

She was guessing that the wound must have penetrated the heart, but even with the dire prognosis that presented, she couldn't give up, could she? Recalling the children's pinched, tear-stained faces was enough to spur her on. There had to be some way she could restore the woman's circulation.

She switched on the car's interior light so that she would be able to see a little better. She removed a pair of disposable gloves from the first-aid kit, along with a small bottle of antiseptic lotion, then took a sharp pair of scissors from her bag. After dousing the scissors in the solution, she began to clean Raeni's skin. She could only pray that the scissors would be strong enough and sharp enough to do the job in place of a scalpel.

In the distance, she heard the sound of the ambulance as she cut into the woman's chest. There was no anaesthetic she could give her, but in Raeni's present state that was probably the least of her problems. Within a minute or two Alyssa had opened up the area and could see the cause of the problem. The pericardium, the sac around the heart, was swollen and stiff with blood, putting pressure like a clamp around the heart and preventing it from pumping.

She heard the ambulance draw up and soon the paramedics were talking to Ross. She looked around and knew a huge surge of relief as she saw Connor coming towards her.

'Oh, Connor, thank heaven it's you,' she said. 'I'd forgotten it would be you coming out with the ambulance… I'm so glad to see you. I really need your help.' A wave of nausea washed through her as the strain of the last few minutes started to make itself felt on her.

'It's okay, Alyssa… Take it easy… Slow down and take a deep breath…' He laid a reassuring hand on her shoulder. His voice and his calm, soothing presence were instantly comforting to her, and she felt some of the tension ease from her. It was only then, as she looked up at him, that she realised Connor might not be as composed as he seemed. His face was devoid of colour and his body was taut, as though he was steeling himself in some way.

'Are you all right?' she asked, and he nodded.

'Tell me what the situation is here.' His manner was brisk, and that was surely understandable. They were dealing with an emergency here.

'I need to remove the blood clot that's formed in the pericardium,' she told him, 'but she'll need anaesthetic and a fluid line, preferably before I do that. We have to act quickly. She may need medication to force the heart muscle to contract.' She'd find out later what was wrong with Connor. For now, their patient had to be their main priority.

Connor was already opening up his medical kit and pulling on disposable gloves. Within a very short time he had put in an intravenous line so that Raeni could be given life-saving fluids, as well as an anaesthetic and other medication. He put an endotracheal tube down her windpipe and connected it to an oxygen supply.

While he did all that, Alyssa carefully began to remove the blood clot and drained away some of the fluid from the pericardial sac. Slowly, as the pressure was eased, the woman's heart began to beat once more, and at the same time blood began to spurt from the wound site. Alyssa placed her finger over the hole to stem the flow.

'We should get her to hospital right away,' she said. 'I'll keep my finger over the hole until we can get her to a surgeon. Will you phone ahead and arrange for a surgical team to be waiting for us?'

'Yes, I will. Are you going to be okay staying with her like that? I could take over for you if you like.'

Alyssa shook her head. 'I'll be fine. I'm just anxious about our other patient. He was very breathless. I didn't get a chance to do anything other than check him out.'

'I think the paramedics started to give him oxygen when we arrived, but I'll go and take over from them while we get this lady transferred to the ambulance. Sit tight and I'll send the paramedics over to you.'

'Thanks, Connor.' On an afterthought she said, 'Will you ask Ross to take care of the children and see that they're handed over to their father?'

'I will.' He smiled at her. 'You're doing a great job. You amaze me, Alyssa. You're a brilliant doctor. I'd be more than glad to have you at my side if I were in dire straits. I can't think of anyone else I'd sooner have with me.'

Her heart jumped a little. It was great that he had faith in her. 'Let's hope that's never put to the test.' She stayed where she was, keeping her finger in place to stop the blood from escaping, but his words warmed her through and through.

A couple of minutes later, the paramedics had placed Raeni on a stretcher, and wheeled her to the ambulance, with Alyssa staying constantly by her side, her hand still in position.

Malik travelled with them, propped up a little by pillows to ease his breathing. There was an oxygen mask over his nose and mouth and his eyes were closed, but it was plain to see that he was suffering a considerable amount of discomfort.

'Did you manage to examine him?' Alyssa asked quietly as the ambulance driver started up the engine and they sped away.

Connor nodded. 'I think there may have been some disruption to the diaphragm,' he said in a low voice. 'When I listened to his chest with the stethoscope I could hear sounds that you wouldn't usually expect to hear.'

'You mean there might be a tear in the diaphragm?'

'That's right. So some of the abdominal organs might have been pushed upwards into the chest cavity. We'll do a chest X-ray and MRI scan to be certain, but I'm pretty sure he'll need surgery.'

Alyssa winced. 'They're both in a bad way.'

'Yes.'

She studied him thoughtfully for a moment or two. 'I didn't realise it straight away, but you weren't quite yourself when you came out of the ambulance. What was wrong?'

'I was fine.'

'No, you weren't. I could tell. What was it, Connor? It couldn't be that you were bothered by the crash, could it? You must have seen things like that many times in your career.'

He nodded, and perhaps he realised that she would persist in her questioning because he said, 'But never when Ross's car was at the scene. When I first stepped out of the ambulance, it looked as though his car was part of the accident. I felt sick to my stomach, imagining that you and he might be injured.'

She sucked in a quick breath. 'I didn't know… I'm so sorry. That must have been awful.'

'It was, but then I found out that you were both okay. That was a tremendous relief. I couldn't bear the thought of either of you being hurt. I don't know how I would have gone on if—' He broke off. He looked uncomfortable, as though he'd said too much.

'If what?' Alyssa prompted him, but he shook his head. 'Nothing. It doesn't matter.'

She thought about it. Was he wondering about how he would go on if anything happened to Ross? Or maybe he was thinking of her…was it possible? Might he care for her more than she dared hope?

Their conversation had to come to an end, though, because by now they had arrived at the hospital and medical teams were waiting in the ambulance bay.

There were separate teams for each of the patients. Raeni was whisked away to the operating theatre and Malik was taken to the radiology department. Alyssa walked with Connor to the emergency room and saw that Raeni's children were there with their father. Ross, it turned out, had gone on to the airport to see if Carys was waiting.

'Heavens, I'd forgotten all about Carys,' Alyssa said in a stunned tone. 'She must be wondering what on earth's going on.'

'I expect Ross will look after her,' Connor murmured.

'Yes, you're probably right.' She was relieved at the thought. 'Perhaps he'll take her for lunch somewhere. That's what I planned to do.'

Connor nodded. 'Don't worry about it—I'm sure Ross will explain the situation to her and help to make her feel welcome. They always got on well together.'

'Good. That's a relief, anyway.'

He led her towards his office. 'I'm still on call for a few hours so I might have to leave at any moment, but I think you should sit down and rest for a while. That must have been a terrible ordeal for you, and yet you stayed in control, doing what you had to do. I'm really proud of you, Alyssa.'

She pressed her lips together. 'I didn't really get a

chance to think about it—until you arrived, and then it hit home with a bang.' They went into the room and he switched on the coffee machine.

'You're a wonderful, skilled doctor,' he said, a few minutes later as he handed her a reviving cup of hot coffee. 'It would be a tremendous waste to the profession if you were to give up on it.'

'I did what I could…but we don't know yet what will happen to her. I may have been too late…'

'At least you gave her a chance of survival. If you hadn't acted as you did, she wouldn't be here now, in the operating theatre.'

Alyssa sipped her coffee. It was good to know that he had faith in her, but could she live up to those expectations? Perhaps it was too early yet to say. She was still very shaken by what had happened.

His pager bleeped and he checked the text message briefly. 'I have to go,' he said. 'Will you get a taxi back home when you're ready? I can give you the number of a reliable company.'

'Yes, I'll be fine. Don't worry about me,' she murmured.

He studied her, his gaze dark and brooding. 'But I do worry,' he said. 'That's the problem.'

CHAPTER EIGHT

'IT MUST have been a terrible shock for you—coming across an accident like that.' Carys shook her head, making her blonde hair swirl silkily around her pretty, oval-shaped face. 'Such awful injuries. Ross has been telling me all about it. And those children—they must have been scared half to death.'

'Yes,' Alyssa agreed, 'that was worrying, seeing how upset they were. It's hard not being able to give them any real news about their mother, but she was still in the recovery room when I left the hospital, and we won't know how she'll be for some time yet. She lost a lot of blood and there are problems with her lungs because of the extent of the injury.'

'At least she came through the operation.' Ross poured drinks for the girls as they sat on the deck, looking out over the sparkling blue ocean. Brown shearwaters swooped and dived for fish, their white underbellies glinting in the sunlight, while black-headed terns cheekily tried to steal their catch.

Alyssa sipped her fruit punch, listening to the clink of ice in her glass. It was good to have Carys here at last. 'Anyway, I'm sorry we had to leave you high and dry at the airport,' she said. 'You must have wondered what was going on. Perhaps you thought we'd abandoned you?'

Carys laughed. 'Oh, no. I knew something must have gone wrong. Ross phoned to tell me he was on his way, and then he took me to the Oasis Club for lunch and drinks. We had a lot of catching up to do, and he told me all about the filming.' She frowned. 'Apparently it will all be over with soon… I expect life will seem fairly drab after all the excitement of the film shoots.'

'You're probably right. I think Ross will feel it quite badly—he thrives on the adrenaline rush.'

Ross nodded agreement. 'Once one project finishes, I'm on the lookout for another.'

As for herself, she would have to think through her options once her contract with the company came to an end. Instead of the relatively easy time she had been expecting, this stint of work in the Bahamas had given her a lot of food for thought.

They chatted through the afternoon, until Connor arrived home from his shift with the ambulance service.

'Hi, there, Carys,' he said, coming on to the deck and greeting her with a warm smile. 'It's good to see you again.' He bent his head towards her.

'You, too.' Carys lifted her cheek for his kiss and, watching them in such a warm, tender embrace, Alyssa felt a sudden sharp stab of jealousy. It was an unexpected reaction and definitely one that she didn't want. It was upsetting that she should respond this way, and it bewildered her. After all, there was no call for it—Carys was her cousin, they'd been close friends all their lives, like sisters almost, and it was perfectly natural for her and Connor to be close to one another.

Even so, she bent her head to hide her frown. Had

her cousin kissed Ross that way, or were these special moments reserved for Connor?

Annoyed with herself, she swallowed some more of her ice-cold drink and put on a smile. 'We were wondering what to do this evening,' she told Connor. 'We thought it might be good to take Carys somewhere special.'

He straightened up and nodded. 'I've been thinking about that. There's a beach barbecue and fire-eating show going on tonight at Smugglers' Cove. That should be well worth a visit.'

'It sounds great,' Carys said, her blue eyes bright with anticipation. 'I vote we go for the fire-eating—just as long as I don't have to try it out myself!'

'I doubt there's much chance of that.' Connor laughed. 'But it should be fun, and there's usually dancing and a whole variety of cocktails to try out.'

'You're leading me down the path to devil-may-care, I can see that,' she told him with a smile. 'But I'm not worried. I'm here to relax and have a good time, and I want Alyssa to do the same.'

'Oh, I will,' Alyssa murmured. 'I'm there in spirit already.' She shot Connor a quick look. 'Why is it called Smugglers' Cove—were there dark and dangerous goings on there at some time in the past?'

'There certainly were. It was the hub of rum-running in the prohibition era. There are lots of caves around there where sailors could hide their booty.'

She smiled. 'It's getting to sound more and more interesting.'

'You'll enjoy it, I'm sure.' Connor went to shower and change, and later, as the sun started to set on the horizon, they all set off to walk along the headland to

Smugglers' Cove. Rounding the bay, they were met by the sound of drums beating out a fast, heady rhythm and by the sight of islanders dressed in vivid costumes, dancing to the feverish beat.

The aroma of barbecued chicken greeted them, and a buffet table had been laid out on a terrace filled with platters of pork, ribs, rice and peas and bowls of salad. It was colourful and appetising, and Alyssa realised she was hungry.

Connor and Ross went to get drinks while the girls found seats at a table and sat down to watch the dancers. Men, bare-chested and athletic, moved to the music, their bodies supple and toned, while the women dancers wore tube tops and flouncy short skirts that flicked up and down as they shifted to the rhythm of the band. There was a fire at the centre of the group, and they took it in turn to light torches, swirling them around, making patterns with the flames.

Alyssa drank tequila sunrise, a flamboyant cocktail with brilliant red and orange colouring, and felt the music deep down inside her, so that when the floor show finished and Connor held out his hand to draw her to her feet, she was ready to dance with him in the traditional hip-shaking, foot-stomping way of the fire dancers. They laughed together, buoyed up by the cheerful atmosphere, and when Carys and Ross came to join them they danced as a foursome.

'I'd no idea you could move like that,' Alyssa remarked, and Connor smiled and tugged her to him.

'You don't do so badly yourself,' he murmured huskily against her cheek. 'You've been tantalising me all night long with those swaying hips and that gorgeous body.'

'Have I really?' She laughed, snuggling up to him. Perhaps the alcohol had gone to her head because all she wanted right now was to be in his arms and it didn't matter to her that there were people all around.

'Yes, you have, Jezebel.' His eyes were dark, glittering with smouldering intent. 'I've been wanting to get close to you all night. I need to have you all to myself.' He looked around. 'What do you say we give these two the slip and go for a walk along the beach?'

'That sounds good to me.' She glanced over to where Ross and Carys were engrossed, deep in conversation. 'I don't think they'll miss us, do you?'

'It doesn't look like it. They've really hit it off, haven't they?'

So they set out to walk back along the beach in the moonlight, kicking up the sand with their bare feet, laughing when the waves rolled in and tickled their toes.

'I think I've had too much to drink,' she murmured, gazing up at the clear night sky. Stars shimmered like diamonds and in the balmy evening the whole world seemed magical. 'My head is swirling, and it's filled with music.'

'That's because we can still hear it, even from this distance.' They rounded the headland and stood for a while, looking out over the bay. A heron was silhouetted against the moonlit horizon, standing on a rocky outcrop, preening itself.

Connor took her in his arms and kissed her tenderly, and it seemed to Alyssa just then that it was so right that they should be together like this. No one had ever made her feel so good, so perfectly at ease with herself and the world.

'Have you had a good time tonight?' he asked

softly, and she nodded, blissful in his arms, not wanting to move.

'I have. I think I've fallen in love with this island,
its people and their traditions.' She'd probably fallen in
love with him, too, and maybe that was what coloured
her judgement, but she couldn't tell him that. He might
feel it was time to gently extricate himself, and she
wanted to stay close to him for as long as was possible.

'I'm glad. I want you to be happy, Alyssa. You were
so sad when you first came here… Not outwardly, but
I think inside you were hurting, though I didn't realise
it at the time. You talked about how you felt about your
work, your relationship with your parents, and your
ex… Do you still feel bad about breaking up with him?'

She shook her head. 'I haven't thought about him in a
long time.' She frowned. 'It's strange, isn't it, how someone can take up so much of your thoughts and be so
great a part of your life, and yet after a while they fade
into the distance?' She thought about that for a while.

'I think perhaps we were never really suited. He
didn't understand me and how important my work was
to me back then. And, of course, when everything went
wrong for me in my job, he wasn't there to support me.
I suppose I started to look at him with different eyes
then, even before he cheated on me.'

Thinking about that was a salutary reminder of how
things could go wrong. She looked up at Connor, his
face shadowed in the moonlight. Could she let herself
love him and put her trust in him? She wanted to, so
much.

He cupped her cheek in his hand. 'I shouldn't have
doubted you when you first came here. I had such pre-
set ideas about the women who'd set their sights on

Ross in the past, and I was judging you without even knowing you.'

'And you don't have those same worries about Carys?' She smiled. 'He seems to be very taken with her.'

'He's always had a place in his heart for Carys. Nothing ever came of it because she sees him for what he is—a man who enjoys life to the hilt and jumps at every opportunity without thinking first.'

'Perhaps he's changing.'

'Maybe.'

'So you don't need to be his protector any more?'

'Probably not. It's a habit I should have left behind long ago.' He smiled. 'I wonder why we're wasting this moonlit night talking about Ross?'

She knew the answer to that. 'Because I've had a little too much to drink and I'm afraid if I let you kiss me I'll do something foolish like fall in love with you.'

He inhaled sharply. 'That would never do, would it?'

'No.' She shook her head. 'You know what they say, "once bitten…"'

'True. But not all relationships have to end badly, do they? Perhaps I hadn't thought about it properly before. I mean, just because your ex let you down, and my parents made a mess of things, it doesn't have to follow that all love affairs follow the same course, does it?'

He swooped to claim her mouth once more and kissed her, deeply, passionately with all the fervour of a man whose emotions were rapidly running out of control. His hands shaped her and drew her to him, tracing the lines of her body with tender devotion.

'I want you so much…' he said raggedly '…so much that it's like an ache deep inside me.'

Her heart seemed to flip over. It was good to know that she could make him feel this way... It made her blood fizz with excitement and filled her with exhilaration to know that he wanted her, and in her heady, dreamlike state she was almost ready to throw caution to the winds and tell him she felt the same way. But self-preservation was a powerful deterrent and just a hint of caution remained, a tiny spark of doubt left to torment her. Perhaps his view of things was changing, but he still talked about affairs, and not about a lasting commitment, didn't he?

It would hurt her so badly if he were to cast her aside once she had committed herself to him. She knew it and there was no escaping the fact. The distress of having to end the relationship with James would be nothing compared to how she would feel if Connor was to go out of her life. She realised now that her feelings for him went very deep, deeper than she'd ever thought possible, and she didn't think she could cope if he were to let her down.

'Alyssa...'

'I know,' she said softly, on a breathy sigh. 'I want you too, but I need to get my feelings straight. I can't let you sweep me off my feet.'

'Are you sure about that?' His lips gently nuzzled the curve of her neck, and slid down along the bare slope of her shoulder. 'It's a very tempting idea. You know there's nothing I'd like more. Ever since the accident, I've been thinking about you and me...how we might be together...'

But before he could kiss her again they heard the sound of voices in the distance, coming ever closer, and Connor sighed and rested his cheek against hers for a second or two. Then he straightened and reluctantly eased himself away from her, still holding onto her hands and looking around to see who was coming along the path towards them.

Alyssa's mind was in a whirl. What did he mean, how they might be together?

'I might have known,' he said, under his breath. 'Ross's timing has always been atrocious.'

'I suppose they decided it was about time to set off for home,' Alyssa murmured, watching his brother and Carys coming closer. 'The music has stopped. It must be very late.'

He laid an arm around her shoulder. 'You're right. I guess we should be thinking about what we can do to entertain Carys tomorrow...unless you want to keep her to yourself?'

She shook her head. 'I think she'd enjoy the four of us being together.' She felt the loss of his arms around her intensely, and she was churned up inside at the interruption, but Carys had come over here especially to see her, and now she felt guilty because of her own dismay at seeing her turn up on the footpath with Ross. She wanted to be alone with Connor right now...but maybe that was not the most sensible idea around.

They went back to the house with Ross and Carys, and since it was so late Ross decided to stay in his brother's apartment overnight.

In the morning, they all had breakfast together on the deck outside Connor's apartment.

'I thought you might like to take a trip around the islands,' Connor suggested, looking first at Carys and then at Alyssa. 'My yacht's moored not far from here—

we could spend the day seeing the sights from on board, take a picnic lunch with us. What do you think?'

'That sounds wonderful.' Carys glanced at Alyssa and she nodded in agreement.

'I think so, too. Perhaps we'd better start getting some food together…and maybe a bottle or two or three…'

Connor shook his head. 'There's no need for you to do that. I'll organise things. You two can just relax and spend some time together while Ross and I see to everything.'

'Well, I'm all for that,' Carys murmured, smiling. 'I'll go and put on some sun cream in readiness.'

'Me, too.' Alyssa turned to go downstairs with Carys, picking up her phone as its ringtone sounded.

She was startled to hear her mother's voice on the other end of the line.

'Hi, Mum, how are you doing?' She signalled to Carys that she was going to take the call out in the garden, and Carys gave her a cheery wave in return.

'I just heard all about the accident you were caught up in,' her mother said, sounding vexed. 'Why on earth didn't you tell me about it?'

'The accident?' Alyssa was puzzled. How would her mother come to know anything about what had happened? Which accident was she talking about?

'On the night of the storm. The car was a write-off, but you didn't say a word. Heavens, Lyssa, you could have been hurt…but you didn't tell me. I'm your mother, and I knew nothing at all about it.'

'I'm sorry. I was fine and I thought it best not to worry you.' She frowned. 'How did you get to hear about it?'

'Well, you know how it is. Your Aunt Jenny heard it from Carys…and Jenny is my sister, after all, so she phoned me and asked, did I know? Of course I didn't. You never tell me anything.'

'That's not true,' Alyssa protested. 'I email you lots of times and tell you all the gossip—I just don't mention anything that might worry you unnecessarily, that's all.'

'Well, you should have told me about that.' Her mother was indignant. 'I need to know that you're safe.'

'I am. Honestly. I'm fine. You've no need to worry about me. It was poor Ross who came out of it with concussion, but he's okay now.' Alyssa was touched that her mother had taken the trouble to phone her. 'I miss you, Mum. It's great to hear from you.'

'We miss you, too, Lyssa. Maybe your dad and I could have a video chat with you when it's your birthday next week? We must arrange a time that's good for the three of us.'

They talked for a few more minutes and Alyssa promised she would let her mother know straight away if anything out of the ordinary happened. In turn, her mother said she would try to keep in touch more often.

'We'll choose a time each week when we can be sure we're both able to get to the phone,' she said. There was a wistful note in her voice as she added, 'Though it would be good if we were able to see you again properly. I couldn't quite take it in when you suddenly upped and left, but your father and I didn't want to stand in your way.'

It was strange, hearing things from her parents' point of view, and when she cut the call a short time later, Alyssa was deep in thought.

'Is everything all right?' Connor asked, on his way

from the house to the car with a large wicker hamper. 'Did I hear you say it was your mother on the phone?'

'Yes, it was…and everything's fine. She heard about Ross's car being written off and wanted to know what happened. She said they miss me. She and Dad are going to call me on my birthday—they want to do a video call that morning.'

His mouth curved. 'That sounds good. Perhaps it won't seem so bad being far away from them if you can hook up by video and actually get to see one another.'

She nodded. 'I suppose so. Though with my contract coming to an end soon I'll have to decide what I'm going to do…whether to stay on here and look for work or maybe go back home. I think my parents would like that.'

He set the hamper down on the ground. He appeared to be stunned. His body became rigid, his shoulders stiff and his whole frame was tense. 'You're not really thinking of going back home, are you?' he said in a shocked voice. 'I thought you said you loved the island?'

Her eyes were troubled. 'I do. But I have to be practical and think about the future. When I came here I needed a break, time to sort myself out. I was trying to decide whether I should give up on medicine altogether. I'm still not entirely sure, but I don't think I can go on straddling the fence for much longer. And if I choose medicine… Well, the fact is I did my training in the UK, so it would seem sensible to go back there to work.'

She didn't tell him the one true factor that would underline her decision-making. She wanted to be near to Connor, to spend her days—and nights—with him. But his track record wasn't encouraging where women were concerned and she'd already seen for herself that things could go badly wrong. Maybe she would feel differently if he gave her some idea that he wanted more than a fleeting affair, but why would he change the habit of a lifetime?

'I can't imagine how it would be without you here,' he said huskily. 'I've grown so used to having you around. You can't mean it...'

'I have to consider it as a real possibility,' she said. She was surprised by how much her words seemed to have affected him. The colour had drained from his face. 'But I still have a week or so before I need to make my decision.'

He nodded, and she said quietly, 'I suppose I should go and get ready for this boat trip. I'm already running late, from the looks of things.' She gestured towards the hamper. 'Have you filled that up already? Surely, you haven't had time?'

'No. That's true, we haven't.' He seemed to make a conscious effort to relax his stance. 'I phoned the catering service in the town and they're going to fill the basket for me. It's only a ten-minute run in the car, so I'll be back before you know it.' His gaze wandered over her. 'You look as though you're ready for the day ahead, anyway. You're perfect as you are.'

'Well, thanks for the vote of confidence.' She smiled. She had chosen to wear white jeans and a lightly patterned blouse that was gently nipped in at the waist. 'I'll just put on some more lipstick and pin back my hair, and then I'll be ready to go. We won't keep you waiting.'

'That's all right. Don't worry about it...but your hair looks great as it is. It always looks good, whether you leave it loose or pin it up, or whatever. I've always thought it was beautiful…that glossy, deep chestnut colour and those gorgeous curls. You look fantastic.'

She felt warm colour run along her cheekbones. 'I'm glad you feel that way. Somehow, with Carys around, looking so lovely, I sometimes feel as though I fade into the background. She's truly beautiful.'

He reached for her, his hands lightly clasping her bare arms. 'So are you. You could never fade into the background. Don't even think it.' He frowned, looking her over. 'You don't have much self-confidence, do you? And yet you have so much to be proud of. All that nonsense about leaving… Maybe I can help you to change your mind.'

She shook her head. 'I don't think that will work,' she said.

'No?' A challenging glint came into his eyes. 'I can see I'm going to have to take you in hand.'

She glanced at the fingers curled around her arms. 'Did you mean that literally?'

'Oh, yes. Definitely.' He had started to pull her towards him when Ross shouted down from the upper veranda.

'Are you going to get that hamper filled,' he said with an amused twist to his mouth, 'or are we going to hang about all morning? Stop fooling around, bro, and get a move on.'

Connor's mouth quirked in mock annoyance. 'I knew I should have sent him back to his own place last night.'

Alyssa chuckled, faintly relieved by the diversion. After all, she couldn't be certain she would be able to withstand Connor's gentle coaxing. 'There are times when I think I must be lucky not to have any siblings.

People talk about rivalry, and you expect it when they're young, but when you grow up…?'

'Yeah, well, a lot of testosterone gets thrown about where men are involved.' He let her go and went to load the hamper in the car. 'I won't be long,' he promised.

He was as good as his word, and it was around mid-morning when they set sail from the marina where Connor's yacht was moored. They climbed into the boat and within a very short time they were cruising the crystal clear waters around the island, with Connor at the helm. Ross mixed rum punch and offered the girls the chance to look through his binoculars at the startling white cliffs in the distance.

After a while, Alyssa went to join Connor at the helm. She handed him an ice-cold lager and he swallowed the drink gratefully.

'Thanks, I was ready for that.'

'I thought you might be.' She pointed to the island in the distance. 'Is that where we're headed?'

'Yes, Ross and I thought it would be a good place to stop for lunch. There's a lovely stretch of beach in a sheltered bay—it's fringed by coral reefs, so it's really one of the most beautiful places around.'

'From what I've seen, the coral is spectacular,' she murmured. 'I didn't think we'd be able to get so close to it, but in these calm waters you can see everything.' She'd seen swaying purple sea fans, pink sea anemones and myriad brightly coloured tropical fish.

'I hoped you would like it,' he said, smiling.

'I do.' She sighed contentedly. 'I'm so glad we came out here today. I wanted to see as much as I could of the reefs and the fish that swim around them. Carys said she was keen on doing that as well.'

'You should have a good chance of that this afternoon.'

They moved slowly through the sparkling turquoise water for an hour or so, and then dropped anchor in the bay of the island they had seen some time ago through the binoculars.

From the deck of the yacht Alyssa looked out at the pristine white sand that bordered the cliffs. Long-billed pelicans made their nesting ground near rocky outcrops, and overhead they could hear gulls calling to one another.

Connor opened up the hamper and produced a wonderful selection of food. There were spiced meats and rock lobster, along with pâté and savoury biscuits, salad and a variety of mouth-watering dips. For dessert they ate fruit tarts with fresh cream—everything had been kept chilled in a cooler and had then been transferred to the fridge on board the yacht.

'Mmm…I could get used to this life,' Alyssa murmured, leaning back in her seat and sipping the highball Ross had handed her.

'Me, too.' Carys stretched out her long, slender legs. 'I've eaten way too much.' She gave Connor a mock glare. 'You're using this weekend to ply me with food—I shall soon be totally fat.'

He laughed. He was sitting by the deck rail and now he cast a glance over her lithe body. 'Oh, I don't think so,' he said. 'You've had that same figure for the last several years—I doubt you're going to start piling on the pounds now.'

'Huh. So you say. How am I supposed to do any work tomorrow? I shall still be stuffed by morning, and it's all your fault for providing such luscious food.'

'Ah, well, I dare say the events management team can do without your input for a few hours…if the local sports club doesn't get their programme for the charity fete for another day or so, it's hardly going to matter, is it? And if Ross's film schedule's held up for half a day because he can't get out of his chair, no one will worry too much.'

'Don't you believe it,' Ross interjected drily. 'The finance department will be on my tail for a week or more.' He made a wry smile. 'Still, I don't suppose it's quite the same as you and Alyssa not turning up for work, is it?'

'I'm not so sure about that,' Alyssa murmured. 'We're not indispensable. There will always be someone skilled and capable who can look after the patients for us.' She looked at Connor. 'Not that I'm suggesting we leave them to it,' she added.

'I don't know,' Ross said. 'If you hadn't been there when those two cars crashed, I doubt Raeni would still be with us. How is she? Do you know?'

'She's still sedated and recovering from the loss of blood,' Connor said, 'and from the fact that her heart actually stopped beating at one point. They haven't managed to restore her heart to a normal rhythm yet, so that's a worry, but she's in Intensive Care, so everything's being done that can be done.'

Alyssa swirled the colourful juice in her glass. 'Did you get to hear anything more about Malik? I rang up yesterday to try and find out, but the consultant was still deciding on the best course of action.'

'There was a tear in his diaphragm,' Connor told her. 'They've decided to operate tomorrow, so we should know a bit more by late afternoon.'

Carys frowned. 'I could never do that job,' she said quietly. 'It would worry me way too much.'

Alyssa nodded. 'That's how I felt when I came over here. I didn't know if I would be able to go on working as a doctor—I thought these last few months would give me the break I needed to help me recharge my batteries.' She frowned. 'But then we had to deal with some real emergencies—something I never expected to happen—and I began to think my career was over. I didn't think I could cope.'

'Do you still feel that way?' Connor was standing by the deck rail, watching her closely.

She shook her head. 'I think I've discovered that I would far rather try to save lives than not to try at all.' She was thoughtful for a moment. 'Things don't always work out the way we want them to in this job, but at least we have the satisfaction of doing everything we possibly can.'

He came over to her and reached for her hand. 'I'm really glad you feel that way,' he said, going down on his haunches beside her. 'I think you've made the right decision.'

She made a faint smile. 'I wasn't so keen when Alex fell from the lorry,' she said quietly. 'But he's beginning to make good progress with his walking, so I guess things are looking up for him at last.'

Lewis hadn't been quite so lucky, though. She'd looked in on him a couple of days ago and the consultant in charge of his case was still searching for a strong antibiotic that would knock the septicaemia on its head. The ones they'd tried so far weren't bringing about the response the team had hoped for.

'Alex should come out of this without any lasting effects,' Connor said. 'He looked really cheerful when I last saw him.' He stood up, glancing out over the side of the yacht and began to tug on her hand, urging her up from her seat. 'Come and see this… I think a shoal of fish must be heading our way. You, too, Carys. You might want to see this.'

They all went with him to the deck rail, Ross coming to stand beside Alyssa, while Connor pointed out the shoal to Carys.

'They don't usually come this close to the surface,' he said softly.

'What are they?' Carys asked. 'Do you know?'

'They're parrotfish—they call them that because of their parrot-like beaks.'

'Oh, I've heard about them,' Carys said, intrigued. 'They use the beak to scrape off coral so that they can feed on algae. They're beautifully coloured, aren't they?' They were blue, yellow and red, flashing brightly as they swam through the water in search of coral. 'I heard they can change sex,' she added in an awed voice. 'That must cause some confusion among the ranks.'

They all laughed and went to sit back on deck. They sipped cocktails and chatted for some time, until Carys reluctantly mentioned that she had a plane to catch in a couple of hours.

'Okay, we'll up anchor,' Connor said. 'I'll drive you to the airport, if you like.'

'Okay, thanks.'

Ross frowned, and Alyssa wondered if he was troubled by his brother's offer. He didn't say anything, though, and when they arrived back at the house some time later, Ross went into the study in Connor's apartment and left Connor to make the arrangements for the journey to the airport. 'I have to make a phone call,' he told Carys. 'You won't leave without saying good-bye, will you?'

'Of course not.' Carys went with Alyssa to the ground-floor apartment. 'I'll be ready in a jiffy,' she told Connor. 'My bag was almost packed before we went out this morning, so I've only a few things to add to it.'

'That's okay. I'll be out on the deck when you need me.'

Alyssa's phone bleeped and she checked the text message that had arrived as they'd walked into the sitting room. 'My mother's arranged a time for us to link up by phone once a week,' she said, looking pleased. 'I wondered if she would remember.'

She chatted with Carys as her cousin finished putting last-minute items into her bag.

'Connor's gorgeous, isn't he?' Carys said, looking around for her make-up bag. 'I was thrilled to bits that he took us out on the boat today. I really wasn't expecting anything like that—just you and me together and a few take-away meals was what I thought when we planned the weekend—and then he went and produced that luxury hamper. Wow, that's the life, isn't it? It'll seem so mundane, going back to my little home in Florida.'

'Yes, I know what you mean.' Alyssa could well understand her cousin's enthusiasm. 'But you do love your home really, and your family is there…that must count for a lot.'

'True.' Carys sighed. 'But he is great, all the same.'

Alyssa chuckled. 'Don't tell me you're smitten. It seems to happen to an awful lot of women, from what I've heard.'

'Yeah…fat chance I'd have there.'

'Anyway, Ross is just as dishy, and he's very keen on you, or hadn't you noticed?'

'Ross?' Carys's eyebrows shot up. 'No way. You're joking.'

'I'm not.'

'You are, too.'

Still exchanging banter, the girls set off to meet Connor up on the deck.

'Oh…I think I left my phone somewhere,' Alyssa said. 'I'd better go and find it.' She was thinking of going with Carys to the airport, so she would need to have her bag as well. 'I'll catch up with you,' she said.

'Okay, no worries.'

It took a few minutes for Alyssa to find her phone, but eventually it turned up beneath a couple of magazines that Carys had put to one side while she was collecting her things together.

She dropped it into her bag and went upstairs to join Connor and her cousin.

She'd expected to hear them talking, but as she approached the veranda from Connor's sitting room she saw that they were very quiet, talking in hushed tones and standing by the rail, their heads close together. Connor put his arm around Carys's shoulder, bending his head towards her, and it seemed at one point as though their bodies almost meshed together.

Alyssa watched them, her mind reeling in stunned surprise. Connor's expression was serious, and Carys was looking up at him with rapt attention.

Alyssa felt a wave of nausea wash over her. Was this really happening? She hadn't mistaken what she'd seen, had she? Now all her dreams were dissolving in the light of that close embrace.

Was he exactly as people had implied, a man who went from one woman to the next? How could he do this? How could he tell her how much he wanted her, make her yearn for him in return, and then casually move on to try his charm on another woman?

He was treating her feelings as if they were of no account, trampling all over them.

She couldn't bear to watch. This hurt went deep, like a knife wound to the heart, and her whole body froze in pain. Her world had collapsed in an instant. What was she to do now?

CHAPTER NINE

'I'LL miss you, Alyssa.' Carys stood beside Connor's car and gave Alyssa a hug. 'We'll have to meet up again soon.'

'We will.' Alyssa was still hurting inside from the shock of seeing her cousin in such an intimate embrace with Connor, but none of this was her cousin's fault so she made an effort to put on a show of cheerfulness. 'I'll come over to Florida for a weekend before I go... and there's always the gala dinner in a few days' time, on Saturday. You have to come over for that.'

Carys nodded with enthusiasm. 'Yes, I'll be there.'

Ross came to say his goodbyes, and Alyssa noticed he held onto Carys's hand for a fraction longer than necessary. 'I was going to offer to take you to the airport myself,' he said, 'but Connor beat me to it. I think I hate him.'

Carys laughed. 'Don't feel so bad about it. There'll be other times. Anyway, I think he wants to talk to me about something—events management stuff for the hospital, and so on, and we can do that on the way.'

'Oh, boring stuff...' Ross grinned and kissed her lightly on the cheek. 'Bye, Carys.'

'Bye, Ross. And if you even think of doing that stunt

with the water-skis, I shan't speak to you. It was bad enough hearing that you'd been virtually knocked unconscious. You've been warned.'

Ross's brows lifted. 'So you do care about me after all? Okay, I won't do it, then. I promise.'

Smiling, Carys slid into the passenger seat beside Connor. Alyssa didn't think for a minute that Connor planned to talk to her about events management, but there was definitely some reason why he'd been so quick to offer to drive her to the airport. She had no idea what that might be, but she was determined now that she wasn't going to go with them to find out. There was the problem of two's company, three's a crowd, to make her think twice about doing that.

But she was still deeply troubled by what she'd seen earlier. Connor had obviously been concerned when she'd said she was thinking about going back to the UK, and perhaps he'd taken that to mean he would have no chance with her. It seemed a bit odd that he should turn his attention to Carys so soon, though, especially since it was clear that Ross was interested in her.

She waved Carys off and went to her bedroom. There, she lay on the bed and tried to think things through. Connor had never looked at another woman in all the time she'd been over here. It just didn't add up that he should start doing it now.

Could it be that she'd misinterpreted his actions? Perhaps she was letting her ex's behaviour influence her unduly. She had a huge problem with trust, and it had coloured all her judgement. But she couldn't rid herself of that image of Connor with his arm around Carys. It had shocked her to the core.

The situation tormented her, and she had no idea how

to resolve the problem. She loved Connor, she realised that now, but it was like a festering wound, believing that he had let her down so badly.

Over the next few days, she couldn't eat, she couldn't sleep, but she tried to lose herself in work, anything to blot out the picture of Connor and Carys together. She couldn't bring herself to talk to him about her worries because he might tell her it was true, and she didn't know how on earth she would handle that without falling apart. It would be a crippling blow.

She went through the motions at work, putting on a brave face for the occasional patient who came into her surgery. When she had some free time she went over to the hospital to look in on the people she had treated.

'Raeni's on the mend, I believe,' the registrar told her. 'Her breathing's improved, and her heart is pumping much more strongly. She seems to have turned the corner.'

'That's brilliant news,' she said, relieved. Apparently Raeni's children went to see her every day with their father, and were beginning to talk about the day when she would go home.

'It shouldn't be too much longer now,' the registrar added, 'two or three weeks, maybe. Of course, she'll have to take things easy to begin with, while everything continues to heal.'

'That's much better than I expected, anyway.' Alyssa thanked him and went to check on Malik, who was recovering on the men's ward after his surgery.

'How are you doing?' she asked him. 'I hear the operation went well.'

'I'm okay...a bit sore, but the doctor said that's to

be expected. I got them to take me over to see the lady who was in the other car. I'm really sorry for the way she was hurt.' He pulled a face. 'I was in a hurry that day because my wife rang to say she'd gone into labour. I was trying to get back home to her.'

'I'm sorry things turned out the way they did.' Alyssa frowned. 'What happened when you didn't get home?'

'A neighbour took her to the hospital.' He grinned, showing white teeth. 'We have a little girl. She's beautiful.'

'I'm glad it worked out all right, in the end, Malik. Congratulations.'

Back on the film set, things were winding to a close. They finished filming the water-ski chase, and she was glad to see that Ross stood back and let a professional stuntman do the action scenes.

'I didn't have much choice,' he told her in a mournful voice. 'I'm pretty sure Carys meant what she said when she told me she wouldn't speak to me. I guess my wild days are over.'

'Poor you.' She patted his shoulder and sent him a commiserating glance. 'You'll have to settle for being a top-notch film producer instead.'

'Yeah.' He laughed. 'I guess that's not so bad.'

A couple of days after that Alyssa closed down her medical centre and locked the door on what had been her sanctuary for the last few months. In a way, she was sad to see it come to an end, but she'd learned a lot about herself and her vocation as a doctor since she'd been here. It had given her a good breathing space and allowed her to sort out what she needed to do next.

On the day of the gala dinner she awoke to a glorious, sun-filled day and decided to go for a walk along the beach before breakfast. It would give her time to think. She needed to sort things out, once and for all.

She gazed around her at the gently swaying branches of the palm trees and let her glance wander over the magnificent sweep of the bay, where the blue water of the ocean met smooth, white sand. It was flawless, a true paradise island...all it needed was for her to find her soul-mate and to live with him here in perfect harmony.

She smiled wistfully and watched the waves break on the shore, leaving lacy ribbons of white foam. She desperately wanted Connor to be there with her.

Over these last few days she'd had plenty of time to think about what had happened on the day when he had taken Carys to the airport. Wasn't it possible she'd got the wrong end of the stick and come up with a false idea of what was going on? Back home, her ex had cheated on her, and ever since then she'd found it hard to put her trust in anyone.

But James was a totally different person from Connor, wasn't he? He'd never been particularly supportive, or understanding, whereas Connor had been there for her every step of the way. He'd never let her down. In fact, he'd gone out of his way to make sure she was safe, happy, and even that she was secure in her work.

She loved him, and surely that meant she had to learn to trust him? Somehow or other, she had to take risks with her feelings, because she didn't want to miss out on being with him.

'Alyssa...'

It was as though, by thinking of him, she'd somehow managed to conjure him up. She shielded her eyes against the sun and looked towards the house, to see Connor coming down the path that led to the beach.

'Hi.' She waved, and waited for him to come closer. 'You're up and about early,' she said. 'I thought this was your day off? I expected you'd be having a lie-in.'

'It is.' He caught up with her and came to stand alongside her, looking out over the sea. 'I heard you moving chairs about on the deck and I realised you'd been going off for early morning walks since your work here finished. I wanted to come with you and wish you a happy birthday.'

Her eyes widened. 'I didn't think you would remember.'

He smiled. 'I did. I was hoping you'd let me take you to the gala dinner—I realised I'd been taking it for granted that we'd go together, but I haven't asked you formally. Will you let me take you? It will be a good way to celebrate your birthday. I'd like to make it special for you.'

She gazed at him, drinking in the sight of him. 'Thank you, I'd like that, very much.' She studied him thoughtfully, hardly daring to say what was on her mind. 'Actually, I wondered if you might ask Carys.'

'She's going with Ross.'

'Ah.' She looked at him from under her lashes. 'How do you feel about that? Do you mind?'

He seemed puzzled. 'I think it's great—she's perfect for Ross.'

She frowned. 'So it doesn't bother you, her being with him?' She couldn't quite take in his easy answers. She hadn't expected this response at all. How could he be so casual and unconcerned if he'd fallen for Carys?

'Why would it bother me?' He was genuinely mystified by her question, and she finally began to relax a little. Had she misjudged him? 'Am I missing something here?' he said. 'You've been acting oddly ever since Carys went home. Is it because you're missing her?'

'I am,' she admitted. She wasn't ready to tell him the true reason. 'We always get on so well together. I sometimes wish we lived closer to one another.'

He wrapped his arms around her. 'She's only a short flight away—or even a boat ride. I could take you over there whenever you wanted to see her.'

She smiled at him. 'That's really thoughtful of you,' she said softly. 'Thank you for that.' It was typical of him that he should make the offer and she was beginning to feel ashamed of herself for doubting him. Surely there was a logical explanation for his behaviour with Carys? The trouble was, she was too embarrassed to ask him about it.

'You're welcome, any time. I want you to be happy, Alyssa.' He frowned briefly. 'Have you decided what you're going to do about staying on in the Bahamas? I hate the thought of you going away. If it's work that worries you, I know there's room for another doctor in the emergency department at the hospital here. There would be no problem getting you in there.'

'Do you think so?'

'I know it,' he said firmly. 'Everyone talks about how much you did for the patients who ended up in the hospital, and because of you they're all recovering. You know about the car-crash victims, they're both doing well. And Alex has been discharged and is walking again with just a stick to help him—sooner or later he'll be able to cope without that.'

'Yes, I saw him the other day. He came on to the film set to say hello to everyone.'

'You see what I'm saying? He's doing fine. And so is Lewis, now that they've found the right antibiotic. Admittedly, it was touch and go for a while, but now he's getting better every day.'

'It just goes to show what a marvellous hospital system you have here.'

He hugged her to him. 'Seriously, Alyssa...it gave me hope when you said you would go on with your work as a doctor. It would have been such a waste if you'd let it all go. But you could just as easily do that work here, couldn't you? You don't need to go back to the UK, do you?'

'I suppose I could stay...but what is there for me here? Why would you want me to stay? You've never wanted to get deeply involved with anyone before this, have you?'

'Things are different now.' His hand smoothed over the length of her spine. 'I dread the thought of you going away. I want you to stay here, with me. Ever since the accident last week, since I saw Ross's car there and thought you were involved in the crash, I've been churned up inside, imagining what it would be like if you weren't around. It was the same when I saw the tree through Ross's windscreen and thought you might be hurt—I couldn't understand why I cared so much. I'd never felt that way about any woman before.'

She lifted a hand to his cheek, scarcely able to believe what he was saying. 'Do you mean it?'

'Of course I do.' He wrapped her fingers in his and kissed the palm of her hand. 'You can't imagine what it was like for me, thinking that you might be injured.

It struck me like a blow to the stomach that I couldn't bear it if you weren't with me.'

Her heart leapt. 'I didn't think it was possible for you to feel that way.'

'Believe it.' It was a heartfelt admission, and she felt his body shudder next to hers. 'And then when you said you were going away, it was like a double blow.' He frowned. 'Alyssa, I know your parents miss you and you miss them—but they could come and visit any time, couldn't they? There's plenty of room for them to stay at the house.'

'You wouldn't mind that…them coming over to stay in the apartment? I mean, it was different with Carys, because you already knew her.'

'Of course I wouldn't mind.' He kissed her tenderly on the lips. 'I want you to stay on and think of the apartment as your own—' He broke off, suddenly intent, searching her face for her response. 'In fact, I'd sooner turn it back into a house and do away with the two apartments.'

'I don't understand,' she said, suddenly confused. 'Are you saying you want me to live with you?'

'Yes, that's exactly what I'm saying.' He ran his hands over her arms, thrilling her with his gentle caresses. 'I want to keep you close, Alyssa. When you told me you were thinking of leaving it made me realise how badly I needed you to stay.' His fingers trailed lightly over her cheek. 'I can't bear to lose you, Alyssa. Will you stay here and marry me so that we can be together for always?'

She pulled in a sharp breath. She wanted to believe that he meant what he said, but her head was reeling from the sudden shock of his proposal. 'But you—you said you didn't believe in commitment… You've never wanted to settle down with any woman.'

'Because I'd never met the right woman until now.' His arms circled her once more and he kissed her, a long, thorough, fervent kiss that left her breathless and sent sweet ripples of ecstasy to flow throughout her body.

'I just know we'll be perfect together,' he said, coming up for air, his voice rough around the edges. 'It won't be like it was for my parents—I'm not the same person as my father. I don't need to go looking at other women because I know you're the one for me. I love you. I thought—' He broke off. 'It felt as though you loved me, too.' He looked at her, his eyes shimmering with passionate intensity.

She smiled, her lips parting in invitation. 'I do, Connor. I do. I wasn't sure you could love me in return.'

'What's not to love? You're gentle, thoughtful, caring…I've never met anyone like you, and I know we make up two halves of the whole. We're right for one another. I just needed to get my head right and see past the mistakes my father made, that's all. That's not going to happen with us. I know that we're right for one another.'

'That's how I feel, too.' She wrapped her arms around him and he gave a deep sigh of contentment, holding her close for a long time while the birds called to one another overhead and the sea lapped desultorily at the fringes of the beach.

After a while, he stirred and said huskily, 'I'd almost forgotten your birthday present. It's in a drawer in the apartment.' He clasped her hand firmly in his. 'Come with me and I'll get it for you.'

They walked back along the beach towards the

house. 'I wasn't sure what to do for the best, but then I talked to Carys, and she said what I had in mind would be just right.' He frowned. 'I hope you like it. I'm still not sure… I mean, I could have…' He stopped talking as she came to a halt and placed her fingers on his lips.

'Whatever it is, I know I'll love it, because you gave to me.' She sent him a thoughtful glance. 'Is this what you and Carys were talking about that day—before you took her to the airport?'

He frowned, and she said, 'I saw you both on the deck. Your heads were close together, and at first I thought…well, it doesn't matter what I thought, but perhaps that was when you were discussing it? Is that why you wanted to drive her there?'

He nodded, but studied her cautiously. 'What went through your mind when you saw us?'

She wriggled her shoulders. 'Nothing. It isn't important.'

He curled his fingers around her upper arms in a firm but gentle clasp. 'You thought I was making a play for her, didn't you?'

She tried to escape from his grasp but he wasn't letting her go until she answered him.

'Okay, yes… It did cross my mind. Only I gave it a lot of thought and decided I had to learn to trust you. If I couldn't do that, we were doomed, and I really wanted us to have a chance.'

He gave a shuddery sigh. 'Next time you have any doubts or worries, talk to me about them. Promise me?'

'I will. I promise.' She gave him a tremulous smile. 'It was hard for me, Connor. I was badly hurt when James cheated on me, and I could see the same thing happening all over again.' She breathed deeply. 'Then

I came to my senses and decided that I was willing to risk everything by putting my faith in you.'

'I will never, ever let you down, Alyssa. Believe me.'

He tugged on her hand and they started towards the house once more. 'Mind you,' he said, almost as an afterthought, 'I had to explain my motives to Ross when I arrived back home. He wasn't at all happy that I'd pipped him to the post by driving Carys to the airport.'

Alyssa laughed. 'Yes, I remember he was very quiet that night.'

They went into Connor's apartment and he went straight over to a bureau in the sitting room and took out a box that was about half the size of a shoebox. He held it out to her.

'Happy birthday,' he said.

She took it from him, gazing at it in wonder. It was beautifully wrapped in gold foil and tied with a pretty silver ribbon. 'It's so lovely, it seems a shame to open it,' she said softly.

'Please do. I really need to know if you like it, if I've done the right thing…I could always…'

She stopped him with a glance and a slight rise of her eyebrow. He laughed. 'Okay, I won't say any more. I've never felt so nervous…'

Carefully, she undid the wrapping and there inside was an exquisite, hand-carved jewellery box, heart-shaped and decorated with an inlaid pattern and delicate enamelling in the shape of a rose.

'Oh, Connor,' she gasped. 'This is beautiful. You made it yourself, didn't you? That's why you were anxious. You shouldn't have been. It's absolutely lovely.'

He breathed a sigh of relief. 'Open it up,' he urged her.

She did as he asked, lifting the lid to reveal a velvet lined interior with sections for necklaces and rings. And in the centre there was another small box, again with an enamelled flower decoration. She lifted it out, and Connor took the jewellery box from her, putting it to one side on a table.

Alyssa's heart began to pound. 'Is this what I think it is?'

He nodded but didn't say anything more, and she carefully opened the box.

Nestling on a bed of silk was a sparkling diamond ring. The gemstones were dazzling, reflecting the sunlight, and the flawless setting took her breath away.

'I've never seen anything so lovely,' she said huskily. 'It's stunning…'

'That's another reason I had to have Carys's help,' he murmured. 'I needed to get the right size, and she said she had a ring that fitted you. We took the measurement from it.'

'No wonder you were so secretive,' she breathed. 'I'd no idea.'

'Let me slip it on your finger,' he said. He smiled. 'Third finger, left hand…' He held up the ring and pulled in a deep breath. 'Will you marry me, Alyssa?'

'Oh, yes. I will. I do love you, Connor,' she said, her voice husky with emotion.

'I love you.'

He slipped the ring on her finger, and they stood by the open doors of his sitting room, arms around one another, gazing at the ring and looking out over the vista of the ocean. Alyssa sighed happily. This was truly their paradise island, and a dream come true.

* * * * *

GET YOUR ROMANCE FIX!

MILLS & BOON
— *blog* —

Get the latest romance news, exclusive author interviews, story extracts and much more!

MILLS & BOON
MODERN
Power and Passion

Prepare to be swept off your feet by sophisticated, sexy and seductive heroes, in some of the world's most glamourous and romantic locations, where power and passion collide.